LUNA DAVID
SAVING
Sebastian

 A CATHARSIS NOVEL

Saving Sebastian

A Catharsis Novel

Custos Securities Series Book 3

Copyright © 2017 and 2018 Luna David

www.lunadavid.com

ALL RIGHTS RESERVED

Cover design by Kellie Dennis at Book Cover by Design

Custos Securities Series & Catharsis Novel emblems designed by Kellie Dennis, property of Luna David

Proofreading provided by Judy Zweifel of Judy's Proofreading

Editing by Miranda Vescio at V8 Editing and Proofreading

Proofreading by Allison Holzapfel at Allison's Author Services

Interior Design by Morningstar Ashley at Designs by Morningstar

Interior Design and Formatting by Flawless Touch Formatting

Warnings

Intended for an adult audience. Contains explicit sexual content. Contains BDSM and mild breath play (neither of which are encouraged or recommended by the author – please adhere to safe sexual practices). No cliffhanger. **Trigger warning: graphic torture, murder, physical assault.**

Trademark and Copyright Acknowledgements

Luna David acknowledges the trademark status of the following trademarks mentioned in this work of fiction:

Dedication

To my readers, for loving my guys as much as I do. Thank you for being patient while waiting for Sebastian and Gideon's story.

To my husband... Forever and always. Yet again, I've failed in my duty of picking your chosen title for my third book, *A Plumber's Hardware: Pipes, Snakes, and Ballcocks*. So close, but I had to go with Saving Sebastian.

catharsis

ca·thar·sis /kəˈTHärsəs/

noun: catharsis; **plural noun:** catharses

definition: the process of releasing, and thereby providing relief from, strong or repressed emotions.

synonyms:

emotional

release, relief, release, venting; purging, purgation, purification, cleansing; abreaction

Chapter 1

GIDEON

Gideon's specialty was knotwork. He loved the feeling of a rope in his hands; the endless possibilities laid out before him, the pleasure it could give, or the pain it could eventually inflict. He'd learned the intricacies of rigging in a past life—utterly unrelated to the life he currently lived. Returning to that life, even just for a short while, felt strangely like coming home, which was exactly why he'd left it to begin with.

Wetwork wasn't what he'd wanted to build his life on—it had chiseled pieces of him away, bit by bit, until he was convinced he no longer knew who he was. In the beginning, spilling blood had been what he did, not who he was. Somewhere along the way that had changed. So, before he could lose himself completely, before he let the adrenaline of his work turn into a killing endorphin rush that would become an obsession, he'd made the decision to leave that life behind him… Or so he'd thought.

He bent and drank some water out of the crude hose he'd attached to the utility sink then shrugged into his previously discarded fleece jacket. His skull cap and ultra-thin leather gloves, donned hours earlier, would stay on until his work was done. Despite the boiler running, the cold was settling back in as his body cooled down from the strenuous activity. He took a seat and admired his handiwork. Flexing his fingers within the confines of the supple leather, rolling his shoulders, and shaking his arms out helped rid him of the aches he'd gotten from the heavy lifting.

Dangling in front of him was a man he'd thought long dead. He eyed his trussed-up, unconscious quarry; his own body relaxing as a maelstrom of thoughts took up residence in his brain. He'd been sent out on what could've quite possibly been a fool's errand. Though he knew that could be a false assumption on his part, and he was certainly getting what he wanted out of the bargain. He was half convinced it was manipulation, pure and simple, a dangled carrot to draw him back in. One thing was for sure, the mindfuck he found himself smack dab in the middle of was almost too *Twilight Zone* to be believed.

He'd agreed to one last op as a favor to his previous employer. To be honest, he'd have been hard pressed to turn it down. As the man he'd just suspended from the ceiling joists of the basement was none other than the man responsible for the assassination of the most trusted men on his SEAL team years ago. The same man who had supposedly been killed in the same ambush that had taken Gideon's men. The fact that he was very much alive—for the time being—and wanted for a completely different string of crimes, just put the icing on the irony cake as far as Gideon was concerned.

But the irony didn't end there. No. Because not only had he been responsible for the death of his teammates, but also for the torture and murder of Naval Intelligence Specialist Mason Alexander, the submissive Gideon had once thought himself in love with. Mason had been tortured for the information that had ultimately provided the man hanging in front of him with the opportunity to kill his men easily, like fish in a barrel. He'd felt the loss of his men and his submissive down deep in his bones. And though he'd eventually come to realize that love wasn't what he'd felt for Mason, guilt and shame were two emotions that he would readily admit to after that day, even if just to himself.

If the dossier he'd been given was to be believed—and he wasn't convinced that it was—his target was also the man responsible for a slew of heinous crimes against hundreds of men, women, and children which was definitely a big part of why he'd accepted the assignment to begin with.

When he'd seen the pictures of the man he was supposed to track, he'd understood the ramifications of the information immediately and exactly why Boone had come knocking on his door. The possibility that the man he'd once trusted with his life and the lives of his team would turn out to be the same man he'd been searching for years later was something no one—himself included—had seen coming.

In fact, he'd been furious when he'd walked into Custos Securities, at the behest of his younger brother Zavier, and been confronted with his former CIA handler, Boone Davies. He'd made a clean break of the CIA, and anything and anyone related to that life, over five years earlier. Boone's arrival was unwelcome. Boone's manipulation of Custos, of his brother specifically, was a step too far that he wouldn't let pass unchallenged.

The call he'd received from his brother had been cryptic, but he'd known from his brother's overly calm tone that Zavier wasn't happy to be making the call, nor was he pleased to be asking him to come into Custos in a professional capacity. The use of Gaelic, a language they'd learned from both sets of grand-parents while growing up and rarely spoken outside of their home, had at least prepared him for an unwanted visitor. The old proverb Zavier used about an uninvited guest arriving unbidden had been spoken quietly as Zavier was ending the call.

He'd prepared himself for someone he didn't want to see, but he'd never have guessed Boone was the man he'd be presented with. Seeing him had thrown off Gideon's equilibrium, but he'd schooled his features and let his displeasure shine through as he stared down the man he hadn't seen in more than half a decade. Boone's chest had risen as he inhaled in reaction to Gideon's stern expression, his eyes immediately cast down to the floor, but Gideon wasn't placated by the token act of submission. Gideon, about to express his displeasure, had raised his gaze to the enormous flat screen TV mounted to the wall in Zavier's office.

His eyes had narrowed as recognition dawned and he'd stared for what must have been minutes at several pictures of the man he'd known as Alan Lewis. The same man that killed his teammates just before walking into a building that exploded into rubble moments later, taking Alan with it, or so he'd thought. Zavier had stood and rounded his desk to take his place beside him to display a unified front to the CIA, but it hadn't been needed. The moment he'd seen the pictures was the moment he'd mentally signed on to whatever it was they'd be asking him to do.

He brought himself back to the present, knowing he needed his wits about him for what needed to be done. He breathed in and out, willing his heart to slow its harried rhythm and his mind to release him of years worth of remorse and regret. In that moment of vulnerability, the strict control he maintained on his features at all times slipped, and some of the bone-deep mental and phys-ical exhaustion showed. As the minutes ticked slowly by, Gideon's composure returned, the chink in his armor shored up and his emotions tucked deep where no one and nothing could reach them. He reclined almost lazily in the unfor-giving wooden chair, watching and waiting for Alan to wake.

He saw it first in the stretching of neck muscles, the slow clenching and unclenching of fingers, and eventually the effort to straighten his spine. He heard it in the increased cadence of breath and the straining of the ropes under his weight. Gideon knew confusion was edging out the haziness of the sedative, and soon enough, the man's small movements would become a full-fledged struggle to escape the ties.

He'd prepared Alan's bindings for durability, not knowing how long it would take to get the information he needed, but knowing he needed to be prepared for a lengthy session. Gideon had kept him fully clothed and strung him up by his lower legs and ankles to the joist above. He'd then used a series of knots and hitches to secure his arms to the same joist, much like a sloth hanging from a tree branch.

As Alan's body did its best to rid itself of the effects of the sedative, Gideon maintained his silence; the only sound in the huge, dank basement was the ancient boiler running in the back-corner room. He saw the moment Alan's consciousness returned. The man stilled completely in his bindings and tilted his head a bit, using his senses to try to find anything that might help him figure out what had happened and where he was.

Gideon let him continue to think he was alone and watched as the man rubbed his head against one of his raised arms, doing his best to dislodge the blindfold Gideon had placed over his eyes. He continued to watch as Alan's struggles with the blindfold seemed to frustrate him and he began moving his jaw and his lips to try to spit out the gag. When that didn't work either, he started thrashing hard in his bindings to test their strength. Finally giving up, he sighed and seemed to slump in on himself, exhausted from his efforts, his whole body heaving as he gulped in air.

Gideon scuffed his booted foot on the floor, knowing the psychological aspect of what was to come was going to be just as excruciating as the physical and reveling in it. Alan stilled then grunted while thrashing around. When Gideon finally stood ten minutes later, he did so noisily, picking up a pair of heavy duty shears from the table. He slowly brought the chair alongside Alan, scraping it across the floor loudly then standing on it—though not close enough to be in danger of getting knocked into by the struggling man.

He gripped Alan's pant leg and used the shears to cut them down the side, revealing the intricate knotwork he'd used for the suspension. The rope was tied tight around his legs, his skin red and angry under the unforgiving jute fibers. The rigging began at his heels, over his snug, fitted leather combat boots, and continued up his lower legs in a spider web effect, ending just before his knees.

Gideon maintained his grip when the man's movements became more desperate. He sliced easily through his briefs and his leather belt then did the same to the other leg, baring Alan's lower body to the cold, damp chill of the basement. He sliced the shirt open, cutting it off from his ribs down, leaving the fabric over his chest, arms, and back where the ropes dug in, holding the shirt in place. Alan was left in the tattered remains of his shirt, his combat boots, and the ropes holding him far above the ground.

Gideon stepped down and tilted his head, watching his victim closely. His voice, though low, sounded loud in the cavernous room. "Cold in here, isn't it?"

Alan let out an angry growl and redoubled his efforts to escape.

Gideon approached again, grasping him just under his chin and tilting his head down. Alan tensed then thrashed in his bindings like a fish out of water. "Uh uh uh. Hold still so I don't cut off anything vital."

Gideon waited patiently as Alan slowly stilled, out of breath. "Much better. Now, I'm going to remove your gag so that we can have a nice chat. Don't concern yourself with being seen or heard. We're far away from any prying eyes or curious ears."

Gideon, one hand still holding Alan's head down by his chin, reached up with his other hand, opened the shears, and slid the bottom blade ever so slowly against Alan's cheek underneath the makeshift gag made of duct tape and cloth and sliced through it. He gently pulled the taped cloth from between Alan's teeth, gripped it tight, and paused for several drawn-out seconds.

He was rewarded when Alan snarled angrily, "Who the fuck—" Which prompted Gideon to yank down hard on the crude tape and cloth handle, earning him a pained shout as the tape was wrenched from around Alan's head. Gideon's hand was full of the ragged remains of the gag that now also included some hair, and if he wasn't mistaken, a bit of skin.

He walked unhurriedly across the room to the table, set the gag down, and made his way back. He stood silently, waiting for the inevitable. Alan tilted his head in Gideon's general direction. "You don't know who you're dealing with! I'm a very powerful man. I'll be missed. My men will be searching for me."

Gideon smirked. "I've been watching you for two months. I found it strange at first that you had no backup, until I realized what it was you were doing. You have no protection here as this isn't where you do business. There's no need to have a security detail during your scouting runs, even less in your own town; not to mention, it would scare the locals. So, there's no one to come to your defense. You don't even carry a mobile phone. I did my homework."

Alan's breath hitched, and he shook his head emphatically. "I check in on a regular basis. I—"

Gideon interrupted, "You make one phone call weekly from a public telephone. You made your call from the market parking lot tonight. If you're missed, it won't be until next week. We have plenty of time."

Alan snarled and wrenched around in his ties again. "What the *fuck* do you want with me? Let me down!"

Gideon straddled the chair, folded his arms on the chair back, and looked up at the struggling man. "Alan. . . Do you mind if I call you Alan? I realize you no longer go by that name, but it's the one I remember you by, so I figured I might as well."

Alan had quietened at that bit of news then expelled a harsh breath and a muttered oath. "Jesus, who are you?"

"Come now. I think that's the question I should be asking you, don't you think?"

"Look, whatever it is you're trying to do, whoever it is you think I am, we can work something out! There's no reason to resort to scare tactics."

"Is that what you think this is?" Gideon shook his head and laughed, but there was no humor in it. "No, this. . . this is much more serious than that I'm afraid."

"Listen, we can—"

"Alan, it's not time for you to talk now, it's time for you to listen."

"Fucking coward!"

Gideon's only reaction was a raised brow that he knew Alan wouldn't be able to see. When he spoke, his tone was bored. "Excuse me?"

"Think you're so tough, tying me up? Hanging me up from the ceiling? Get me down! Show yourself! You obviously know me, so let me see your fucking face!"

Standing, Gideon picked up the shears again and approached. That time when he grabbed Alan's chin and pulled his head back down, the man didn't move. He slid the bottom blade of the shears below the duct tape and fabric covering his eyes and easily cut through it. Wasting no time, he yanked the blindfold off the same way he'd done the gag; the angry, pained cries not even registering as he turned and set what was left of the blindfold next to the gag scraps.

Turning around, he made sure Alan got a good long look at him. As he watched the color drain from the man's face, Gideon figured recognition had dawned, and with it, the reality of what was to come. Gideon picked up the dossier he'd been given, spun the chair around, and sat, taking his time.

"Now, let's see here." Gideon opened the file and thumbed through it almost casually. Finding what he was looking for, he pulled out some gruesome photos of several of the victims. "Why don't we avoid beating around the bush and I'll show you exactly why I'm here. Besides the fact that you killed my men."

He held up a glossy eight by ten of the broken body of a little girl. "This is Elira, a little nine-year-old Kosovan girl who was stolen from her family about a year ago and funneled into a human trafficking syndicate that you're *very* familiar with. She was purchased, forced into sexual slavery, her body branded and used until it was unable to withstand anymore. She was found dead and nearly unrecognizable from a brutal beating in an alley in downtown Dubrovnik, Croatia."

Gideon continued, reading the information on the back of each picture, providing the gruesome backstory of every victim in the file, each one carrying the same unique brand which was one of the only things tying all the victims together. When he was done, he stood and set the folder aside, picking up the shears again. At that point, he knew Alan's body was in pain; being strung up for any length of time wasn't easy on one's muscles and joints.

Though the man remained silent, a green cast tinged his skin after viewing the photographs of the mutilated bodies. Gideon could see the tension, the now palpable fear causing full body shakes. He wondered idly if the man cared one iota that the people he'd helped kidnap had gone through much worse.

He approached Alan and slipped the shears under the neck of what was left of his shirt and began cutting. When he reached the rope between his shoulder blades, he cut through the bindings easily, ignoring the jerky movements of the man.

Stepping away quickly, he watched as the tightly weaved knotwork he'd created all along the length of Alan's arms lost its grip as his weight pulled his body from it. As the man's now fully naked body swung from the ceiling, he swayed like a pendulum from his trussed up legs, finally crying out. Gideon approached again, grabbed an arm and wrestled it behind Alan's body then grabbed the other. He snapped a pair of handcuffs on his wrists and stepped away.

"What do you want? *WHAT THE FUCK DO YOU WANT?* You don't need to do this. We can come to some type of agreement. I have lots of money. I know powerful people. Whatever you want, I can make it happen. There's no reason you have to go through with this."

Gideon ignored him and headed to the sink where he turned on the cold tap, filling up the hose he'd attached. Picking up the spray nozzle, Gideon approached the man that was still talking to him, still begging, but the words didn't break through his concentration. He clicked over to the jet spray option and pelted the man's body with a hard blast of icy water as he swayed from the rafters. The begging continued as he drew closer, holding the spray lever down with a firm grip.

Alan was shivering from the cold and moaning. His broken words loud now that the water had stopped. "What do you want? What do you want? What do you want?"

He continued asking the same question over and over until Gideon bent down and looked in the man's eyes. "Why don't we chat about the contents of the briefcase you've been carrying around with you for the last two months, and go from there."

Alan's eyes widened, and he began shaking his head no at an almost frenetic pace. "No. No. No. No. It's not… That's not mine to give. It's not mine."

Alan continued to shake his head no, muttering about the case not being his. Gideon raised the nozzle again and drenched the man with another punishing icy spray. As Alan shivered, teeth chattering, and still tried to argue about the briefcase, Gideon walked behind him to the far corner of the basement. He reached the old boiler room and flung the door open, approached the mammoth old machine, pushed down the huge handle, and gingerly drew the small, heavy metal door open. He began sweating immediately from the flames.

He picked up the crowbar, putting one end directly into the flames. He headed back to the dangling man, walked around to his front, and held the scorching crowbar close to his face, cluing the man in to what was to come. Alan released his bladder and started to jerk in his bindings, crying out then begging. Gideon grimaced at the stench of the man's piss, grateful he'd avoided being hit with it.

As there was no useful information to be gleaned from Alan's indecipherable noises, Gideon raised the crowbar and slid it in the space between the man's upper thighs and held it there while Alan did his best to stay still as he continued to moan and beg. The truly warped part of Gideon conjured up an image of the children's game *Operation*. He touched the scorching metal to his trussed-up victim's inner thigh, and the screaming began.

After he was sure there would be quite a large brand left behind, he crouched down and whispered, "I think I'll give you a brand in every location each of the victims had one. What do you think? Little Elira had one on her pelvis, didn't she? Let me ask you this, are you the one that brands them before sending them off to the syndicate to be sold like chattel?"

At that point, Alan was a blubbering mess and the crowbar needed to be heated up again. Gideon went back to the boiler, taking his sweet time, whistling while he worked. When he walked around to Alan's front, he ignored the pleas and held the scalding bar to his pelvis. "The location of the briefcase's contents, Alan. You give me that, everything stops."

Deciding not to wait, Gideon lifted the bar and moved it to his neck, below his ear, and the answer he wanted finally came as Alan flinched away from the burning metal. "Okay, okay! No more, please! *PLEASE!*"

"Where is it? I know you emptied the case, where did you put its contents?"

"It's under my mattress!"

Gideon shook his head in admonishment and tsked him as he walked toward the boiler again. Heating up the bar, he walked back to Alan, dragging the bar along the floor. Placing the newly heated-up metal against Alan's left pectoral, Gideon yelled to be heard over Alan's cries of pain. "Let's try this again, shall we? Keep in mind you'll be left swinging here until I return with the contents. If you're lucky, the trip back to your place won't take long enough for both of your hips or knees to pop out of their sockets. Though the pain from the blood gathering in your head will be substantial, I have it on good authority that it won't cause death for many, many hours."

Alan mumbled something between cries. Gideon lowered the bar and moved closer. "Again."

"Vacuum."

"What about it?"

The crying continued, and Gideon raised the bar again which had Alan sputtering. "In… Ins… Inside vacuum bag."

Gideon huffed out a humorless laugh, eyes narrowed. "Quite the effective hiding place, you better hope you're not lying to me."

Alan moaned, "Please let me down… *Please*."

Gideon squatted down to Alan's eye level and rubbed his thumb hard over the fresh brand on Alan's chest. The man moaned in agony. "Use this time to imagine what other things I could do to you. Better yet, think of the pain all of your victims have gone through over the years and what ideas I might have gleaned from just looking at the photos of their dead and mutilated bodies."

Alan continued to wail as Gideon stood. He headed toward the doorway to the stairs and leaned the crowbar against the wall. As he headed up the stairs, he called out to Alan. "I'll be back. Eventually."

Chapter 2

SEBASTIAN

Sebastian Phillips, sunglasses donned and hoodie up, slid into the Lyft car and quietly thanked the driver for picking him up. He pulled on his seatbelt and reached into his shirt pocket for the dose of Valium and Vicodin he'd put there earlier, swallowing them down with a drink from his water bottle. He slid in his earbuds and thumbed his way to the Spotify mix he'd made long ago for days like these.

His foot tapped out a rhythm to the first song, more from nerves than any desire to participate in the music itself. No matter how many times he went through with his doctor's appointments, he couldn't shake the tension it brought. His hands shook a bit as he rubbed his sweaty palms back and forth on his bouncing knees.

He was dropped off without fanfare in front of the building that housed his doctor's office. He always arrived early so he had plenty of time to wait and let the meds kick in before his treatment. He was highly susceptible to medications and combining them got him as relaxed as he was able to get without being knocked out completely.

As he neared the check-in desk, he smiled as he watched Suda, the receptionist. She was a tiny little spitfire, always talking animatedly with her hands. She wound down the call when she saw him and took her headset off.

"Hi, Suda."

She grinned. "Sebastian, you handsome boy. Come, let me check you in."

He handed over his debit card to take care of his co-pay and took a seat in the waiting room. Suda came out several minutes later to bring him an ice roller and wish him luck. He fiddled with the handle of the frozen rolling cylinder that closely resembled a mini paint roller. It was used to roll over the skin for the numbing effect of the ice before treatment and the management of swelling after.

He began to use it on his face and neck, absentmindedly thumbing through people's comments on his Instagram account. Just shy of twenty minutes later, he was called into one of the treatment rooms where the machine was already humming, making his hands start to sweat again with nerves.

He waited; buds in his ears with the music on stun to drown out the noise and icing his skin with the roller. Ten minutes later, Dr. Perez came in the door with a couple of interns. She said hello and introduced them, but he was awful with names and so nervous he forgot them almost immediately.

The fact that he was at a hospital at all had him extremely on edge. Even though he wasn't technically on the hospital campus but at a satellite location, he still hated every second of it. The mild nausea he was currently experiencing began the moment he got out of the car and would continue until he was back outside. Ever since he was little and had been taken over and over again to a hospital for different treatments, he'd grown to hate and fear hospitals.

Dr. Perez was just shy of six feet tall which put her several inches taller than him. She was beautiful, her loose dark curls winding their way down her back to her waist, but best of all, she had a wonderful bedside manner. While it always seemed the interns were gawking at him, she was always gracious and kind, which went a long way with him. She was very pregnant and put her hand at her lower back and stretched.

She smiled at his raised eyebrows. "I was due three days ago." When he winced, she threw up her hands. "Right? So I figured I might as well keep working because maybe that will trigger him to make his grand entrance."

He chuckled. "Good luck and congrats."

She smiled and patted the hand he had on the armrest. "Thanks." She opened his file on her iPad and looked him over critically. "So, I'm seeing some improvement. Would you agree?"

He shrugged noncommittally. "I see myself every day. I have no clue."

She picked up the mirror from the nearby rolling tray, tilted the iPad towards him and flipped the screen for him to see the pictures she'd taken before the last treatment, and then held up the mirror. He supposed, if he looked hard enough, there was a difference that could be seen, but again, he shrugged. She gave him a patient smile and warned him they were going to increase the intensity of the treatment.

He clenched his shaking hands into fists but nodded his head as she stood up and chatted with the interns. He continued to use the roller until she asked him to remove his shirt. Once his hoodie and shirt were off and in a ball in his lap, she took the roller and set it on the tray.

When she approached him again, he could see that she had a hand down by her side hidden from view. He looked up at her and when they made eye contact, she smiled in understanding. "You ready?"

No. He nodded his head. "Yeah."

He closed his eyes, and she proceeded to inject his facial tissue with lidocaine to provide some numbness. She injected three shots in his face and two inside his mouth to numb the area above his lip. Dr. Perez rubbed the areas to spread out the medication, and he relaxed a bit, knowing that part was over. The female intern prepared the ocular shield, and he put his buds back in and cranked up the music.

The seat was raised, and the back reclined. He closed his eyes and did his best to ignore it when the other intern lifted his eyelid and slid one of the shields directly onto his eye, pulling both lower and upper eyelids over the shield to keep it in place. She covered his other eye with gauze.

He practiced his deep breathing exercises, doing his best to calm his racing heart. No matter the drugs in his system, his tension was unavoidable. He jumped in his seat when the doctor let out a blast of the cold air connected to the laser. Voice muffled by his music, he imagined she apologized for scaring him but didn't take out his buds to find out.

When she patted him on the shoulder a second time, he knew well enough to brace himself for the onslaught. He gripped his shirt in his hand like a stress ball. No matter how many times he'd had the treatments, the first ten or so pulses from the laser always had his whole body reacting, every pulse like a rubber band snapping against his skin. After that, he was able to settle into the treatment and keep himself from jerking in his seat.

With a pulse nearly every second, she was able to get quite a lot of each area done fairly quickly. Inevitably, after about a hundred pulses or so, he was usually in need of a break. At that point, the machine's depth and strength levels needed to be changed anyway, as the doctor moved on to his neck then later on his shoulder and chest.

Between treatment areas, the doctor and her minions would usually go out and treat another patient then come back. He was usually there for a couple hours, but it was either that or subject himself to it more often with separate appointments for each treatment area. He didn't even want to think about having to be there more than he already was, so he stuck it out and did the whole treatment in one go.

When he was finally done, exhaustion had set in as it always did after a treatment. He was given a couple ice packs and was on his way home, so he could well and truly crash. As he stepped out of the Lyft outside of his house, his movements were lethargic. Sunglasses donned and hoodie up again, he made his way slowly to his front door. Upon entering, he stripped off everything from the waist up and headed to the kitchen for some fresh ice packs and acetaminophen. His energy was nearly gone, and he wanted to lie down.

As soon as he was on the couch—soft ice packs covering the treatment areas for the pain and swelling—he pulled the blanket off the back of the couch, draping it over his chest and legs. His two cuddly, little Egyptian Mau kittens snuggled up on his chest under his chin. He scratched them between the ears until they purred for him then settled his hands on their tiny bodies and promptly passed out.

Chapter 3

GIDEON

Gideon left the old automobile tire production and distribution center on the outskirts of Timisoara, the city in Romania that Alan currently resided in. As he arrived at Alan's home, he got out to open the gate then pulled through, shutting it behind him and parking in front of the single-story house.

Alan's car was nearly ten years old, his home outwardly appeared as run-down as those nearby, and once he entered the house, Gideon could see he had very little in the way of technological advances. The fact that the man didn't have a cell phone was just one more thing on the list of WTF-isms the man had going on. He began to search the small house, quickly finding the vacuum in the tiny closet just off the kitchen.

He pulled the heavy vacuum out of the closet. It was an older canister style number, so he knelt and flipped up the top of the vacuum's body where the bag was housed. He lifted the bag, which was attached to the filter housing with a round rubber connector.

Once he detached the connector and lifted the vacuum bag, he flipped it over and discovered a cut in the back by the top. He slid his hand in and was surprised to grip a handle of some sort. He pulled out whatever it was he'd grabbed but couldn't have prepared himself for the item he held in his hand.

He fell back on his ass and stared at the small branding iron in his hand. It matched the brands he'd seen on the victims' bodies. He dropped it as if he'd been burned, and his stomach turned as he pulled out a small blow torch. Dropping it angrily by the iron, he shoved his hand back into the bag and removed three full manila envelopes, each with the number thirteen written on the front in thick, black marker, and finally, four black plastic film canisters.

He replaced the bag, attaching the rubber connector properly before closing the lid and putting the vacuum back where he'd found it. He got up, walked to the dark room, and turned on the light, filling the room with a red glow. He began a more thorough search of the room and all the photography supplies than he'd done in the beginning, gathering up about ten more film canisters.

He gathered everything into a small shopping bag and left the house. He took his time driving back to the distribution center, knowing the wait would increase the anxiety, not to mention the pain, Alan would be subjected to. When he arrived, he took the steps leading to the basement and picked up the crowbar, quietly approaching. Alan, eyes squeezed tightly shut, was moaning softly, and despite the small boiler door being left wide open, shivering from the cold.

He slammed the crowbar down on the wooden table, causing the man to cry out in shock. He stacked the envelopes on the table beside all the film canisters, tossing the iron and torch down on the table with a clatter, pulled the chair up, and sat. "Let's see what we have here. Care to walk me through it, or do I get to be surprised?"

Alan growled and began thrashing in his bindings again, spittle flying as he yelled out his frustration. "Fuck you! *FUCK YOU, MCCADE!* I'm not saying shit!"

Gideon pulled the first envelope forward. "Well, I don't think you're going to have to. I think I have what I need right here, don't you?"

Gideon set about discovering what he'd unearthed from that vacuum bag. Ignoring the piteous noises across the room, he opened the first notebook and slipped into a nightmare. An hour later, eyes scratchy, headache brewing, and utterly horrified by what he'd learned, Gideon stood slowly. Swallowing down bile, he was thankful he hadn't had anything to eat since lunch. He'd have lost it for sure.

He knew it would be bad, and he'd seen some of the worst the world had to offer, but those disturbing acts of unbelievable violence with such blatant disregard for human suffering were almost more than he could handle—and he could handle a lot. He knew how to compartmentalize better than most, and he never let emotions cloud his judgment, but what a mindfuck.

Taking several deep breaths, the nausea subsided, and Gideon reached toward the other side of the table. He wrapped his fingers around the leather handle of the sjambok and approached Alan. He watched the man's eyes widen in horror as he tested the pliability of the whip, grabbing both ends and bending it nearly in half.

It was three feet in length, the leather handle was about an inch thick, and the body, made out of thick, black, pliable plastic, tapered down to around a quarter of an inch. "So, how's the head feeling? It's painful being hung upside down for any length of time, isn't it?"

Alan's moans stopped long enough for him to spit out, "Go to hell!"

Gideon lowered the whip down along his side and tapped it repeatedly against his lower leg hard enough to make a loud thipping noise. "I had quite a bit of evidence coming into our little meeting today, but your treasure trove of material here is exactly what we needed to help shut down the syndicate for good. There's still a lot that doesn't make sense though. That's where you'll come in handy. I want information, Alan. But what I need to know is if you're going to make this *easy* or if you're going to make it *fun*."

Alan crunched his stomach muscles and threw himself backwards, succeeding only in making himself sway back and forth. He growled in frustration and bit out, "I already told you, I'm not saying shit."

Gideon chuckled humorlessly. "Well, we both know that's not true. Don't we? Your vacuum was a veritable fount of information. Thanks for that, by the way." Tap, tap, tap. "What I don't quite get are the locations for the other dead, branded bodies. The ones in your—for lack of a better word—district all stem from Southeastern European countries and tie back to your meticulously kept records."

"I'm not saying shit!"

Gideon continued as if he hadn't been interrupted. "But there are so many others in my dossier whose locations range from South America to Africa to Asia. Which leads me to believe that you are *not* who the CIA desperately wants you to be... No." Tap, tap, tap. Gideon circled him. "I don't believe for a second that you're Diabo Feio. I think you're one tiny, little cog in a very big machine." Tap, tap, tap. "So, Alan, why don't you enlighten me? Who *is* Diabo Feio?"

A terrified look had etched itself across Alan's face. "*FUCK YOU!*"

"It's gonna be like that, is it?" Tap, tap, tap. He circled the man again. "You should have gone with *easy*, Alan. But I guess you prefer *fun*."

The first crack of the whip against Alan's side elicited a howl like none Gideon had ever heard. And a burst of satisfied warmth wended its way through him when he realized he was exacting a small bit of vengeance for Alan's many victims. He hadn't tortured anyone with a sjambok in years. And it *was* an instrument of torture, and not the type of torture he enjoyed inflicting on willing submissives at his club. No, the sjambok—for him—was, and always would be, a method of torture from his past life, used as a means to an end.

Putting his whole weight behind the blow, he admitted to himself he may have let the contents of the vacuum bag color the intensity and strength of his swing. He'd never before let his personal feelings get in the way of his duty, but that man proved to Gideon—like none of the others before him— he was not the robotic killing machine he'd once been dubbed.

There was nothing robotic or unemotional in him now. As he landed his fifth blow, each one leaving a long bloody welt on the once clean canvas of Alan's skin, he called out another of the names of the man's victims on his downward swing. Before moving onto the next hit, he detailed everything the coroners could glean from each of that victim's many injuries. He'd read the CIA's file so many times, he had the facts memorized, doubtful now that they'd ever leave his mind.

Ignoring Alan's pained shouts, Gideon continued on—name…lash…list of the victim's injuries…lash…name…lash…list of the victim's injuries…lash. As he lifted the whip up for the ninth time in preparation for a blow across the man's right pectoral, the blood humming in his ears finally ebbed enough to allow him to hear that the groaning and moaning had become a desperate plea. "Please, no more. Please. I'll tell you whatever you want to know. Just please, no more."

Gideon lowered the whip down along his side again, wiped the whip along his pant leg, a smear of blood left in its wake, and pulled in several deep breaths. He was sweating, and his muscles were bunched. He shrugged his shoulders and moved his head back and forth, loosening the tightness there. One more deep breath in and his calm was restored.

He circled his prey, admiring the marks he'd left behind, and settled in front of him. As he focused on the red-rimmed, bloodshot, and teary eyes of his target, he tapped the whip against his leg again, eyes narrowing as Alan's body jumped involuntarily with each slap. He waited in silence and was finally rewarded.

"I don't know who he is, and before you tell me that's bullshit, it's the fucking truth. None of us know who he is." Alan struggled, handcuffs clinking together as he adjusted his arms behind his back. "You gotta let me down, man. I'll tell you what you want to know, but you gotta get me down. Please, it hurts. Everything hurts."

"It's supposed to hurt, Alan. I was trained by the very best to ensure that it does. And that answer is not gonna cut it, I'm afraid." He raised his arm again without warning and brought it down on Alan's chest while calling out another child's name and their many injuries.

"Oh god, stop. Just please. Stop. I'll tell you everything. I'll tell you everything!"

Gideon nodded. "I thought we might be able to come to an agreement. Let's start with your current employer then you can clear up a few issues from our shared past."

Stepping back, Gideon folded his arms across his chest, sjambok still in his hand, now wedged under his armpit and pointed upwards. He tilted his head, watching as Alan's eyes followed the movements of the whip and raised his brow when the man's eyes finally met his again. Alan mumbled unintelligibly. Gideon stepped forward, unfolding his arms, and saw Alan flinch violently as the whip was brought down to Gideon's side once again.

"What did you say?"

Alan squeezed his eyes shut, his face scrunched in pain, tears falling. Gideon watched, indifferent, as the man seemed to gather himself enough to be able to talk. "He knows who we are, but he never uses our names. He calls us his 'cem'—his one hundred men. I'm lucky number thirteen."

Gideon recalled the number thirteen being on nearly everything in those envelopes. He watched as Alan closed his eyes and took several deep breaths. Keeping them closed, he continued. "We each have a region. We funnel the children in with strict orders to never pull in anyone older than twenty. We mark them with his brand so it's visible in photos. We take the pictures, process them ourselves, and write on the front of the eight by tens where they came from and where they are going."

Alan continued to tell Gideon what he knew. What was clear was that he didn't know anyone else's side of the business. He was kept in the dark about anything that he didn't need to know but was able to give enough to Gideon that they'd eventually be able to find Diabo Feio after gathering more of the "cem" to provide enough information to dismantle and destroy the syndicate.

With the last of his strength, Alan explained what he'd done to the men on Gideon's team and to Mason all those years ago.

As Alan wound down, his words were coming slower, pain etched in the lines of his face, exhaustion not allowing him to continue. Gideon set the sjambok down on the table, picked up the blowtorch and approached Alan. He switched it on and brought the flame near Alan's cheek, providing enough heat to get the nearly unconscious man's attention. Alan's lids slid slowly open, too fatigued to react quickly, even while the flame heated his face. "Is there anything else I need to know?"

Alan whined and tried to shake his head. His answer was barely a whisper. "No."

Gideon tucked the torch in his back pocket and took out his blade. He'd gotten the information he needed. All that was left to do was finish the job. As Alan was close to losing consciousness completely and was beyond comprehension at that point, he quickly slit the man's throat and stepped back several paces, waiting patiently until the end.

Afterwards, he stripped down to his socks and underwear, pulled on some fresh clothes and shoes, and a new pair of gloves. He took his bloody clothes, along with the tattered remains of Alan's, to the boiler and tossed them into the flames along with the knife he'd just used. He closed the door of the huge machine, wishing, not for the first time, that the opening was large enough for Alan's body, but knowing he'd have to leave it and trust that it would be taken care of properly.

He shut the door to the boiler room, gathered everything he'd brought into his military duffle, and shouldered the bag as he climbed the stairs, leaving what was left of Alan behind. Pulling his sat phone out of his pocket, he dialed and waited.

Boone answered on the third ring. Gideon dove right in. "The men you put on me have a mess to clean up."

"I didn't—"

"You did."

"Wait, a mess? You were supposed to bring him in! We need everything he's got on this fucking syndicate, Gideon! You fucking took the guy out? That wasn't what we agreed—"

Gideon snarled. "We didn't agree to shit! You dangled this guy in front of me knowing I'd reel him in like a fish. Well, I reeled him in and gutted him. If your boys are fast and industrious, they'll have him in pieces fairly quickly and make good use of the boiler room."

"Boiler room?! What the fuck? Gideon, listen—"

Gideon's voice was more of a growl when he responded. "No, you listen. You dragged me back into a life I no longer want and a mess you know very little about. Your two best men just became my fixers. That should keep them busy long enough for me to get gone. If one of them remains on my six, you'll have another mess that needs cleaning, and you won't get any of the information I have."

"Gideon, you need to be debrief—"

"I'll come to you when I'm goddamned good and ready."

He hung up before Boone could do more than grunt and exited the back of the building. He walked several blocks west and hotwired a car to get him to the city center where he picked up a cab to the airport. He was in the air and headed out of the country within three hours, exhausted and needing a shower that would have to wait for one of his many pit stops before his final flight home. His patience with the day—let alone the past two months—had worn thin.

The trip home was a long one. There was a lot of what he called "traveling hopscotch," which was part of his routine. Lots of flying in no discernable pattern with multiple IDs until he arrived at his final destination. It was probably a precaution he no longer needed to take, but there were many reasons why he was still alive after spending a majority of his career killing people for a living, and that was one self-protective habit he refused to change, no matter how tiresome.

Chapter 4

SEBASTIAN

It took two days for the swelling around Sebastian's right eye to diminish enough to see out of again. He'd taken some sick time from work and managed to get himself past the worst of the pain and swelling since the Wednesday treatment. When Monday rolled around, he was back to work. His stress level was high as he had a couple appointments at the hospital to do composites of two different suspects with two different victims. As he approached room one hundred seven in the emergency department, he rubbed his sweaty hands on his pants. He was about to enter, but he heard escalated voices.

"...with us, and that's all there is to it!"

"Absolutely not, young man! You're newlyweds! The last thing you need is your grandmother staying with you and cramping your style."

"Nana, you can't just go home. You've got a cast, and you can barely walk, how are you going to do anything for yourself?"

"It's only one arm. I'll be fine."

"It's your right arm and your knee is messed up! You won't be able—"

He heard a deeper voice interject in a much more muted tone.

"But, she—"

More muted talking, the deeper tone calm but firm. Sebastian found himself stalling outside of the room, not wanting to interrupt, enjoying listening to the muted voice even though he couldn't make out much of what was being said.

He nearly jumped out of his skin when someone tapped him on the shoulder. Whirling around, he glanced way up into the questioning eyes of a doctor who looked ridiculously like one of his previous clients.

The man, arms folded across his chest, smiled politely at him. "May I help you?"

SAVING SEBASTIAN: A CATHARSIS NOVEL

Sebastian gestured behind him to the room. "I'm the police sketch artist from San Francisco PD. I have an appointment but didn't want to interrupt."

The doctor's brows rose. "Interrupt?"

Just then the woman spoke up. "What are you going to do, wipe my ass for me?"

Sebastian's eyes popped wide, and he nearly sputtered when the laughing doctor clasped his elbow and turned him back towards the door. "That's our cue."

Sebastian let out a soft gasp and tried to pull his arm free as he frantically whispered, "What? No! That's not our cue! That should never be anyone's cue!"

His protests fell on deaf ears as he was unceremoniously, but gently, dragged into the hospital room. He barely had time to register the fact that not only was a McCade dragging him into the room, but another McCade was already there before the curtain beyond the door that the doctor had pulled to the side swished back in place and partially covered him.

Zavier and his partner, Braden, sat beside the hospital bed. Though they both had their eyes on the doctor and hadn't seen him before he stepped behind the curtain. A small smile flitted over Sebastian's face. He'd really liked Braden when he'd done a composite sketch of the man's stalker. At least a year had passed since then, but he still remembered meeting both men that after-noon, and the quick comradery he'd felt with Braden.

"Braden, you know she just wants to go home so she can be waited on hand and foot by her male harem. Isn't that right, Nana?"

The woman Sebastian now knew to be Clara Cross, his 1:30 p.m. appoint-ment, laughed. "Finnegan, darling! Come give me some sugar."

As Dr. McCade hugged the petite woman, Sebastian did his best to back-track and escape the little family reunion that was happening. He figured he'd just wait outside for a bit and give them some time. His messenger bag had other ideas, however, and clunked loudly against the door. As his face grew hot with embarrassment, he pulled the door open just as he heard the hanging curtain being yanked back. Dr. McCade grinned at him, raised a brow in chal-lenge, winked and walked back to Mrs. Cross.

Sebastian turned and smiled uncomfortably at everyone else in the room, hating the attention he'd just brought on himself, and waved self-consciously before he fumbled behind him for the door handle and pulled it open, again. "Uh, hi. I have an appointment with Mrs. Cross, but I'll come back."

He watched as Braden and Zavier stood, a surprised look on both of their faces. Sebastian continued to try to give them the privacy he was sure they'd prefer and began to back out of the door. Braden reached out toward him beseechingly. Zavier, soothing Braden, ran his hand up his partner's spine and clasped the back of his neck. Sebastian had seen the gesture the first time they'd met, and his heart pinched watching it again. He wanted that.

When Zavier spoke, Sebastian stopped. "Sebastian Phillips, right?" When he nodded, Zavier placed a hand on his own chest. "Zavier McCade. I'm not sure if you remember, but you helped us with the composite sketch for Braden's case. Please, stay."

"I re—" Sebastian cleared his throat and tried again, his voice barely above a whisper. "I remember."

Of course, he remembered. The man was impossible to forget. That, along with the faux flirting and joking around he'd forced himself to do to relax Braden into being comfortable when he had to draw the man who was terrorizing him, had Sebastian red faced with embarrassment.

He found it nearly impossible to make his escape at that point, held still by some invisible force. Looking down, he fiddled with the cross strap of his bag and avoided eye contact with the enormous man. There was just something so arresting about him. A low-level hum ran through Sebastian—just like he remembered from the first time he'd met him—a sensation he only ever got at the club. It made him wonder about the relationship dynamic between Braden and Zavier. Knowing that was none of his business, he tucked his curiosity away.

Mrs. Cross tilted her head examining him and beckoned him closer. She was a tiny little thing and looked rather frail on the bed. She touched her face, indicating his. "Are you all right?"

He glanced away and nodded. "Yes, ma'am. I'm just fine."

She only nodded then asked, "You gonna work some magic and help me remember more than I think I will?"

Sebastian smiled. "I'll do my best, ma'am."

She scoffed at that. "Call me Clara or Nana, young man. I've never met a sketch artist before. Come sit and chat with me."

He approached the bed, not knowing quite where to sit. Zavier reached out his hand and they shook, putting him a bit more at ease. "It's good to see you again, Sebastian. Why don't you take my seat, and I'll head down to the café with Finn and see if we can't scrounge up some mediocre coffee."

Sebastian cleared his throat again and nodded. "Thank you."

He set down his heavy messenger bag beside the chair Zavier had vacated and was about to speak to Mrs. Cross when she spoke to Zavier's brother. "Finnegan, I wanna get outta here."

Dr. McCade sat on the edge of the mattress and clasped her casted hand in his, kissing her fingers. "I'll be back in a bit, and I'll look at your chart and see what's what. Maybe we can blow this popsicle stand and ride off into the sunset. What do you say, beautiful?"

Sebastian couldn't help but smile at the scarlet tint flushing the woman's cheeks as she giggled. "Oh, go on with you then."

Dr. McCade grinned and leaned forward to buss her cheek. He stood, winked at Braden, and walked toward his brother. Both men exited, and he found himself transfixed by the two tall, self-assured men. By the time he turned back towards Braden and Mrs. Cross, they were both grinning at him knowingly.

Blushing again, he reached out to shake her hand, and she reached up with her left hand and clasped his, making the embarrassing moment seem a bit less awkward. He reached over to Braden to shake his hand and answered the man's wide grin, feeling a warmth in his chest when the other man clasped his hand in both of his and squeezed.

When Braden let go of his hand, he scooted behind Sebastian and picked up his messenger bag with a grunt. "Good lord, Sebastian, what have you got in here? Rocks?"

Sebastian smirked. "Yes. Pet rocks, actually. It's my thing. I bring them to all of my appointments."

Braden laughed as he'd expected and handed over the bag. "Here, sit closer to Nana so you can work with her on the sketch. I'll sit in the other chair."

Sebastian nodded and took the proffered chair. "Mrs. Cross, how are you doing?"

The woman huffed. "Please, call me Clara at least. Mrs. Cross sounds so formal. To tell you the truth, I've been better. That rat bastard came outta nowhere! Yanked my purse from my arm. I lost my balance and fell. Got all scraped up and I've got a broken arm that they said may take up to ten weeks to heal. I was about to leave and I got a little dizzy, so now they're checking everything under the sun. Drawing blood, asking about my medications, taking my blood pressure every other minute. I mean, really!"

Braden sighed. "Nana, they just need to make sure everything is okay before you leave. You weren't steady on your feet and your knee is very swollen, add in the blood pressure issue and they just want to dot all the I's and cross all the T's."

"Well they can leave my I's and T's alone, as far as I'm concerned. They want me off my feet with my leg elevated for a couple of days. And if that isn't bad enough, I had to cancel my date tonight because of this. Ira is in high demand, and that broad Irma is gunning for him. She's constantly reminding him that their names are so alike that it must be fate. Fate my ass! He better not go sniffing around her while I'm on my ass with my legs in the air."

Sebastian hid his smile behind his hand and had to fake a cough when a laugh nearly escaped after he heard Braden let out a muffled, "Jesus Christ."

He knew he couldn't look at Braden, or he'd continue to laugh, so with some effort, he got himself under control. "I'm so sorry, Clara. Maybe we can pass the time drawing what you remember of the suspect and you can leave soon after?"

She agreed, and he flipped open his bag, pulling out his supplies. "So why don't you walk me through your day from the moment you woke up, and we'll go from there."

She looked at him confused but did as he asked. When she got to the mugging, she made a dismissive noise in her throat. "I don't remember much except hitting the pavement. Then when I looked up, I saw him glance back at me before he turned and ran. Another woman stopped and called nine-one-one and stayed with me until help came."

Sebastian talked her back around to what she'd seen and began from there. Eventually, he had to get out his facial identification catalogues—the pet rocks in his bag—to help jog her memory. He spent about an hour and a half on the sketch, and when he was done and showed her the final results, her eyes popped wide. "Wow, you're really good at this. I never would've thought I saw as many details as you got out of me, but that's him."

He grinned at her enthusiasm. "I'm glad. You did great. Most of the time, people don't have confidence in what they've seen or if they'll be able to explain it to me in a way I can use, but usually, I can get more out of people than they think."

He never knew how successful his appointments would be, nor how long they would last, and depending on the type of crime involved, he'd schedule more or less time with his clients. Most of his time was utilized making the client comfortable. He had to build a certain level of trust with each person in order for them to relax enough to remember details they never thought they knew or had subconsciously buried in their minds.

He absentmindedly thanked Clara for her time while he unfolded his legs and leaned down to place the rendering in his completed sketches folder so it wouldn't get bent. He put his catalogues away as well and stood up to stretch. He tugged the legs of his jeans back down, zipped up his hoodie, yanked up the hood, and hooked his sunglasses in the V of the hoodie's zipper. Distractedly he continued to get ready to leave and slid the strap of his bag over his head, tightening it against his chest.

He leaned to clasp Clara's left hand and gave it a quick squeeze. "You did great, Clara. I hope Ira realizes what a catch you are and brings you flowers and waits on you hand and foot. If he's smart, I'm sure he'll do just that." He reached into his back pocket and pulled out a business card. "Now, if you remember anything else or have any questions for me, give me a ring, okay?"

She took the card and clasped his hand before he could pull it away. She tugged him down to her level and gave him a kiss on the cheek. "Thank you, Sebastian. You were very patient with an old lady such as me."

Blushing, as he'd never had someone kiss his cheek like that, he grinned self-consciously and did his best to move the focus from himself. "I don't see any old ladies in here, do you, Braden?"

He turned, seeking the man's eyes and found himself looking at a bemused Dr. McCade, sitting where Braden had been with an iPad balanced on his crossed leg. Beside him was a hospital reclining chair where Braden sat on Zavier's lap. He blushed even deeper, realizing that he'd been so intent on his work that he'd had no idea the other men had returned.

He cleared his throat, embarrassed. "Sorry it took so long. I'll get out of your hair. I have an appointment in..." He checked his watch. "About twenty minutes with another client that I need to prepare for."

He made his way toward the door and was nearly able to escape when

Braden stopped him with a question. "Sebastian, do you like coffee and pastries?"

Caught off guard by the non-sequitur, he paused before answering. "Um. Yes, I do."

Braden stood and approached him, handing him a card. Sebastian saw Sugar n' Spice Café on the front and looked up questioningly. Braden took it from his fingertips and flipped it over, handing it back. "I wrote my cell number on the back. I co-own the café with my friend Maya. I'm the pastry chef there. Maybe when you've got a break in your schedule someday, you can come visit and we can have a coffee."

Sebastian was taken off guard. He knew the name of the café as it was where his friend Zoe worked. It also sounded as if Braden wanted to befriend him, and as he wasn't really familiar with that feeling, he found himself at a loss. He stared at the card, turned it over again, and rubbed his hand over the penned number on the back. He realized after several long, drawn-out seconds he needed to respond in some way. He smiled shyly at Braden who looked concerned. "Thank you. That sounds nice."

Braden smiled in return, and Sebastian tucked the card in the front pocket of his jeans. He didn't have much time and needed to watch a few of his visual retraining videos on his phone before his next appointment.

Sebastian tossed back a bottle of water from a vending machine in the cafeteria. He had about fifteen minutes before he had to meet his next client. Taking Braden's card out of his pocket, he smiled when he realized that Braden had taken Zavier's name, that fact not surprising him at all.

He flipped over the card and ran his finger over the handwritten mobile number again. His heartbeat sped up when he unlocked his phone and went to his contacts. Nearly empty, his list contained several people at the station, the number to the art co-op where he rented a studio for his other work, the number to the laser center where he had his treatments, and finally Zoe, the only person on the list he would call a friend. A small smile flitted over his face as he added Braden's number to his short list of contacts.

Chapter 5

SEBASTIAN

It had been a while since Sebastian had been to the club. He'd had his last laser treatment, and then gotten caught up with work. He'd made plans earlier in the week to go to Catharsis on Saturday night with Zoe, but she'd cancelled earlier in the day because she'd caught some kind of bug. He was disappointed because she was always fun to be with, but he needed an outlet that night and wasn't going to skip it.

He faked his way through social situations which didn't lend itself to making many friends. Pretending or playing a role was something he'd had to become adept at from an early age when he'd figured out that having a crush on the cute boy in the Sunday school class at his parents' church wasn't normal for boys his age.

He pulled on his skintight mesh, long-sleeved black shirt, adding his leather chest harness over the top of it. He clipped on the bottom part of the harness to the chest portion, his naked cock framed nicely by two leather straps that connected and crossed under his sac and wrapped around the underside of his ass cheeks and back around to just above his hips where they were connected to a metal ring.

He put on his wide leather cuff bracelets that could latch to the metal rings on the harness at his hips, if a Dom chose to do so. He slid on his black, skinny stretch jeans that had black leather patches everywhere, some with zippers on them. Last, he pulled on his scuffed-up eight-eye Doc Martens and looked at himself in the mirror.

As always, he avoided looking at anything above his neck, and the critical once-over he gave himself was just that, critical. He mostly kept mirrors around so he could check to see he wasn't leaving the house with a zipper down or something else embarrassing that would make matters even worse. Shrugging, and knowing that staring at himself in the mirror wasn't going to improve matters, he threw on his black hoodie, zipped it up to cover his chest harness completely, and tossed up the hood. He didn't want to deal with even more side eyes than necessary out in public.

He stepped outside just as his Lyft driver pulled up in front of his place. Hopping in the back, he buckled the seatbelt, and put his buds in. His knee bounced with nervous anticipation. Never knowing what he was going to find at the club, or if he'd find anything at all, was a source of tension for him every single time. The anticipation for the possibilities of what could happen was sometimes the only anticipation he felt some nights.

Putting himself out there with Doms was much easier for him than trying to make friends with the other subs. His shy demeanor and inability to meet most people's direct gaze was actually a benefit in the BDSM lifestyle. That didn't mean he had Doms clamoring for his submission—far from it—it just meant that it wasn't panic attack inducing.

With other subs, he had to figure out what to say and when to say it, with Doms, they did the talking, and he spoke only when asked a direct question. Even he could handle that. But it was never a given that he'd get a proposition. There was often a lot of indifference where he was concerned, and if he did garner enough interest for a scene, it was never enough for a repeat performance.

Sometimes he wondered if it was worth it, getting all worked up for the possibilities of something happening then coming home so often without so much as a flogging. He'd stop going for a few weeks, but then he'd realize that during those self-inflicted breaks he'd have no physical human contact of any kind besides handshakes with clients, and ultimately he'd return to see if he could get his needs met.

He yearned for human contact more than he'd ever admit to anyone—even if it was just the touch of a tawse, a whip, or a cane to his skin. But yearning for something didn't mean it would happen, and more often than not, it would feel like he'd take anything he could get in order to make it through another week. It had become like a drug, and he never knew when he'd get his next fix. Sebastian knew deep down he was lucky to receive the few scenes he got and consoled himself with that.

He looked out the window to the street passing by and realized he was only a few minutes away from the club. He stopped the music on his phone and opened the club's app. Checking in and flagging himself available for play, he took a look at who else was playing that evening. Several of the Doms he'd scened with before were there, but his heartbeat picked up when he noticed several Doms that he'd never met before. He clicked on their profiles to see what their preferences were and was happy to see there were no red flags that would push up against his hard limits. Perhaps he'd have a successful night after all.

He stepped out of the Lyft car and walked towards the front door, surprised to see no one else out front. Not that the place was the type to have a line around the corner—it was members only, and fairly exclusive—but it was a Saturday, one of its busiest nights, and usually Sebastian arrived at the same time others were heading inside.

He'd been a member for three months, and the club itself had only been open for about eleven. Years before, it had been a gay dance club that had eventually failed as the location hadn't kept its clientele loyal when there were more trendy and upscale clubs popping up all over the place in other parts of the city. Rumor was, the new owner had come out of nowhere, bought the whole warehouse, and dove into renovations before the ink was dry on the permits. It had been a long renovation, and though the outside of the warehouse had gotten a facelift, it still had that old industrial feel.

People wouldn't walk by and think the place was a BDSM club. The front door was a huge, antique looking, solid sliding metal door. The large, stainless steel letters above the door were backlit with warm yellow lighting. Sebastian would have bet his next paycheck they were heavy and made by an artist, not your run of the mill sign maker.

There were no bouncers outside to draw attention to passersby, though there was one inside, or at least that's what he thought the paradox of a man was that always manned the reception desk when he visited the club. He approached the door and typed his personal code into the keypad, unlocking the door. Putting his weight behind it, Sebastian pulled the heavy door open along its slider, stepped in, and pulled it shut behind him. He turned and smiled at Khaleo, the lone occupant of the club's foyer entrance.

Rather than the stereotypical huge musclebound barbarians with black t-shirts and shit-kickers with arms crossed menacingly over their chests, Khaleo was about five-ten and always had on a pastel color of some kind. Tonight, it was a button-down pink dress shirt. Sebastian could never tell what nationality he was, but his skin was a flawless golden-brown color, his hair short and dyed bright lavender.

He always wore makeup that was expertly applied and artfully done. Some nights, he looked like he was ready to perform in some kind of sci-fi adventure stage performance. He was a particular level of beautiful that would often be termed feminine, but there was something in his eyes, an awareness, an edge, that kept one from thinking he was anything but masculine.

He'd actually drawn the man several times over, from memory. The first time he did so, he realized the man seemed remarkably laid-back, almost tranquil, but the more he looked, the more Sebastian thought he was so much more than the club greeter and began to assume he was more than likely a bouncer.

He smiled to himself as he remembered one drawing of the beautiful man he'd done where he was a ninja superhero comic character in black spandex from head to toe, leaping through the air as he chased down a villain. When Sebastian approached, he glanced up and saw Khaleo's raised eyebrow at his expression, and quickly schooled his features, glancing back down to the floor.

"Good evening, Sebastian."

"Good evening, Sir." He didn't know if the man was a Dom, a sub, neither, or a switch, so he always went with that honorific to be safe.

He stepped forward and raised his left arm. Khaleo slipped a lime green paracord adjustable bracelet on his wrist, signifying he was submissive and available for play. Not everyone utilized the club's app for the purpose of meeting members, and even when they did, pictures were not provided until personal messages were exchanged and both parties approved and sent their own picture from their phone.

He headed into the submissives' locker room and used the app to get into his assigned locker, locking his stuff in it with the touch of a button to his phone. Making his way out of the locker room, he walked toward the main area which was called the Tranquility Room, directly to the enormous L-shaped bar.

Grateful to find an available seat where he could easily turn and observe the goings on, he waited patiently until one of the bartenders noticed him. A few minutes later, Taryn stood before him, smiling shyly. He chuckled softly as he realized what a pair they were, both nearly unable to meet the other's gaze, trying to communicate without having to say a word.

Her voice was raised just enough to be heard above the low noise level of the club's main bar area. "What can I get you, Sebastian?"

He smiled and pulled out his phone, opening the club's app and navigated to his drink code. Holding it out to her, she scanned the QR code from his phone and one of the two alcoholic beverages allowed per visit was removed from his account. "Vodka tonic, extra lime, please."

Nodding, she got to work on his drink. He knew she was a submissive because he'd seen her wrist cord before when she wasn't working. He'd also seen her in a few demo scenes. She was a striking woman with naturally red hair that was cut in a short pixie style; enormous, beautiful green eyes, artfully smoky; and clear gloss on her plump bow lips. Handing over his drink, she smiled again and moved on to her next customer.

He scanned the darkened room, enjoying the view. As he sipped leisurely on his drink, he relaxed. He wasn't in a hurry, so he left his phone on the bar instead of perusing the profiles of the new Doms to see if they were available for play. He loved the aesthetics of the enormous club.

This room was dimly lit, as was the whole club, including the locker rooms and the elevators. Sebastian supposed it was for ambiance, but whatever the reason, he loved it since it helped him feel more at ease and less on display. Along two walls of the room were large, semi-circular booths, each with a gorgeous burnt orange glass pendant light hanging above it, providing enough lighting to see the other occupants, but only just.

Though it wasn't a restaurant, along with its vast array of drink options, the bar did serve small, select dishes. Depending on one's mood, people could order cocktails and fancy hors d'oeuvres or specialty coffees and pastries. Sebastian thought of the room as the heart of the club. It was the place people came to meet up, to socialize. There was always a quiet hum of energy, and everyone, following some unspoken rule, kept their voices pitched low.

In addition to the booths, there were seating areas dispersed throughout the whole room surrounding a moveable center stage that held nightly scenes. They were either scenes between Doms and their subs who wanted an audience, or between Club Masters and subs in order to demonstrate a particular implement or kink request. The stage was scheduled to be used sometimes once, sometimes twice, a night, and otherwise could be used at whim by people spontaneously wanting to have a scene where others could watch or participate. He'd never gotten up on the stage and didn't have any desire to do so.

The area, when not used for demos or scenes, was mostly used for visiting, a gathering place for before or after play. What Sebastian loved most was the occasional glimpse of a Dom giving his sub aftercare. It wasn't the only place for it, but when it happened, everyone respected the Dom's space and gave the couple privacy. He'd often get caught up watching those private interludes, recognizing it for what it was, yearning. As he continued to sip his drink his gaze fell on such a couple.

He watched as the Domme took care of her female submissive. The scene was intimate, the Domme, a statuesque woman in red leather pants, black spiked heels, and a gorgeous black corset, leaned back on a low-slung leather sofa, her tiny sub curled up in her lap, blanket wrapped around her. Sebastian watched as the Domme murmured quietly to the sub, Sebastian seeing the sub's occasional nod. He smiled as he watched the Domme run her hand over the sub's hair and ghost her lips over the sub's forehead. One of the servers approached and brought them both glasses of water. The Domme bringing the straw to her sub's lips, taking nothing for herself.

"It's fun to people watch here, isn't it?"

Even though the comment wasn't loud, Sebastian hadn't been expecting anyone to speak to him, so he'd nearly jumped out of his skin. He was surprised enough to look directly into the eyes of the man who'd spoken to him, he felt the subtle challenge in the man's gaze and automatically looked down. Warmth, mostly from embarrassment, colored his cheeks. "Yes, Sir."

"I'm sorry, I didn't mean to startle you."

The man glided his hand lightly over Sebastian's forearm. Something in Sebastian wanted to pull away, but he knew that wasn't a smart move. Beggars can't be choosers, after all. So, he kept his arm where it was, grabbed his drink with the other, and tossed the remainder of it back. Taryn had apparently been keeping her eye on his drink and approached again. He tapped the rim of his glass, and opened the app, pulling up the QR code. Once it was scanned and he had another drink in his hand, Sebastian turned a little more towards the man who had finally taken his hand off of his arm.

"What's your name, boy?"

Sebastian shuddered, confused why he didn't like it when *that* man called him boy, especially when it was something he usually longed to hear. "Sebastian, Sir."

"Sebastian, how long have you been a member here?"

"Three months."

"Mmm, not long then."

"No. You, Sir?"

"I'm pretty new as well."

Sebastian nodded, knowing he'd never seen him before. The man leaned closer, invading his space. "What were you looking at so intently out there?"

Everything in Sebastian was telling him to move away, but he didn't dare. He cleared his throat instead. "Oh, just a couple on one of the couches."

The man jutted his chin out towards the room. "Which one, boy?"

Sebastian felt compelled to glance towards the Domme and her sub again. "The Domme, giving aftercare to her sub, to the left, just there."

The man stayed in his personal space making goose bumps skitter up his arms. "You into voyeurism?"

Sebastian let out a slow, uneasy breath, trying not to draw attention to the fact that the man made him unusually uncomfortable. "Not particularly, Sir."

The man sat back in his chair all of a sudden and gave him more space. With that space, he felt more at ease, and they continued to chat for a while about the club and its members, about the clothes people were wearing, about his limits, and finally, about the club app.

Things started feeling much better to him, his chest wasn't tight with anxiety, and he began to feel really relaxed. He glanced at his drink and smiled when he realized it was empty. He was happy the alcohol had helped him feel so relaxed. He hadn't wanted to turn down the one man that had shown him interest in weeks.

"…me what it can do, boy."

Oops, he'd missed something. "I'm sorry, Sir, what did you say?"

Sebastian was sure he was wrong about the man's jaw clenching. "You said the app can do so many things. Will you show me what it can do?"

"Uh, yeah, sure."

Fumbling with his phone, he slowly keyed in his code. Not exactly feeling nimble-fingered, he chuckled at himself. Shaking his head to clear it, he opened the club's app, showing the man how he could check in, look at people's profiles, open his assigned locker, and use codes to get drinks.

He clicked on another icon and opened the floor plan of the club, showing him all three floors. The middle floor was the one with the entrance, the floor above that, housing the private rooms that were purchased by those that could afford the exorbitant prices for a permanent space, and the basement floor where people danced and got crazy and also where people signed out voyeur rooms. He was about to shut it down when the man pointed out a few icons. "What are these?"

"Oh!" Excited to show off what it could do, he clicked one of the icons. "You can actually search to see what rooms are available and when. You can check out rooms from anywhere from thirty minutes to two hours for scenes. Isn't that cool?"

He grinned and looked at the Dom, expecting to see an impressed look on the man's face but was confused when he was faced with what he thought was annoyance. When the man saw he was looking directly at him, he raised a brow, his expression morphing into a strange smile. "Seriously? How?"

Sebastian nodded his head. "Yeah, uh, like if you click on the private rooms icon, it takes you to a list of the private rooms by name."

"Private rooms?"

Sebastian cleared his throat. "Yeah. So, the rooms downstairs are set up so that people can watch the scenes, and the ones up here are set up so that they are private, and no one can watch."

"How can you tell they're free?"

Sebastian scrolled through the list and frowned. "Well, none of the private rooms are free right now. Busy night, I guess."

"And the ones downstairs can't be private?"

Confused by the questions, Sebastian shrugged. "Uh, well. From what I remember you can make them private by marking it as a closed scene."

The man nodded. "Are there any of those open?"

Sebastian backed out of the private rooms list to click on the voyeur rooms list and saw the Interrogation Room was open. He tilted his phone towards the man. "Looks like this one's available, see the green dot next to the room name?"

"Show me how to check it out."

"Oh, okay. Do you want to get your phone out, so you know how next time?"

"Forgot my phone."

Sebastian frowned. How had he even gotten by Khaleo, without checking in? Confused, he rubbed his palm over his forehead, not sure why things were so muddled. "But, how did you—"

Abruptly, the man stood. Annoyance written across his face. "I guess you aren't interested in being my sub tonight."

Sebastian, hearing him say "my sub"—words he so very rarely heard—and seeing his only chance at a scene slipping away, stood up as well. Reaching towards the man to stop him from leaving, he got a bit dizzy and pitched forward into him instead. "I'm sorry, Sir. I'm not sure what's wrong. Please, I want to scene with you. Let me check out that room."

Sebastian, fingers moving slowly not understanding why he felt so strange, was startled when the phone was pulled out of his hands. He watched as the man checked out the room and listed it as closed for observation. Another of those strange smiles ghosted over the Dom's face. "There, now we'll have privacy for a couple hours."

Sebastian smiled, no one usually wanted to spend that long with him. Maybe he had found someone that would want him more than one time. "Thank you, Sir."

The man merely grunted and headed towards the alcove that hid the stairs and elevator. Once they got into the elevator and were headed down, the Dom turned his way. "Where is the Interrogation Room?"

Sebastian held his tongue again when he wanted to question why the man didn't know where he was going or seem to know what he was doing. "We'll come out in the main bar area downstairs, turn to the right, and head back into the hallway where all of the voyeur rooms are located."

When the elevator doors slid open with a soft ding, they both stepped out into the alcove and walked into the main bar area called the Liberation Room. The Dom turned to head towards the voyeur rooms, and Sebastian bumped into someone when he rounded the corner. He gasped and nearly fell. The Dom turned and threw him a dirty look, grabbing his arm above his leather wrist cuff and pulling him into his side. Sebastian turned back to apologize to whoever he'd bumped into and saw the club's trainer/manager watching him. He pasted a happy smile on his face and waved, mouthing "sorry" and hoping he didn't draw any more attention to himself.

The Dom pulled him along, arm wrapped around his waist, squeezing him a bit too tightly. When they got to the room, he tried to open it, but it was locked. "What the fuck?"

Sebastian couldn't help it, he sniggered, pulling out his phone. "You have to get the temporary room code that's assigned to you when you check the room out."

Again, the phone was yanked out of his hand and the arm wrapped around him was removed as the man entered his phone code. What? "Hey. . . How'djaknow—"

The Dom narrowed his eyes challengingly at Sebastian. "Don't you remember telling me?"

"What? No. I—" Another wave of dizziness hit him, and he leaned on the wall. He tried to sort out his jumbled thoughts but couldn't remember them talking about his phone code. "I don't think—"

"There we go. Come on, boy. Let's have some fun."

When Sebastian hesitated, the man grabbed his upper arm and propelled him inside, shutting the door behind him with a slam. Sebastian stumbled and nearly fell, thinking to himself that he wasn't having any fun at all.

Chapter 6

GIDEON

Gideon made his way around the Liberation Room, thus named because it was a place of complete liberation and physical abandon. The only rule in the room was there was no domination and submission play, nothing that would require a safeword because it would never be heard nor seen there.

The music was deep and full of the vibration and thump of the bass, people writhed on the dance floor, fucked against the wall, made out in the booths, and gave head in the corners. There were no tools of the trade allowed; no whips, handcuffs, or ball gags. Nothing but an enormous dance floor surrounded by booths, tables and chairs, sofas and armchairs.

He'd wanted to create a place where people could go wild and be free to be themselves, even if this was the only place they'd ever have that feeling. At first, he'd worried that people would get out of control, and always had undercover bouncers mingled with the others on the dance floor, keeping an eye on things.

Strangely enough, the room he thought would give him the most trouble, caused him the least amount. It seemed that just the simple fact that he'd provided the place for people to go wild, kept everyone from becoming out of control. It was a strange feeling of giving and receiving respect in turn, and he hadn't regretted creating the space for it once.

He had no doubt that the two-drink club limit was a big part of what kept things under control. He often found himself down there more often than not. When he remained upstairs in the Tranquility Room, he was constantly being approached by submissives desiring his attention.

He wouldn't run himself through subs at his own club. He scened with them, he did a lot of demos, and he kept his eye on the goings on around every single inch of his club, but he remained set apart. It kept him in check, kept his strongest desires at bay, but allowed him to feel a part of it regardless.

He admitted to himself that he felt a strange longing to be in the throng of dancers, participating in the sexual free-for-all, but being the owner both allowed him to keep himself removed mentally and required him to keep himself distant physically. It was enough, for now, to be involved peripherally. If that changed in the future, so be it, but keeping himself removed kept him in his comfort zone and others from getting too close.

As he rounded the dance floor for a third time, checking on the writhing bodies and the couples and throuples making use of the couches and booths, he heard his club manager, Roarke Ramirez, speak to him through their security earpiece. "Master G, I need you to meet me at the Interrogation Room, immediately."

Gideon responded that he was on his way. Tension mounting, he hurriedly pushed himself through the throng of people. Roarke was a cautious man and didn't raise flags without good reason. Rushing down the hall to the room in question, he saw his manager there at the security panel. He keyed in his code as Gideon neared him and the door to the right of the room in question opened up, allowing them into the voyeur area adjacent to the room in question. They kept the light off as they walked to the huge two-way mirror.

The room was partially set up as a police interrogation room, hence the name. Outfitted with a metal table with handcuffs attached to the center and metal chairs with their own handcuffs attached to the sides, it also housed a number of other tools of the trade, including a spanking bench and many instruments of sexual pleasure and torture.

He was confused as to why Roarke had called him in. There was a submissive, trussed up on the bench, facing away from the mirror, his head completely covered by a loose hood. The scene wasn't alarming, at first glance. The Dom's cock was hard and sticking out from his fly, wrapped and from the looks of it, lubed. Nothing overt was off. The scene—like many others that occurred on a nightly basis in that room and others like it down the hall—didn't signal any of Gideon's warning bells.

That was, until Roarke turned the sound on so they could listen to what was going on. He knew immediately why he'd been called in when all he heard was the whisper of the cane as it arced through the air and was brought down with enormous force on the boy's skin.

It was more a feeling that something wasn't right, rather than anything visually alarming. "Check the feeds. I want eyes on this guy from the second he arrived. He's not a member, I'd remember his face, so he's got to be a visi-tor. And get the feeds on whoever signed him in as a guest. Who's the boy?"

"Sebastian, Sir."

"The one you've been telling me about?"

"Yes, Sir."

"Get the feeds for him as well."

"Yes, Sir."

Gideon waited as Roarke spoke into the mic that was connected to his security earpiece. He relayed his directives and then nodded at Gideon that their in-house security team was working on it. They didn't have on-site video and audio security personnel, as of a couple of months prior, they'd paid Custos to manage that for them, off-site. He had two dedicated Custos employees to monitor their feeds live every night they were open. So far, they'd had no call to pull the footage in all the time they'd been open. That they had to do so tonight pissed him off and new security measures would be put in place as a result to keep it from happening again.

"You've seen the boy in scenes. Is he usually this quiet?"

"No, Sir. That's why I called you to observe. Everything about this feels off because I know Sebastian's reactions. He ran into me when he came down from upstairs. He turned around to see who he'd knocked into and the guy didn't let him stop. Sebastian tried to smile and say sorry, but was being pulled away from me."

"Was he resisting being pulled away? Did he look distressed?"

"No. He didn't appear to be resisting, but he didn't appear to be excited either, which is unlike him. He's the most eager to please sub I've ever tested. Also, unless he's told not to make a sound, the Dom knows when Sebastian is enjoying what's going on. His noises are beautiful to hear."

As they continued to observe, the whisper of the cane was still the only sound to be heard and the only movement being made was that of the Dom, no reaction to the cane's blows at all. "Is he a masochist?"

"I don't think so, Sir. He can take a lot, but I believe it's more about pleasing the Dom."

Suddenly, the boy began to jerk in his bindings, and it was immediately apparent he wasn't playing. There was no give in his ties, and it just appeared the boy was flopping around in an unsuccessful attempt to escape. It stopped a few seconds later then again, there was no movement at all.

They heard a growl from the man with the cane. Gideon got another good look at the man's face and the anger there made his blood run cold. He was moving before he even realized it. As he ran into the hall to the other door, he heard the man yell, "You ugly little fucker! If I'd have known you were such a freak, I'd never have wasted my time on you!"

Gideon keyed in his master code and shoved angrily at the door. It flew open with a loud bang and the man jumped, lowering the cane. "What the fuck? Get the hell out! This is a private session; you have no right to come in here!"

Gideon ignored him completely, his eyes never leaving the boy's small frame. It hadn't moved when he'd thrown the door open. When the man raised the cane as if he was going to continue, Gideon spared the man a glance. "I wouldn't if I were you."

"I'll do whatever the fuck I want! I paid good money to visit this dive tonight, and I'm gonna get my money's worth!"

As if to prove his point, he lowered the cane in a swift arc. Gideon moved quickly, catching it in his palm, and yanked it towards him. The man, still holding onto the other end, stumbled forward. Gideon gave another yank and the guy finally let go. "Fuck this shit. I'm outta here, he's not worth it anyway. Fucking freak."

Gideon glanced back and gave a slight shake of his head. Roarke moved into the room and shut the door behind him, effectively blocking the man's exit. As the guy began to rail in indignation at being locked in, Gideon blocked him out and focused on the boy in front of him.

As he rounded the bench and gently pulled the hood from the boy's head, he realized he had a ball gag in his mouth and his eyes didn't open when the hood was removed. His cheek was slightly swollen and pink, causing Gideon to clench his teeth in anger, wondering if he'd been slapped. His heartbeat kicked up several notches when he ran his fingers through the boys long, dark bangs and he still didn't respond.

Making quick work of the bindings connecting his legs to the bench, he went to work on his arms and stilled at the terrified moan that ripped through the room. The boy was shaking his head violently as if trying to say no, to safeword, to stop what had been happening to him.

Suddenly, he started to gag and Gideon nearly lost ten years off his life as he scrambled to trigger the quick release clasp on the ball gag so the boy could

SAVING SEBASTIAN: A CATHARSIS NOVEL

vomit without choking himself to death. Internally cursing the other man to the pits of hell and annoyed with himself that he hadn't taken it off first thing, Gideon held the boy's head as he retched on the floor. The mess that hit Gideon's shirt and pants was a small price to pay for the boy's safety.

When the sub was done getting sick, Gideon used the bottom of his t-shirt to gently wipe away his tears and anything left on his face, all the while murmuring to him. "You're all right. You're safe. I've got you. Nothing else is going to happen to you, boy. You're safe now."

He looked at Roarke to ask him to get some water, but the man was already on it, walking towards him with a bottle in his hand. As he did so, Gideon watched as the asshole tried to beat a hasty retreat when he saw the door was no longer being manned. Gideon watched him with narrowed eyes as he tried the door only to realize it was locked from the inside. He started yelling again, about his rights, about who he was, about what he'd paid, and on and on, but Gideon didn't spare him another glance.

He was worried that the boy seemed so out of it. When his eyes had closed again after he'd gotten sick, Gideon guessed what had happened and the anger rolling through his body was burning out of control. He finally worked the restraints off the boy's arms, leaving him where he was for now, as there wasn't a more comfortable place for him to rest in the room.

He looked at Roarke and the man came to him immediately. He ran his hand through the boy's hair again, giving him soft, reassuring touches. When he lifted his hand Roarke nodded and took his place, continuing to touch the unconscious boy as Gideon approached the man who now stood pacing by the door.

"The first thing you're gonna do is open up that cabinet over there and get out the cleaning supplies. You're gonna clean every single drop of that vomit off the floor until it sparkles. Then you're gonna sit down at one of the chairs and allow Master Roarke to handcuff you to the table."

"The fuck I am!"

As if the man hadn't spoken, Gideon continued. "Then you're going to wait, patiently, until the police arrive to take your ass in."

"You can't keep me here! Do you know who I am? You have no right to keep me against my will! I did nothing wrong! That little freak was begging for it! He wanted to be beaten! Let me the hell outta here!"

Gideon got into the man's space, his chest wedging the asshole against the door. Putting his back to the cameras, he pulled the ever-present knife out of his pocket, holding it up just enough for the man to see, his eyes going wide. He brought up his other hand, grabbing onto the man's chin and tilting his head up and back at an uncomfortable angle, the knife down low, against the fly the coward had tucked his dick back into at some point.

He leaned down next to his ear and spoke in a guttural whisper. "You'll never harm any of my subs ever again, here or outside of the club. If you do, I'll hunt you down, torture you within an inch of your life, cut off your cock and balls, and shove them down your throat. I've done it before; I'll do it again. That's the last warning you'll receive from me."

"Master G."

The words, softly spoken, brought Gideon out of his angry haze. He turned and approached the bench again, surreptitiously tucking the knife away. The boy was trying to move, his actions slow and disjointed, as if he couldn't make his muscles work. He tried to raise his head but ultimately didn't have the strength. Gideon saw his eyes flutter open and then close again.

After several moments and a monumental effort on the boy's part, his eyes finally cracked open to half-mast and he looked around, confused, and disoriented as he began mumbling. Gideon had to lower himself to one knee to make out what he was saying.

"Red. Red. Red. Red."

Gideon's heart broke at the sound of the wounded boy, his litany of safewords continuing as Gideon looked up into the eyes of the man that had done that to him. The man paled at his venomous glare, understanding the danger he was in. Gideon ran his hand through the sub's hair, keeping it there, rubbing his head softly. With his other hand he began to touch his back, his arm, his shoulder, so gently, murmuring that he was safe. The boy finally stilled.

Gideon wanted to get him out of there, but the other rooms were booked this time of night, and he didn't want to draw attention to the situation and humiliate Sebastian. He'd be damned if anything else happened to make matters worse for him if he could help it. And as much as he wanted to find him a more comfortable place to be, his back, ass, and thighs were too damaged to move him more than once. He'd get things settled as quickly as possible and hopefully the ambulance would arrive quickly.

Gideon looked up at Roarke. "Call nine-one-one. We need him drug tested. I'm pretty sure he's been roofied. We also need a rape kit done—"

The man, his hand still guarding his cock after Gideon's threat, choked out his denial. "I didn't rape him! I never got the…"

Gideon stood, glaring at the man. "Never got the what, the chance? You pathetic piece of shit. We'll see if that's the case." Gideon glanced back at Roarke. "Regardless, we need to get him to the hospital."

"No." The whispered word, so weak and thready was repeated. "No."

Gideon bent down. "What is it, boy?"

"Nospital. Plee."

"Sebastian—"

Fear in his eyes, he slowly, painstakingly shook his head. "No, no."

Gideon let out a pained sigh and nodded his head. "No hospital, but I'm having a doctor come and check you out, understood?"

Sebastian opened his eyes again, just barely enough to gaze at him directly and nodded. Gideon's heart squeezed at the fear and sadness he saw there. "You're safe with me. I won't let anything happen to you."

Sebastian's slurred thank you had Gideon's fingers reaching out again to gently card them through the boy's hair. It was as if the single act of getting those final words out had sapped the last of his strength, and Sebastian closed his eyes again. Angry that they were in that situation, he stood and paced away. Pulling his phone from his pocket he called his brother.

"Gideon?"

"Yeah. Finn, I need your help."

There was a stunned silence on the other end of the line before Finn finally responded. "Anything."

Some of the tension left his shoulders. "I have a boy here that needs a doctor."

There was a pause as Finn put things together. "You're at the club?"

"Yes. I think he's been roofied, and there's also a possibility he's been raped."

"Jesus. Gideon, take him to the hospital. I'll meet you there."

"He doesn't want to go."

"He needs to, Gideon."

"Please, Finn. He asked me not to, and I promised I wouldn't. He's been through enough tonight; it's imperative that I don't break his trust after what he's been through."

Finn sighed. "So, a urine test and a rape kit."

45

Gideon took a deep breath. "Yes."

The way he answered must have given him away. "What aren't you telling me?"

"He's been caned."

"What the fuck does that. . . wait, you mean beat with a cane?"

Gideon's pause was answer enough. Finn let out a frustrated huff. "Christ, Gideon. Okay. I'll be there as soon as possible."

"I'm taking him up to my place. Use your code."

"Okay, see you soon."

"Finn?"

"What?"

"Thank you."

Finn let out an exasperated sigh. "You're welcome."

Gideon rubbed a hand over his forehead. Not having control of the situation was getting to him. He hated the censure he could hear in Finn's voice, and because it was so unlike his brother, he could hardly hold it against him. He was angry at himself for allowing this to happen in his own goddamn house.

His brother didn't understand the world he lived in, but regardless of that fact, it was the first time he'd felt Finn's disapproval since he'd told his family about his club. Gideon knew Finn wasn't upset because of the club itself, but that someone had gotten hurt on his watch, and as he felt the same disappointment in himself with the situation, all he could do was make it right and make sure it never happened again.

He was about to place a call to Zavier, but the phone rang in his hand. "You've heard."

"They're pulling the feeds for all three men. Is the boy okay?"

Knowing Zavier understood the BDSM lifestyle, he felt more at ease speaking with him about it than he did with Finn. "I think so, but I'm not sure. Finn's on his way. Would you trust that detective you worked with at the SFPD?"

"Detective Miller?"

"Whoever the guy was that worked on Braden's case."

"Yes, but he's no longer in the SVU."

"Shit."

"Let me check and see if I have his old lieutenant's number."

Gideon nodded, knowing his brother kept meticulous records and would find the information. "Yeah. Listen. Watch the feeds and call him. Explain to him what happened and have him send someone to pick up this asshole. Even if it's just a beat cop, I want them to know who they're dealing with and I want this taken seriously. Sebastian's not going to be up to talking to anyone tonight, so we'll probably just need someone to come and arrest the guy, and Sebastian can hopefully answer questions in the morning."

He finished his conversation with his brother and hung up the phone. He glanced at Roarke, whose eyebrows were raised in question. "Zavier?"

"Yeah. Listen, can you deal with him? I need to get Sebastian out of here and up to my place. He can't stay on this fucking bench any longer."

"Yeah, of course. I've got a couple more of our guys out in the hall. Let one of them escort you to the elevator."

Gideon nodded and gently grasped Sebastian's shoulders, tilting him back on his knees on the bench and holding him upright until he could gather his shoulders in one arm and scoop his other underneath his knees. The whimper that escaped the boy's lips escalated his rage. Gideon murmured softly to him and his heart lodged in his throat when Sebastian's body tensed and the most beautiful amber colored eyes opened to gaze steadily at him. "You're gonna be okay. You're safe with me."

He felt the tension leave Sebastian's body as they continued to look at each other, something indefinable shifting in Gideon's chest. Sebastian finally nodded at Gideon, closed his eyes, and leaned his head on Gideon's shoulder. When Gideon got to the doorway, Roarke met him there with a blanket and tucked the edges gently around the boy's small frame. He stirred, sucking in a breath, scared by that action alone, but settled again when Gideon murmured reassurances that he was safe.

The door was opened, and one of his security guards walked in the room to help Roarke, another waited for him to exit with Sebastian and closed the door after him. Gideon nodded at the guard dressed in Dom gear and allowed him to lead them through the throng of people in the Liberation Room and to the elevator. When they were safely ensconced inside, Gideon carefully entered his passcode into the keypad, and they were whisked up to the top floor that acted as his home.

Chapter 7

GIDEON

Gideon carried Sebastian to the bedroom, gingerly pulled the bedding back, and placed him gently down on his stomach. He dimmed the lights so they wouldn't bother the boy if he regained consciousness and headed out to the kitchen to get a bottle of water and some pain meds for him when he woke.

When he heard movement on the bed, he ran back to the bedroom to see the boy's body shaking. A few moments later he vomited again all over the pillow. Gideon put the water and pills on the nightstand and leaned in to lightly rub the boy's shoulder. When he sucked in a scared breath and pulled away, curling in on himself, Gideon whispered to him and he finally settled.

Making sure Sebastian wasn't in danger of backing himself off the bed, Gideon quickly turned the heat up in the bedroom and headed into the attached bath. Wetting a washcloth with warm water, he carried it back to the bed. He gently wiped the boy's face off and exchanged a clean pillow for the soiled one. Not knowing what else to do, and not wanting to make matters worse, he sat at the foot of the bed, his hand clasping the boy's calf just to reassure him that he wasn't alone. He leaned his other elbow on his knee and put his head in his hand.

When he heard Finn arrive a few minutes later, he stayed where he was, not wanting to leave Sebastian alone again. His brother entered the room, pulling his medical bag from across his shoulder and placing it on the floor. Gideon watched as Finn approached, seeing the anger gather in his eyes and the muscles in his jaw clench as he took the boy's battered form in from head to toe.

Gideon let his head fall again, rubbing his eyes. "He's mostly been unconscious since we got to him. He roused enough to try to speak his safeword and to tell me no hospital. He's vomited twice now. Once downstairs and once up here. I washed his face off and exchanged the pillows but I didn't want to do anything else because I didn't know what that would do to any evidence."

Finn crouched down by his bag and rifled through it, pulling out what he needed, he glanced up. "I'm not equipped to process a rape kit here. I'll leave a sample cup for him to urinate in so we can test him in the morning for anything he might have been slipped tonight. Some date rape drugs only stay in the body for twelve hours, others up to seventy-two, so as soon as he wakes, have him try to give you a sample. I need to check his vitals. Help me turn him to face me."

They both did their best to flip Sebastian over without hurting his backside further. Once he was facing them near the edge of the bed, Finn put his stethoscope in his ears and got down on his knee. A huff of air, expelled in surprise, caused Gideon to glance at his brother's face. Finn glanced from the boy to his brother, and back again. "Jesus, Gideon. It's Sebastian Phillips."

Gideon jerked his head back in surprise. "How do you know him? Have you treated him before?"

Finn shook his head and rubbed a hand back and forth over his mouth. "No. He's... I just met him recently when Braden's grandmother was mugged."

"Nana was mugged?"

Finn nodded. "Yeah. I was at the hospital checking on a few patients when Zavier called me."

"Is she okay?"

"She will be. Broken arm, a few lacerations and contusions, and a knee strain that's going to keep her down for a bit, which she's grumpy as hell about, but nothing permanent."

Gideon nodded absently, hoping her recovery was quick. He got a kick out of Braden's grandmother and hoped they found the person that mugged her. "But, what does that have to do with Sebastian?"

Finn sat back on his heel and draped his arm over his other knee. He lifted his chin towards Sebastian. "He's a composite artist for the SFPD. Did the sketch of Eric for Braden and came into the hospital to do Nana's sketch that day. He's brilliant at what he does. Seems like a nice kid. I guess I shouldn't be surprised that he's a submissive at your club."

As Finn sat up straighter and began the process of checking Sebastian's vitals, Gideon's forehead creased in confusion at his brother's last comment. "What do you mean by that?"

Finn continued working as they chatted. "He was just very shy. Wouldn't meet my eyes, was uncomfortable around most everyone in the room besides Braden."

Gideon nodded his head, knowing that explanation closely coincided with what Roarke had said about Sebastian before Gideon had even known who the boy was. He was about to ask Finn something else when his phone rang. Looking at the caller ID he answered Zavier's call immediately.

"What have you got?"

"Jesus, Gideon. I know you will regardless, but please treat this boy well. Did Finn get there already?"

Gideon stood up to pace. "Yeah. He told me you guys know him. And you know damn good and well that I'd treat him well regardless. He was my responsibility before it happened, and even more so now. It happened in *my* house, Zavier. That won't go unpunished."

"I know. We—"

Gideon interrupted, not wanting to be rude but unable to wait. "Have you seen all the tapes? I need to know if he was raped, Zavier."

"No. No, he wasn't raped."

"Thank fuck!" Gideon's knees went out in relief and he barely managed to land his ass on the bed at Sebastian's feet. His hand gently clasping the boy's calf, his thumb lightly stroking his soft skin, not even aware he was doing it.

"That asshole did drug him, though. We've found that much on the tapes. We're trying to get a better angle on it from a few other cameras. We want it to stand up in court, along with the boy's testimony."

Gideon nodded and then realized Zavier couldn't hear him. "Yeah. Do everything you can do to get this guy. I want a copy of what you find from the moment the guy arrives with his friend, and the moment Sebastian arrives. Send them to me immediately."

"Will do. I know you're aware that he was caned, but the guy also did his fair share of pushing the boy around. At one point, when he wasn't moving fast enough, the guy yanked on his arm and Sebastian fell into the table and hit his hip pretty hard. The asshole didn't even give him time to finish getting his pants off, which he was reluctantly and uncoordinatedly doing after he tried to tell the guy he was no longer in the mood."

He didn't even realize he'd growled low in his throat until he got a strange look from Finn and Zavier commented on it. "Take it easy. We'll get him. We've got audio on it as well. You've covered your bases."

Gideon cursed. "I'm not fucking worried about me."

Zavier sighed. "You know I didn't mean it that way. I want this asshole to go down and go down hard. This boy... He's just... He already means a lot to Braden, and he doesn't even know him that well, yet. There's a vulnerability, a fragility to him, yeah? Whatever you need from me, you've got it."

Gideon's shoulders sagged. "Yeah. Yeah, I know. Thanks."

They said their goodbyes and Gideon stared at his phone for several long moments before he glanced towards Finn. "He wasn't raped."

Finn nodded, having pieced it together himself. "That's good. It means we don't have to do a rape kit at the hospital. His blood pressure is a little low. I'm going to stay for a while to make sure we can get it under control. If it goes too low, he could go into shock. I'd like to clean up his wounds. With the blood smeared all over, I can't tell which welts are bleeding and which are just swollen."

They slowly moved the boy onto his stomach so they could take care of his injuries. Gideon made quick work of the harness and then the mesh shirt. There was blood under the shirt they needed to get to before they could settle him in for the night. As he drew off the shirt he noticed some light purplish red marks on Sebastian's shoulder and neck.

He moved Sebastian's hair away to see more of it and saw that the light marks made their way up in a splotchy pattern under the boy's beard and onto his right cheek. It was what Gideon had thought was swelling, and possible bruising in the fluorescent lights in the Interrogation Room, but now looked less noticeable.

"Finn?"

He turned to face his brother and gestured to the strange marks. "Do you know what could have caused this?"

Finn leaned over the boy, looking at Sebastian's neck and shoulder. "It's a port-wine stain."

"A what?"

"A birthmark."

Gideon's brow furrowed. "Is it painful?"

Finn gave his brother a soft smile and shook his head. "No."

Gideon glanced once more at the unconscious boy. Unable to help himself, he leaned over and ran his fingers over Sebastian's dark hair, its texture as soft as silk. The more time he was around the submissive, the angrier he got at what had happened. Glancing down at the boy's ravaged back, ass, and thighs, he clenched his fists and faced his brother again.

"What can I do to help?"

Finn glanced at his fists, causing Gideon to release them and take in a deep breath. Finn clapped him lightly on the back. "We'll clean and treat his wounds then you can ice them. I'll stay until his blood pressure stabilizes."

Gideon nodded, and they got to work cleaning the boy up. When all was said and done, the blood had made things look worse than they were. Afterwards, Gideon went and grabbed a few bags of frozen veggies and wrapped them in thin kitchen towels. He came back and placed the bags on the worst of the swollen welts left by the cane and covered the boy up with his sheet, pulling the duvet up to cover his legs as well. Finn and Gideon picked up all of the medical supplies, turned the light off in the room, and headed into his kitchen.

Gideon grabbed them both a bottle of water from the fridge, hitching himself up on the bar and watched as Finn finished packing up his supplies. They'd both been quiet while cleaning and treating the wounds, and he thought the silence might veer towards the uncomfortable if he didn't speak up. "Thank you for coming."

Finn looked up from his bag, his brows drawn together. "I'll always come if you need me. You know that, right? I'm sorry if I've made things uncomfortable between us. I—"

Gideon shook his head. "Finnegan, you haven't made things uncomfortable, I have. I know my. . . sexual proclivities probably freaked out everyone in our family." He chuckled and rubbed the back of his neck. "Well, besides Zavier, I guess. I wasn't going to tell you guys about the club at all, but I figured news would travel back to all of you anyway. I'm not ashamed or embarrassed by anything, but I usually don't talk about it. I'm working on that. I had to keep secrets from you guys for far too long."

Finn nodded solemnly. "This is the longest conversation we've had in a really long time."

"I'm sorry for that. I've been back for a while, I just find it hard to join in on the conversations at family dinners. I want to be there, I was just guarded for so damned long, it's like I still don't know what to say, so I don't say anything at all."

"'Cause you were just *so* chatty when we were younger."

Gideon snorted. A joke from Finn at his expense; god, how long had it been? "True."

Finn chuckled then seemed to grow serious again, rubbing his hands over his face. Gideon's heart squeezed, thinking his brother might be disappointed in him, or worse, disgusted with him, but when Finn looked back up Gideon was surprised to see laughter mixed with embarrassment on his brother's face.

"Oh, and just to allay your fears about you freaking everyone out in our family, let me tell you a little story. A couple of weeks ago, Dad asked me to stop by the house to help him move a few pieces of furniture. Mom bought an antique writing desk to replace the one she has in her office. I knocked when I came in through the side door, gave Buckley a few treats, and let him outside with his Kong. I heard Mom and Dad upstairs in her office and headed that way. Dad's bent over her old desk, pulling out the drawers to make it easier to move the damned thing. You know how massive it is, right?"

When Finn glanced at him, Gideon smiled and nodded as he raised his bottle of water for a drink. Finn continued, his cheeks turning red with embarrassment. "So, Mom's telling him to let her empty them first before he 'messes everything up' and Dad says, 'Baby, I'm not gonna mess up a damn thing. You keep complaining, and Daddy's gonna have to bend you over his knees again and make that gorgeous ass of yours all pretty and red.'"

Gideon choked on the gulp of water he'd just taken, his eyes watering as some of it shot up his nose. He coughed for a full minute and finally glanced over at Finn who handed him a paper towel, his eyes wide and face still red, but now he was nodding in commiseration. "I swear to Christ, Gideon, my ears were bleeding. She started to respond to him, but I hightailed it outta there so fast I nearly blew my cover tripping over my own two feet down the stairs."

Gideon shook his head, closed his eyes, and rubbed his hand over his mouth. "I just threw up a little in my mouth. What the hell did you do?"

Finn made a horrified face and threw up his hands in defeat. "What could I do? I went to the downstairs bathroom and washed the shame off of my hands in lieu of a full-on shower, splashed water on my face, and tried unsuccessfully to convince myself it was all a nightmare. Needless to say, I made an enormous amount of noise calling out to them from the foyer before going back upstairs and pretending I didn't just die a little inside from hearing that."

Gideon had started laughing when Finn mentioned needing a shower, but when Finn was done, his laughter had turned into guffaws and both of them could barely breathe by the time they were done. Gideon rubbed the tears of mirth off his cheeks. "I'll take 'Things I never wanted to learn about my parents for three hundred, Alex…'"

Finn, wiping his own face, shook his head. "No fucking kidding."

Gideon gave Finn's shoulder a good hard shove. "You're an asshole for telling me that."

Finn chuckled. "I had to share my pain. *First,* you tell us you've randomly purchased a BDSM club, and *then* I'm horrified to find out the shenanigans Mom and Dad are into. I was *not* going to suffer alone!"

Gideon shook his head and tossed back the rest of his water. "Still an asshole, but I'm sorry I dropped that on you guys the way I did."

"I'm not. I'm glad you told us. We don't think of you differently, you know that, right?"

Gideon shrugged. "When I called you earlier, I know you were upset—"

Finn tilted his head and raised a brow. "You think I was acting like that because of the club?"

Gideon shook his head. "No. I know you're okay with the fact that I own the club. You were upset because I let it happen—"

Finn raised his hands. "Whoa, no, Gideon. If you'd have known, you'd have stopped it. You didn't *let* anything happen, and I know damn good and well you'll deal with it. I was pissed off that someone in your club, a *submissive* in your club, was assaulted and drugged. Submissives put a lot of trust in the Doms at clubs like yours from what I understand. I was pissed that someone would do that under the guise of domination and submission."

Gideon's eyes popped up. "Finn, is there something you wanna tell me? Are you interested in the lifestyle?"

Finn's face burned bright red. "No. At least, I don't think I am. I just started reading about it after you told us, that's all."

Gideon hopped down from the counter and yanked his younger brother into a tight embrace. "Never was a topic you discovered that you didn't want to learn everything about." Pulling away, Gideon clapped Finn on the back.

"You never know. You might find yourself interested in some hands-on learning. If you are, let me know and I can help."

Finn's eyes bugged out of his head, his expression horrified, making Gideon laugh. "Jesus, Finnegan. I wouldn't be the one to teach you. I have a Master on staff that coordinates the training needs of our members."

Gideon shook his head when Finn let out a relieved breath. He grinned sheepishly. "Okay, well, I'll be sure to let you know."

"You do that. So listen, why don't you sleep on the couch?"

"Where are you gonna sleep?"

Gideon shrugged. "Well, the couch is a sectional, so it's probably big enough for both of us, but I can sleep on the floor in my room to keep an eye on him. I've slept in worse places."

"True enough, but you're getting on in years, ya know."

Gideon made a rude noise in the back of his throat and pushed his brother. "You're not that much younger, Finnegan. Let me go grab you some bedding for the couch."

"I'll come with you and check his blood pressure again. I'll set my alarm to wake and continue to check it throughout the night. Once it's stabilized, I'll head home. I have an early morning surgery, so I'll need to leave before you're up anyway."

Finn checked Sebastian's blood pressure and it had improved slightly. Gideon handed over the bedding for the sofa and gave him some toiletries. He brushed his teeth and grabbed a couple pillows and a blanket for the floor.

He'd only been down there for about thirty minutes when Sebastian cried out in his sleep. When he whispered his safeword, his voice shaky, Gideon sat beside him on the bed, placing a gentle hand on his slender shoulder. The boy calmed immediately. After a few minutes, he lay back down on the floor.

A couple hours later Sebastian's cries woke him again. That time when Gideon sat gently beside him and placed a hand on his shoulder, the boy curled into him and held on. He tried to wait it out, but Sebastian didn't seem inclined to let him go.

Eventually, he scooted down a little, so he wasn't sitting in such an uncomfortable position. He did his best to maintain his distance and was thankful the boy was under the blankets while he was on top of them. And although his intention was to stay until Sebastian moved away from him, it never happened, and he eventually became exhausted and fell asleep.

Chapter 8

SEBASTIAN

Sebastian's body felt heavy, and an exhaustion like he'd never felt before had him barely able to open his eyes. He was warm and comfortable, but he knew something wasn't right. He felt completely disoriented and fuzzy. He had no idea where he was and why. He breathed in deeply, unable, or perhaps unwilling, to open his eyes to reality. His senses were enveloped by the most wonderful smell. It was woodsy, warm, and citrusy. He stretched to get himself closer to whatever it was that had his mind and body humming and found a soft, warm spot to nestle into.

He grabbed onto whatever it was and snuggled in, drifting off again. Waking later, though he had no idea how much later, he rubbed his face against warm cotton, inhaling that scent again, and letting out a little moan of satisfaction when he felt strong arms envelop him. Mmm, he must have had a good evening at the club, followed by an even better night, if those strong arms and heavenly scent were anything to go by.

Nuzzling his face into the crook of what he realized was the neck of the man whose arms were wrapped protectively around him, he hummed in the back of his throat and tightened his hold around the man's back. He cast his mind back to the night before and couldn't remember anything after securing his belongings in his locker.

Strange.

He put it out of his mind for the moment and concentrated on the feel of the arms wrapped around him. They were strong, unusually so. He could feel the muscles under his cheek as his head rested on a very solid bicep. He felt the impressive back muscles where his hand gripped and ran his hand up and down the solid length of it. Jesus, it seemed to go on forever.

Not able to wait any longer to find out who the mystery man was that held him so protectively and yet so gently, he slowly pulled back, unable to keep the hope from flaring up in his chest. As he withdrew, the man's arms loosened and allowed him to lean back far enough to glance up. What he saw there had him gasping in horror. Tears sprang to his eyes as he pushed himself away, completely bewildered. The hope that had, mere seconds earlier, flared bright in his chest, withered and died.

Feeling nausea roil in his stomach, he scuttled back, tangling his legs in the bedding. He shook his head, trying to reach out. Sebastian nearly pitched himself off the bed but grabbed the bedding and held on until he could wrestle one of his legs out of the blankets, which was when he realized he was completely naked. He cried out then, unable to help himself. "*No!*"

"Sebastian!"

Nearly sobbing, he shook his head hard, lost his grip on the sheet, and fell off the edge of the bed only to yelp in surprise as the pain on his ass registered for the first time. He reached around to feel the multitude of welts and anger built up inside of him. The pain and horror of the last few minutes coalescing into an unavoidable vortex. "What did you do? What did we. . . Oh, god. Oh my god! *Where is he?*"

An incredulous expression passed over the man's face. "Who?"

Sebastian lost it then, full out lost it. "*WHO? Your husband!* Where is Braden? How *could* you? How could *we?*" He covered his mouth and shook his head, trying to erase the truth of what he'd apparently done.

The man slid across the bed as he sat frozen in place. He kneeled down in front of Sebastian and reached his hand out to grip his wrist. "Calm down."

Calm *down*? Before he even knew what he was doing, his other hand flew out and slapped the man across the face so hard the noise was like a shock-wave in his own head. He gasped and covered his mouth with his now stinging hand. Holy shit, he'd never hit anyone in his whole life. Not once. What the fuck was going on? "Ohgodohgodohgod. Nonononono."

He shook his head again and realized he was going to be sick. He looked around frantically and saw the bathroom to his left and scrambled in that direction, nearly tripping over a blanket and pillow on the floor as he stumbled his way to the toilet.

He distantly heard, "...you're confused."

He lost whatever was left of his stomach contents. What the hell was there to be confused about? He continued to dry heave long after there was nothing to expel and sobbed into his folded arms, knowing he'd ruined the closest thing he'd come to the beginning of a friendship in longer than he could ever remember. As he flushed the toilet, he felt a gentle hand on his shoulder and drew back in anger and disgust, sprawling on his ass gracelessly. Ouch.

"Don't touch me! Just stay away from me, Zavier."

"Look at me, boy."

Training, so ingrained into his psyche he was unable to ignore that deep Dominant voice, had him lifting his eyes. Expecting to see guilt or shame, he was utterly speechless to see understanding coupled with a sad smile. He looked down at the floor.

A gentle finger tilted his chin up, and he once again looked into the eyes of a man he'd somehow thought he could trust. Devastation was eating him from the inside out. A gentle hand cupped his cheek, but before he could look away again, the deepest, most concerned voice he'd ever heard held him captive.

"Sebastian, I'm not Zavier. I'm Gideon, Zavier's older brother."

Wait. . . What? No. That couldn't be right. He stared hard at the man who he would have sworn was Zavier. There was no way. Only…maybe. He looked deeply into the man's eyes, aquamarine, not Zavier's electric blue. His dark brown hair, a bit longer, making the slight curls visible. Jesus, what had he done?

He reached forward and gripped the man's wrist in one hand and pushed his long sleeve up his forearm. His breathing became erratic and he grabbed the man's other wrist and did the same thing. No tattoos. None. Oh my god. And he'd hit him!? He jerked this head up and took in the red handprint still visible on the gorgeous man's cheek.

Reaching up, he ran his fingers lightly over the mark he'd left on Gideon's face, glancing at his dark beard, much fuller than his brother's. What the fuck was going on? He quickly pulled his hand back, crossing both arms over his chest, realizing again that he was naked in front of one of the most enormously built men he'd ever seen, a bit more muscular than Zavier, the differences between the two men obvious once he looked hard enough.

He brought his knees up to cover himself more thoroughly, wrapped his arms around them, and pulled them flush with his chest. He avoided the man's eyes at all costs. "I'm sorry I hit you, Sir."

"I'm not."

That threw him for a loop and he looked up at Gideon, incredulous. Gideon shook his head and said, "You were protecting Braden and standing up for yourself. There's no reason for you to be sorry."

Confusion etched its way across Sebastian's face. "What happened last night? How did I get here? Why can't I remember anything?"

Gideon grimaced. "You were roofied. We caught him before he could do anything worse than stripe your backside with the cane. I'm just sorry we weren't fast enough to keep that much from happening."

Sebastian squeezed his eyes closed, wanting to shut out the words he'd just heard. He shook his head and rubbed his hands over his face and realized he really needed to relieve himself. His face grew hot. "Um, I need to..." He glanced at the toilet.

Gideon held up a finger and stood. "Hold that thought, Finn left a urine sample cup here. We need to test it to figure out which drug you were given."

Sebastian felt queasy again. Of course, Gideon had called his doctor brother to come help the drugged unconscious stranger in his home. Muttering a few choice expletives under his breath, he waited on the floor feeling humiliated beyond belief. When Gideon returned with the cup, he squatted in front of him and held onto the cup when Sebastian went to take it out of his hand. Sebastian looked up, his eyes questioning. Gideon reached out and rubbed his thumb over Sebastian's bottom lip, effectively freeing it from between his teeth. "You have nothing to be embarrassed about."

Sebastian pulled the cup from Gideon's grasp and averted his gaze. Gideon stood, giving him space. "After you get a sample in the cup, there's a paper bag on the counter you can put it in and some fresh towels in the linen closet just there." He pointed out the closet and headed toward the bathroom door. "Go ahead and get a shower if you'd like. I'll grab you a shirt of mine to wear. Your pants and shoes were brought up by one of my guys, along with your hoodie and your wallet from the locker. Take your time. I'll be in the kitchen making some breakfast. Come out when you're ready."

With that, he was out the door, and Sebastian stood awkwardly, holding the sample cup and staring after Gideon in consternation. His stuff was brought up, meaning what, that they were above the club? Sebastian shook off his confusion, knowing he wouldn't get the answers he needed by standing in the bathroom. He took care of the sample and took the proffered shower. He scrubbed himself raw, knowing that he'd need to ask Gideon for more details, but wanting to rid his body of any possible residual traces of the asshole that had apparently drugged him.

When he was done, he toweled off and checked the bedroom to be sure it was empty. He knew Gideon had already seen him naked—that ship had sailed —but if he could avoid the further humiliation of baring his naked, damaged ass yet again, he might trick himself into believing he could keep his dignity somewhat intact. He walked into the empty bedroom and found his clothes as well as a shirt and some boxers of Gideon's on the bed.

Forgoing the use of Gideon's things, because then he'd have to wash and return them— and let's face it, stringing along his humiliation for days wasn't on his wish list—he pulled his pants on slowly, unable to avoid the tight jeans rubbing against the raw skin of his ass. He pulled on his socks and boots and then donned his hoodie, zipping it all the way up, covering as much skin as possible.

He ventured out of the bedroom into what looked like an enormous, open floor plan loft. He smelled freshly brewed coffee and what he thought were toasted bagels. Crossing his arms over his chest, he approached Gideon, who was smearing a bagel with cream cheese in what Sebastian could only call the most masculine, modern kitchen he'd ever seen; all clean lines, glossy blue lacquer cabinetry, and white quartz countertops surrounding stainless steel appliances. He glanced around the rest of the enormous room, spying the elevator and right next to it, the stairwell.

Gideon surveyed him, his perusal feeling strangely intimate, his eyes finally raising to meet Sebastian's. "Feeling better?"

At Sebastian's shrug, Gideon lifted the knife he'd been using and quirked a brow. "Hungry?"

"No. Thank you."

Pointing the knife at the bar stools, Gideon resumed his task then poured two cups of coffee, assuming correctly that Sebastian would sit as expected. Gideon placed one of the coffee mugs in front of him and stood opposite him. Lifting the bagel, he speared Sebastian with a look. "Take anything in your coffee?"

Sebastian shook his head and wrapped his cold hands around the mug, studying the aromatic brew and avoiding the man's gaze. Taking a deep breath, he plunged ahead, knowing that if he was going to make a quick escape he needed to know what happened. "How did I get here? And where is 'here,' exactly?"

"Well, this is my loft, obviously, and I carried you up here from my club."

At that, Sebastian jerked and coffee sloshed over the edge of the cup, burning his skin. He managed to hold in the hiss that wanted to escape, but it was close. Carried? From *his* club? Jesus fucking Christ. Taking a deep breath, he shook himself out of his daze and managed to murmur an apology about the mess. Leaning over the bar, he grabbed a paper towel, wiping his hand off and then the countertop. Stuffing the trash in his pocket, he looked up when Gideon's soothing voice broke into his thoughts.

"Sebastian, are you okay?"

Tucking his hands in his lap he nodded and said, "Yes."

"You'll call me Sir, boy."

Chills worked their way from his hairline to his toes and shivers followed close behind. His face grew warm as he nodded. "Yes, Sir."

"Better. Come."

Sebastian walked around the island and watched as Gideon turned on the tap. "Run your hand under the cold water."

Sebastian did as he was told, some of the pain receding. The hair at the back of his neck stood on end as he felt warmth at his back. Gideon reached into his pocket and pulled out the dirty paper towel, tossing it into a drawer beside the sink that was apparently a trash can. He reached around Sebastian and gripped his wrist, removing his hand from the water to turn it this way and that. Sebastian held his breath as Gideon's chest brushed against his upper back, barely any space separating them.

Gideon's hold was gentle as he moved Sebastian's hand back under the water. And another shiver went through Sebastian when Gideon leaned down and whispered in his ear. "Better?"

Sebastian nodded and cleared his throat as shivers wracked his body again. Jesus, did he have to give himself away so easily? "Y…yes, Sir."

"Good. You need a refill?"

"No, Sir."

"Grab your coffee and sit at the table so we can talk."

They sat next to each other, Sebastian taking the side of the table closest to the exit door. Gideon dove into his explanation. "My club manager, Roarke, called me to the Interrogation Room which is where he'd found you with a man he'd never seen before. You'd bumped into him, and he'd watched you head into that room and checked up on you. He felt uneasy about your reaction times and how your interactions appeared from the double-sided mirror."

Sebastian let go of the coffee mug and put his hands in his lap where he could fidget nervously without an audience. Gideon continued, "When I got there, I didn't like the look of the man. He was angry, and you weren't responsive. We entered and got him away from you, realized you were unconscious, and called the cops to come get the guy."

Gideon glanced down at the table under which Sebastian's hands had formed tight fists which were shaking. He tilted his head at Sebastian and asked, "Are you all right, boy?"

"Yessir," he responded, quickly without thought.

Gideon's eyes narrowed, but he didn't question Sebastian further. He continued, "Apparently, he was a visitor of one of the members. I contacted my security company and had them look at the video from the moment you arrived and the moment he arrived until we found you. He slipped something into your drink at the bar then proceeded to get you downstairs and into a room. He was pretty rough with you from what I understand, so you might have some bumps and bruises. I got you off the spanking bench and carried you up here. Finn came by and checked on you. You had low blood pressure, so he stayed until around four a.m. when it finally stabilized. He slept on the couch, and I was sleeping on the floor in my room to keep an eye on you, but you had a couple nightmares and I tried to soothe you. The second time, you held on pretty tight when I tried to leave, so I slept on top of the covers beside you."

So, he was the one that had inched closer until he'd practically rubbed himself all over the man. *Great*. He wasn't sure he could take much more humiliation. He looked down at his lap as his face heated, yet again. "I'm sorry I...um, groped you while I was asleep, Sir."

Sebastian's head popped up when he heard a snort, his eyes widening when he saw the grin on Gideon's face. "You're a class A snuggler. I'll give you that."

"Jesus," he muttered as he scrubbed his face with his hands then pushed his chair back, thinking now would be the time to make his escape; before Gideon revealed anything else that might put the cherry on top of his mortification sundae. Before he could stand, Gideon's hand was warming his knee.

"We still have things to talk about, boy."

Jesus, that voice was going to do him in. He let out a slow breath, shoulders sagging. "Yes, Sir."

"With the urine test and the video that I got from Zavier—"

Sebastian's dismayed exclamation cut into Gideon's explanation. "Zavier? He saw the video footage?"

Gideon's eyebrows raised. "Yes, Sebastian. We're taking this very seriously and Custos, my brother's company, provides the club's security. He was notified immediately that something happened at the club. He's not going to leave it up to his team when his family is involved."

Rubbing his hands on his jeans, Sebastian nodded, all the while cringing inside. He swallowed reflexively. *Could things get any worse? Oh wait. . .* "So, you saw the footage?"

"Yes. Are you all right?" The pitying look Gideon gave him nearly sent Sebastian running for the exit again, but he stayed put, clenching his shaking hands together under the table.

Sebastian answered by rote, as he always did when someone asked if he was okay. "I'm fine, Sir."

Gideon looked like he didn't believe him but continued, regardless. "All right, well I wanted to make sure we had the proof you'll need, so I watched it to make sure we had everything."

Sebastian's voice broke on his response. "The proof *I'll* need?"

Gideon's voice was deep and soothing as if he was trying to calm and encourage Sebastian at once. "To press charges."

Sebastian's mind blanked. "Charges."

"Yes. The man drugged you and assaulted you, Sebastian. He needs to be held accountable."

Sebastian's heart was beating so hard he thought it might burst through his chest. He shook his head. "I… I don't…"

Gideon leaned forward and pulled Sebastian's clasped fists into his hands, slowly unwrapping each finger from their death grip. He leaned his elbows on his knees and held Sebastian's shaking, sweating hands in his, rubbing the backs of them with his thumbs. "I would strongly encourage you to press charges, Sebastian. He shouldn't be able to get away with what he did and move on to another target."

Gideon paused, and though Sebastian's eyes were squeezed shut, he could feel Gideon's gaze on him. "I can't order you to press charges, boy. We have no contract, and you're not mine to influence, at this point. Though, after talking with Roarke about your situation, I think you and I have some things to discuss. So, we'll leave that possibility open for now."

His situation? Nope. That was the last straw. He could take a lot but discussing a pity contract was the last thing he ever wanted or needed to discuss with anyone. Jesus, how had things gone so wrong? Tugging his hands from Gideon's grasp, he stood. He shook his head and forced his voice to be calm as he stared at Gideon's chest. "No, thank you. A discussion isn't necessary, Sir. But I'll think about pressing charges."

With that, he turned and made a beeline to the stairwell door he'd spied earlier. He ignored Gideon when he called his name not once, but twice. When he got to the door he put his palm against it and stopped, turning slightly toward Gideon but still avoiding his gaze. "Thank you for helping me last night."

He unlocked the bolt and swung the door open, escaping into the stairwell and down the stairs at record speed. Once he was out on the sidewalk, he started off in the direction of a coffee shop he'd seen down the street from the club, ordering a Lyft to pick him up on the way.

Chapter 9

GIDEON

G ideon sat at the table, wondering how he'd fucked things up so badly. The boy had practically run for the door and from the sound of his footsteps before the door had closed behind him, he *had* run down the stairs. Shaking his head at himself, he stood and dumped the remains of his bagel in the trash and poured out the dregs of his coffee and Sebastian's virtually untouched mug. He ran the conversation over in his head, still unsure what he'd said or done to have the stricken look take over the boy's beautiful features.

He put the dishes in the dishwasher and headed towards his bathroom to take a long shower. He couldn't get their conversation out of his mind and knew he needed to figure out what the fuck he'd done wrong and fix it, which was easier said than done. Something was pushing him not to let Sebastian slip through his fingers.

The boy was beautiful, his eyes haunting and the first thing he noticed. He had eyelashes for days, making his already big eyes look even bigger. His trimmed beard only highlighting the lushness of his naturally dark red lips. His hair was longer in front and fell forward into his face. It was a dark mahogany, shiny and thick, and Gideon just wanted to run his fingers through it.

He was smaller than Gideon was used to, but more enticing as a result. It played greatly into his inner alpha Dom and his protective side. The boy had beautiful ink as well. The tattoos were intriguing. He hadn't been joking when he'd mentioned contracting with Sebastian, and he hoped to fix things so that they could talk about it.

Toweling off his hair, he heard noises coming from the other room and hurried to get himself dressed, hoping that Sebastian had come back. He headed out to the loft area, basketball shorts donned and a t-shirt in his hand. He found his brother and his husband making themselves at home in his kitchen, Braden unboxing what appeared to be some of his pastries. The hunger he thought he'd lost when Sebastian fled made itself known when his stomach protested loudly, causing Braden to smile and look his way. "Is he still here?"

Shoulders sagging, Gideon shook his head. "No. I'm pretty sure I fucked up somehow, but I don't know what I did."

Zavier turned on the electric kettle and pulled Braden's favorite tea out of his brother's cabinet. He got a cup ready and dug out the tea infuser, filling it with the leaves. Gideon joined them and ground some fresh beans for another cup of coffee to pair with the pain au chocolat he hoped was in the box Braden was unpacking onto some of his plates.

Braden took the plates to the table and sat, crossing his arms over his chest and crossing his legs, settling in for what appeared to Gideon might be a dressing down. "What happened?"

Gideon sighed and walked them both through what had happened, beginning at the part where Gideon had allowed a sleeping Sebastian to snuggle up to him. When he was done, he had to laugh at the confused look on his brother's face and the utterly annoyed look on Braden's.

Zavier shrugged and said, "I dunno, man. Your guess is as good as mine."

Braden made a rude noise in the back of his throat. "You two are so much alike and equally clueless."

"Well, tell me how to fix it, and I will. I gotta track down his address and go see him today. He'll need to be interviewed by the cops since the asshole that assaulted him is gonna get sprung if he doesn't press charges."

When Braden was done explaining how he thought their conversation might have sounded to Sebastian, he felt like a total prick. The last thing he'd wanted to do was make Sebastian feel like any discussion they would have regarding a contract between them was because Roarke had basically told him Sebastian couldn't find his own Dom which wasn't what had been said at all.

He pulled Zavier aside while Braden cleaned up the box of pastries and the plates. "I want to know everything about the one who assaulted Sebastian and the person who got him in, down to their blood type and shoe size. The more dirt the better. If charges don't get filed, they'll still be dealt with."

Zavier readily agreed, completely on board with his request. Afterward, he saw his brother and Braden out and got changed into something more suitable. Gideon logged onto his laptop and into the club's system to get Sebastian's address. He was on his Harley minutes later, heading across town to the address Catharsis had on file.

When he pulled up to the old row house that was listed as Sebastian's residence, he paused, taking in the old, yellowish green paint that had seen better days. The house looked like it could use some work, but the neighborhood was in an area that had begun to see some gentrification, so Gideon figured a new coat of paint would go a long way. He sighed, realizing he was using delay tactics to avoid the conversation ahead.

He parked the bike and walked up the steps to Sebastian's door, knocking and hoping Sebastian wasn't going to slam it in his face. When the door opened and he got a look at Sebastian, wearing old, threadbare jeans low on his hips with a hole in the knee, no shoes or socks, and a fairly fitted, vintage concert tee for Echo and the Bunnymen, his mouth went dry. The boy was beautiful, and he'd be kidding himself if he denied his desire to get him in a contract.

Sebastian hadn't realized it was him yet, he was distracted by the tiniest kittens Gideon had ever seen. One scurried past Sebastian's feet across the door's threshold, and the other jumped comically out of the boy's hands while he tried to juggle the furry little monster as he hopped towards the ground like the cat was one of those slippery water snake toys that you couldn't keep your hands on.

The grin on Gideon's face morphed into a full-blown laugh as Sebastian yelled after the kittens. "Slap and Tickle, get back inside!"

He was just quick enough to glimpse the shock on the boy's face as he bent down to retrieve one of the rebellious little fur balls. Gideon schooled his features as he handed over the kitten he'd picked up then went back to pick up the other one that had managed to dig its nails into his pant leg and make it nearly to his knee. As he brought the tiny little ball of fur close to his face and looked into its eyes, Gideon glanced back at Sebastian and asked, "Is this one Slap or Tickle?"

Appearing dumbfounded, Sebastian looked at the tiny kitten in Gideon's hand and glanced back at him, murmuring, "Tickle."

Gideon tucked the kitten into the crook of his arm like a football and held it there, giving Sebastian a gentle, non-threatening smile. "Mind if we come in?"

Looking a bit like he'd been cornered, Sebastian nodded. "Yeah, okay."

Gideon stepped into Sebastian's home, smiling as he took in his surroundings. Feeling tiny pinpricks of pain, he glanced down to see the little monster doing its level best to climb up his chest. He gently pulled the kitten away from his shirt and turned it around in his hand, nuzzling its neck against his cheek and kissing it on the head before putting it down on the floor to play with its little sibling.

Gideon gestured to the couch in the living room to their left and asked, "Can we sit down and talk for a few minutes?"

Sebastian, hands shaking, crossed his arms over his chest, tucking his hands into his armpits, probably thinking he could hide the tremors. Gideon stepped up to him, moving into his space, his heart squeezing when he saw the boy's shoulders hunch. "Sebastian, have I given you reason to fear me?"

Sebastian shook his head. "No."

Gideon nodded, whispering, "Boy, I'd never hurt you." He let a small grin escape before he continued, "Unless you asked me to."

At that, Sebastian's eyes shifted away from him. Heat suffusing his cheeks, he stepped back, putting some space between them as he gestured toward the living room. Gideon gave him the space he seemed to need and made himself comfortable on the couch as Sebastian sat on a chair across from him, pulling his legs up against his chest and wrapping his arms around them. "What can I do for you, Sir?"

Seeing Sebastian's defensive posture made what he would say next all that much more important. "I fucked up earlier, Sebastian. I wanted to apologize."

The surprise that appeared on the boy's face had him wondering at the kind of people taking up space in Sebastian's world. "It's fine, Sir."

Gideon raised a brow at that. "It's not. I didn't handle things very well. I didn't even really ask how you were feeling and if you were doing all right."

"I'm fine, Sir."

"Fine, huh? If that was the case, why did you leave the loft so fast?"

Sebastian blushed and started pulling at the strings hanging from the hole in the knee of his jeans. "I figured we were done and wanted to get home."

"Try that again, boy."

Sebastian's head flew up and he stilled. "What?"

Gideon shook his head. "I said, try that again, but tell me the truth this time. Why did you leave so quickly, Sebastian?"

Sebastian looked down at his knees and mumbled. "It doesn't matter, Sir. I'm fine, all right? You don't need to—"

Gideon leaned forward, his deep tone cutting through Sebastian's prevarications. "Boy, look at me."

Sebastian's eyes popped wide as he followed Gideon's instructions and his jaw clenched before he answered. "Yes, Sir."

"Why did you leave my loft so quickly?"

"I'm not sure I want to press charges, Sir."

"And?"

"I don't want to have to drag myself through a trial where I'm attacked for what happened."

Gideon nodded, his voice soft when he replied, "That's understandable. Why else did you leave?"

Sebastian shook his head, avoiding Gideon's gaze. "No other reason, Sir."

Gideon growled, low in his throat, his patience wearing thin. Sebastian was telegraphing his thoughts and feelings with his every move, and Gideon was frustrated more than was probably warranted. "Get on your knees in front of me, boy."

Sebastian was up like a shot and kneeling in front of Gideon in record time, hands palm up on his knees, head bowed. Gideon clasped his chin and tilted it up until their eyes met. "You've lied to me for the last time, Sebastian. Is that understood? I can read your tells, and I know when you're not being truthful. If we move forward with a contract—"

"I don't want a contract with you, Sir!"

Gideon narrowed his eyes at the boy's outburst and tilted his head. "You're telling the truth. Now tell me why."

The stubborn set to Sebastian's jaw nearly made Gideon smile. Nearly. He kept his hold on Sebastian's chin which seemed to annoy him.

Sebastian sighed then asked, "Why does it matter, Sir? Are you going to force me into a contract?"

Gideon kept his face impassive. "Why, boy?"

"I don't want a contract because you feel sorry for me, okay? Jesus, I'm humiliated enough as it is. The last thing I need or want from you is a fucking pity contract!"

Even though Braden had come close with what he thought Sebastian might have been upset about, it still made Gideon feel like a complete bastard for not handling matters more delicately, especially after the night the boy had had. Gideon leaned forward, his features softening.

His voice was a low murmur when he finally replied. "You have absolutely no reason to be humiliated. Do you have *any* idea how angry I am that you were drugged and assaulted in *my* house? I wanted to crush the guy and probably would have if you hadn't needed me. Your humiliation is a form of self-blame, Sebastian, and I can't have that. You are not at fault here."

When Sebastian glanced down, avoiding his gaze, Gideon gently squeezed the boy's chin until their eyes met again. "The man that drugged and assaulted you is at fault. Hell, I'm at fault for allowing members to occasionally bring guests without thorough background checks which is a policy I'll be changing immediately. That man will never step foot in my club again. The man that brought him is also banned. I'm taking this shit seriously, Sebastian, and I can't have you blaming yourself for what happened."

Sebastian frowned. "You're not to blame."

"That's debatable. But let's talk about the pity contract, shall we?"

"Look, Gideon… Sir. I appreciate your help last night. And I'll get back to you when I decide if I'm gonna press charges. But other than that, I'm fine. I'm sure Roarke told you some sob story about how I can't find a Dom or something. I appreciate your willingness to take one for the team, as it were, but it's not needed."

"Sebastian—"

"Sir, please? I know it might seem like it, but I'm not desperate. I'd really like to retain at least a modicum of my dignity and self-respect."

Gideon narrowed his eyes, his voice deep and rough when he replied, "Are you done, boy?"

A shudder traveled its way over the boy's small frame. "Yes, Sir."

"Let me make several things perfectly clear. I don't sign contracts out of pity. I don't sign contracts with club subs, period."

Sebastian's surprise was evident when his eyebrows nearly reached his hairline. "Then why?"

"Roarke told me that you're a natural submissive. That your training prior to joining was thorough, and that you have great instincts. He got the impression that you're seeking a contract but that you haven't found a Dom you're interested in. Hell, he's tempted to take you on himself, but he doesn't feel like he'd be able to give you the time you need with him being the manager at

Catharsis as well as the club's trainer. He's been trying to figure out who to pair you with, but frankly, he doesn't think the Doms who are free are right for you. He asked me to meet with you—"

"Exactly! He feels sorry for—"

"Enough, boy."

Gideon felt bad when his frustrated tone made the boy jump, but he was done with the interruptions. At Sebastian's, "Yes, Sir," he continued, "He asked me if I had the time to meet with you to see if I might have someone in mind for you or if I was interested in signing one with you myself. I have to admit that he spoke highly of you, but I didn't think I was going to extend that offer to you until I met you."

"I... What?"

Gideon shook his head. "I get the feeling you don't understand your own appeal. You're a stunning man, Sebastian, and you're beautiful in your submission. But, you need to think about whether or not you want to sign a contract with me. This isn't just about what *I* want, this is about what *you* want. I'm happy to sit down with you and discuss what I'm looking for in a submissive, but I'd like to give you time to come up with your own list of the things you need and want from a Dominant."

Sebastian just stared at Gideon like he didn't understand what was being said. Besides his facial expressions and the involuntary shudder earlier, the boy hadn't moved a millimeter since he'd knelt between Gideon's legs. He had to admit, the boy made quite the picture. Gideon's hands were itching to get all over him.

He tried to reason why Sebastian had a poor opinion of himself, and he couldn't do it. There was a beauty and innocence about him that seemed untarnished in many ways. He couldn't put a finger on it, but he knew he wanted to get to know the depths of Sebastian, find out what made him tick, what made him lose control, and what made him squirm and come apart.

"So, let me just ask so we can decide if we're moving forward. Do you have any desire to have further discussions with me about a possible D/s contract?"

Sebastian still didn't say a word, his eyes were still just as wide as he nodded, mutely.

Gideon smiled and moved his thumb from Sebastian's chin to rub it back and forth over Sebastian's lower lip, causing the boy to suck in a surprised breath. "Words, boy."

"Yes, Sir. I'd like to discuss it further."

Gideon's smile spread even wider. "Good. For now, I'd like to curb this discussion, give you time to sort out what you need and want. We can come back to it in several days. All right?"

Still dazed, Sebastian nodded again. "Yes, Sir."

"As much as I don't want to have to bring it up, I do think we need to talk about the assault and pressing charges. I know you don't remember what happened, but it's all on video, so he can't exactly deny the charges. Do you feel like you want to see the video?"

When Sebastian blanched and gave an emphatic shake of his head, Gideon held up a hand. "If you're going to press charges, it might help to remember what happened."

"I… I don't think…"

"You have my support, and the support of Custos backing you. Video proof, and by the end of the day today, proof from the lab that's testing your sample. It would be a cut-and-dried case."

"I don't want… I'm not going to press charges, Sir."

"Sebastian…"

Sebastian shook his head again and looked down at his hands in his lap. Gideon could see the desire he had to move, to squirm. He didn't. But he did look back up, directly into Gideon's eyes, when he answered, "Sir, I work for the SFPD. And, while I'm out, and not ashamed of it, I don't make it known that I'm part of the BDSM community. I don't think it would negatively impact me as much as it would, say, a cop, but it's not a theory I want to test."

Gideon nodded his head. "I can understand that, but if you need a guarantee that your job won't be affected, the chief is a close family friend. I can get his assurance that it wouldn't be an issue. You would be protected, boy."

Sebastian took a deep breath as if gathering himself for a fight. When he met Gideon's gaze again, his spine straightened. "Thank you, Sir. I appreciate that, but frankly, I don't *want* to remember. I'll be more careful going forward when drinking at the bar. It could have been much worse, I get that, but it wasn't, and I just want to call it a lesson learned. I've had stripes like these on my back before. They'll heal. It's not worth it to me to go through that."

"Sebastian, he drew blood."

"I know, Sir. But, if I had to testify, they'd destroy my character because I'm a sub. They'll say I wanted it, deserved it even for being at the club in the first place. I get that it's not likely with all the evidence that I'd have to testify, but it might come down to that, and I just don't want to put myself through it. I'm sorry, Sir."

A small smile made its way to Gideon's lips. "I can't say I'm not disappointed because I want him to be held accountable, but I can work on that angle myself. You've thought about it, and you've made the best decision for you. I'll make some calls, and he'll be released."

Sebastian sat, staring at Gideon in shock. "You're not going to try to change my mind or push me to do it?"

Gideon shook his head and answered, "No. You're an adult, your reasons are sound, and it's your choice. I'm going to go and make some calls though. I'll let the police know you're not pressing charges. I never gave them your name to begin with, so we'll see if we can avoid using it at all. I'm going to make sure that the friend who brought him in, and the asshole himself, are blacklisted from BDSM clubs, both locally and statewide. Once we know there's an abuser posing as a Dom, the community closes its ranks to protect our own. Are you feeling all right? Do you need anything before I go?"

"I'm fine. I don't need anything. Thank you, Sir."

Gideon stood and held his hand out to Sebastian who took it and stood at Gideon's silent command. "You're welcome." Gideon clasped his chin in his hand then rubbed his thumb back and forth over that full lower lip again. Stepping back, he pulled out his wallet. "Here's my card. Put my number in your phone and call me if you need anything. Think about what you want out of a contract with me, boy. Download the standard contract from the Catharsis app so you have a starting point. I'll be in touch in a few days to discuss it."

Sebastian took the card, his hand trembling a bit. He glanced back up and nodded, thanking him again. Gideon made his way out of Sebastian's place and glanced at his phone when it vibrated at an incoming call. Clenching his jaw, he hit the power button to ignore the call but made another one immediately.

"Zavier, I need you to take that video and blur out everything that identifies Sebastian and send it to me. Sebastian won't press charges, so the guy will be out on the streets soon. I want to make it harder for him to slip into clubs like mine and continue to assault subs. I'm going to call the chief right now to let him know what's going on so we don't have cops asking too many questions about Sebastian." Gideon paused as his brother responded, pulling out his keys. "Yeah. Perfect. Thanks. I also need to take a trip to finish that job I recently handled, so I'll be out of touch for a few days. Thanks, man."

Ending the call, he got on his bike and took off for home, frustrated that he needed to tie off the loose end before it started to unravel further, but knowing he didn't have a choice.

Chapter 10

GIDEON

The house was relatively nondescript compared to those surrounding it. The neighborhood—well established, with immaculate landscaping—was full of large ranch style homes. The landscaping was meticulous though Gideon thought it rather understated compared to the neighboring houses.

Knowing everything about that was purposeful, Gideon had to hand it to the man; he was nothing if not methodical even in his choice of real estate. The anger Gideon felt towards him dissipated a bit once he was face to face with those idiosyncrasies. A soft spot he'd forgotten he had for his former submissive came to the forefront of his mind upon remembering the man's almost pathological need for secrecy, order, and privacy.

The one thing that had drawn Gideon's attention on his first visit was the gate surrounding the property. Made to look relatively benign so that it fit in with the others close by, it boasted hidden cameras and extensive security measures. It stretched its way across the driveway, keeping unwanted vehicles from getting too close, and continued around back, surrounding a pool flanked by dark brown wide-plank composite decking. Everything surrounded by a dense wall of tall, orderly arborvitae that bordered the fence and was pruned within an inch of its life.

A simple call to one of Zavier's men at Custos took care of the pressing problem of bypassing the high-tech security system. He'd tested it out the day before, when he'd searched the house thoroughly. His findings disturbing him, making him realize his fears had been justified. The home was meticulously organized with an utterly unlived-in feel that had him thinking the worst.

It was around 5:30 p.m.. The neighborhood was alive with people returning from their busy days. Gideon had rented the same model Range Rover Autobiography that he owned as it would fit into the neighborhood without drawing any undue attention. He parked right out in front of the house and pulled out his military duffle. A woman glanced his way as she pulled into her driveway. He waved and got a flirty little wave in return. He went so far as to open the mailbox and pull out the mail, tucking it under his arm. He headed up the walkway and made as if to fish out a set of keys which were really a few lock picking tools.

He had the door open in less than a minute and was inside the house a moment later. He sent one last wave to the woman who was still watching him as he closed the door. Deactivating the alarm, he whistled a tune as he walked into the kitchen and dropped the mail on the countertop and gathered some stuff from the fridge that would grill up nicely for dinner.

Tossing his dinner on the grill, he stripped down to his boxers and dove into the pool. He swam laps and checked on his food, ravenous by the time it was ready. Halfway through his meal, he sensed someone behind him. "Put down the gun, Boone." He cut another piece of steak. "Thank you for the meal by the way. Great marinade on the rib-eye."

Savoring the piece he just put in his mouth, he smiled as he heard an angry growl behind him. "What the fuck are you doing here, Gideon? You were supposed to show up at my office three days ago. You fucked with my case, and I need that report. I need everything you were able to get before you fucked me over with your vigilante bullshit. I've been scrambling with my superiors to come up with an excuse for Alan's death. If I don't—"

"I think there's been some kind of misunderstanding, Boone." Polishing off a bite of sweet potato, he pushed his chair back and grabbed his beer. Taking another pull from the bottle, he leaned back and swiveled the chair to face his former submissive and CIA handler. "I no longer work for the Special Operations Group of the CIA. That means that doing the CIA's bidding is no longer part and parcel of my daily life."

"Look, I get it, but—"

As if Boone hadn't spoken, Gideon continued, "You made a mistake dragging my brother's company into your business. You won't utilize members of my family to get to me ever again. Custos Securities is not in the business of government sanctioned black ops. Not because they can't, but because they won't. Zavier took that meeting because he knew I had a right to turn you down or accept your proposition myself. He will not afford you the luxury of coming into his world ever again. That was an asinine bridge to burn."

Boone crossed his arms defensively over his chest. "All right, I get it,

Gideon. What do you want from me? The only way I knew I could get your attention was by going through Zavier. The upper echelons are scrambling. This syndicate is out of control. We need to take it down, and you fucked up! The unsanctioned hit isn't going over well. I need to pull you back in for a debrief. I need you to meet with my superiors, and we need to strike while we've got the upper hand."

Ignoring him, Gideon shook his head. "Don't make that mistake a second time, Boone. My family stays out of it. You've pushed too far this time."

Boone threw his hands in the air. "Jesus, come on! Who cares about that? I did what I had—"

Gideon stood slowly, his steely eyes burning bright, causing Boone to stop talking. Gideon leaned in, his voice lowering an octave. "I care. I care that you came unbidden back into my life and used my family to do it. Never again, are we clear?"

"Gideon—"

"*Are we fucking clear?*"

Gideon was surprised when Boone's body gave in involuntary shiver like it was responding to the tone Gideon used, and not his words.

"Yes, S... Gideon."

Gideon was concerned that Boone reacted so swiftly to his authoritative voice, wanting to call him Sir. How long had it been since he'd scened to have such a visceral reaction to something so simple as Gideon's tone? To figure that out, he'd have to shut down the business conversation first. "Let's table this discussion until later."

Boone shook his head and huffed. "Gideon, this is my work we're talking about here. I need that information."

Gideon softened his tone. "Boone, you know I wouldn't be here unless I had what you need for your superiors. But I think we have more important things to discuss. Shop talk will wait until this evening."

Boone sighed, obviously not looking forward to Gideon checking in on that part of his life. "Fine."

Gideon lifted his brow at the disrespectful petulance coming from Boone. He nudged the man's chin up until Boone met his gaze and he spoke quietly but sternly to get things moving in the right direction. "Do you want to try that again?"

Boone shuddered and sucked in a breath. "Yes, Sir."

"There you go. Now, are you hungry, pet?"

A slow, shaky breath eased from Boone's lips, the final switch having been flipped with the use of the submissive endearment. "I'd rather serve you first. May I heat it up for you, Sir?"

"Thank you, yes. On the grill, please. Not in the microwave."

"I remember, Sir."

"Take care of it, and while the food is on the grill, present yourself properly to me."

"Yes, Sir."

Gideon waited for the natural fluidity he was used to seeing when Boone was in submissive mode. It had been absent from the man just minutes before, so he hoped it would return once he was put in his place. However, as he went about heating up Gideon's food, it didn't show, and the man seemed to be searching for it, unable to find it. A sadness came over Gideon, and he hoped his assumption was wrong, but he had to ask. "Pet, when did you last scene?"

Boone stilled all movement then his shoulders slumped, answering Gideon's question. "You don't have to worry about me, Sir."

Gideon knew they couldn't go any further until they specified their terms. "Boone, while I'm here, do you agree to adhere to our previous contract's stipulations as my temporary submissive? We won't go any further, if you don't. I want to help you, but if you're unwilling, I won't force you."

Gideon watched as Boone took a deep breath and squared his shoulders. "Yes, Sir. I agree."

"Do you have our old contract at hand?"

"Yes, Sir."

"Get it please, and a pen."

"Yes, Sir."

Gideon saw him glance at the grill. "I'll take care of it, pet. Go."

Gideon flipped the steak, and Boone was back in less than a minute. Gideon sat and wrote out a quick temporary addendum stating that they would both adhere to the previous contract's stipulations while he was with him temporarily. They both signed it, and he handed it back to Boone.

"So, with the contract being a healthy reminder, what happens when I ask you a question?"

"You expect an immediate answer."

"That's right. So, I'll ask again. When did you last scene?"

Boone sighed and answered, "It's been a while, Sir."

"You're trying my patience, pet."

Boone sighed. "I honestly can't recall, Sir. It's been some time. Don't worry. There have been several scenes since you left."

"How many is several?"

Gideon saw Boone's grip on the grilling tongs tighten as he moved his food back on the flames. "Around ten?"

"You're asking me? More than ten or less than ten?"

"Less than ten."

"I've been gone for five years."

"I'm aware, Sir."

"In all that time, you've scened less than ten times and had no other contracts?"

"Yes. I... I have issues with trust."

Gideon sighed and rubbed his hand over his stubbled jaw. "I'm aware, pet. When I asked you before I left if you were in love with me, you told me no. Were you telling me the truth?"

Boone turned swiftly, eyes wide, meeting his gaze. "Yes, Sir. I swear. It's just..." His gaze returned to the ground. "I tried. It just never felt right."

Gideon watched Boone's shoulders slump again, and his heart went out to him. No matter what went on between them professionally, Gideon would always set everything aside to be what a sub needed and at that moment, the sub needed him. "I'm going to call someone—"

"No! Sir, please. I'm dealing with it."

Gideon stood taller, crowding the sub. "Present yourself to me. Now."

Boone turned and dropped the tongs on the counter and was on his knees in seconds. His legs were spread shoulder width apart, hands on his thighs, palms up, head forward, and eyes cast down. His stance was nearly perfect, and Gideon could see that as nervous as he was, he was also reveling in his submission. He tapped his finger on the middle of the sub's back, and Boone instantly squared his shoulders. "Why did my words have bite?"

"I interrupted you, Sir."

"How many of my rules have you broken in the last ten minutes?"

Boone paused, thinking. "Three, Sir."

"List them, please."

"I did not treat you with respect. I did not answer your question immediately. And I interrupted you."

"You have been too long without a scene if you are behaving in such a manner. This is not how I trained you, Boone. We'll discuss punishment later. If I were you, I would be paying very close attention to my behavior tonight. Please stand and make sure you aren't burning my dinner."

"Yes, Sir."

He got quickly to his feet and checked on the food. Gideon sat, contemplating the evening ahead. They had much to discuss, but he wasn't about to let business be the only thing being dealt with that night. Moments later his food was back in front of him, freshly heated and smelling wonderful. Boone kneeled in resting pose to his right.

After several bites, he paused to glance at Boone. Knowing it had probably been hours since he'd eaten, he cut a succulent piece of meat and placed it at Boone's lips which dutifully remained closed. Boone only opened his lips and took the bite when Gideon said, "Eat, pet."

He spent the remainder of his meal sharing bites with Boone. When he was done, he pushed his chair back and stood. Boone didn't move a muscle, his training having finally, fully kicked in. "You may stand. I'm going to go take a nice long shower. You can fix yourself something if you're still hungry."

"Yes, Sir." Boone stood.

When Boone bent to clean up the mess from the table, Gideon stilled his hand on the dinner plate. "Pet, did I ask you to clean up?"

Boone shook his head. "No, Sir."

"You will leave the mess. Fix yourself something to eat. When you have done so and eaten, come see me. Do I make myself clear?"

Nodding, Boone said, "Yes, Sir."

Gideon grabbed his duffle and walked into the house. He took his time, knowing that Boone had to still be hungry and would feed himself and seek him out immediately, hoping he'd be permitted to clean up. When he was done with his shower and dressed more comfortably in loose fitting basketball shorts and a fitted t-shirt, he placed a call to an old friend.

The familiar deep voice answered. "Hello?"

"Connell."

"Gideon?" Surprise laced his response.

"Yes. How are you?"

Connell let out a low rumbling chuckle. "I'm doing well. This is a wonderful surprise. To what do I owe the pleasure?"

Gideon smiled. "I might need to call in a favor."

"Tell me."

"Are you still located in D.C.?"

"I am."

"Are you. . . encumbered?"

Connell paused on the other end of the line. "I'm not."

"Are you. . . reluctant to become so?"

Another pause then a slow exhalation. "I'm not."

Gideon couldn't tell if Connell's reactions were wary or interested. "If I gave you an address, would you have time to drive to McLean in the next day or so?"

"I can make time. What am I walking into, Gideon?"

"I have a pet in need. He was my sub over five years ago. We were not in love, we were colleagues that fell into a...comfortable contract, I guess you could say. I didn't know he was struggling, but I should have checked, and that's on me."

"Gideon, I know you well enough to know you didn't just carelessly walk away."

Gideon grunted. "Be that as it may, he didn't utilize the resources I arranged for him. He's not seeking what he needs because he feels as if he's unable to build trust. Because of the sensitivity of your career, I believe you may be a good fit for him as he would have similar issues and be unable to discuss his work with his Dom."

After a pause, Gideon heard Connell audibly exhale, knowing the man was allowing him to hear it finally made him feel like he'd made the right choice. "I would be happy to meet with you both."

Connell's response relieved some of the stress he'd heaped upon himself when he'd realized his former pet had been struggling. "How does dinner tomorrow evening sound?"

"It sounds good. Though I won't be able to make it out that way until around seven p.m."

"That should be fine. Connell, please understand, I'm not trying to be a matchmaker here. What I need to find is a Dom he can trust. He's adrift and needs a guiding hand from someone able to give him the time he needs. If you don't have time to dedicate to a needy pet that denies that neediness at every turn, please tell me now."

"I have the time."

"Good, I think you'll be a good fit for him. When I ended our contract I thought of you, but you were in your own contract so I never made contact."

"You could have called me regardless. I could have helped you make necessary arrangements. But I guess that's neither here nor there. If you feel that we would be compatible, at least from the standpoint of a standard contract, I'm willing to discuss things with you both."

They made arrangements for the following night and spent a couple minutes catching up. Finally, at ease once again, Gideon thanked his old friend and hung up the phone.

Chapter 11

SEBASTIAN

Sebastian had mostly recovered from that weekend's ordeal and could finally sit on his ass without being in too much pain. When Monday came around, he'd made his way back to the hospital yet again for another composite sketch. When he was done, he had some spare time and called Braden to see if he could stop by to see him at work. When he got off the phone, he couldn't help but smile. Braden's enthusiasm was contagious.

The Sugar n' Spice Café was an eclectic mix of relaxed chic and trendy hipster. Sebastian walked through the doors without a preconceived idea of what he'd find and fell in love with the atmosphere immediately. His friend Zoe was a barista for the café, but he'd never known Braden was a co-owner. The room was long and narrow with the counter and pastry cases running down the right side.

The smell of the place was ambrosia to his senses, so good he could nearly taste it. There was the coffee, of course, but he could also smell some fruity teas. But best of all, it smelled like what you'd hope the world's best grand-mother's kitchen would smell like: flour, sugar, butter, chocolate, cinnamon, and vanilla.

He approached the counter and jumped when he heard a strange sort of growling yawn then looked toward the window where a huge dog bed was set up with the name Thor on it, on top of which sat a gorgeous German shepherd that was, in fact, yawning. Upon further inspection, he saw the dog had a service vest on with a tag on it that read, "Please, do not pet me. I'm a service dog, and I'm working."

Wow, how cool was that? He grinned as he watched the dog bite a little at his foreleg as if gnawing at an itch then he rolled to the side to grab a huge red rubber toy of some sort in his teeth, emitting some happy growly noises as if he was talking to the toy while he was chewing it. Sebastian found himself laughing, as he imagined what the dog was saying. "Hello, toy. You are mine. I'm going to eat you. You taste good. Nom nom nom."

Shaking his head at himself, Sebastian moved to the counter, feeling a bit self-conscious. The grin Maya gave him was welcoming, and he couldn't help but smile back.

"Hi, how can I help you?"

"Uh, Braden said—"

Maya's smile got bigger if that was possible. "Sebastian?"

Sebastian nodded. "Yes."

"Want something to drink?"

"Uh, yeah." Sebastian reached into his back pocket to pull out his wallet.

Maya shook her head. "Nope. No charge. What can I getcha?"

"Oh, no. Please let me pay." He held his card out to her.

She shook her head no again and replied, "Nope. Your money's no good here. You've helped Braden and Nana. Please, it's just some coffee. What can we make for you?"

Sebastian could feel his face heating up, and a warm feeling lodged itself in his chest. "Uh, okay, thanks." He glanced up at the handwritten chalkboard menu with its beautiful cursive scripted concoctions written in chalk paint in various colors, trying to find what he wanted. "Do you have a caramel mocha?"

"Yep, salted caramel mocha. I'll get that going for you and bring it back. You can get whatever treats you want in the kitchen."

Sebastian's brows rose. "In the back?"

Maya smiled and pointed to the end of the counter. "Yep. Come on around the counter there and go right through the swinging door behind me. You'll find Braden in the middle of a batch of snickerdoodles."

Sebastian headed the way she'd indicated, suddenly nervous. He'd assumed Braden would come out to chat with him for a bit and that would be that. Heading back into the kitchen felt more familiar than they were, and his nerves were making themselves known.

He wiped his hands on his pant legs as he walked through the swinging door. He found Braden, earbuds in his ears, the cord trailing down his back connected to the phone in his back pocket, just like he did at his tattoo studio. Not wanting to surprise him, Sebastian stayed off to the side until he was within Braden's eyeline. When Braden looked up, Sebastian waved self-consciously.

The grin that spread over the other man's face went a long way towards settling his nerves, and he watched as Braden pulled the buds from his ears, letting them drape over his shoulders. He wiped his hands on a towel, took his apron off, and tossed it into a bin by the door. Sebastian didn't know what to make of the hug he found himself in until Braden spoke up, "Are you all right?"

Pulling away, his face now aflame, his posture became defensive as he crossed his arms over his chest. It was at that awkward moment Maya came in the back carrying his mocha. She took one look at them both—eyebrows raised in surprise—set the coffee down on the countertop and backed away, nodding at Sebastian's word of thanks. When he turned back toward Braden, he was sure his expression was pained. "So, you saw it too?"

Braden's brows drew together. "Saw what?"

"The video of what happened."

Braden started shaking his head, and when his eyes got comically big, Sebastian relaxed a bit. "God, no! No, Sebastian. Zavier would never do that. We were just heading to bed when the call came in from downstairs. All I knew was that someone at the club had gotten assaulted. He left immediately and came home hours later, looking so upset. I pried your name out of him, but nothing else."

"Well, that's something, I guess."

"Sebastian, he was worried about you. So was Gideon, and so am I. That's all."

Perplexed, Sebastian asked the first thing that came to his mind. "Why?"

"What do you mean, 'why?'"

"Why was everyone worried about me?"

"What..." Braden looked as confused as he felt. "Why wouldn't we be? You were roofied and assaulted, Sebastian."

Feeling suddenly vulnerable, Sebastian stuffed his hands in his pockets. "But you don't know me."

"I'd like to. You're here, right? I know you enough to know that I wouldn't want something to happen to you and feel worried about you when it does."

Sebastian didn't understand that last part, and his face must have shown it because Braden continued, "Look. I had hoped that you'd call. I was excited today when you did. We seemed to get along the couple times we've met, and I'd kind of hoped we'd become friends."

"You did?"

"Yes! Why do you sound so surprised?"

Sebastian shrugged. "I don't really make friends very easily. Or at all, really."

"You don't have friends?"

Sebastian shrugged again. "Not really. I mean, ironically, I'm friends with Zoe, your barista, but that's kind of it."

"Zoe's great, she's one of my favorite people. Look, I'm glad you're here, it's as simple as that. I hope we can become friends if we get along as well as I think we will. Does that work for you?"

He found himself nodding. "Yeah. That works for me."

Braden smiled. "Yeah?"

Sebastian laughed. "Yeah."

"Awesome. Okay, I'm at a good stopping point, so I can take a break. Let's head into the break room and chat for a bit. You said you had some questions for me. But before that, what can I get you? We have scones, cookies, croissants, cinnamon buns, and muffins. You name it, we probably have it, so pick your poison."

Sebastian laughed again, and feeling sort of light and happy suddenly, decided to go for decadence. "I want a huge cinnamon bun."

Braden laughed as well, and they both smiled at each other. "Warm and extra gooey?"

Nodding, Sebastian agreed, "Oh yeah."

Braden got to work, and the next thing Sebastian knew he was fast approaching a sugar coma in the break room of the café and couldn't, for the life of him, remember a time he'd felt so carefree. While they both drank their coffee, and he indulged in the sticky, sugary confection that he'd probably never recover from, they chatted and began to establish the beginnings of the friendship they'd both been hoping for. Their conversation hovered around the safe and simple at first; their daily routines, how Nana was doing, Braden and Zavier's wedding, and the café. But finally, they came to the reason for his visit: the McCades.

Chapter 12

GIDEON

Gideon was just about to head to the front of the house when he heard Boone approaching. Sitting on the bench at the end of the bed, he watched as Boone entered the room. When the man's eyes finally reached his, Gideon opened his legs wide and waited. Boone's eyes drifted closed on a relieved sigh, and he settled into resting pose, tucked between Gideon's legs.

Leaning slightly forward, he cocooned Boone with his bulk. "I'm sorry I didn't check to make sure that you were taken care of when I left."

When Boone began frantically shaking his head no, Gideon's clasped it in both hands, tilting Boone's head back so that he was looking directly up at him. Their faces were mere inches apart, ensuring the sub's eyes stayed on his.

The sadness on Boone's face wrenched at Gideon's heart. "Ours wasn't a love match, but you know I cared for you deeply. Your pragmatic reaction to my leaving the job and ending our contract convinced me there wouldn't be any issues and you'd utilize the resources I set out for you when I left."

"Permission to speak, Sir."

"Granted."

"I'm fine. Truly. When the contract ended, I was no longer your responsibility."

"Ending the contract wasn't a mutual decision. When I wanted out of the job, I should have left it and stayed with you until you were fully settled, until we were both in agreement about the contract ending, rather than me advising you it was over."

"It was your prerogative, Sir. It was stated in the contract that either party could cancel the contract at any time. I'm a grown man. I can take care of myself."

"You've proven that. Your home is beautiful. You've gotten the promotion you wanted."

"How do you—"

He shook his head, and Boone quieted. "Clearly you're able to take care of yourself. But, Boone, in so many ways you're not living, you're existing. You're a man that needs to serve, and you've taken no steps towards finding someone to kneel for."

"It's not as easy as all that. I—"

Gideon interrupted. "Hush now. I've already made a call." When Boone's head began another frantic shake, Gideon's hands tightened on the man's head. "Settle."

The stern command, though spoken quietly, did its job. The man stilled and calmed immediately. "Have I damaged you so much you've lost your trust in me to take care of your needs?"

Boone closed his eyes then slowly opened them. "No, Sir. I trust you."

Gideon leaned forward and kissed Boone's forehead. "His name is Connell. I trust the man with my life. I'll entrust you to his care. I'll be asking you to give the gift of your submission to him. If things between you don't work out as I think they will, I'll ask that he takes on the responsibility of ensuring that until he finds someone you'll be happy to serve, he will act as your Dom. Do you understand?"

"But what if he demands—"

"Pet, he works for the Secret Service. He'll be unable to share the details of his job, just as you are unable to share the details of yours. He'll make no such demands. He doesn't know you work for the CIA, let alone what division you work for. What you both speak of about your respective careers is up to you."

Shaking his head again, Boone tried to argue. "But…"

"Boone, think carefully on this before you answer. Are you scared, or are you telling me no?"

Boone took a deep breath and let it out slowly. "I'm scared, Sir."

Gideon nodded, proud of the sub. "The decision is made. He'll be here for dinner tomorrow evening at seven p.m.. If you must go in tomorrow, you'll be home at five p.m. to ensure you're ready. Understood?"

"I might need to stay—"

"Working twelve or more hours a day is over, pet. You'll be getting out the contract we signed years ago. He'll understand the agreement we once had. The rules you adhered to then, you will most likely adhere to again. And if what I remember about Connell holds true, the rules may be even more strict."

Rather than the slumped shoulders Gideon expected, he was rewarded with the sub raising his head, stiffening his spine, and straightening his shoulders. It was as if Gideon's words relieved him of a burden weighing him down. Boone's face was more serene than he'd seen it since the moment Gideon had walked into Zavier's office at Custos a couple months back and found Boone there. The man was nearly buzzing with renewed energy.

"Yes, Sir."

Smiling, Gideon gave permission for him to react freely. "Relax, pet."

A smile spread across the sub's face as he slowly wrapped his arms around Gideon's waist and laid his cheek against his chest. Relaxing into the hug, Gideon wrapped his arms around the sub and whispered in his ear. "Proud of you. I'm sorry you've been struggling. I won't leave until I see you settled with Connell. I'm going to make a demand, however, and it's very important there are no prevarications."

Pulling away from Gideon, Boone nodded. "Yes, Sir."

"If things don't work out with Connell, you will allow him to fulfill his obligation to me and to you, by finding you someone suitable. Is that understood?"

"It's not *that* bad, Sir."

Gideon narrowed his eyes. "You've lost weight, Boone. Your skin looks sallow, your eyes shadowed. Perhaps you're allowing yourself a good solid meal for dinner, but I'm guessing breakfast and lunch are hit or miss. You're not sleeping well, and I'd be willing to bet even the sleeping pills on your bathroom counter aren't working their magic. You're working yourself to death, and your OCD is rearing its ugly head."

"I just get overwhelmed and making sure everything is in its place makes me feel some measure of control."

Cupping Boone's chin in his hand, Gideon tilted his head back up. "I know, pet. But though this house is beautiful, you've not made it yours. Where are your knick-knacks, your framed photos and artwork? I know how important those things are to you."

Boone sat back on his heels and rubbed his hands over his face. He composed himself and moved back into resting pose. "I haven't had the energy."

"We're going to change that. Right now, I want you to quickly clean up after our meals and get yourself showered and more comfortable, so we can get some business out of the way."

"Yes, Sir."

When Boone was done with his shower and had himself redressed in comfortable clothes, he got down on his knees beside the bed, waiting for further instruction. Now that the awkwardness of his switch to submissive mode was gone, his need to please was enormous. Gideon almost hated bringing him out of his submission to talk business, but it couldn't be helped. What he could do, however, was make sure that Boone knew he would be well taken care of going forward.

Chapter 13

SEBASTIAN

"What kind of man is Gideon?" Sebastian knew he wasn't being subtle, but he figured he shouldn't beat around the bush and act coy about his desire to know more before he signed a contract with the powerful Dom.

Braden contemplated him for a moment then quirked a soft little smile. "That's a relatively simple question for a fairly complex man. I don't know a lot of the fine details. Nobody does, really. He keeps himself separate, distanced. Yet, for all of that detachment, he attends every family function if he's not traveling. He doesn't talk a lot, but I get the feeling that he listens to everything and sees more than most."

Sebastian pulled his feet up on the chair, placing his crossed arms on top of his knees, he rested his chin on them and admitted, "I haven't signed a contract with a Dom in a really long time. I've had a total of two conversations with Gideon, and he's asking me to sign a contract with him."

Braden smiled. "And that makes you nervous?"

Sebastian shrugged. "In a way it does, but not for the reasons you'd expect. I'm nervous that I'll fail him. I'm nervous that I'm not good enough. And I'm nervous that I'm *not* nervous about him."

Braden's eyes popped wide in surprise. "He doesn't make you nervous?"

Sebastian shook his head and replied, "No. His voice calms me, and the few times he's touched me, it felt the same. I know it sounds weird, but when he uses his Dom voice, it's like everything in me stills. I can't explain it."

"No, you're explaining it perfectly," Braden chuckled. "That's exactly how it feels when Zavier does that with me."

A thought occurred to Sebastian, and he voiced it before he could think better of it. "So, Zavier is your Dom? Are you members of Catharsis?"

Braden shrugged. "I don't really think of him as my Dom." He blushed and continued, "I mean, he dominates me, so I guess he is, right? But it's nothing formal, just the roles we fall into. We don't want a contract between us, we just do what feels natural. We haven't known for very long that Gideon owns Catharsis, but since we found out, Zavier and I have discussed joining."

Sebastian smiled knowingly and nudged Braden's knee with his foot. "Don't be embarrassed. I think it's great. And to be honest, I've heard Zavier speak to you and seen the way you react to him. He uses the same tone as Gideon does when he's being toppy, so I kind of wondered."

"I guess I'm kind of intrigued with the idea of the club and what it's like there, but I don't know that I'm ready to scene in front of others or if I'll ever be ready for that."

"You don't have to scene in front of others, there's a lot of private rooms. I've never been to a club quite like it. He's kind of turned the typical dungeon type of club on its head and really made it more of an experience, a place for anyone to feel at home, whatever their kinks. Have you been there to check it out?"

Braden shook his head. "Not yet. I want to. Now that I know you're a member, maybe we'll plan to come the next time you're there."

They grinned at each other. "Sounds like a plan. I'm still curious about Gideon, but I don't want you to feel like I'm giving you the third degree."

"I don't feel like that at all. But like I said, he's a complex guy and extremely private. I get the feeling there's a lot to be uncovered there, a lot of potential, but it would take a lot for him to open up, to trust someone enough to do so."

"Oh, I don't know about all that. I guess I just want to know if I need to be worried about the type of Dom he is. I don't really know him at all."

Braden gave him a gentle smile. "One thing I'm sure of is there are some universal truths about the McCades. They're all very protective and nurturing. I'd swear it was ingrained into their DNA. So, my guess is you'll probably be hard pressed to find a better Dom for you than Gideon. He'll meet your needs, both mentally and physically. It's the emotional part that might not be there at first. He'll keep himself emotionally distanced from you. It'll be up to you to break through the barriers he's erected. Maybe, just maybe, you'll be the one to be able to do that."

"Oh, no. That's not…" Sebastian cleared his throat and continued, "That's not gonna happen. It'll just be a simple Dom/sub contract. There won't be anything emotional or romantic about it."

After a long moment of giving him a thorough once-over, Braden shrugged and said, "We'll see. You never know what might happen."

Sebastian shook his head emphatically. "No. I don't... That won't happen."

Confusion and, if he wasn't mistaken, sadness marred Braden's face, but he smiled when he replied, "Okay. But either way, if you came here today to ask me if you could trust Gideon to be a good Dom and to treat you well, I'm telling you that I have no doubts he'll be a wonderful Dom and he can be trusted to be good to you. I trust him nearly as much as I do my husband, and that's saying something, as I trust Zavier with everything that I am."

With that, a weight lifted off Sebastian's shoulders. He hadn't known how much Braden's opinion would matter to him, but as soon as he had it, he knew he'd be signing the contract with no reservations. He was about to thank Braden when he heard a familiar voice in the kitchen, and he smiled as Zoe walked around the corner and into the breakroom.

She stopped and her mouth dropped open. "Sebastian, what are you doing here?"

He grinned and replied, "Hey, Zoe. I came by to talk to Braden. How are you feeling?"

"I'm better. I didn't even know you two knew each other."

Sebastian nodded and replied, "I met him through work."

Her eyes popped wide, and she grinned at Braden. "You got a new tattoo?"

Braden's face turned comical in its confusion, and he asked, "No. What are you even talking about?"

"Oh. Sorry, Sebastian." She looked at him, guilt-ridden.

"It's okay. I don't mind him knowing."

"Yeah?" With that, she pulled her long-sleeved shirt off and Sebastian laughed at her unashamedly stripping down to her spaghetti strap tank at work. She pushed the tank top up to her ribs and did a little twirl, showing off the ink he'd put on her skin.

Incredulous, Braden asked, "Wait, you're a tattoo artist, too?"

Sebastian blushed and nodded, watching while Braden pulled Zoe towards him and slowly spun her around as he took in the ink on her stomach, her back, her shoulders, and her arms. The more he looked, the more Sebastian became self-conscious, wondering what Braden thought of it all.

"Oh my god, Sebastian! I've always loved her ink, but I've only seen her arms. You're so talented! They're gorgeous. I'm going to have to get one from you, and when Zavier finds out, forget about it. You've just gained a lot of customers. His men are gonna want some work, too, I'd be willing to bet."

Sebastian smiled and blushed at the compliments, shrugging. "Thanks. I just do it as a side job on the weekends to earn a little extra money."

Zoe snorted. "You've got people clamoring for your ink and more work than you know what to do with. You could quit your job and make a living off it. You know you could!"

The way the conversation was heading made him feel uncomfortable, so Sebastian just shrugged it off and went with his usual excuse about his work at the SFPD. "I like helping people."

Zoe smiled and rubbed his shoulder. She pulled her shirt back on and asked, "So, you just dropped by to chat?"

"I needed to talk to Braden about Master G."

Zoe's jaw dropped. "You mean owner of Catharsis, Master G?"

It was Braden's turn for a jaw drop. "You're a member there too? Are you a Domme or a sub?"

"Sub, but wait! What about Master G?" She glanced back at Sebastian. "And why would you be asking Braden?"

Sebastian, growing uncomfortable with her stare, rubbed a hand over his scruff. "He asked me to sign a contract with him. And Braden's kinda related to him, so…"

"*WHAT?*"

Sebastian hunched in on himself, not understanding her reaction. Crossing his arms over his chest, he just looked at her while she glanced back and forth from him to Braden and back again. He was used to feeling unworthy, but she'd never made him feel like that before, and he wasn't sure how to react.

He didn't understand Gideon's interest either, so he guessed her confusion was warranted. Trying to shrug it off, he downplayed the danger he'd put himself in that night as much as possible and quickly outlined what had happened at the club, so she'd understand why Gideon felt he had to offer a contract. When he was done, the horrified look on her face made him squirm.

"Are you fucking serious? Sebastian, are you all right?"

"Yeah. I'm fine."

"That's horrible! I'm so sorry. Maybe he wouldn't have approached you if I'd been with you."

He shrugged. "You were sick, and it just would have happened to another sub. I'm fine and it's over. Better me than anyone else."

"What the hell does that mean? It's not better that it happened to you! It shouldn't have happened to anyone!"

"But it did, and it's over. I'm fine."

Zoe looked as if she wanted to keep talking about it, but huffed, shaking her head. She turned her attention to Braden and asked, "So what's this about him being related to you?"

"Gideon is Zavier's brother."

Zoe dropped into a chair next to him and let out a woosh of breath. "So, Gideon is Master G? Huh. Well *that's* crazy! God, and *HOT!* I've met him here a couple times. Lord those McCade genes are phenomenal! I never made the connection. I only knew of Master G by name. Subs love him, and they all want to sub in scenes with him when he does a demo, but I've never seen him do one myself. We've only been members for about three months, and he's always seemed like an enigma."

Braden nodded. "Yeah, he was out of town for a couple months recently, so that makes sense."

Suddenly, Zoe grinned and glanced at him. "So the Dom that everyone wants, wants you? Why doesn't that surprise me?"

Her comment made him feel a bit better about her earlier reaction, and he relaxed his defensive stance. "Surprised me."

Zoe snorted indelicately. "That's because you've never watched yourself submit. You really should. It's so effortless for you, and you're so damned gorgeous; you're an obvious choice for him. Sign that contract, like, yesterday. I might have to tape you both sometime."

Humiliated just thinking about it, he shook his head. "No way in hell. That's the last thing I want to see."

Zoe shook her head, popped up from the chair and kissed his cheek. Still surprised by her penchant for being so physically demonstrative, he hunched his shoulders and inched away, but at that point, she'd already turned and walked out to the kitchen, tossing behind her, "Gotta get my ass up front or Maya will have my head! Love you guys!"

Braden called out, "Love you, Boop!"

When she'd swished through the door to the café, Sebastian looked at Braden in amusement. "Boop?"

Braden grinned. "Don't you think she looks like Betty?"

Sebastian chuckled and nodded, having seen the resemblance himself, down to her clothing choices. He just never would have thought to call her by a nickname. He didn't think their friendship was close enough for that kind of familiarity. "Yeah, I guess she does."

Braden tilted his head and raised his brows and asked, "So, do you feel better about signing that contract now?"

"Yeah. Thanks for your help."

"You're welcome. Maybe we can make plans to hang out and do something soon. Would you like that?"

Sebastian—surprised by Braden's question, but happy the feeling was mutual—nodded and stood up to get going. He checked his watch and realized he needed to hurry to make his next work appointment. "Yeah, I would. I need to get going to my next appointment. Thanks for making time for me and feeding me. Not to mention answering all of my questions."

Braden moved in and hugged him, surprising Sebastian yet again. "Anytime, Sebastian. I think we're gonna become good friends."

Sebastian smiled and nodded, feeling suddenly lighter knowing Braden wanted to hang out again. He left with a spring in his step, hugging Zoe on the way out and waving at a smiling Maya who told him to come back anytime.

Chapter 14

GIDEON

Gideon slid to the edge of the bed and clasped Boone's wrist with his other hand, placing his finger over his pulse as he whispered quietly in his ear. "I'm going to pull you out of submission so we can have our discussion about the syndicate. But first, we'll discuss your punishment."

Gideon closed his eyes as he felt Boone tense up and heard the nearly inaudible catch in his throat. As the sub's heart rate increased under his fingers, Gideon spoke softly. "Settle, pet. I've got you. What has you worked up, your punishment or coming out of submission?"

"Coming out of submission, Sir. It's been so long since I've felt like this, I just. . ."

"You don't want it to stop."

A relieved sigh escaped. "Yeah."

Gideon gripped the sub's shoulder which relaxed him quite a bit. "Once we're done hashing out the details, you'll be in total submission until I hand you over into Connell's care. Does that lessen your anxiety?"

"Yes, Sir. Thank you."

"Good. So, if you have meetings tomorrow that you can't cancel or call into, you will be permitted to attend those meetings and then return. Your punishment tonight, for breaking three rules, will be threefold. Why is that?"

Boone let out a shaky breath. "The punishment fits the crime, Sir."

"That's right, pet. You're doing so well." Gideon felt the slow return to a normal heart rate and felt Boone's body relax more fully into him. "One of your punishments will be an essay of sorts. I want you to write a letter to your new Dom. Once I've introduced you to him, you'll present properly and give him your letter. You'll offer to read the letter aloud to him, or he can choose to read it on his own. Any questions?"

"What do you want in the letter?"

"Ultimately that's up to you, but there are some key points that must be there. One, you need to explain the rules from our contract and why I made them. Two, you'll explain what your everyday life is like from the time you get up in the morning to the time you go to bed and which rules you are breaking. And three, you'll explain what you need from him as your new Dom. You will include our contract so he has a copy of it and can adjust it as he sees fit. Any questions?"

"When will I write the letter?"

"Tomorrow morning before work, after you've had a good night's rest of at least eight hours of sleep."

"Yes, Sir."

"Another punishment is ordering dinner in tomorrow."

"May I speak, Sir?

"Yes."

"I'd like to make a good first impression and cook for Connell, Sir."

"I know that, pet. That's why I'm considering it a punishment."

"Yes, Sir."

Gideon watched Boone's shoulders slump, but he didn't change his mind. He knew Boone would stress himself out until he was too wired to function if he had to cook some elaborate meal for a new Dom, so not only was he punishing Boone, but he was keeping him from being too worked up to connect with Connell. Two birds, one stone.

"Good. Your last punishment is that you'll be unpacking each neglected box of personal items downstairs in the basement and bringing the items you want to use in your house up one thing at a time and finding a home for them and returning for the next item."

"One at a time, Sir?"

"One at a time. When you're not in meetings tomorrow, that and the letter are all you will do. If you don't have enough time to finish the job tomorrow, you will make the commitment to finish it before the weekend is over. You will also not be allowed to clean your home for Connell."

Boone let out a little groan before he could stop himself. "Yes, Sir."

"Do you know why I tacked on the last bit?"

Boone let out a frustrated sigh that made Gideon smile. "Because, Sir, it would be a case of polishing the cannonball."

"That's right. Explain why that is."

"Because my house is clean already and to clean it thoroughly again, prior to having company, does not add value and is a compulsive behavior that I utilize as a coping mechanism to avoid dealing directly with my perceived problems in my life."

Gideon chuckled, tightening his hold on his shoulder. "That was very specific, but all true."

"You drilled it into me, Sir."

"Good. Why don't you grab us some water and meet me in the dining room? We'll need the table to spread everything out."

Gideon grabbed his duffle and made his way down the hallway. He pulled out everything he'd taken from Alan's home as well as his own notebook where he'd kept a journal and timeline of the events that occurred from the moment he'd taken on the assignment, written in his own version of shorthand. If found, no one would be able to decipher it which was exactly the point. As he walked into the dining room, he thought about how things would go tonight, but also about how things had gone between them so many years ago.

The dynamic between them when they were working was always professional. They both drew very deep, dark, unmistakable lines between their work and their play. It was a rule they'd both set and had stuck with, at all costs. They both respected the hell out of each other though their skillsets were completely different. Boone never looked at Gideon like just another hired gun, and Gideon never looked at Boone as just another desk jockey.

It was one of the reasons they'd worked so well together. Boone wasn't the reason he'd left, in fact, he was one of the reasons he'd stayed so long. They made a solid team and worked effortlessly together, but ultimately, Gideon had to leave Boone's world behind, or he'd have lost himself completely.

Gideon heard footsteps approaching and pulled himself out of his reverie. When Boone came into the room carrying two tall glasses of ice water and a bowl wedged between his arm and side, Gideon stood to help him and couldn't help but grin. "Frozen grapes? I thought you only kept them in your freezer back then because of me."

Boone chuckled. "No, you totally got me hooked on them. I almost panic when I run out. It's an addiction. I blame you."

Gideon laughed, enjoying the more relaxed Boone. He hoped the man would be able to get back to that after their discussion, knowing Boone wouldn't like the tactics he'd be using. He set the grapes down in the middle of the table and went back to the other side to sit down. All the info he had gathered, everything he'd brought with him, was still lined up in front of him on his side of the table.

When Boone sat down, he rubbed his hands together and looked at Gideon. "Okay, let's see what you got."

As he reached across the table to slide some of what Gideon had towards him, Gideon placed his hand on the envelopes. "We need to have a discussion, Boone."

A look of wariness passed over Boone's features. "Gideon. . ."

"I need you to listen to me first."

Boone narrowed his eyes. "I'm not gonna like this, am I?"

Gideon shook his head. "No, you're not."

Boone sat back abruptly, his hands clenched on top of the table, and waited. Gideon folded his hands on top of the envelopes. "There's a man I need you to find. His name is Lars Janssen. He was the one that gave the orders to take out my SEAL team. Alan worked for him."

Boone shook his head. "Gideon, I can't just put resources on a guy that isn't part of a case I'm working. You know damn good and well that every single penny spent these days is dissected and put under a microscope."

Gideon nodded and passed Boone an envelope. "I do know that. I also know there are ways around it. You can add his name to your file for this case. No one will know. That envelope has all the info I was able to get on him from Alan."

Gideon watched as Boone opened the envelope and looked inside. "Jesus, Gideon, there's hardly anything here!"

Gideon watched as Boone tossed the envelope down. "Do you want what I was able to get from him about your case, or not?"

Boone's hands clenched into fists, knuckles white. "You can't be serious."

Gideon leaned back in his chair. "Oh, but I am."

"You fucking asshole! We had an agree—"

Gideon narrowed his eyes and tilted his head. "Watch yourself, Boone. Think back to our conversation in Zavier's office. The file was up on his TV screen so we didn't have to waste time with small talk. Smart move on your part because it hooked me immediately, just like you knew it would. But I was very careful with my words. I asked for the dossier, you handed it over. You said you needed him found and brought in. What did I say?"

Gideon watched as Boone glanced away, eyes unfocused, as he tried to remember. Boone's face morphed into anger. "You said, 'I'll deal with him.'"

"And what did I do?"

Boone's jaw clenched. "You dealt with him."

Gideon's eyes glittered as he nodded. "I did."

Boone growled and picked up the envelope again, taking its meager contents out and sorting through it. "This is fucked up, Gideon. You led me to believe—"

"I did no such thing, Boone, regardless of how much you wish I had. You were on a mission to pull me back in. You didn't take the time to think your methods through or to take even a second to wonder at my easy capitulation. You know me fairly well. The navy taught me a lot, the SEALs even more, but your division of the CIA took my education to a new level. All I did with Alan was utilize my training."

Boone scoffed. "Your training included following orders, protocol."

Gideon shook his head. "First of all, I was never given orders back then. That wasn't the agreement. I was provided information, and I did the jobs I was assigned, my way. Second, I didn't sign anything. You never officially re-hired me or contracted my services. I haven't been paid a cent, and I neither need nor want your money. You dangled a goddamned carrot in front of a killer, Boone. A killer you helped create. What did you expect to happen?"

"You know what I expected!"

"He killed my men! He'd have been dead by my hand already if I hadn't been told by the brass that he'd died the same day my men did. You're lucky it wasn't worse. Did you know I was fully trained by *your* people to revive so I could kill someone a second time? What was their philosophy? Ah yes, it's a method that gives the enemy false hope and incentivizes them to give up more information."

The color drained from Boone's face, and he rubbed it with his hands. "Jesus, Gideon."

"You can't blame an animal for doing what it's been conditioned to do. I may be five years out, but that conditioning will never go away. That's my cross to bear." Gideon sat back again, took a deep breath, and then a drink. "So, do we have an agreement, or not?"

Boone let out a deep sigh, shoulders slumped. "Yes. Yes, we have an agreement. I'll put resources on him."

Gideon nodded and passed everything he had across the table knowing Boone was a man of his word and would do his level best to come through for him. They spent hours going through everything he'd brought, piece by piece. The fact that the syndicate was much bigger than Boone and his superiors had thought didn't go over well.

When he was done providing Boone with a rundown of his time and findings, he sat back in his chair. Boone was a brilliant strategist and Gideon knew he'd hash the information out in his own head six ways from Sunday before he felt like he knew the information backwards and forwards. There wasn't a submissive bone in his body when he put on his CIA cap. It was only in private that he needed the release submission provided him.

Boone scrubbed his hands over his face several times, leaned back, and looked up from his notes. "So, we've got more information than we had, but we've still got a ways to go. The one hundred men only meet every six months when they're given their new assignments and new locations. It's the weekly phone calls that are confusing... Jesus, he's just making them call in to fuck with them. To keep his leash tight. I bet the number you have here just leads to an answering service that doesn't even have any inkling of what these guys are calling about."

Gideon nodded. "I doubt Diabo Feio needs the information they're calling in. It's a mindfuck. They call the number and give a couple code phrases, depending on if things are going well or not. If things aren't going well, they probably send someone to dispatch them. My guess is someone completely unrelated to the whole thing is answering and passing the information along to someone else that's only peripherally involved."

Boone shook his head in disgust. "He's smart, really smart."

Gideon nodded in agreement. "He covers his bases and is gonna be really hard for you to find. He leaves no trail. None. They get their assignments and never communicate directly with him until that six-month assignment is up and even then, only peripherally. They have no cell phones, they use no email, and they don't use cloud drives. They have notebooks, pens, and paper maps. Christ, they process their own fucking photographs. Diabo Feio is off the fucking grid. They meet at a predetermined place six months later and get their new assignment, and so it goes. That may be your only chance. You've got your work cut out for you."

"You're talking as if... No. Gideon. . ."

"I'm out, Boone. I've been out for five years. That hasn't changed."

"We need you for this. You're the best. I need to pull you in."

"I'm not coming in. I won't do it, Boone. I can't."

"What do you mean, you can't? You've just proven you can! It's not what we wanted, but you dealt with it. You dealt with it." He looked at Gideon, his gaze imploring. "Gideon. . ."

Gideon shook his head, sadly. "I have about an ounce of humanity left in me, Boone. That's about it. I'm out, until you find me Lars Janssen. I need you to accept that." Gideon stood and looked down at him. He stared at Boone, unblinking, until he finally got a frustrated nod of acceptance. "I'll give you another two hours to go through the information I've given you. When those two hours are up, I want you back in submission. I'll expect to see you in resting pose in the living room where you'll spend an hour on your knees while I do some work."

Boone shook his head. "We don't have to—"

"An ounce, Boone. You'll submit to me because you need it. That ounce of mine requires that I take care of your needs. It was never your goal, and I allowed it, but regardless of those facts, you've assisted in siphoning off huge chunks of my humanity, don't deny me that last ounce, too."

Boone, looking thoroughly gutted, rubbed his hand over his mouth and nodded again. Gideon left and took an hour long run, showering afterwards. He gathered some supplies from his duffle and took them to Boone's living room where he began his own prep work for the following evening. When his work was done, he put his supplies away and got out his laptop to check on things at the club. Signaled by Boone's movements in the dining room, he turned and watched as Boone walked towards him.

"Can I get you anything, Sir? I still have your favorite whisky."

Happy Boone was already out of work mode and into submission mode, he smiled. "Yes, pet. That would be great. Get a book for yourself if you'd like."

Boone shook his head. "No, thank you. I just want to shut my mind off."

Gideon nodded and watched as Boone went to the kitchen and poured him his drink. When he came back, Gideon tossed a pillow on the floor and watched as the man kneeled on it and held the drink out to him. When Gideon took it, Boone settled into resting pose, leaning against Gideon's leg. It was a familiar scene for them, as Gideon had Boone sit the same way most nights years ago to get Boone ready for the stress of the next day. Gideon touched him on the head, and Boone settled even more into a good headspace. They sat like that for an hour while Gideon finished his work.

Afterwards, Gideon drew Boone into a hug, and he knew by the man's shudder and tight hold that he'd needed the contact. Gideon urged him to get a good night's rest and gathered his gear, tossing it into the nearest guest bedroom. He'd have thought nothing of sleeping in with Boone not even a week ago. He wouldn't have had sex with him then, but he'd have slept in the same bed, giving the sub physical closeness after being in submission for several hours for the first time in too long.

However, the hug would have to do. He didn't want to confuse their inter-action as that was no longer his place in Boone's life. Gideon had kept his punishments non-physical and non-sexual for exactly that reason. He wanted to get Boone's mind back where it needed to be. But, after meeting Sebastian, he felt it was a betrayal of what he was hoping to build with the boy. Surprising even himself with that train of thought, Gideon stripped down and went outside to swim for an hour. After another quick shower, Gideon decided to let his mind and body rest.

Chapter 15

SEBASTIAN

The electric whirring of the tattoo gun filled the space of his studio. Saturdays were always busy for him because he scheduled as many tattoos as he could possibly fit in, beginning at 9 a.m. and ending sometimes as late as 9 p.m. if he had sufficient time to take a couple breaks. He was lucky he was ambidextrous and had trained himself early on to be able to tattoo with both hands equally well. It allowed him to give one hand a rest while using the other to continue.

He lifted the gun and swiped the blood from the skin of the woman's left breast that he was working on. He noticed once he did she shifted to get more comfortable. He tapped her to get her attention, and she pulled out her earbuds. "Jenna, do you need a break? I'm happy to stop working for a bit. You've been lying in that same position for an hour and a half."

She nodded and said, "Yeah, thanks. Sorry, if I could just walk around for a few minutes that would be great."

"Are you feeling chilled?"

She lifted her shirt that had been covering her right breast. "Yeah, a little. Can I get one of your smocks?"

"Of course, I'm sorry I didn't think of it."

He wheeled himself back and pulled out a cotton shirt that resembled a medical gown—with its opening in the back or front, depending on what was needed—but was waist length and long sleeved. He had multiple options depending on what part of the body he was working on and needed access to. He found that having the smocks—especially when people were exposing sensitive areas—helped keep people at ease. He cursed himself for not thinking of it sooner.

She slipped it over her shoulders and tied it in the front and took a walk around his studio checking out his work he had framed and drinking from a glass of ice water he'd gotten her when she arrived for her appointment.

"I've been so happy with your work. I can't wait for it to be done. My girl-friends all want a tattoo from you, by the way."

Sebastian—in the middle of doing some exercises for his fingers and wrists, not to mention stretching out his back—tensed and glanced in her direction. She smiled over her shoulder at him. "Don't worry. I gave them your card and told them you're booked and mostly help people with scars they want to cover up. I figured I'd let you weed through the requests you get and choose what you want to do."

He relaxed and nodded. "Thanks. Yeah, after word got out, I've got more work than I can keep up with and only take on those that I feel I can help in some way. You ready to get back to it?"

She nodded and climbed back onto the tattoo bed. He raised it up so he could work on her while standing for a bit and got going. As he neared her scars, he paused and touched her arm, causing her to pull out an earbud. "I'm getting closer to your scar tissue. Do you want a stress ball or some gum or candies to chew on to help manage the pain?"

She shifted and took a deep breath. "Yeah. Can I use your stress boobs and get a stick of gum?"

He chuckled, remembering how she'd laughed at his collection of dirty stress balls. His big bowl of balls ranged from cocks, of both the penis and poultry varieties, and boobs to testicles and eyeballs, and pretty much any other kind a warped mind could think of. She'd loved squeezing the shit out of the stress ball boobs he had, telling him it was only fitting, as she was there getting her double mastectomy reconstruction scars covered with his ink.

He could tell by the way she kept tensing up he was working on a particu-larly gnarly bit of scar tissue. She'd told him at their first appointment it was better for her if he kept working through the tough parts rather than taking breaks in the middle of it because it just prolonged it for her that way. He fully understood the desire to power through, so he didn't let up and did his best to keep his pace steady.

It was her fourth appointment with him, and he hoped it would be her last though she didn't know that. Some of her scar tissue was a little thicker in some areas, and he had to go over it multiple times before it took the ink like he needed it to. She was lucky her scars were susceptible to tattooing. Some people didn't have the kinds of scars that lent themselves to ink.

He hated being the one to let down a client that had pinned all their hopes of fixing the damaged landscape of their skin on him. He always made sure people understood before making an appointment that full coverage wasn't possible for everyone. He was always able to help in some way by utilizing artistic design, brilliant color, and unique shapes and movement to camouflage the scarred area. But some scars simply didn't take ink.

Those were the times he'd go home emotionally wrecked when a client would cry at their dashed hopes. Some would leave, too upset to work with him after learning they couldn't have what they wanted. Others would stay, still eager to accept the best he could give them. They'd make a new plan together, one that perhaps wasn't what they'd hoped for, but would help them in some small way to move past the painful ordeal that their scars represented.

He finished some of the shading on the brightest orchid of those he'd inked into her skin. Traces of blood bloomed where his needles had just been and he wiped them away, along with traces of ink. Glancing up, he caught her as she opened her eyes and met his. He grabbed his spray bottle of green soap and sprayed it over her tattoo, wiping it off gently with a fresh paper towel. He helped her up and walked her to the huge standing framed mirror he had leaning against the wall. "Today's your last session, so unless you see anything you don't like, you're all set to go."

Before getting a good look at herself in the mirror, she asked, "Really?"

He nodded, gave her a gentle smile, and then nudged her toward the mirror. He gave her as much privacy as he could with them both occupying the same room. He began to clean up the area, wipe down the table, and dump the ink cups in the trash. When he heard sniffling, he turned around and headed back her way, heart rate spiking. He'd feel awful if she wasn't satisfied. "Is there something you're not happy with?"

As he approached, he noticed she'd taken off the smock and was regarding herself, wiping tears from her eyes. She turned away from the mirror, fresh tears coursing down her face and pulled him into a hug. Stunned to have a half-naked woman in his arms—a first for him, for sure, and completely disconcerting—he returned the hug a bit stiffly. "Uh, Jenna? Is everything okay?"

As he patted her awkwardly on her upper back, she gripped him still tighter. "Sebastian, I love it! It's amazing! So beautiful and vibrant. The nipples look so impossibly real, but the orchids, they're better than I could have dreamed. I can't even see the scars at all. You're a miracle worker!"

Sebastian blushed as she pulled away to look at herself once more. "I'm glad you like it."

She shook her head. "I don't like it, I love it! Look how beautiful you made me!"

He stepped back and waved his hand, brushing away her statement. "Nah, that was all you. I just added a splash of color, that's all."

"A splash of color? That's a whole lotta splash, Sebastian. I'm so grateful to you. You have no idea the change this will make in my life. Really, truly."

"I'm glad. Come on over here, and we'll get you wrapped up."

After cleaning and wrapping her tattoo, he handed her back her shirt, and she took it and pulled it over her head as he made himself busy, putting everything away. When he heard her picking up her handbag, he turned toward her with his aftercare directions.

"Oh, I don't need this, I'm pretty sure I have the last one still."

He smiled and said, "Humor me."

She grinned and took it, slipping it into her handbag and hugging him again before he could prepare himself. He hugged her a bit more comfortably that time around, seeing as she was fully clothed. "Thank you, again. I can't even express how happy I am with it."

Pulling back from her, he smiled. "That's always the best compliment. I'm pleased you're so happy. Give it a couple weeks to heal and contact me if there are any issues or touch-ups you feel you'd like me to make."

She nodded, heading toward the studio door and waved before she left. He continued to clean up after the session; tossing his instruments in their packets, he placed them in the autoclave and started it up. He double checked everything was in its place and locked up for the day. Stopping at the Italian café just down the street from his studio, he grabbed a cup of zuppa Toscana and a chunk of Italian bread before getting in his ancient car to head home. He never wanted to cook for himself after a long day of tattooing. He just didn't have the energy for it.

He felt good about the work he'd gotten done that day and was glad he'd have a short day of only two clients the next day. They were both substantial time sinks, but he'd be able to get out in the late afternoon and have some down time before the new week began.

Walking in his front door, he was greeted by Slap and Tickle. Setting his dinner on the coffee table he picked them both up and gathered them close, enjoying the feel of their furry little faces rubbing against his short beard and loving their little mewls for attention. He set them down in the kitchen and proceeded to do his best not to step on them while they wound their way in and out of his path as he opened some fresh wet food.

He looked down as they attacked their smelly meal with gusto. He hated the stuff and only fed it to them when he was gone for a particularly long day, but they were putty in his hands afterward and always curled up with him on the couch and watched a little television after he ate to relax before bed. Drifting off on the couch, he remembered the way Gideon had nuzzled Tickle against his face and kissed him on the head before he set him down. He couldn't help but wonder if Gideon would treat him with that much care.

Chapter 16

GIDEON

Boone adhered to Gideon's rules for the day. He wrote the essay before he started working. He'd had to go in for meetings but had come home immediately afterward to begin unpacking his personal things in the basement and bringing them upstairs, one at a time. Gideon received a call from Connell earlier in the day. Unbeknownst to Boone, Connell had been able to get out of a late meeting and now planned to arrive earlier. Their previous contract stipulated that adding another person into a scene was at his discretion so that's what they planned.

When five thirty rolled around, Boone, thinking he had plenty of time, was still bringing things upstairs and finding places for his favorite artwork and trinkets. He looked tired, but if the smile was anything to go by, happy about making his house a home.

Gideon entered the kitchen where Boone was hanging a clock. "You've got five more minutes, so clean up what you can of your mess in the basement."

"Yes, Sir."

"I want you to present in the living room when you're done."

"Yes, Sir," Boone said as he walked towards the basement to clean up.

Gideon left him to it and went to quietly unlock the front door. He then got what he'd need and brought it to the living room. He turned on some background music, something soothing and not distracting, loud enough to muffle some noise but not detract from their scene, nor drown out a safeword. He sat in a large armless side chair, waiting the last several minutes for the sub to finish up. When Boone walked into the room, rubbing his sweat dampened hands on his pants, Gideon sat still. He watched every movement as Boone took off his clothes and presented himself properly in the middle of the room.

Gideon stood and walked toward Boone. He crouched down, using his finger to raise Boone's chin up, though the sub's eyes never moved above his chin. He reached around to his back pocket and pulled out a blindfold and saw Boone let out a satisfied sigh when he saw it.

"Look me in the eyes before I blindfold you." When their eyes met, Gideon clasped Boone's chin firmly in his hand. "This scene is going to be intense. I'll stay within the boundaries of our previously agreed upon limits. Do you trust me with your mind and your body?"

"Yes, Sir."

"What are your safewords?"

"Green for go. Yellow for slow down. Red for stop, Sir."

"Use them if you need to, pet."

"Yes, Sir."

He tied the blindfold over Boone's eyes, and grabbed one of his coils of jute, his favorite rope for bondage. He much preferred natural fibers because they held more securely than synthetics, allowing fewer knots and very little stretch which made it perfect for suspension rigging.

"Hands clasped behind your head, elbows by your ears."

Gideon folded the rope in half, hooking the loop between the folded together middle fingers of Boone's clasped hands, utilizing them as a sort of hook. He worked each side of the rope down opposite sides, creating beautiful hitching down each wrist to the elbows.

Halfway down, he drew each rope from one elbow over to the other and worked the remainder of the rope down the opposite upper arms, bringing the ropes together at the shoulder blades, connecting two Olias knots in the center with a small button knot. He continued wrapping them around Boone's upper chest, hitching and knotting them together between Boone's pecs in a large, flat button knot then letting the ends of each rope fall straight down to his crotch.

Gideon continued on, drawing the ropes through his legs and around his ass cheeks, and after a couple more hitches, brought the ends together at his back. The intricacy of the hitches and knots on the arms, juxtaposed by the simplicity of the rigging around his body, made a striking contrast and left his body open and available for what was to come.

It was six o'clock when he tied off the rope. He felt a presence behind him and slowly turned, seeing Connell standing there and knowing he'd probably been there for several minutes, watching him finish up but not wanting to disturb him. Gideon approached him, and they shook hands silently, pulling each other into a tight embrace.

They turned to face Boone's back and slowly made their way around the sub until they were both crouching in front of him. Knowing the silence—only cut by the music in the room—was contributing to Boone's tension, Gideon looked at Connell and nudged his head towards Boone. Gideon watched as Connell took his cue and reached towards the sub and tweaked both of his hard nipples in turn.

Boone's cock, semi-hard prior to that, perked up even more. Gideon, glancing over at Connell, smiled at the intense look on the man's face as he eyed the sub who would soon—if things went as planned—become his. If the fire in his eyes was any indication, there'd hopefully be more than a contract between them in the future. Boone's breath began to saw in and out of his chest, the situation exciting him, obviously sensing Gideon's closeness but not knowing what was to come.

Both Doms smiled and Gideon leaned forward. "Check in, pet."

Boone let out an expulsion of air, his face serene. "Green, Sir."

"And so it begins."

A blissful smile settled over Boone's face. "Thank you, Sir."

Both Doms stood. Gideon led Connell over to the small pile of things he'd prepared for the scene but had tucked away out of the pet's sight. He picked up the paracord flogger he'd made years ago for Boone, the falls each ending in a monkey fist knot, the center of each holding a marble. He handed the flogger to Connell and placed his hand on his old friend's shoulder, letting him know to stay where he was.

He picked up the leather ottoman that sat in front of one of the room's side chairs and approached Boone. He put the ottoman down in front of him. "The ottoman is in front of you, pet. Lean over it and rest your chest on it. Expose your back and ass to me, legs spread as wide as you can handle them comfortably. That's it."

As Gideon stepped back, Connell moved forward. He ran a soft hand over Boone's head, over his trussed-up hands, and down his back to his ass in one long, soft caress. Gideon smiled as he saw Boone shiver. Connell stepped back, hitched the handle of the flogger at the small of his back in the back pocket of his pants, untucked his shirt and unbuttoned his sleeves at each wrist, rolling them up. The act delaying the scene shortly to build tension and also putting the Dom in the right headspace for the flogging ahead.

He'd forgotten how much he enjoyed watching Connell work a sub over and fell into the rhythm of the dance with the other Dom, staying back several steps but following the man around Boone's body, nearly feeling the work himself, the sense of the flogger in his hands. When Connell was done, he made eye contact with Gideon and nodded. Gideon moved in, taking over his part of the dance. "Check in, pet."

Boone let out a very shaky breath. "Oh god, Sir. I…"

Vaguely concerned, Gideon leaned in and slid his fingers softly down Boone's back. "Deep breath, in and out. Talk to me."

Boone took in a deep breath as ordered. "I'm sorry, Sir. It feels…" Another deep breath, in and out. "It feels different, Sir. I don't know how to explain it. Maybe it's just because it's been so long. I don't know…"

Gideon turned to Connell, eyebrow raised, small smile on his face. Understanding from the sub's tenor that he was feeling good, but needing him to verbalize it, he turned back to the sub. "Good different or bad different?"

"Shit, Sir. Sorry. Green. Very green, Sir."

Gideon chuckled and looked at Connell, grinning even wider when the man straightened, a bit of pride stiffening his spine. He pointed out the three-foot nylon snake whip he'd found in Boone's play stash earlier that day, another piece of equipment he'd made years ago. He nodded when Connell picked it up. Gideon trailed his fingers down Boone's back again. "You're doing good, pet. Going to continue."

The shivers that ran through Boone made Gideon smile and nod at Connell again. The sub let out a small moan. "Thank you, Sir."

"Sit up, pet."

Boone raised himself off the ottoman, spine straight. Gideon moved the ottoman away. "Beautiful presentation. You're not permitted to come, understood?"

Boone dragged in an unsteady breath. "Understood, Sir."

Again, he silently switched places with Connell, and the man began a warm-up with the snake whip; the sound of it lashing through the air made Boone moan before it had even touched his skin. When Connell finally let loose with his first lash, a gentle precursor to what was to come, the sub cried out in surprise, followed by a long moan. As the whip got a workout, so did

Boone. Connell kept the strikes from being too harsh. Not knowing enough about Boone's limits, Gideon could tell he didn't want to take the chance of rolling right past them and forcing the sub to safeword before they'd even met.

Connell worked his way around Boone's body, never lashing in the same spot twice, leaving beautiful crisscrossing red lines covering him from torso to knees. Gideon, needing to stay back from the whip, watched Boone carefully, watching his every facial expression. When he saw the sub's face relax and the cadence of his breathing even out, he knew Boone was flying. As he was about to make a move toward Connell, he realized his old friend had seen it too and was slowing the lashes down. When he finally stopped and moved back, Gideon moved in.

"You took that so well, pet. Proud of you."

His response more whisper than anything. "Thank you, Sir."

Gideon stood and turned toward Connell who had the lube bottle in his hands. Gideon moved back as Connell moved in, getting on his knees behind the sub. As Gideon watched, Connell reached around to tweak Boone's nipple with his left hand and clasped Boone's rigid cock in his right. Gideon sat in the same armless chair he'd been in earlier and watched as Connell masterfully edged the sub many times over before glancing at him and nodding.

Gideon stood, crouched beside Connell who had resumed his stroking, and whispered in Boone's ear. "Come, pet."

Both Doms watched in satisfaction as Boone's cock let loose a torrent of cum which arched up then fell. He moaned as the cum continued to shoot in volley after volley until the last remnants of it dribbled over Connell's fist. He watched and waited to see if Connell would require his assistance to loosen and remove Boone's bindings. Knotwork wasn't Connell's thing so he wanted to assist, if needed.

He needn't have bothered though, as he watched Connell make quick work of it, leaving the blindfold for last. Both Doms watched as Boone shrugged his shoulders, rolling them and shaking out his arms to relax the muscles. When he'd settled, Gideon backed up but kept an eye on Boone's reactions from a distance.

When Connell kneeled in front of Boone on one knee and removed the blindfold, Gideon watched as a myriad of emotions passed over the sub's features. Shock and confusion came first, as he looked into Connell's eyes for the first time then over to Gideon and back again.

Gideon heard his breath start to hitch as he stared at Connell, unmoving. Gideon stepped forward but Connell held up his hand to stop him from approaching. The sub continued devouring every feature of Connell's as if he might disappear if he blinked or looked away for even a second.

Gideon heard Connell whisper, "Be at ease, boy."

Gideon watched in amazement as tears coursed their way down Boone's cheeks. He could see the indecision pass across Boone's face, his body tense, and then surprise wended through Gideon as Boone's body relaxed fully and he nearly launched himself into Connell's arms, kissing the man for all he was worth. Gideon let out a relieved sigh and a quiet chuckle, and he watched Connell's arms wrap tightly around his new boy as he savored their passionate kiss.

As they pulled apart, Connell reached and wiped Boone's tears away. They spent several long drawn-out moments staring into each other's eyes, both smiling. "Good boy. I'm going to go get you some water. And then we'll give you the aftercare you need."

Gideon murmured, "There's a couple cold bottles in the fridge."

Connell nodded at Gideon as he walked out of the room. Gideon picked up the blanket from the back of the chair and approached Boone. He kneeled, wrapping the blanket around him, holding it clasped in front of Boone as he used his other hand to raise Boone's lowered face. Their eyes met and the hope Gideon saw there went a long way in assuaging his guilt.

Gideon kissed his temple. "He's a good Dom, pet. And an even better man. He'll be what you need, and I think you'll be exactly what he needs. Can you trust me enough to trust him and give him a chance?"

Boone's eyes widened, and he nodded quickly, his body tense once again. Gideon smiled gently. "Relax, pet. I need to hear the words."

Boone took a deep breath and once more, launched himself forward, this time into Gideon's arms. As Gideon held him, Boone's body trembling. Gideon's body relaxed at Boone's words. "Yes, Sir. I trust you enough to trust him."

Gideon pulled back and looked at Boone. "Good. Then I'm not gonna stick around. I think you both need the time and the privacy to figure out how to move forward together. Oh, and you might wanna order that dinner."

Boone's laugh warmed Gideon's heart. Boone nodded. "Thank you, Sir. Truly. Thank you so much."

Gideon cupped Boone's cheek and smiled. "You're welcome, pet. You'll be in contact with me, I trust?"

Boone nodded his head, chuckling at Gideon's not so subtle reminder of their agreement. "Yeah… I mean, yes, Sir. I will."

Gideon nodded and stood. He headed towards the front door, meeting Connell on his way. He saw the surprised look in the man's eyes as he opened the door to the coat closet and removed his duffel. As he hitched it over his shoulder, he approached the other Dom. He kept his voice low, just between them. "He'll push you at every turn. He's stubborn as a mule and needs a strict hand to keep him in line. He's got a copy of our contract for you and a hand-written letter for you as well. Call me in a week or so. I'd like to know how things are going."

Connell reached out to shake his hand. "I will. Thank you, Gideon. We'll make it work. He's in good hands."

Gideon nodded. "I know he is. Take care of him. He needed more than I could give him back then, and even more now."

As Connell reassured him that he would, Gideon opened the front door and walked out, suddenly ready to be home again. If things went his way, he'd soon have his own sub to Dominate, and he'd be kidding himself if he didn't admit to the warmth spreading through his system at the thought of his boy.

His. Boy.

And just like that, his heart rate kicked into a fast cadence in anticipation and excitement as he realized that for the first time in his life, he was thinking of a sub as his boy rather than a pet, and had been from the very beginning.

Chapter 17

SEBASTIAN

The call had come on a Thursday night, right after he'd gotten home from a long day at the station. He'd been putting the finishing touches on his salad when his phone had vibrated in his pocket. He'd added Gideon's number to his phone, wondering if the trend of adding people to his contacts list was going to continue and uncomfortable with the fact that he'd wanted it to, even as it'd scared him.

He'd been half thinking he'd never hear from the man again, half knowing and fearing he would. Pulling the phone out of his pocket, he'd glanced at the caller ID, and his heart had lodged in his throat when he'd seen Gideon's name pop up on the screen.

He'd cleared his throat before answering. "Hello?"

"Boy." Even through the phone, Gideon's voice had him inhaling and closing his eyes. That one word. Fuck. It had zinged straight to his cock like a physical touch.

His breath had grown shaky when he'd answered, "Yes, Sir?"

"How are you doing?"

"Uh, I'm good, Sir."

"Good."

"Um, how are you, Sir?" Jesus, could he have been any more inane?

Gideon had chuckled, sending shivers down his spine. Good lord, had he ever reacted like this to anyone from a simple telephone conversation? No. No, he hadn't. Fuck.

"...this weekend?"

Shit, shit, triple shit. "I'm sorry, Sir. Could you repeat that?"

There'd been a pause that had kicked up Sebastian's heart rate. "Do I have your full attention, Sebastian?"

His name, instead of boy, fuckity fuck. "Yes, Sir. I apologize for getting *distracted."*

"Forgiven. I asked if you were available this weekend."

"The whole weekend, Sir?" Had his voice broken, just a few days before turning twenty-seven? Kill him now.

He'd obviously pushed Gideon's patience to its limit. "Yes, the whole weekend."

"I... I... I'm sorry, Sir. I have appointments on Saturday that I can't reschedule." Stuttering. Really? It had just kept getting better. *"I'm free Friday evening after work and all of Sunday, Sir. And I had a floating holiday I needed to make use of, so I'm off Monday as well."* Which had been true, for the most part.

"Hmm. Okay, let's do this, I'm going to come over to your place after work on Friday. We're going to hash out the contract over dinner. Then, when your appointments are over on Saturday, I want you to come by the club. Understood?"

"Um, okay, but I might not be done with work on Saturday until later at night."

The long pause after that bit of information had Sebastian feeling nervous. "You have to work late at night on Saturdays?"

"Yes? Um, yes, Sir. Sometimes." He hadn't thought it prudent to explain about the tattooing at that point.

"All right. What time should I be at your place tomorrow? I'll arrange dinner."

"Is six okay?"

"Yes, that's fine. See you tomorrow."

He'd gotten goose bumps up and down his arms at the low gravelly voice, and his breath had hitched. *"Yes, Sir."*

There'd been a pause and then what Sebastian would have only called a low growl. "And, boy?"

Sebastian had whispered, *"Yes, Sir?"*

"I know we haven't signed anything yet, but are you willing to take instruction from me right now?"

Holy hell that had gotten him hard. *"Yes, Sir."*

"I want you to edge yourself nearly to orgasm tonight, as many times as you can handle, but do not come. Do you understand, boy?"

He'd let his breath out in a whoosh, unable to care if Gideon had heard him. "Y-yes, Sir."

"Good boy. See you tomorrow evening."

"Goodnight, Sir."

"Goodn—"

The knock on Sebastian's door brought him out of his reverie. Throughout his workday, he'd played the previous night's conversation and his own edging sessions over and over in his mind. He couldn't stop thinking about Gideon's orders given in his deep, stern voice. He'd gone up to bed right after scarfing down his salad and had spent thirty minutes bringing himself to the brink of coming only to back off at the last moment. He stood from the couch, keeping Slap and Tickle in his hands so they wouldn't try to escape again.

Gideon was a sight for sore eyes. When he opened the door, he watched as Gideon slowly took off his sunglasses, a hungry look in his eyes, his full lips sensuously curved. He looked Sebastian up and down, eyes stopping at the kittens who were held fast in Sebastian's grip. His curved lips turned into a broad grin as he reached out, plucking Slap out of his hands. Gideon brought the kitten against his chest and pet the little monster.

His hair looked like he'd dragged his hands through it multiple times, and his beard looked so soft Sebastian wanted to touch it. Gideon wore a fitted, navy blue, long-sleeved cotton shirt that outlined every single bulging muscle. His shirt ended and Sebastian couldn't help but look at the bulge in Gideon's slate gray tactical pants. If that was what he looked like soft, Sebastian gulped at the thought of what he was hiding behind the placket of his zipper. The fitted pants ended nearly touching the ground around the base of some enormous black, leather shit-kicker biker boots.

Good lord this man ticked all his boxes, hard. Some of which he didn't even know he'd had until he'd latched his gaze on the man before him. He leisurely trailed his eyes back up the muscular man and turned beet red when he realized Slap was sitting on Gideon's shoulder and they were both looking at him with quizzically tilted heads. Humiliation warred with amusement at their matching gazes and his lips twitched before he could stop them. A smile spread across his face as he backed away from the door and finally managed to speak. "Sorry, Sir. Please come in."

Gideon walked through the door and clasped Sebastian's chin, tilting it up so their eyes met. "How many times did you edge, boy?"

Goosebumps broke out all over Sebastian's arms. "Nine, Sir."

Gideon grinned wolfishly. "That's a good boy. I'm assuming you didn't come?"

Sebastian blushed. "Correct, Sir."

Gideon nodded, lifted a bag Sebastian hadn't noticed, and said, "Good. Where can I set this for later?"

Curious, and dying to look inside, Sebastian pointed to his entryway table. He watched as Gideon put the bag down before he turned toward Sebastian and said, "Let's get comfortable."

They sat facing each other on the couch, the kittens wandering back and forth between them. "Do you need to bring them with you?"

"I... What?"

Gideon smiled. "Slap and Tickle. This weekend?"

What did he think Sebastian did when he usually went to the club? "Oh, uh... No, that's okay. I can just feed them when I get home."

"But will they get into trouble, missing you? They seem the mischievous types."

Was this man for real?

"No, they should be fine."

"Okay, well think about it. You can bring them if you'd like."

To the club? What was going on? Confused, he went along with it, figuring he'd eventually catch up. "Thank you, Sir."

"You're welcome. Now, let's talk about the contract. Do you have a copy printed out?"

"Yes, just here." He leaned over and gave Gideon a copy of what he had.

Gideon shook his head, a confused look on his face. "Sebastian, this is the short contract between a Dom and sub that have repeated, casual scenes in the club only. We need the full contract between Dom and sub. Did you print that out?"

A lightning bolt of anxiety skittered its way from his prickling hairline to his spine on down to send frissons of electricity through his limbs, lifting the tiny hairs. What? He shook his head in denial. "No. I thought you wanted me to print out this one."

A look he couldn't discern passed over Gideon's face, making his discomfort palpable. "Sebastian, what is it you think we're discussing tonight?"

"Signing the contract so that we can do scenes together."

"Where?"

"The club?"

Sebastian was out of his element, and before Gideon could answer him, a knock sounded on his door causing him to jump. He went to stand up but Gideon stayed him with a raised hand and walked towards the door. "It's dinner. I've got it."

When he walked back in carrying wood fired pizzas from a local pizzeria that Sebastian was very familiar with, he stood and led Gideon through the dining room into the kitchen. He pulled out plates, napkins, and utensils. After getting them both ice waters to drink, they sat back down on the sofa, digging into their side salads, pizzas still in their boxes. Gideon had actually ended up getting the one that Sebastian always ordered from them, so he was happy with that. When he'd eaten his salad and one small piece of pizza he set down his food and watched, amused, as Gideon ate everything he'd ordered.

When he nudged his pizza toward Gideon, the Dom opened the box, his brows drawing together. "Was it not good?"

"It was great. It's the kind I always order for myself. I had my fill. Go ahead."

The look of consternation was still there. "Sebastian, you ate a small piece of pizza and a side salad."

Sebastian smiled and shrugged. "I don't need that much."

Gideon grunted, biting down on one of Sebastian's pizza slices, and mumbled, "You could stand to gain a few pounds."

Sebastian stilled, that old, all too familiar feeling of not being good enough wending its way through him. Had it ever left? He had to stop this now if it was going to beat him down mentally. He did enough of that on his own and had worked hard at extricating himself from others that helped him with it. His voice shook, when he finally replied, and he grew annoyed at his inability to be strong when standing up for himself. "Gideon, I won't sign a contract with you if you're going to insult me."

Surprise etched itself across the Dom's features. "Sebastian, I didn't mean it as an insult. I like everything I see." Gideon paused, as if letting that sink in. "Everything. I just want you to be healthy."

Sebastian felt the truth of those words and let them settle him and nodded. "All right."

"I think there's been a misunderstanding between us, here."

Sebastian crossed his arms over his chest and leaned back into the corner of the couch as far away from the big man as he could get. He didn't know what was coming but he wasn't sure he was going to like it.

"We're not signing a contract for a couple scenes at the club. When I mentioned coming over this weekend, I didn't mean to the club, I meant to stay with me Saturday night through Tuesday morning. At the end of the weekend, we'll decide if we're compatible and have built enough trust to sign a six-month contract."

Sebastian's eyes popped wide. "Oh."

"Were you under the impression that I wanted to sign a contract for scenes at the club only?"

Eyes still wide open, Sebastian only managed a nod.

"Are you against a longer-term contract?"

"I…I don't know. I don't think so, but that's not what I thought this was about. I guess I'm confused. I don't know what a six-month contract would entail. What you expect from me, what we expect from each other."

"That's what the full contract lays out for us. We can make it what we want. It's a guideline only, a starting point."

"Um. Okay. I can go up and print that out."

"Why don't you do that, and I'll clean up."

Sebastian looked down at both empty pizza boxes and smiled, happy Gideon had gotten enough to eat. He got up and headed up the stairs, waking his laptop. Once he located the contract and sent it to his printer, he sifted through the pages, nervous and excited all at once. He didn't know if it would work, in fact, he had serious doubts that it would, but it was more than he ever thought he'd be offered, so he was going to do his best to be exactly what Gideon wanted in a sub.

Handing a copy of the contract to Gideon, he took his seat opposite him on the couch. They went through the beginning pages that outlined the Dom's role and the sub's role. Sebastian really liked that it outlined that the Dom would take care of the sub's needs, ensuring they were taken care of, mentally and physically, when in the Dom's care. Both Dom and sub sections called out the need for each person to have respect for not only the role the other played but for their choices and autonomy. Sebastian got the feeling this contract wasn't the standard contract used at most clubs or between most Doms and subs. His regard for Gideon increased as they moved through the pages.

When they reached the proposed schedule page, that's when his palms grew damp. That was where the issues would begin, he knew it. He was convinced Gideon wouldn't want to sign a contract with someone that worked so much and didn't have that much time to give to his Dom. But, when he explained that his job kept him pretty busy and that his schedule varied every week depending on the workload and sometimes involved travel, Gideon just shrugged as if it wasn't a concern and said they'd go week to week and figure things out as they went along.

Sebastian smiled and a weight lifted off his shoulders. They went through each other's hard and soft limits, finding them fairly compatible. There were a couple pages on the self-care habits expected of the sub, and when Gideon said he expected him to be trimmed up top but keep his balls and ass shaved or waxed, a nervous thrill shot through Sebastian.

He knew most Doms and subs had sex when they were contracted, but as he'd only expected to scene in the club, he truly hadn't thought sex would be part of the equation, or rather, he didn't think it would interest Gideon. Hearing Gideon explain what he expected of Sebastian's self-care habits surprised the hell out of him, so maybe he'd been wrong.

They moved through the self-care sections that dealt with exercise and eating and Gideon looked up. "Is this a sore subject?"

Sebastian shook his head, not wanting Gideon to think he tripped out about either topic. "No, Sir. It had nothing to do with that. I just don't want to get myself into a situation where I'm insulted and belittled."

Gideon narrowed his eyes at that. "Have experience with that, do you?"

When all Sebastian did was shrug, Gideon looked like he wanted to press the issue, but in the end, he didn't which was a relief. But that relief fled upon seeing Sexual Intercourse emblazoned across the top of the next page. Okay, that was a bit of an exaggeration, but it felt like that.

There were two boxes. The first of which stated: No sexual intercourse will occur between the two parties. The second of which stated: Sexual intercourse will occur between the two parties then further outlined possibilities for limits or stipulations regarding said sexual intercourse.

He cleared his throat. Wanting Gideon to know he had no expectations and didn't assume the man wanted him like that, he spoke up, "We can check the first box, Sir."

He watched Gideon's reaction closely and confusion set in when the man didn't react at all besides staring at him quietly. He felt like he had to explain himself. "Um, I just mean that I'm not expecting anything. I understand if that's not what you want from our arrangement." When Gideon's eyes narrowed, he realized what he'd omitted. "Sir."

He looked down at his lap and distracted himself with petting Slap and Tickle and scratching them behind their ears. He jumped in surprise when Gideon growled out, "Put the kittens on the floor."

Sebastian's eyes popped wide, and he did as instructed. No sooner were the kittens on the floor than he was yanked down the length of the couch by his ankle until he was lying flat and Gideon was lying on top of him. They were face to face and Sebastian's heart was racing, his breath coming in pants. *Holy fuck, how had Gideon managed that maneuver? And was Sebastian crazy to think that was the hottest thing he'd ever experienced?*

Gideon loomed over Sebastian, gently clasping Sebastian's left leg around the calf and wrapped it around his upper thigh and did the same to Sebastian's right leg. Sebastian couldn't help it, he tugged Gideon even closer and crossed his ankles over Gideon's ass. Heat flared in Gideon's eyes, and Sebastian began to rethink his offer of checking the first box.

Gideon wedged an arm under Sebastian's back, tugging his shirt up in the process, gripping his neck. They were a hairsbreadth apart, their eyes locked on each other, Gideon's aquamarine gaze intense. If Sebastian didn't get his breathing under control, he was going to pass out.

His mind shut down when Gideon's hips began a slow undulation.

"What do you feel, boy?" Gideon's hips rolled into his once again, making Sebastian gasp and grind his own hard cock against Gideon's. "Answer me."

"Your cock, Sir."

"Does it feel good?"

Sebastian's yes, was more an exhalation than a fully formed answer. He closed his eyes when those magical hips undulated against his again.

"Who's it hard for?"

Sebastian's eyes popped open, meeting Gideon's. Unable to answer, all he could do was gasp in another breath and pray he didn't embarrass himself by coming in his jeans.

"Who's it hard for, boy?"

"M-me, Sir?"

"Say it again. Who's it hard for, Sebastian?"

"Me, Sir."

"That's right, you. There is nothing I want more than to sink myself fully into your tight little hole. I want you, every inch of you, Sebastian. Don't doubt it."

Sebastian's eyes rolled back in his head when he heard the growly whisper in his ear. He began to rub up against Gideon faster, unable to stop himself. He used the leverage of his ankles still locked together at Gideon's ass to rub his hard dick against the Dom's.

"You like that? You gonna come for me, Bastian?"

Dear god, more whispering. He'd never been called Bastian before, but suddenly, he never wanted to be called anything *but* Bastian by the man. Well, that and boy because that pushed his buttons too.

"That's it, boy. Take what you need from me. Mmm, goddamn those hips can move."

Sebastian couldn't stop the whimper if he tried.

"Can they move that fast while you're riding my fat cock?"

Jesus, the man would be the death of him.

"We're gonna find out, aren't we, boy?"

When he could no longer control his movements, he cried out, "Sir, please?"

Gideon bit down on his earlobe and growled, "Come for your Dom, boy."

White lights flashed behind his eyelids, and the longest orgasm he could ever remember having had him convulsing as volley after volley of cum shot out of his cock into his pants, leaving him limp and panting. His gasping breaths eased, his heart rate slowed, and the orgasm haze had him nearly asleep, the only thing keeping him awake was the weight of his Dom on top of him.

As the minutes ticked by, he grew embarrassed, not wanting to open his eyes and face the man that had just brought him more pleasure than he'd had in longer than he cared to admit without even touching his dick. He didn't even know why he was feeling so self-conscious, or rather, didn't want to admit it was because he'd come so quickly and in his own jeans. For fuck's sake.

"Open your eyes."

When he did, his Dom's eyes were crinkled at the sides, his smile one of contentment and satisfaction. "Thank you, Sir."

His blush bloomed fast, and he cast his eyes down to Gideon's lips. Lips that lowered and took his before he even had time to take a breath. Before he could contemplate that this was their first kiss, it was over like it had never been. He glanced up into Gideon's eyes again and smiled, shyly.

"You're welcome."

"Can…can I return the favor, Sir?"

Gideon slowly extricated himself from the grip of Sebastian's legs and sat down on the couch by his feet, facing him. Pulling both of Sebastian's feet onto his lap. "No, we still have a few things to discuss. Let's move on to safety so we can wrap up talk of the contract."

Sebastian nodded, grabbed the contract and saw that safewords were up next. Gideon left it up to Sebastian what safewords he wanted to use. They moved on to discussing the three-month STD screening schedule required by the club's bylaws. They'd each recently had a full one completed. Gideon said he was willing to use condoms that weekend before they signed the contract and Sebastian agreed, mouth going dry at the thought.

He asked for a copy of his last full physical, including blood test results regarding his overall health so he could see for himself that he was in good health. He said if the results were all at healthy levels, he wouldn't push about his diet and exercise. Sebastian swallowed back his panic at sharing his medical information. Gideon must have seen it in his eyes because he paused and looked at Sebastian until he was unable to hold Gideon's gaze.

"Do you have any serious medical issues that will impact or be affected by our play that I need to be made aware of?"

Sebastian ran the wording of that question over and over through his mind and breathed a sigh of relief when he could look Gideon in the eyes and tell him the truth. "No, Sir."

Sebastian's pause must have made Gideon uneasy because he asked, "You sure about that?"

Sebastian nodded quickly. "Yes, Sir."

Gideon nodded, and Sebastian breathed out a sigh of relief as they turned to the last full page before the signature page. Feeling excited about the possibility of being in a contract with this larger-than-life man if he could only get through the long weekend ahead keeping the Dom's interest, Sebastian was itching to sign on the dotted line. Gideon watched him closely, making Sebastian uncomfortable under the scrutiny. Sebastian set aside the contract, realizing Gideon had something on his mind.

"I need to explain some things to you before we go any further."

"Okay."

"This contract if we sign it after this weekend is all we can have together. I'm not good with relationships. It's not what I'm looking for. I want to say that now, so you understand that going in."

Sebastian shrugged, not surprised in the least. Relationships didn't happen for him. He wasn't what people termed "a catch." Not having much to offer anyone kept him well insulated from romantic entanglements. "That's fine, Sir."

"I'm a good Dom. You'll get what you need from me there. I'm also very physically demonstrative, even playful and affectionate with my contracted subs. It's important to me that I not only meet your needs in a dungeon setting, but also in the bedroom."

Sebastian grinned. "If the hot frotting session we just had was anything to go by, I can agree with that, Sir."

Gideon chuckled. "Brat. I just mean that I'm the type of person that likes to touch and be touched. It's important to have that connection between a Dom and their sub. I think all too often it's missing. But if I hold you while you're sleeping or touch you casually while we're talking, I can't have you confusing my affection for love."

"I don't have a problem with that."

"I'll want my hands on you, often, and I'll want to bend you over every surface in my home. But I won't be taking you out to dinner or sending you flowers at work. I won't be buying you gifts for special occasions or asking you out to the movies. We won't be spending holidays together, as that's a time for family and I don't want to blur those lines. I don't want to confuse you or have you hoping that I'll change my mind. That's not gonna happen."

Sebastian's smile remained. "You don't have to worry about me expecting more from you, Sir."

Gideon's eyes narrowed. "You sound pretty sure of yourself. Why is that?"

Sebastian thought about how to say it in a way that wouldn't pose further questions. The blame was at his feet. He'd never be the one someone chose for their forever. He'd long since made peace with that and knew it to be true like he knew the sun would rise in the morning and set in the evening. "I'm not built for that, I guess. I've never been a romantic relationship sort of guy."

When Gideon stared at him for several drawn-out moments as if challenging and assessing what he'd said, Sebastian held his breath. Only when he realized that Gideon could see what he needed to see in his eyes did Sebastian relax.

Gideon nodded. "Okay, that's great. I'm glad we're on the same page."

Sebastian smiled and kept his gaze on the larger man, loving the soft touches he was absentmindedly giving his feet. Moving Sebastian's feet off his lap, Gideon pulled him onto his lap to straddle him. Sebastian's shirt—still hiked up from Gideon's roving hands—revealed his stomach, and he watched as Gideon's eyes traveled down his chest to his navel. He looked down as well as Gideon reached out his hand, gathering some of the cum that had escaped his jeans on his fingers.

Sebastian watched as Gideon looked at his own fingers and licked his lips. He thought Gideon was going to lick it off which would have been so hot but got even more turned on when he used those same fingers to open Sebastian's mouth and slide them in. Sebastian gripped onto Gideon's wrist and wrapped his lips around Gideon's fingers, his dick giving a jerk in his pants as it tried, and failed, to get hard again. It was a close thing though, as Gideon's growl nearly did the trick.

"Clean them off, boy."

Once he did, Gideon went back for more until his stomach was cleaned of his own spunk. When Gideon finally pulled his fingers out of Sebastian's mouth for the last time, he gripped his face in both hands and pulled Sebastian down for a kiss that stole his breath. His Dom's tongue swept in as if searching for any lingering essence of Sebastian's cum. He gripped Gideon's muscular arms to keep from just floating off in blissful euphoria.

Gideon drew them apart and Sebastian tried again. "Please, can I make you come, Sir?"

Gideon smiled, kissing him one more time. "Tonight was for you. The next time I come, I'm gonna be buried balls deep in your tight ass. Which brings me to the bag I brought with me."

Shivers wracked Sebastian's body at the promise of what was to come, and he could do nothing but nod his head. Gideon stood, and he locked his legs around his Dom. He used a hand to push Sebastian's hair away from his face. He tried to turn his face away, uncomfortable being on display in front of the gorgeous man and having him see all his flaws up close and personal.

But Gideon's grip was firm, and he drew Sebastian's gaze back to his.

Kissing Sebastian on the lips then ever so softly on both cheeks and his forehead, Gideon set him back on his feet and gripped Sebastian's hand in his as he walked them both towards the table.

He handed the bag over, and Sebastian peered inside the paper gift bag and saw several boxes. Pulling them out, he realized he was the proud owner of a new bottle of lube and four different sizes of butt plugs, the last of which had his eyes popping wide. If the size of that one was any indication, he better be taking things seriously. He put the items back in the bag and set it down, unsure what to say. Gideon drew him back in with a palm to his ass and a smirk on his face.

"Beginning tonight, for a couple hours, I want you wearing the smallest one. By the time Sunday morning rolls around, I want you to be able to take the biggest one for that amount of time. Think you can do that for me?"

"Yes, Sir."

"Good boy. No coming or touching yourself between now and tomorrow night at my place unless it's to wash, shave, plug, or relieve yourself. Is that understood?"

Sebastian nodded. "Yes, Sir."

"Pack enough clothes to stay until Tuesday. You can leave early from my place to drop Slap and Tickle back at home before work."

Sebastian sounded like a broken record and tried to hide his grin. "Yes, Sir."

After a quick spank to Sebastian's ass, Gideon growled, "Be good for me."

Sebastian couldn't hide the grin at that comment. He nodded and watched as Gideon walked out of his place, making his way to an enormous boxy and expensive looking SUV. God the man was sex on wheels; big, heavy duty, all terrain wheels, apparently.

Fuck him sideways, he was gonna fall hard for the man. It could be quick and painful, or it might take a while, but he knew without a doubt in his mind it was only a matter of time. Shrugging, he picked up Slap and Tickle and began to walk upstairs to bed, all the while telling them he knew what he was getting himself into, knew it would end with his heart broken, but that he wouldn't want to miss the ride, no matter how much it broke him when Gideon ended it.

GIDEON

Earlier that day, he'd met his brother at the Custos Securities offices, and they'd had a discussion regarding Lars Janssen. He'd given Zavier all the information he had on the man, including everything he knew about what the man had done to his team, regardless of the fact that it was classified. He was hiring CS to find him, and he wanted Zavier to be armed with all of the info he had available.

Zavier argued about the hiring, refusing to take payment, but they all had each other's account information, and when he threatened to pay him personally instead of paying CS directly, he'd acquiesced. Then, Zavier shocked the hell out of him and offered him a position at CS. Apparently, they could use a man with Gideon's background, and the offer was open-ended.

When he tried to explain why he'd gotten out of the business, Zavier reminded him that doing what he assumed he'd done for the CIA was different than what they did at CS. Gideon said he'd think about it, feeling conflicted since a part of him wanted to join their ranks, against his better judgement.

When Zavier compromised and said he'd take him on as a consultant, Gideon said he'd try it out. Why that appealed to him, he didn't know but thought perhaps keeping his mind sharp, rather than physically going out on jobs, might do him some good. Though he wondered if he was just seeking a reason to say yes.

Gideon passed the time working that evening while he waited for his boy. Sebastian had said he didn't know when he'd be done, but the fact that it was nearing ten o'clock didn't sit well with Gideon. They'd agreed that when he arrived, he'd head directly up to Gideon's loft and key in the same code he used at the club.

He received a system text that someone had keyed into his loft, and he walked to the front desk to let Khaleo know he was leaving and not to disturb him unless the place was burning down. He also explained that Roarke was covering until Tuesday. At Khaleo's raised brow Gideon smirked and took the elevator to his loft. He didn't need to explain himself, and his club was like the proverbial grapevine, it would be known soon enough that he'd signed a boy.

He glanced at his watch, saw that it was nearly ten fifteen and shook his head. He didn't like the fact that Sebastian worked weekends. He got the distinct feeling that the boy was holding back information from him about any number of things, but he wasn't going to push. Yet. As the bell dinged and the door slid open, both kittens stopped playing with their toys, and their tails puffed up as they both started doing a sort of scared side shuffle that had Gideon chuckling as he stepped into the room.

The elevator closed and the kittens sped toward him, winding around his feet as he squatted to pet them both. They tumbled over each other trying to hop up on his knee, and he gazed at Sebastian. His boy was leaning against the back of a chair, amusement sparkling in his eyes as he watched Gideon interacting with his little terrors. His shy finger wave did things to Gideon that he'd have to think on later.

He continued to give the kittens attention but kept his eyes on Sebastian. "You wearing a plug, boy?"

The blush pushed even more of his buttons, and he smiled as his boy nodded and said, "Yes, Sir."

Gideon, still squatting with the kittens, rested his elbows on his knees as he gazed up at his boy, grinning. "You look good enough to eat."

Sebastian's blush deepened, and he turned his face away, avoiding eye contact. Gideon watched as an emotional wall came up, insulating his sub from any unwanted compliments he didn't believe were genuine. He'd have to work on that.

"Speaking of eating. Have you had dinner?"

"Yes, Sir."

"Good. Come on into the kitchen, I'm gonna grab a beer, and you can look through what I've got to see if you want anything."

Sebastian followed him quietly, and when Gideon pulled a beer from his fridge, he left it open for Sebastian to look through. He saw a spark of interest then a sideways glance at Gideon before he shrugged and said, "I'll just take water."

"Nope."

That brought Sebastian's focus directly on him. His eyebrows reaching toward his hairline. "Pardon?"

Gideon grinned at his boy's proper response and used the neck of his beer bottle to point at the fridge. "You saw something that interested you in there. Go ahead."

A blush crept up his boy's neck to his cheeks and Gideon smiled wider, wondering what on earth could garner that much embarrassment from his refrigerator. He frowned when Sebastian insisted that water was what he wanted. That wouldn't do at all.

Setting his beer down, he lifted Sebastian up and sat him on the countertop, watching as the boy wiggled to get his plug-ladened ass comfortable. He smiled and wedged himself between the boy's legs. Watching his eyes dilate when he wrapped both of his legs around his waist like he'd done the night before sent a little thrill through Gideon. He loved how Sebastian responded to him.

He leaned in and trailed soft kisses up Sebastian's neck, smiling when he felt his whole body shiver. Kissing his way to his ear he whispered, "What's got you blushing in my fridge? Hmm?"

Before Sebastian could respond, Gideon kissed his lips and pulled back. "We're not gonna move from this spot until you tell me. I'm a very patient man, Sebastian."

Sebastian huffed, blushing again. "You'll laugh."

Gideon laughed. Guilty as charged. And reveled in the fact that Sebastian felt comfortable enough to shove him away playfully.

"See? I told you, you'd laugh!"

"You haven't even told me what you want yet!"

"Well, I'm not gonna tell you *now*!"

Gideon snuck back in between the boy's legs and tested a theory from a response he'd gotten the night before, digging his thumb lightly into Sebastian's ribs. When the boy squeaked and tried to shove him away again, he dug his fingers into Sebastian's other side until he was squirming and trying desperately to get away from those tickling digits.

"CHOCOLATE MILK!"

Gideon stopped his torture in complete surprise. A laugh escaping before he could stop it. *"What?"*

Sebastian's mouth dropped open at his audacity. "See?! You laughed!"

Gideon gripped the edge of the counter, leaning into Sebastian, the top of his head resting on Sebastian's shoulder, hiding his face as he kept laughing. "I'm not! Really. I'm not."

Sebastian gasped and tried to shove him away. "You so are!"

He shook his head and cleared his throat, finding himself completely surprised, pleasantly so, that he was having so much fun. When was the last time he'd had fun like that? His expression serious, he gazed into Sebastian's eyes, his own twinkling with mirth. "I'm not. I promise. This is serious. Chocolate milk is serious business. Hang on."

He went about getting out a long ice cream spoon and the largest glass he could find. He filled it with milk and got the chocolate syrup out of the door of his fridge and proceeded to brandish it high above the milk glass, squeezing a ridiculous amount of chocolate into the glass with a flourish.

Setting the syrup down, he held up the spoon to be examined by Sebastian who was now crossing his arms over his chest, eyes narrowed, doing his level best not to laugh. When he nodded, Gideon proceeded to take said spoon and stir in the chocolate, the milk changing color gradually until it was as dark as he could possibly get it.

When Sebastian moved to pick it up, Gideon held up his finger and turned to a drawer. Back a second later, he was brandishing a plastic, bright blue, loopy straw with a penis as the tip, and Sebastian lost the fight and finally let loose his laughter. When Gideon handed him the huge glass of chocolate milk, he took it with greedy hands and started drinking from the penis with outrageously exaggerated enjoyment, making Gideon laugh again.

When he finally stopped drinking, the glass was half empty, and Sebastian smacked his lips. "Ahh! Sooo good! Thank you, Sir."

Completely charmed, and thoroughly enjoying himself, Gideon replied, "You're welcome. I'll keep it stocked for you."

Sebastian tried his best to look stern. "See that you do."

They grinned at each other a few more seconds then Gideon remembered the box of pastries his brother had given him earlier. He snagged them from the counter and opened them, watching as Sebastian's eyes widened comically and he reached in the box, but then yanked his hand back out, looking up at Gideon. "May I, Sir?"

He smiled gently and nodded, loving hearing Sebastian call him Sir. "Please. That's why I opened the box. Braden made them."

They snacked on the sugary confections quietly for several minutes, and Sebastian took another long drink from his glass then looked at him seriously. "Um, Sir?"

Gideon smirked. "Yeah?"

Sebastian looked down at his drink and back up again, grinning. "Don't think I'm gonna let it slide that you have an electric blue, loopy penis straw in your kitchen."

Gideon threw his head back and laughed. "Well, see. . . There was this party. . ."

"Uh huh, sure. I've heard it all before!"

"You've heard a story about an electric blue, loopy penis straw party favor before?"

"Who hasn't?"

"I'm gonna go out on a limb and say, probably most people."

Sebastian smirked at him and asked, "Okay, so there was this party?"

Gideon set aside Sebastian's glass of chocolate milk and lifted the boy off the countertop. He grabbed the milk and his beer in one hand and clasped Sebastian's hand in the other, leading him to his large chocolate brown leather couch. They both sat, facing one another, and Gideon handed back Sebastian's tall glass of diabetes.

"There was a bachelor party for a gay couple at the club several months back. There was penis themed everything. We had a lot left over, so I put them in the storage room at the club. Occasionally, Khaleo is up here to see me, and he took to bringing some of those penis party favors up and hiding them in my loft. Every once in a while, I'll come across one of them, and most of the time, they end up in my kitchen so I can gather them and bring them back down to the club."

"I like Khaleo. Even more now, after that story."

"Yeah, you say that now, but eventually, you're gonna find something penis related where it has no business being, and you're gonna wonder about the guy's mental health."

They grinned at each other, and Gideon took Sebastian's empty glass, setting it down on the side table and leaning in close. "You gonna lapse into a sugar coma while I'm trying to talk to you?"

"I hope not, Sir."

"You and me both, boy. So, I'd like to propose something this weekend."

He wrapped his hand around the back of Sebastian's neck, tugging him closer so he could kiss the boy's neck as he talked, causing him to squirm. "Mmm… Yes. What? Okay."

Gideon chuckled and finally pulled back. "I think we need some time to establish trust with one another before we sign the contract. I'm proposing that this weekend isn't about Domination and submission, or at least that's not all it will be about."

Sebastian crossed his arms over his chest. "Okay."

"I'm gonna leave a lot of it up to you. Tell me what you want, what your fantasies are. I'll do the same. The more we trust each other with saying these things out loud, the more we'll trust the other with our physical limits."

Sebastian grimaced. "That's gonna be hard for me. I don't like taking the lead."

"You don't have to lead, boy. You tell me what you want, I'll make it happen. Maybe by the end of the weekend, you'll feel more comfortable being spontaneous with me."

Sebastian looked doubtful, but shrugged. "All right. We can try it."

"Good boy. Do you feel brave enough to tell me one of your fantasies, or do you want me to start?"

Sebastian bit a fingernail and gazed at him. Gideon pulled his hand away from his mouth and kissed it, holding it there so the boy couldn't continue. When he finally answered, he wouldn't meet Gideon's eyes. "Could you…" Sebastian cleared his throat. "Could you start first, Sir?"

"All right. I noticed that you're uncut. I'm cut and I love foreskin play. So I want to do some of that this weekend."

Gideon loved the blush that bloomed on Sebastian's face and smiled when he nodded enthusiastically.

"I'd like that, Sir. Umm…" Sebastian blushed and continued, "I've always wanted to shower with someone. I know that sounds stupid—"

"Not stupid, it sounds amazing. I can't wait to see what you look like all sudsy and feel you all slicked up from head to toe."

Sebastian glanced up through his bangs, a shy smile on his face. Gideon made a vow right then and there that he was going to do his level best to keep a smile on his boy's face. He was a beautiful man, but when he smiled, he was another level of gorgeous. He hated that he was going to wipe that smile away with his next request, but he wanted to see how Sebastian reacted to it.

"I'd like to get a couple pictures taken of you." Before he'd even finished the sentence, Sebastian was shaking his head, looking horrified at the thought. "Hear me out, boy."

At Sebastian's dour expression and curt nod, Gideon continued, "The black and white photographs on the walls of the Tranquility Room—"

"NO!" Head shaking, Sebastian repeated, "No way, Sir."

Gideon had known, at least on some level that it wouldn't be Sebastian's favorite request, but he didn't know how deep rooted his self-consciousness and poor self-image went. His voice got stern with his next command. "Sebastian, I said hear me out. I'm not finished yet. I won't ask again, boy."

Eyes cast down, Sebastian's tone was sullen when he replied, "Yes, Sir."

Gideon couldn't keep the grin off his face and nearly let loose a chuckle before he stopped himself. He was glad the boy didn't see it, or he was sure to have a brat on his hands. Straightening his features into a firm expression, Gideon continued, "I'd like to get some pictures taken of you for the Tranquility Room. The pictures there were all taken by Khaleo. He's really good at what he does. You'd have the final say in what you would allow us to hang up. If you don't like any of them, they don't get put up. In the end, if you don't like any of them, you keep them. Every shot, every proof, everything."

Sebastian looked up, his expression less distressed. "Can I think about it?"

"Yeah, of course."

Sebastian nodded and murmured his thanks. When he looked up again, Gideon scooted closer on the couch. "What else do you want to try with me? What other fantasy can I fulfill?"

His boy bit his lip and gave him such a hopeful expression, Gideon's heart twisted. "Um, I've been tied up before but never suspended. I heard that you're a Master Rigger."

"I'd never call myself a Master of anything. The fact that I'm called Master G in the club is still a bone of contention between me and my staff."

"I'm sorry, Sir."

"Don't be. I'll admit that I specialize in knotwork because it's a passion of mine, but I don't follow any particular school or teaching of the practice. What people call Kinbaku or Shibari is an artform, and I'd never presume to be an artist."

"But you love it."

It wasn't a question which Gideon thought was pretty perceptive of him.

He had his sub's full attention, and he loved the honest openness the boy had on his face. "I do, yes. I've been tying knots since I was little, and then later in the military which is also where I started practicing BDSM, leading to my interest in knotwork."

"So, you taught yourself?"

Gideon shrugged. "I guess, yeah. I worked with several trainers to learn the proper way to practice safe suspension techniques, but the knotwork just came from me loving the look of it. I don't have a predetermined plan before I begin, so each session is different. My knotting and rigging is based on what I know works, what holds well and what I think looks visually pleasing against the skin of whatever submissive I'm working with at the time."

"I haven't seen you do a demonstration at the club."

Gideon shook his head. "I very rarely do public knotwork scenes; it's personal for me. If I do it, I try to keep it private, in a training session with another Dom or with a sub that requested it of me personally. I'd love nothing more than to get my ropes on you, boy."

"Really?"

"Really. How about tomorrow before the club opens?"

"I'd love that, Sir."

"Good. Can you promise me something?"

"Yes, Sir."

"Can you think about my request to get some pictures taken of you? I'd love to capture you in suspension."

Suddenly uncomfortable, Sebastian dropped his gaze from Gideon's and rubbed his hands on his jeans in a nervous gesture. After a few drawn-out seconds, he nodded. "Yeah. I'll think about it."

"Good boy. Come on." Gideon stood, clasping Sebastian's hand and pulling him up from the couch. "Let's get you in the shower, and we'll check to see what size plug we're working with."

Gideon grinned when he heard a moan behind him.

Chapter 19

SEBASTIAN

On Sunday morning, Sebastian sat on a chair at one of the bar tables, knee bouncing, while he chewed nervously on his thumbnail. He had no idea what he'd been thinking, agreeing to this. He felt hot all over one minute and freezing the next. Regret coursed through him like venom.

He watched as Khaleo got set up for what was rapidly turning into a full-blown professional photo shoot, rather than the "few photos" he thought it was going to be. If he didn't end up with a twitching eye or a nervous tick by the end of the shoot, it would be a small miracle.

The man's lavender hair which was usually styled in a high fauxhawk that was oftentimes wild and sticking up at interesting angles wasn't styled at all, and lay angled forward over his forehead, coming to a point near the tip of his nose. Every once in awhile, it would annoy the beautiful man and he'd swipe it back out of his face as he set up more and more photographic equipment. He'd met them in the club, arriving via the elevator, which had thrown Sebastian until Gideon had told him that he lived on site in one of two apartments on the fourth floor of the building.

Gideon came back from his office carrying a long military looking duffle bag slung over his shoulder. He approached Sebastian, setting the bag down, an understanding look on his face. "You're nervous. Would I be right in assuming that the cameras are making you the most uncomfortable?"

Sebastian looked up at Gideon, let out a shaky breath and nodded. "Yes, Sir. I know it's stupid—"

Gideon crouched down in front of him, taking one of his hands in his own much bigger one. "Your feelings are never stupid. Let me ask you this, do you use the standard red, yellow, and green safewords for play here at the club?"

Confused, Sebastian answered, "Yes, Sir."

"So, I'm saying this now,because we're about to have our first scene together, but I also want it to be true for everything that happens between us. You can always use your safeword with me. Always. Do you understand?"

No. "Yes, Sir."

Gideon squeezed his hand. "What I mean is, we don't have to be playing for you to use your safewords with me. If we're getting to know each other and I ask something too personal or that makes you uncomfortable, say yellow. If I'm crossing boundaries with my requests of you while we're apart, like the edging session I had you do, you can call me and safeword. And if I ask something of you, and you agree but later change your mind," Gideon tilted his head toward Khaleo and continued, "use your safewords."

When Sebastian only nodded, Gideon went on, "You know that safewording isn't a bad thing, right?"

"Yes, Sir. I just would never have used them outside of a scene."

"It's a simple way for you to easily communicate with me that things aren't all right with you. That's all. We don't know each other very well, yet. That'll change, but these types of relationships aren't easy. Yes, we have rules, a contract, but that doesn't make everything simple. I won't magically know everything you're thinking. Just think of it as a tool to use within the boundaries of our relationship."

Some of Sebastian's tension left him, and he nodded. "Okay, yeah. That makes sense."

"Good boy." Gideon tilted his head to indicate Khaleo again. "And how are you feeling about this?"

Sebastian blew out a breath and admitted, "I was a dark amber before we started talking. I'm more of a chartreuse, now."

Gideon chuckled at that. "So, you were in between yellow and red and now you're in between green and yellow."

Sebastian laughed at himself. "Yes, Sir."

"Let's see if we can't make that a solid green. Come on."

Gideon grabbed his bag and clasped Sebastian's hand. They walked toward Khaleo's setup and Gideon placed his bag on top of the bar table, tugging Sebastian along with him toward the man who was now ready to turn this into the photoshoot of Sebastian's nightmares. When they approached, Sebastian realized the other man had some buds in when he pulled them out of his ears and smiled at them.

"Hey, guys. I'm really excited about this. I've often looked at your features and seen you playing a few times and have wanted to photograph you, Sebastian." He glanced over at Gideon. "The fact that I get to do it while Master G is your rigger, just makes it a bonus. He never lets me take his picture."

That surprised Sebastian, and he glanced over at his Dom. "Really?"

"Really."

Sebastian grinned playfully up at Gideon, head tilted. "Are you feeling like dark amber, or chartreuse, Sir?"

Gideon laughed and swatted him on the ass. "I'm a solid green, brat. How about you?"

Sebastian glanced over at Khaleo, and suddenly, verbal diarrhea of the worst sort began coming out of his mouth. "I've drawn you."

What the fuck, Sebastian?

Khaleo pulled back, surprised. "You've what me?"

"Drawn you. I'm an artist."

Khaleo seemed to look at him with new eyes. "Well, we're gonna have to talk about that in more detail later."

Sebastian nodded and did his best to ignore the voice inside him telling him no. Absolutely, unequivocally, no. *Ignore it.* He could do this. Gideon was excited. Khaleo was excited. He wouldn't let them down. He could do this. He took a deep breath and looked up at Gideon and lied. "Green, Sir."

"Good boy. Take off your clothes and put them on the chair."

While he undressed, Gideon opened his duffle bag and pulled out a black canvas messenger bag. He turned and watched Sebastian finish, lust in his eyes. As Sebastian squirmed under the scrutiny, Gideon clasped his chin, lifting it for a soft kiss. When he pulled back, he rubbed his thumb over Sebastian's lower lip and said, "Come."

They both stepped up onto the large, raised stage that had been moved against the wall for their scene. Gideon approached the table in the middle of the stage and tossed the bag on the end of it. "Stand facing the table, a few feet away. That's it. Take a deep breath and center yourself, arms behind your back, each gripping the opposite forearm, head bowed."

Sebastian complied, fighting down the sick feeling in his stomach. One of his biggest fantasies was about to happen, and all he could think about was that fucking camera. Shut it down. Think of something else. Their shower the night before. They'd had amazing hand jobs and blow jobs, a lot of kissing and exploring of each other's bodies with hands, lips, tongues, and teeth. His nerve endings had been on fire, and he'd never felt anything so sensual as Gideon's hands and mouth on his skin while warm water cascaded over their bodies.

He saw something flash before his eyes, and he flinched, still unable to tuck his unease away. He glanced up surreptitiously and was caught red-handed by Gideon smirking at him, eyebrow raised, and he realized he needed to pay attention to what his Dom was doing. He'd unraveled a coil of rope with a flourish, the long lengths of jute uncoiling in a spiral arc in the air which is what had caused Sebastian to give a start and come back to himself. Not the camera. Yet. Glancing at the table, he saw a heap of meticulously coiled ropes, several carabiners, what he thought was an anal hook sticking out of the bag, and a lot of other metal pieces he wasn't familiar with.

He had to get out of his head, or he'd miss everything. Taking a deep breath, he let it out slowly, centered himself again before he whispered, "I'm sorry, Sir."

Gideon approached slowly, Sebastian's downward gaze caught the center line of the rope in his Dom's fingers, the two lengthy falls in an uncoiled heap at their feet. There was something just so masculine about those large, muscular hands holding the rope like that, he shivered just thinking of them wrapping him tightly in ropes. He could do this. He wanted it so bad. If it came with the price of the pictures, he'd do it.

"I need you present with me for a few more minutes then you can let your mind drift."

"Yes, Sir."

"Because I want the photographs to reflect not only your beauty, but the beauty of the bindings against your skin, I'm going to start on some intricate knotwork that can stand on its own. It will make for some beautiful stills before we begin the suspension. Safewords, Bastian?"

"Red, yellow, and green, Sir."

"Good boy. Use them if you need to. Get your arms as comfortable as they can be as I'll be binding them behind your back. Because this is your first time, if you have questions, feel free to ask. If you feel any pinching or too much discomfort, if anything doesn't feel right, I expect you to safeword. This will take some time, and I won't have you hurt because you didn't want to bother me. Understood?"

Safeword. DO IT! "Yes, Sir."

"Let's begin."

No sooner had Gideon said those words than Sebastian saw Khaleo in his peripheral vision and heard the telltale snicks of the camera. His heart rate spiked and he sucked in a breath that didn't quite make it to his lungs. *No. Please, no.* Taking a step back before he could stop himself, he turned away from the camera, unable to catch his breath no matter how hard he tried. And he tried. Harder and harder, over and over. Shaking his head, he whispered, "Yellow."

What. The. Fuck, Sebastian?

He watched, as if in a dream, as Gideon lowered the rope down to his side and stepped back away from him. Off to his left he saw that Khaleo had lowered the camera so it hung from the strap around his neck and stepped back off the stage. Sebastian's vision grew fuzzy, and he was bent at the waist, hands on his thighs, when who he assumed was Gideon showed up in his blurred field of vision. Which meant his Dom was on his knees in front of him. *Please, no.* He shook his head, gulped in some air and shook his head again.

He tried to say, "I'm fine," but he was afraid it hadn't sounded like that at all.

He heard Gideon talking but couldn't make out the words and tried to ask, "What?"

Hands clasped his face softly, and Gideon's voice finally made it through the cobwebs. "Look at me, Bastian. Focus on me. You're fine. I've got you."

Squeezing his eyes tightly closed, he took a few more gulps of air before he could respond. "I'm okay. I'm sorry. I'm okay."

Sebastian felt Gideon's bearded cheek against his own and heard his calm voice in his ear. "Slow your breathing. Focus and slow your breathing down."

It took several minutes, and as time ticked by, his humiliation grew. *God, he was such a freak.* Gideon pulled away slowly so they were face to face. Focusing on the huge Dom who was literally on his knees for him was the hardest thing he'd had to do in a long while. He got down on his own knees. He couldn't stand above a kneeling Gideon; he wanted, no needed to be looking up at him. "I'm sorry. I'm okay now. Let me try again. I can do it. Please. I want this."

Gideon's hand grasped the side of his neck "Shhh. Bastian, calm down."

"No, really. I'm fine now. Green. I want this."

"Slow down. Let's take one thing at a time. Why did you safeword? Was it the pictures or the rope?"

Sebastian looked down at his lap. "Pictures, Sir. I'm sor—"

"Khaleo, come here, please."

"Yes, Sir."

Sebastian shook his head. "It's okay, really."

Khaleo approached and crouched beside them, camera still around his neck. His actions had Sebastian wondering inanely if he actually was submissive and feeling the same about standing above Gideon.

Gideon tapped the camera and asked, "How many pictures did you take?"

"About ten, Sir."

Sebastian's breathing kicked up again, and from the look in Gideon's eyes, he knew it. Gideon nodded towards him and said, "Show him the pictures as you delete each one."

"Yes, Sir."

Sebastian looked at Khaleo and shook his head again. "You don't have to do that. I didn't say red, I said yellow. Please. I agreed."

Gideon pinched his chin lightly and turned his face towards him. Their eyes met and the compassion he saw there nearly broke him. "You safeworded, Sebastian. Asked me to slow down to figure out what was bothering you. I take that very seriously. I would never use pictures that caused you distress. You're obviously not ready. I shouldn't have pushed. We're deleting the photos. If you ever feel comfortable enough, we'll try it again later."

"I'm sorry. I thought I could do it. I knew I'd hate it, but you both wanted it, and I wanted to give you what you wanted. I've never reacted like that. It took me by surprise."

"That makes both of us. Please watch while he deletes the pictures. I don't want you having any doubts."

Sebastian watched as Khaleo deleted everything he'd taken and said, "Thank you. I'm sorry to have wasted your time."

Khaleo smiled. "It wasn't a waste. I learned that you've drawn me. That was well worth it." He stood and headed towards his camera bag. "I'll leave you two alone. Please text me, Sir, when you're done here, and I'll come down and clean up my equipment before we open."

"Actually, Khaleo, why don't I help you break it all down so we can give Sebastian a few moments to catch his breath."

Fresh embarrassment reddened his cheeks, and he shook his head. "I don't need—"

Gideon silenced him with a look. "Catch your breath, boy. You can sit and rest or rifle through everything I brought down with me if you want and ask me questions about anything that's there. We'll be done here in a couple minutes."

Knowing better than to argue, he nodded and murmured, "Yes, Sir."

Chapter 20

GIDEON

While he wanted to give Sebastian a breather, he felt like he needed one himself as well. He should have been able to read him better and shouldn't have pressed to do the photos so quickly. As he helped Khaleo with the camera equipment, he realized just how much he wanted his contract with Sebastian to work out. The boy was sensuality personified, and he just knew there was so much untapped potential there; he couldn't wait to discover it all. What he thought would be a simple act of him giving his sub an erotic showering experience the night before, had turned into something he knew he'd never forget.

He slowly undressed Sebastian, reveling in seeing his gorgeous body, really for the first time. Having only looked at his body in a clinical way prior, he'd paid no attention to the beautiful lines of his willowy body, the soft hairlessness of his torso, the supple play of muscles under flawlessly smooth skin, or the way the pinkish birthmark that the boy seemed to loathe highlighted his slender neck and the soft curve of his shoulder.

Once he got the boy fully undressed, he allowed Sebastian to do the same to him, chuckling at the wide-eyed wonder in reaction to the size of his engorged, cut cock. His eyes were comically big, his jaw dropping open, and then he bit his lower lip and licked it in such an unconsciously carnal way that it nearly did Gideon in.

When the boy finally glanced up at him, he smiled, his excitement evident, and whispered, "I see why you wanted me to prep with the plugs. I thought the biggest one was wishful thinking on your part, but now I'm not so sure it's enough."

Gideon threw his head back in laughter, enjoying the sparkle in his boy's eyes and the teasing and playful tone in his voice. "We'll get the biggest one in tonight for a couple hours and then again in the morning before the rigging."

The disappointment that wrinkled the boy's brows and made him pout at having to wait, reassured him. "You won't miss it tonight, that's a promise."

When Sebastian sighed and nodded in response, Gideon led them into his large shower enclosure that boasted three showerheads, one of which was detachable. As it was the boy's fantasy, he allowed Sebastian free rein with his body, and he came alive with his eagerness to touch and taste every inch of Gideon's skin. He couldn't remember a time he'd experienced such an amalgam of sensory stimulation and denial.

It seemed his boy had a bit of devilishness in him. No sooner would Gideon sink into a relaxed feeling of boneless bliss at the remarkably strong hands making putty of his muscles than he was brought nearly to peak when taken into the boy's tight fist and hot mouth, repeatedly, an edging torture that made him weak in the knees. Sebastian went so far as to ask permission to rim him. Gideon couldn't remember the last time someone offered him that. As a rule, he didn't bottom, but the rim job Sebastian gave him was a thing of existential beauty that had his cock leaking copious amounts of precum and his breath sawing in and out of his lungs while asking for more of his boy's tongue.

When Sebastian finally came around and took him into his mouth, using a soapy finger to mimic the feeling of his tongue on his asshole, he was nearly vibrating with need. The boy couldn't deep throat him, but he made up for it with an enthusiasm that made Gideon thankful the boy had chosen to join his club. Using his other hand and his talented mouth, Sebastian gave him the best orgasm from a blow job he'd ever had. He came down the boy's throat, nearly too blissed out to see the look of ecstasy on Sebastian's face at receiving his Dom's load. So. Fucking. Beautiful.

He dried his boy off then himself, walking them back to his bedroom and tossing Sebastian on the bed. His boy giggled so playfully Gideon found himself pouncing on the smaller man and tickling him just to hear more of that sweet, carefree sound. That led to a bit of spirited wrestling until they were both a bit breathless and grinning at each other. Just then Slap, or maybe it was Tickle, clawed his way up onto the bed, batting at Sebastian's damp hair and trying to lick it.

He picked the kitten up, walked him across the room, and put him on the floor outside the door just as the other one slipped right past his defenses, making a giant leap and clinging precariously by his little claws from Gideon's duvet. As he watched that happen, the other one darted back in, and soon, he was standing by his bed, hands on his naked hips watching the kittens climb over Sebastian and make a beeline to his damp hair again, chewing on it like it was a tasty treat, the boy trying not to laugh at his mock, thunderous expression.

Skirting the end of the bed, Gideon leaned over and lifted both cats in front of his face, "Can't have you in here tonight, little monsters, my boy needs some attention."

As he walked back into the bedroom, muttering, "Gonna have to buy some kinda cat jungle gym or some shit to keep them busy and out of our hair," he glanced up to see that Sebastian's cock which had been deflated only moments ago was now hard as a rock, pulsing with the beat of his heart and nearly kissing his stomach. He glanced up at the boy's face and saw that he'd propped himself up on his elbows and was looking at Gideon with such desire he did a double take.

Gideon tilted his head and asked, "What's got you so hard?"

Sebastian bit his lip and shook his head, but Gideon wasn't having any of that. He crawled across the bed, wedging his thigh between Sebastian's, resting his weight on his side. He took the boy's cock gently in his hand, clasping it in his loose fist just under the head. He pulled down to slowly, torturously reveal the gorgeous flared head by sliding back the foreskin, eliciting a moan. "Don't make me ask again, boy."

Sebastian collapsed on the bed and covered his eyes with one of his forearms. When he kissed Sebastian's upper arm, he'd lifted it, glancing sheepishly at Gideon, his grin self-deprecating when he admitted, "You called me your boy, Sir."

Confused, Gideon said, "I've called you boy before."

Sebastian shook his head. "Not just boy, you said, 'my boy,' Sir."

Gideon smiled, enjoying the fact that saying those words triggered such a physical reaction with Sebastian. He'd already made the decision in his head that he wanted the man underneath him to be his boy, possibly more than he'd wanted anyone in his life. "You wanna be my boy, Bastian?"

Sebastian's grin slipped away, and he nodded quickly.

Gideon needed the words. "Yeah?"

His boy let out a shaky breath and nodded again. "Yes, Sir."

Gideon nodded. "That's good, because I want you to be my boy."

He barely had the words out before Sebastian clasped his face and kissed him with a passion born of desperation as Gideon continued his gentle pumping of the boy's cock, loving the feel of his foreskin sliding under his hand. They kissed for an age, caresses slowly changing from soft and tentative to rough and frantic. But Gideon didn't want Sebastian to come anywhere other than his mouth, so he pulled away and was just about to move to get the largest plug he'd spoken of earlier when Sebastian's palm on his chest stopped him, a pretty blush tinting his cheeks.

His boy cleared his throat and whispered, "Can I try something?"

Curious, Gideon nodded. "Whatever you want."

Biting his lip, Sebastian's blush deepened. "Where's your lube?"

Gideon got up and pulled a bottle out of his nightstand drawer and handed it over. Sebastian asked him to sit on the edge of the bed. Intrigued, he did so and was quite happy when Sebastian straddled his lap. He gripped the boy's round ass cheeks in his hands and gave them a squeeze, dragging him closer so he could take those pouty lips with his own. Sebastian had other ideas, however, and clasped Gideon's face in his hands, pulling away from the kiss and backing away a bit on Gideon's lap.

He took the cap off the lube and held it over Gideon's straining erection, dripping a small bit of the lube on Gideon's cockhead and doing the same on his. Sebastian's slender fingers began to softly rub the lube over every millimeter of his glans, leaving no spot untouched. This was Sebastian's game, and he'd let him play it, but damned if he didn't want to flip the boy over, crawl on top of him and rut him like a wild animal. Those soft, tentative teasing touches were going to kill him.

He watched, transfixed, as Sebastian rubbed the lube onto his own cock-head and then glanced shyly up at him, his bottom lip between his teeth. Gideon thumbed the soft flesh out of the boy's mouth and kissed him, taking that bottom lip between his own teeth instead. When they parted, Sebastian looked down and scooted back a tiny bit more on his lap. Head down, the boy held their cocks, kissing the tips together and holding Gideon's shaft still as he ever so slowly slid his foreskin over the tip of Gideon's cock.

Fuck. Him. Sideways. Docking?

Jesus Christ, Sebastian was full of surprises. Gideon could do nothing but sit still and watch as the sexiest boy he'd ever seen fully engulfed his fat glans and a bit of his shaft with his own foreskin. When Sebastian gripped both their *cockheads in his hand and began to jerk them off, Gideon nearly exploded right then and there.*

He'd never experienced the feeling of another man's foreskin on his cock. The lube and the feeling of the softest, slickest layer of skin sliding over his hypersensitive glans was nearly more than he could take. A full body shudder consumed him, and his boy looked up, their eyes colliding.

Possessiveness like he'd never felt before settled over him like a warm blanket, and he found himself reaching up to grip Sebastian's throat, just enough for him to physically feel his submission. His boy's eyes slid to half-mast, and his breathing picked up, grip tightening and quickening on their joined cocks. When Sebastian moaned and pushed his neck harder against Gideon's hand, Gideon took the cue and gripped a little tighter. The boy started rolling his hips causing their cockheads to slide up against each other over and over, sparks of sensation emanating from tip to shaft and zinging into his ball sack.

When Sebastian leaned forward again, Gideon tightened his grip just a fraction more and leaned their foreheads together. He growled and let out a harsh whispered command, "Hold your breath for me, boy."

When he heard Sebastian gulp in a deep breath then hold it, he placed his other hand on top of his boy's and gripped harder, the friction of the lube, the butting cockheads, the docking foreskin, Sebastian's thrusting hips, and their double fisted grip holding everything together was building him toward release faster than he cared to admit. When he heard mewling escaping from behind Sebastian's sealed lips, he tugged on Sebastian's throat, drawing him closer and whispered in his ear. "Come for me, Bastian."

Sebastian let out a strangled cry, and Gideon felt hot cum spurting against his oversensitive glans and dripping out from around the edges of Sebastian's foreskin. He came unglued, pulled his cock from the slick sheath, and began frantically pumping his shaft, wanting to brand the boy with his cum, claim him in some primal way. When he glanced into his boy's eyes and saw his struggle not to take a breath, he whispered, "Breathe, boy."

When the boy sucked in huge gulps of much needed oxygen, the evidence that he waited until Gideon gave permission sent chills throughout his entire body, and he lost any and all control he had. He painted the boy's chest with ribbons of his cum, grunting as a final spurt escaped and again, he looked into Sebastian's eyes. His boy grew shy suddenly and looked down at his lap.

Immeasurably moved by the trust Sebastian had just shown him, he gathered him in, hugging and reassuring him. "So good. You did so good, boy. I'm so proud of you."

The praise must have released a lot of tension the boy had been carrying because suddenly he was shaking in his arms. Gideon gathered him still closer and began to rock them back and forth, banding an arm around his lower back and holding him flush against his chest as he used his other hand to caress the smooth skin of his back. "Shh. I've got you. You were amazing, Bastian. Such a good boy."

When Gideon felt Sebastian's grip tighten around him after his praise, he knew he'd reached him. He continued caressing and holding his new sub, emotions running rampant through him, knowing they were doing the same to Sebastian. When the adrenaline finally ebbed, he could feel Sebastian go limp in his arms. He laid him down on the bed, leaned over him, and kissed his soft lips.

After the emotional release Sebastian had, Gideon cleaned him up, lubed him up, and slowly, painstakingly inserted the largest butt plug, praising his boy throughout. He left it in as they each went through their bedtime routines and climbed in bed. At about the thirty-minute mark he removed it, promising Sebastian it would go back in first thing in the morning.

The memories from the night before were so vivid it was like watching a movie reel of their evening. As he finished breaking everything down with Khaleo, he thought about how proud he was of Sebastian, trusting him enough to be spontaneous and try something new. Gideon knew he wanted the suspension rigging, but as he made his way back over to his boy, he was still unsure if they should continue with the session.

He helped Sebastian onto the table, wedged himself between his legs, and cupped his face. "You safeworded to slow me down, and for that I'm grateful. But, Sebastian, I need you to understand that I would have been just as happy if you'd safeworded before you were having a panic attack. More so, actually. And with red, not yellow. Or even if you'd told me a straight out no, last night."

Sebastian nodded, looking ashamed. "I'm sorry. I wanted to please you because you were doing the rigging when you don't normally do it for people, and it was our first scene. I wanted to slow down and see if I could try again so I could be what you need."

Gideon's shoulders slumped. He'd obviously not explained himself properly if the boy felt like he had to repay him for performing as a proper Dom should. He lowered his forehead to Sebastian's and let out a slow breath. Pulling back, he kissed Sebastian's temple and said, "I'm sorry. That's not what I meant when I explained it to you. I meant to say that I don't like performing it in public with subs that I'm not contracted with. Does that make sense?"

Sebastian nodded again and then, as if thinking better of it, he shook his head. "No, Sir."

Gideon smiled. "Good boy. Thank you for being truthful. Rigging is a personal thing for me, so I don't want to do it as a show, as a scene for all to see, because I want to connect with the person I'm rigging. Doing it in front of an audience cheapens it for me."

Sebastian nodded. "That makes sense."

"I wanted to do it for you and would have suggested it if you hadn't brought it up. This contract is for both of us. I want both of us to get our needs met."

When Sebastian merely nodded, Gideon continued, "I'd happily perform a public rigging scene for you, anytime, if that's what you needed from me."

Sebastian shook his head and said, "No, Sir."

"I didn't think so. Just don't feel like you have to repay me for doing my job, all right? Never feel like you need to do something for me so that I'll do something you want. I don't want it to feel like we're bartering to get what we need."

Sebastian scrunched up his face in distaste, shaking his head. "No, I don't want that either."

"It's a give and take, of course it is, but I'd do what you needed even if I didn't get anything out of it but seeing you submit beautifully for me, and I have a feeling you'd do the same to please me. Isn't that right?"

Sebastian nodded. "Yes, Sir."

"Good. So why don't we go upstairs? We'll make lunch and decide what else we'd like to try today. We can—"

Sebastian reached out and gripped his waist, gazing up at him imploringly. *Goddamn, those gorgeous eyes. The boy was going to be the death of him.* Sebastian interrupted his thoughts. "Can't we continue?"

Gideon followed Sebastian's gaze behind them where he'd dropped the rope. "Sebastian, you had a panic attack and were struggling to breathe. I don't think—"

"Please, Sir. It was only because of the camera, and I said yellow, not red. Please. I want this. I *really* want this."

Gideon gazed at him silently for several long moments. He reached up and slid the back of his hand down the boy's soft cheek. "You've interrupted me twice now, boy."

The horrified look on his sub's face was priceless. "I'm so sorry, Sir. Normally, I wouldn't…" He stopped himself and shook his head. "There's no excuse."

Gideon almost felt bad for him, so dismayed by something so insignificant. "You're forgiven. Normally, I'd punish you for that, but we haven't discussed it, nor have we signed the contract, so punishment at this point isn't fair. I just want you to be one hundred percent certain you still want to proceed."

Sebastian waited several beats, ensuring he was done talking, making Gideon smile. "Yes, Sir. Please, I really want you to do it."

Gideon gave him another long look before he finally acquiesced. As his boy moved back in place, he picked up the rope at the marked midpoint. By the time he stood, Sebastian was in position and fully erect once again. He was a gorgeous sight, his tattoos were beautiful, skin supple, and Gideon took him in, taking his time, walking around one side and back again, loving the fact he had to do nothing to fix the boy's posture.

Gideon hooked the midpoint of the rope over Sebastian's head, settling it on the back of his neck. Seeing the desire and—finally—the peace on the boy's face went a long way in helping him settle quickly into a good headspace. A calm came over him as he wound ropes snugly against soft, beautiful skin; the repetition of movement, the familiarity, quickly easing him into Dom space.

As he worked, he thought about what a paradox the boy was; a surprise, really, in so many ways. Shy and full of insecurities, funny and kind, strong and brave. Roarke had described him as the boy who was quiet, followed orders beautifully, naturally submissive, reserved, and seemed to have a sadness that he kept locked deep within him.

Roarke was a very good judge of character. Gideon wasn't about to argue with his insights, but there was so much more to the boy that stood before him; a flush of excitement pinking his skin, his beautiful, uncut cock fully erect. Recovering quickly from his panic, he was giving in so beautifully to the eroticism of the moment. Sebastian had a depth of character and sense of humor that he enjoyed.

Gideon knew he was going to have a hard time resisting the temptation of more with the boy. More emotion, more intimacy, and more commitment. But he'd do it, for Sebastian, if nothing else. His past was too big a stain on his future to involve anyone in his life on a permanent basis. But he could be a good Dom to a boy like Sebastian, and maybe that would be enough for them both.

As Gideon neared the end of his second length of rope, he gazed down at the butt plug, reveling in the fact he'd be taking it out soon enough to fuck his boy for the first time. He headed back to the table to gather another coil, satisfied so far with the intricate, crisscross patterns he'd been able to create across Sebastian's smooth skin. His boy's arms were now snug behind his back in an atypical box tie knot, as a tie-in to the elaborate webbing on his chest and back.

He slowly walked around Sebastian, checking the bindings, ensuring there was no pinching. Leaning in, close to his sub's ear, he whispered, "Check in with me, Bastian. Any discomfort or tingling in your limbs?"

A shiver wended its way through Sebastian's body, letting him know how much his voice affected him. "No discomfort or tingling. Green, Sir."

"That's my boy. We'll continue then. I'm gonna pick you up and put you on the table so I can bind your legs. You're doing beautifully."

When he was done with Sebastian's rigging, his boy's legs were frog tied and connected to his chest harness, keeping him folded in two and wide open. He walked to the side of the stage, grabbing the hanging cord with the control switch at the end, and lowered the metal suspension frame from the ceiling so that it was within reach. When he got back over to Sebastian, the boy was vibrating like a bow string in anticipation.

"Check in, boy."

At the deep sigh he let out, Gideon leaned in and clasped the back of Sebastian's neck. He took a deep breath and replied, "Green, Sir."

"Good boy. We're gonna get you suspended then. Use your safewords if you need them."

"Yes, Sir."

Gideon decided he wanted Sebastian in horizontal suspension, face up. Gathering his supplies, he worked on getting everything ready to suspend his boy from a swivel attached to the frame. He'd use a couple small rigging plates so that he could evenly distribute Sebastian's weight with enough suspension lines to avoid too much discomfort and any nerve damage. He was always extremely careful when performing bondage suspension and took it very seriously, but he felt an additional responsibility with Sebastian. A need to bring his boy a pleasure like he'd never experienced while keeping him protected and safe.

When he finally used the control to slowly lift Sebastian's weight from the table, he heard the quick intake of breath and a giddy moan escape him at finally being suspended. Gideon moved back, away from his boy, and watched as he moved incrementally in his bindings, testing them, and moaning again when he realized he was well and truly captured. When the swivel allowed his boy to twist a bit towards him, their eyes locked and the hunger in his sub's eyes was unparalleled. Gideon had started him out with his lower body at a slightly higher angle, his head therefore a fraction lower. He pressed another button and he was lowered incrementally, until Gideon had him right where he wanted him.

"Please, Sir."

"Please what, boy?"

"Please, take me. Please."

"You want my big cock in your tight little hole?"

Sebastian sucked in a breath and nodded. "Please. Please, Sir."

"You beg so nicely. I want to hear more of it, boy."

As Sebastian continued to beg and plead, Gideon slowly tugged his shirt up to his ribs. Unbuckling his belt and unfastening his jeans, he breathed a sigh of relief as he lowered the waistband of his boxer briefs below his sac, releasing his hard cock from confinement. He approached his boy—who'd been watching his every move—belt buckle clinking against his pant leg with every step.

He swiveled Sebastian around. The boy's face was right in front of his cock, the long expanse of his throat exposed as his head tipped back towards the floor. Good boy that he was, he didn't take any liberties, but let out a whimper and begged to taste him. "Stick out your tongue. That's it."

Gideon smacked his cock several times up against his boy's tongue and then touched the tip of his cock to the tip of Sebastian's tongue, causing the boy to moan as he did his best to get as much of Gideon's precum on his tongue as he could. "You want more of my cock, boy?"

"Yes, Sir. Please."

"You're gonna get what you want. Open that throat, I wanna see my cock sliding into it. And take a deep breath, you're gonna need it."

The boy obeyed immediately, sucking in air like he was starving for it then holding it. Gideon slid his cock deep inside his boy's hot, wet mouth. It wouldn't fit all the way in; that would take practice. Practice, he was going to ensure, made perfect. That didn't stop him from pushing as much of it in as would fit. He felt his cockhead slip into the boy's open throat, and he trained his eyes on it, watching the muscles move as he swallowed around him, taking more in until Gideon could see the outline of his cockhead in the boy's throat. Nothing could have stopped him from placing a palm against it to feel himself there.

He brought his other hand behind the boy's head, holding him there for several long beats until he felt Sebastian's body do its best to expel the intrusion. Pulling back, he kept his hands in place and tilted the boy's head up so their eyes met. "I'm gonna fuck that throat. We need to condition it to take all of me, understand?"

Sebastian nodded as much as he could within Gideon's hold, and whispered, "Yes, please, Sir."

Gideon growled at this easy acceptance and grated out, "That's right. You want it now. Soon enough, you're gonna need it. Open up."

When that tongue appeared again, he slid back in and held his head steady as he fucked slowly in and out of his boy's throat. On the way out, he made sure he pulled back far enough to allow for the boy's desperate gulps of air and then slid right back in. No rest for the wicked.

He went on like that for a while longer, feeling the boy's saliva sliding down his shaft and slipping down his sac. He'd be willing to bet there was some at his feet. The thought of it had him pushing in a bit deeper, eliciting a moaning gag, prompting him to pull all the way out so he could tilt Sebastian's head up. When they made eye contact, Sebastian had tears in his eyes from the strain.

"That's my good boy. You're doing so well. I want more, but I'm not sure you're ready."

"Please. Please, let me try, Sir."

"Damn, Bastian. I don't think I've ever heard sweeter begging in my life. I'm gonna let you try. I wanna see those lips straining around my fat cock; that throat taking me in. Deep breath."

His sub sucked in a desperate breath and moaned as Gideon's cock slipped past his lips. He slid in deep, waited for that first swallow around his cockhead then used his hands to hold his sub's head as he pushed in deeper than he'd been. He held himself there, a little longer that time, letting the boy gag around him twice before pulling out.

He leaned down and licked his way into Sebastian's hot mouth, reaching up and grabbing the ropes crisscrossing over Sebastian's abdomen. When he'd had his fill, he tipped his sub's head back down with a hand cupping his chin and looked up at his fingers that were swirling in his boy's precum that had pooled near his belly button. Glancing down at the floor, he saw the drops of Sebastian's saliva that had slid off his own cock and balls. Bringing his face alongside Sebastian's, he whispered in his ear, "You're dripping for me, boy. You like that cock in your throat, don't you?"

His voice was rough from the workout when he answered, "Yes, Sir."

Gideon stood and squeezed Sebastian's cock, giving it a few good tugs before pushing it back towards his ass and letting it go. He watched it spring back and smack his stomach, and he grinned at the boy's sweet moan and the sight of the thin shiny thread of precum now connecting the tip of his cock to his abdomen.

He let his voice reflect his desire when he whispered, "I'm gonna pull that plug out and slide my cock deep. That what you want, Sebastian?"

His sub moaned, nodding. "Please. I want you to fill me up, Sir."

"That's what I want to hear."

Gideon swiveled the boy about ninety degrees and made some adjustments so his head was much higher than his ass. He pulled a condom from his pocket and rolled it down his shaft while Sebastian looked on. When his boy moaned and his head fell back, Gideon gripped his hair and lifted it again. When their eyes met, the blown pupils spoke of his boy's readiness. He kissed him and said, "Check in with me, boy, before we go any further."

Sebastian closed his eyes ever so slowly, and when he opened them again, the desire Gideon saw there had his heart skipping a beat. "Green. Please, Sir."

Gideon nodded and kissed Sebastian's hairline, breathing in the sweet scent of his own shampoo on the boy's soft, beautiful strands. Possessiveness shot through every nerve ending in his body, and he pulled the single use lube packet from his pocket. He spun Sebastian's gorgeous round ass his way, a thrill snaking through him as he took in those beautiful globes separated by the base of the largest plug he'd purchased to prepare his boy for his cock.

He separated his cheeks with one hand and clasped the plug's base in the other, slowly pulling it out and nearly moaning himself when he saw Sebastian's ring of muscle give way to the large body of the plug. When it slid easily the rest of the way out, he watched as his boy's stunningly perfect hole stayed open for several moments before slowly shrinking back, his beautiful pucker expanding and contracting incrementally, as if trying to grab him and pull him in.

Opening the lube packet with his teeth, he squeezed some on his thumb and forefinger. Swiping his thumb over that gorgeous wrinkled skin a few times and pressing the pad of it against his entrance, Gideon smiled as the boy's body was wracked with shivers, and he let a whimper escape. He rubbed the lube from his finger over the hole then brought his thumb back against it, pressing in and growling when the boy's hole practically sucked it in, as if begging for more.

Unable to wait another minute longer, he poured a generous amount of lube in his palm and slicked up his cock. He squeezed some down the boy's smooth crack and used his thumb to rub the lube into the boy's hole. Gathering more on his finger, he slid it in, preparing Sebastian for his cock. Grabbing the spider web rigging on the boy's chest, he held Sebastian still as he moved forward. He used his other hand to guide his cock to Sebastian's waiting hole and pushed his cockhead against Sebastian's entrance.

When he realized Sebastian was subconsciously tensing up, he stilled his body, dragging his cockhead up and down the boy's crack, and whispered, "Open for me, boy. Bear down as I push in. Don't fight it, welcome it."

It seemed to be all the boy needed to loosen up and relax. He felt a kind of unfurling of Sebastian's muscles and then his head was past the rings of muscle, and he was being drawn into the tightest, hottest hole he'd ever entered. He inched in incrementally, not wanting to hurt Sebastian, but his body was urging him to pound into the boy until he came, screaming out Gideon's name. He'd never seen anything as beautiful as Sebastian's ass milking his dick.

"Goddamn. Your hole is so greedy for my cock, sucking me in. You're gonna take all of me. Open that little hole for me a bit more."

Pulling back out a couple inches, he eased back in three and so it went until he was fully seated and his boy was moaning incoherently. Easing in and out fully several times assured him that Sebastian was ready. He grabbed onto his boy's hips and slammed home. The shouted, "Yes!" had him grinning and doing it again, eliciting a, "Oh fuck! Yes!"

"So good. Take it."

Slamming in again, he heard his boy mumbling and had to quiet his own breathing to hear him. Sebastian, eyes closed, head thrown back, was asking for more, over and over. He realized in that moment he wanted—no needed—to see his boy's eyes and slowly, torturously pulled almost all the way out, leaving Sebastian panting and begging for his cock and finally raising his head again to look at him.

Before he could say anything, Sebastian groaned, "Gr-green, Sir. More, please."

Gideon grinned when Sebastian assumed he'd wanted him to check in. He hadn't. He'd known the boy was green by the sweet moans and begging. No, he'd wanted Sebastian's gaze, and his eyes narrowed as the sub closed his and whispered more pleas. His voice was stern when he finally grated out, "Keep your eyes on me, boy."

When those eyes popped open and Sebastian gave a small nod, Gideon slid back inside that hot, tight hole and began a torturously slow undulation of his hips as his boy, arms tied behind his back, legs tied open and close to his chest, looked on, helpless to do anything but take what Gideon gave him. The longing in Sebastian's eyes, the hitch of his breath, and the sight of that sweet tongue licking his lower lip had Gideon quickening his pace.

"Tell me how much you want my cock. How good it feels. Tell me what you need."

Sebastian released a sweet hum, and Gideon didn't think he could ever tire of hearing his boy's reactions. In fact, he wanted to hear more of them, but he was happy to hear Sebastian's strained voice a second later.

"Want it, Sir. So big. It feels so good, so good."

"Yeah?"

"Mmm, you're so big. It hurts. Hurts so fucking good. I need. . . I need. . ."

"What do you need, Bastian?"

"More, Sir. Harder. Faster. Please."

Without saying another word, Gideon slammed his hips forward, growling and losing his calm façade. As Sebastian cried out but kept his gaze on him, Gideon moved his hands from the boy's hips and gripped the rope rigging high on Sebastian's chest and used it as an anchor as his hips took up a frantic, pounding pace. He gripped Sebastian's hair at the base of his neck, tugging on it, holding it tight in his grip, the boy hummed and several yeses fell from his lips.

Gideon refused to tear his eyes away, no matter how much he wanted to close them at the sensations. He wanted to feel and see everything. Revel in the experience of watching his boy fly, eyes still on him, but glassy and unfocused.

That's what did it. That's what tipped him over, and his hips sped up until he was sure they'd be a blur to anyone watching and he growled, his pace faltering, rhythm lost as his stomach clenched, and he flooded the condom deep inside Sebastian's ass. He rode it out, pace increasing again as Sebastian's ass tightened on his cock.

He looked down and saw the boy's cock drip more precum. Letting go of Sebastian's hair, he slowly slid his palm under the boy's cock, barely touching it. Wrapping his fingers around that gorgeous steely length, grip still barely there and feather soft, he slid Sebastian's foreskin back to reveal his cockhead and whispered, "Come, boy."

When he felt Sebastian's cock jerk in his palm, satisfaction in the form of chills radiated from his core to his extremities, another volley of cum joining the rest in the condom. He hadn't been sure the boy would be able to come without any pressure on his cock or that the barely there grip was enough, and he knew he'd be working hard to make him come with absolutely no stimulation in the future.

Sebastian's whole body shuddered, and those slightly higher-pitched, moaning sighs escaped with every spurt shooting out of his cock until it was spent. Only then did Sebastian's gaze leave his, when he could no longer hold his head up and it tilted back. Knowing he was flying, floating in subspace and an orgasm high, too blissed out to feel more than that blissful euphoria, Gideon slipped out of him as quickly as he could manage without causing pain or yanking him out of his trance-like state.

He made quick work of his condom, fastened his pants and belt, and pulled the table back under Sebastian, needing to get the boy out of his bindings as quickly as possible. He knew he'd never been bound for so long, nor as completely, let alone suspended. And while Gideon knew he'd been completely safe and the boy would be fine, he'd still be sore and feeling it for days. The most important job Gideon had, besides honoring the trust Sebastian granted him with his mind and body, was aftercare, and he took his responsibility seriously.

As his boy continued to drift, he quickly used the corded controller to lower Sebastian down to the table's surface to remove the ropes. Making quick work of removing the many suspension lines connecting him to the frame, Gideon then removed the rest of the ropes, sitting Sebastian up to help shake out his arms, rubbing them down to bring circulation back.

When he had him completely free of the rigging, Gideon slid his arms under his boy and picked him up. Sebastian murmured to him incoherently and rested his head on Gideon's chest. He got him up to his loft and lay him on the side of the bed against a mound of pillows, murmuring that he'd be right back. He grabbed several bottles of water from the kitchen and brought them back, opening one and handing it over. While Sebastian drank, he gathered some massage oils and a towel.

Gideon took a few pulls from his own water bottle and set it down. Taking Sebastian's empty water bottle from him, Gideon laid the towel out on the middle of the bed. "Lie face down on the towel."

Sebastian's half-lidded eyes and crooked smile let him know the boy was still flying. He was slow to turn over onto his stomach. Once there, he was boneless, arms at his sides, eyes closed. "Bastian, check in with me, please."

Gideon heard a dreamy sigh before the boy finally answered, his words slurring a bit. "Mmm. Green, Sir."

"Good boy. Rest now, I'll massage the achiness from your body as much as possible then get you in the tub."

"Mmmhmm."

Smiling, Gideon got to work on the boy's back side and then turned him over to rub down his front. While Sebastian wasn't sleeping, he was drifting in and out. After his body was fully rubbed down, Gideon got up and turned on the faucets to fill the gigantic tub. He added in some scented Epsom salts and went back to lie with Sebastian, cuddling him and murmuring praise. He told him how proud he was of him, how good he'd done and continued to do while his boy clung to him, subspace making him needier and less guarded than he'd normally be.

He carried Sebastian to the tub and got them both in, he settled his boy between his legs in the steaming hot water and ran his hands gently over his soft, slick skin. He couldn't remember a feeling of contentment so strong in years, maybe ever. He leaned his cheek on the crown of Sebastian's head and let himself come down from his own high.

Chapter 21

SEBASTIAN

Sebastian was on cloud nine, or maybe even cloud ten. Eleven? Was there even a cloud eleven? He'd have to look that up. Sitting gingerly at his desk on Tuesday morning, he thought back on the last two days. He didn't have a client for another hour, and he'd already caught up on the work he'd missed on Monday. He had some projects he could work on, but he found himself daydreaming while staring blankly at his computer screen. It had turned out taking one of his floating holidays on his birthday wasn't a bad idea after all. He couldn't remember having a better birthday.

He was used to either working on his birthday or being alone. He mostly didn't acknowledge it. It passed by each year, if not unnoticed, uncelebrated. And he was okay with that. He had to be. It had been that way since his sixth birthday, the first year he'd had one of his episodes—as his mother called them —in front of other people.

His mother, not one to do much for birthdays in the first place, had finally allowed him to invite a friend over for a sleepover. Before his best friend's mom even left, he'd had one of his "episodes" and his best friend and his best friend's mom were both so horrified, they left immediately after, making their apologies and saying it looked like he wasn't feeling well and they'd have to reschedule when he was feeling better.

They hadn't. His best friend had told everyone in their class what happened, and he'd struggled to make friends from that day forward. Children's cruelty and people's inability to accept those who were different didn't bode well for making new friends, let alone winning popularity contests. It was a good thing he was an introvert. Or perhaps he was an introvert because of things that happened during his childhood. That was a nature vs. nurture debate he didn't have the desire to sink energy into.

The cupcakes his mom had allowed him to buy with his own allowance at the store that day had disappeared. He found them accidentally when taking the kitchen trash out to the garage bins the following afternoon. She'd said they shouldn't celebrate birthdays anyway. That what happened was God's way of ensuring they only celebrated the birth of Jesus Christ. So, from then on, birthdays had gone uncelebrated throughout his childhood and into his adulthood. He hadn't really tried to break the habit. He'd had no reason to celebrate because, really, who celebrates alone? And it wasn't like he'd celebrated the day before, either. Not really. He might have looked at himself in the mirror after waking up and given himself a mental, "Happy Birthday!"

Maybe Gideon thought his smile was only for him, and truthfully, it mostly was. When he came into the bathroom with a cup of coffee for Sebastian and stood behind him, kissing his neck, Sebastian silently thanked whatever powers that be that this year he'd at least have a good birthday.

He hadn't mentioned it to Gideon. Gideon had said no flowers, gifts, or dates, and truthfully, he wouldn't have expected them anyway. So, he kept it to himself and was grateful just to spend the time with the beautiful man that had chosen him—for reasons he still didn't understand and maybe never would—to sign a contract with. The day was great, the night before even better. The rigging Gideon did had far surpassed anything he could have dreamed up.

He barely remembered Gideon carrying him upstairs. He'd never gone into such deep subspace before. And he couldn't remember ever having come so hard with almost no stimulation. Before he knew what was happening, he was being asked to turn over, and Gideon was digging into his sore muscles with practiced precision, finding each and every sore spot he had and working it until it was gone. By the time he was done, Sebastian was a boneless, incoherent mess. He wouldn't be able to stand if he wanted to, so it was good that Gideon carried him to the tub, surrounding him with nearly scalding water and his arms. As aftercare went, it was definitely a first. Not that he was complaining.

He knew his body would be sore for a couple days after a scene like the one they'd just shared. He was between Gideon's legs, caged by his raised knees, his own arms hooked over Gideon's thick, muscular thighs, and when he finally came more fully into himself, he couldn't keep his hands to himself and rubbed them up and down Gideon's shins. He leaned to the side then tilted his head to look back at the gorgeous man behind him.

"There you are."

Sebastian blushed and smiled. "Hi."

"Hi, yourself. How are you feeling?"

"Good. Exhausted, but really good, Sir. Thank you."

"Good. I'm glad. And I'm happy you're back with me again. I want to finish washing you."

Sebastian could feel his blush deepen, but a thrill shot through him and he nodded.

"Good boy. Lean up, I wanna wash your back."

And on it went. The amount of firsts Sebastian experienced that day made him giddy. He thought it prudent to pinch himself, but truthfully, he didn't want to wake up if it was a dream.

Gideon got out and dried himself quickly then helped him out of the tub and held up a towel, warm from the hot towel rack. He took his time and dried every inch of him, even getting down to his knees to dry his feet, again worrying Sebastian with the wrongness of his Dom on his knees for him. It took everything he had not to get down on his own knees until Gideon stood.

That discomfort only continued, as Gideon hung up the towel and moved him to stand in front of a full-length mirror. Practiced in avoiding looking at himself in the mirror, he gazed at the man behind him, easily twice his size, and would have continued to feast his eyes there if Gideon hadn't demanded otherwise.

He leaned down and whispered in Sebastian's ear, "Look at the lines on your body caused by the ropes. They're beautiful. You're beautiful."

Curiosity had him seeking himself out in the mirror, if only to see the lines Gideon was referring to. He was glad he did. They were everywhere, and they were brilliant. He reached up, almost convinced he wouldn't be able to feel them, that they weren't real. But when he ran his fingers over his chest, he could feel the indentations, the little bumps that the rope left, awed by the pattern.

He hadn't paid attention to what he looked like in the ropes, just how he felt, and he'd felt amazing. He almost wished he'd allowed Khaleo to take the pictures. Almost. Before he could stop himself, he admitted as much to Gideon as he blushed, yet again. He was ordered to stay where he was as Gideon left the bathroom. Moments later, he returned with Sebastian's phone, handing it over and asking him to put his code in.

Once he did, Gideon took the phone back, stood directly behind him, and cupped his chin in his hand, tilting Sebastian's head back against Gideon's chest and took a picture of them as Gideon kissed the top of his head, whispering again that he was beautiful. The only reason Sebastian didn't tense was because it was his phone, his camera, his album, and he could control where the pictures went and who saw them.

Gideon handed his phone back, and they walked into the bedroom where Gideon helped him get dressed then told him to rest for a bit while he made lunch. He started to protest but a stern look from his Dom had him acquiescing. No sooner did he follow instructions than Gideon was back, chuckling at his inability to even lift his body enough to get up and join him in the kitchen for lunch.

However, when Gideon said he'd bring lunch to him in bed, Sebastian was up like a shot, unwilling to have the man wait on him even more than he already had. One thing was for sure, Gideon took aftercare seriously, and Sebastian couldn't help but enjoy every single minute of it, racking up even more firsts with the pictures in the mirror, and the massage.

They spent the rest of the day being lazy and getting to know each other a bit, though strangely they both kept from sharing too much of their personal lives. They fell into a pattern of safely talking about what things they liked to do, the food they liked to eat, and the places they'd like to visit. They discussed their favorite songs, movies, and books. And covered silly topics like what was their favorite color, what they'd wanted to be when they grew up, and whether or not they liked mustard on their sandwiches. They both did, and the spicier the better. Though pepperoncini were a bone of contention.

When Sunday night rolled around, Sebastian found his back snuggled tight against Gideon's front in a spooning that felt more like a cocooning the man was so enormous. He couldn't remember a night when he'd had such a peaceful sleep. He was a cold sleeper, and Gideon, it turned out, was a furnace and kept him warm from the top of his head to the bottom of his feet. Sebastian snickered when he rubbed his freezing feet on Gideon's shins and the man jumped and cussed a blue streak, saying he was made of ice before drawing them between both of his calves to warm them up.

The following morning, his birthday, started off with a hot shower that soothed some of his achiness from the rigging of the day before. He was sad to see nearly all the rope impressions on his skin were gone but his sadness didn't last long when he was permitted to go down on Gideon again in the shower.

He was bound and determined to be able to deepthroat the man's whole cock, eventually.

A huge part of the day was going through the contract again, point by point. They added several caveats toward the end. They both wanted to avoid talking much about their personal lives, hoping to keep them separate and not blur any of those lines. Sebastian was happy with that adjustment. He was very uneasy about sharing too much about his personal life including his past and his medical issues. He was being truthful with Gideon when he said there was nothing medically that would impact or be affected by their play, so he felt reassured that there wouldn't be further questions regarding those issues.

They also both agreed that should either of them feel like they weren't getting what they needed from the contract, they could end it at any time, no questions asked. Sebastian knew he wouldn't be the one to end it, and he was okay with not asking Gideon any questions about it when he decided to move on. He didn't have any misconceptions that more would come from their contract, nor did he think the six-month time designation would ever be reached. He figured, if he was lucky, he'd be able to enjoy having a contracted Dom for a couple months and be happier for it.

He'd seen the part of the contract talking about monogamy and glanced at Gideon, biting his lip, "It's okay if you don't want our arrangement to be monogamous."

Gideon, confused and angry, replied, "We're getting retested so we don't have to wear condoms. You can bet your ass you won't be fucking anyone else."

Sebastian's eyes popped wide and he shook his head. "No. That's not... I'm sorry, Sir. That's not what I meant. I don't want to be with anyone else. I just don't expect you'll want to limit yourself to just m—"

Incredulous, Gideon growled out, "Limit myself? What kind of asshole do you think I am?"

Sebastian's mouth dropped open. "No, Sir. I'm sorry. I didn't mean to imply—"

Gideon held up his hand to cut him off. "Our contract will be monogamous, on both sides. End of discussion. Understood?"

All he was able to do was nod, wide eyed, which caused Gideon to soften a little and give his hand a squeeze. "Bastian, I don't want anyone else. If I did, I wouldn't be signing a contract with you. All right?"

Sebastian gulped, nodding again. "Yes, Sir."

He vowed to himself then and there that he'd do his best to ensure his sexy Dom didn't need anyone else. Though he was still surprised, he admitted to himself that he was secretly thrilled Gideon wasn't thinking of getting his needs met elsewhere.

Once they signed the contract, he wrote out the following week's schedule for Gideon, and though his Dom had given him the side eye about working Saturday, he arranged for them to have two weeknight sessions and for Sebastian to come over Saturday evening after his work was completed and stay until Monday morning. Sebastian decided then and there to begin tattooing Friday evenings so he could reduce his workload on Saturdays. It would take some adjustment but would be worth it until Gideon ended their contract.

They had dinner after their contract was signed, and then Gideon had ordered him to strip and kneel naked on Gideon's huge, square brown leather ottoman in his living area facing the couch, behind which was a wall of windows. His pulse raced as he looked out toward the other buildings that were taller than the one he was in. He couldn't see in their windows, so he hoped they couldn't see in Gideon's, but in the end, even if they could, he wouldn't change a thing.

When Gideon returned, Sebastian heard several thunks as multiple things were dropped on the hardwood floor behind him. He'd heard him approach but hadn't expected the clatter of equipment. It made him nervous, it made him giddy, and it made his cock stand at attention. The hairs on the back of his neck stood up and he shivered when that deep commanding voice quietly ordered him to bend over, face down, knees on the edge of the ottoman, arms straight back by his sides.

He knew by the position it would be precarious after a few minutes and take all of his concentration to keep his knees on the ottoman's edge without slipping off, especially when he started to sweat, and he knew he would. His forehead was on the ottoman and Gideon murmured he could turn it to the side and lay his cheek on the leather. He did so and found his back arching more, and his ass a bit higher than it had been.

Not five minutes later, his ankles and wrists were bound by leather cuffs. Left wrist cuff chained to left ankle cuff, the same done on the right side. His knees were spread, and he found himself suddenly feeling shy that his ass was sticking so far up into the air, right in Gideon's face as he finished fastening the leather restraints. He couldn't keep a moan from escaping as Gideon gripped his ass cheeks and spread them wider, swiping his tongue over his ready hole.

"Whose beautiful ass is this?"

"Yours, Sir."

"That's right. And what do you think I'm gonna do with it, boy?"

Sebastian's breath caught at the sexy smirk he could hear in his Dom's voice. "Re—" He cleared his throat and tried again. "Redden it, Sir?"

"Beautiful and smart. I'm a lucky man, aren't I, Sebastian?"

When he didn't respond, he got a smack on his ass, and Gideon growled, "You answer me when I ask you a question, boy."

"Yes, Sir."

"What am I?"

"Lucky, Sir."

"Why is that?"

"Because your sub is beautiful and smart."

"Who is beautiful and smart?"

Sebastian let out a shaky breath and answered, "I am, Sir."

"That's right, my beautiful boy. And look at you, bent over for me, skin so flawless. It's gonna look stunning with my marks."

Sebastian's heart rate sped up when he heard what he thought was a flogger whooshing through the air. It never made contact, and he figured Gideon was warming up and heightening Sebastian's tension levels. He did his best to relax. Drew in and let out a couple deep, slow breaths. The noise of the flogger got faster, and Sebastian could envision his Dom making a figure eight in the air, warming up his muscles.

He was startled out of his musings when his Sir asked, "Safewords?"

"Green, yellow, and red, Sir."

"Use them if you need them, Bastian."

"Yes, S—"

The rest of the word was cut off with the strike of the flogger to his upturned ass. Before he could take a full breath, there were two more on the same exact spot. As he took in a deep breath and let it out, Gideon fell into the figure eight rhythm Sebastian had guessed at earlier. His left cheek getting a strike then his right, and on it went. It wasn't painful, but when his focus needed to remain on keeping his knees on the edge of the ottoman and his ass *was getting warmer and warmer, he found it difficult to sink into any type of subspace. He didn't for a second believe that was accidental.*

"Your skin is pinking up so beautifully. You're doing great, Bastian."

At the praise, he relaxed a bit more. As soon as he sank into a headspace where he could at least focus less on his precarious position and more on the feeling of the flogger making his nerve endings sing, Gideon changed tactics and stood near his head, focusing the flogger's aim at his back. And again, as soon as he could fall into that headspace where he could begin to float, Gideon moved behind him again and focused on his upper thighs.

"I can see you struggling. You can do this, Bastian. Breathe in and give me another thirty seconds, boy."

He took a deep breath then another, but he wasn't sure he could take much more, and his legs, though not in too much pain, were shaking from keeping them in position. He hadn't moved a muscle, but it was costing him, and he let out a groan as he realized he was going to have to call out his safeword to slow things down when he couldn't hold on any longer.

Before he could say his safeword, the flogging stopped, and he could hear Gideon's words of praise as he moved quickly to unhook his wrists from his ankles. "Move slowly. Don't rush to get up."

He slowly moved so he was lying flat, legs dangling off the edge of the ottoman. He brought his arms up to drape over the other edge near his head and moaned as his muscles were allowed some relief. He was lying in a puddle of his own precum and on top of his ridiculously hard cock, but he didn't have the energy yet to move.

He opened his eyes and saw Gideon crouch down beside the ottoman. He ran his hand up Sebastian's shoulder and into his hair. "You took the flogging so well. Do you have it in you to turn over on your back? If not, we can call it done and get you into the bedroom so I can rub you down."

Sebastian saw the admiring glance Gideon gave his body, and before he could answer, Gideon's hands skimmed down his back and he took his left ass cheek in his palm and squeezed. "Oh, fuck. Mmm. Sir."

He reached over and squeezed the other cheek, and Sebastian's hips involuntarily began rutting against the leather beneath him. He let out a groan when Gideon smacked his ass. "None of that, boy. Answer my question before I start to get impatient."

"Yes, I can turn over, Sir."

"That's my good boy. Do you need help?"

Sebastian shook his head and answered, "No, Sir."

He slowly maneuvered himself onto his back, wincing as the heat of the flogging met with the warmth of the leather he'd just been lying on. He didn't know where Gideon wanted his arms, but he didn't have to wait long to find out as he pulled them above Sebastian's head, and chained them around the leg of the ottoman. He did the same to Sebastian's ankles. He could move if he needed, the chains weren't tight. The slack allowed him to squirm and from the look in Gideon's eyes, he'd be squirming a lot. He kept his eyes on his Dom as he stepped away and leaned down to pick up a riding crop.

Sebastian's eyes rolled back in his head when he realized what Gideon had in mind. Goddamn he wasn't sure he could take it. Did Gideon think he was a machine? *Fuck, he was gonna have to safeword and damned if the thought didn't make him miserable enough to somewhat deflate his erection.*

He sucked in a breath when he heard Gideon tsking his disapproval. "No, no. That just won't do. We can't have you soft for what I have in store for you, boy."

Fuck, fuck, fuckity fuck. The man was gonna kill him.

Gideon chuckled. "Such language. I'm not gonna kill you, boy. That's a promise."

He'd said that out loud? Double fuck. *"Sorry, Sir."*

"Forgiven. We're gonna get you nice and hard again, and then I'm giving you the freedom to come when you're ready. Understood?"

"Yes, S—"

FUCK! He needed to remember that his new Dom liked to surprise him before he was ready. The crop landed on the underside of his cock and had him arching up as much as the chains would allow. Before he could recover, he had another slap on his cock then one on his balls. He squeezed his legs together before he could stop himself but realized Gideon knew he'd be doing so and had landed two more volleys, one on each nipple. He gasped and moaned and damned if his cock wasn't as hard as steel.

"There we go. Damn, Bastian, you keep surprising me. Look at that pretty cock, dripping for me, hard as a rock."

He gave Sebastian's cock several slaps on both sides, lightly this time, enough to drive him wild with need. Two hard smacks on his nipples again, and he actually felt his precum pulse out of his slit with his heartbeat. "Oh god, oh god, oh god."

"Yes, boy. Let me hear it."

Sebastian panted when Gideon slid the crop down his cock to his balls then smacked them repeatedly. But when Sebastian went to squeeze his legs together this time, he realized Gideon's knee kept his legs wedged open. He wasn't going to be able to protect his balls and the groan he let loose couldn't be contained.

"Beautiful. Fucking beautiful, boy."

Three more smacks up and down the length of his cock and he shouted, "Sir! Oh god. Oh fuck, Sir!"

Gideon walked around the ottoman toward his head, kneeled down, and whispered, "Breathe in." His Dom covered his mouth and nose after he'd done so and growled out, "That's it, boy."

When he'd first seen breath play on the contract, Sebastian had been intrigued. He'd always been interested in it, but had never done it before. He realized once he thought about it that he had a habit of holding his breath when he was in some scenes and almost always when he was masturbating.

When he'd admitted as much to Gideon, the Dom's eyes had gotten heated and Sebastian had gotten hard seeing his reaction. Gideon assured him that he would never take it too far, nor would he ever put him in danger, always making it possible for him to take a breath if needed and mostly just playing with the psychological aspect of it, rather than realistic asphyxiation play.

Sebastian nearly lost his mind when Gideon slowly tickled his sack with the tip of the crop, smacked his nipples again, and then went after his cock with that thing like it had pissed him off. He needed to breathe, and his eyes rolled back in his head when he realized he wasn't permitted. Gideon must have seen his need because he removed his hand from Sebastian's mouth and placed it on his throat, providing pressure, a pressure that thrilled him.

Sebastian shouted and couldn't have stopped himself from shooting if he'd tried. He didn't know what he yelled, everything was a jumbled mess in his head and though he'd cried out he still hadn't breathed in. He was in pain, he was in ecstasy, he couldn't make heads or tails of what was going on with his body.

Gideon's whispered, "Breathe now, Bastian," had him drawing in greedy gulps. He was vaguely aware that he still hadn't stopped coming and felt some hit his chin and his cheeks. He could feel his pulse in his cock and it continued to drip onto his stomach as his cock bobbed in the aftermath.

He looked up into his Dom's eyes and smiled at the awed expression on the man's face. He tried to speak but his throat was raw, and he watched as Gideon brought his other hand up, wrapping both his hands around Sebastian's throat. The possessive look in Gideon's eyes and the soft grip he kept on Sebastian's throat would linger in his mind for quite some time. He grinned wider as his Dom growled and took his mouth upside down, still gripping his throat.

When he had pulled away, Sebastian thought it was over until he felt the soft rasp of his Dom's tongue on his cheeks, then his chin, and then his chest, licking the cum off his skin. Fuck, was this man for real? Sebastian didn't think a sexier Dom existed and just as he was sucking in a breath at the teeth biting into his nipple, those lips were back on his and he'd give anything to touch his Dom in that moment.

<hr>

W hen Gideon had placed an ornate wooden box in his hands that morning, Sebastian didn't know what to think. He glanced up at Gideon from his seat on the edge of the bed and watched as his Dom got on his knees in front of him.

When he shook his head at Gideon and looked down at the box, Gideon asked bluntly, "What's got you shaking your head?"

He'd blushed and shaken his head again. "Nothing, Sir. What's this?"

When he looked at the Dom's stern expression, he bit his lip then laughed at himself, realizing how ridiculous he must look and finally admitted, "You keep getting on your knees for me." He sighed and glanced back down at the box. "It feels wrong."

"Why? Because you're convinced as my sub you should always be below me?"

Sebastian shrugged. "Yeah. I mean, I'm serving you, not the other way around."

"You don't think I do the same for you?"

Sebastian tilted his head in confusion and shook his head. "You should never serve me."

Gideon chuckled at that and said, "Of course I should. We're serving each other. We just do it in different ways. You're offering your service to me as my submissive. But I'm also offering my service to you as your Dominant. We're equals in this, Sebastian."

"You really believe that?"

"Fuck yes! I absolutely do. I can do nothing with you, to you, unless you have given your express permission. That power is in your hands. You know this."

Sebastian nodded. "Yeah. I mean, I guess. I just never thought of it that way. That doesn't seem right."

"I'm giving you what you need, just as you are doing for me. If that isn't service, I don't know what is."

A warmth filled Sebastian and he glanced down at the nearly forgotten box in his hands. He traced a pattern on the lid, trying to keep his hands busy, trying to. . . Nope. He reached up and gripped the back of Gideon's neck and tugged him forward so he could ravish his Dom's mouth.

When Gideon's lips curved and he chuckled under Sebastian's passionate kiss, Sebastian blushed, bashful at his own uninhibited reaction. Gideon clasped his face in his hands and gave him multiple chaste kisses on his lips and pulled away, a gorgeous smile lighting up his face, the honest joy in his expression surprising Sebastian and making him grin in return.

"We good?"

Sebastian nodded in response and glanced back down at the box, muttering, "We're good."

"All right, boy. Open your gift."

He glanced up at his Dom then back down as he flipped the lid up. He gasped and reached to touch then pulled his hand away and looked up at Gideon. "Sir?"

His Dom's expression grew serious and he reached around and took one of the items out of the box. The one that had his heart racing and his eyes stinging. He sucked his lips into his mouth and breathed in through his nose, doing his best to control his emotions as his Dom clasped the gorgeous black metal chain around his neck. When it was on and Gideon settled back down on his heels, he touched it in awe.

"It matches the black metal bracelet on your wrist, so I thought you'd like it. And as collars go, it's not obvious, so you can always keep it on."

Sebastian lost a bit of his color and covered the medical alert bracelet on his arm but recovered quickly when his Dom, obviously not noticing his distress, continued. "You'll wear my temporary collar and cage while we're in contract. I want you in chastity at all times when you're not with me. I had this one made for you, but if it isn't the right fit, we'll get it adjusted. I guessed at the measurements, so we'll have to see. They're both made of black titanium, so they're corrosion resistant and hypoallergenic. I wasn't sure if you had any metal allergies, and I wanted you to be able to bathe with them on."

Sebastian's heart raced again as he thought about the gorgeous cage. He'd never worn one and when they'd talked about it, he'd hoped to be able to try it, but hadn't dreamed he'd be wearing one twenty-four seven while contracted with Gideon. Jesus. A contract, a fucking collar, *and* chastity? What alternate reality had he stepped into? His life had taken a detour he'd never expected and fuck if he didn't hope he never found his way back on course.

Remembering that morning with great fondness, he found himself touching the smooth, uniquely shaped links of the chain around his neck. Nearly jumping out of his chair when his captain, Jon Conway, came and rapped loudly on his doorframe before striding into his tiny office, a thin box under one arm. "Sorry to surprise you there, Sebastian. You looked like you were a million miles away. I just heard from Captain Baxter at Cupertino PD. They're gonna need your help this afternoon."

"Sir, I'm booked at one p.m. and four p.m. I won't be able to drive down there, do a sketch, and make it back in time."

"How about a two thirty appointment via video conference?"

Sebastian sighed. "Sir, I don't have. . ." He looked up, the box in his captain's hand held out towards him. "No way!"

His captain laughed and placed the box on his desk. "There was a lot of grumbling about this, but in the end, you were right, it will cost them less money in travel and faster turnaround time. Don't say I never did anything for you. Once you get set up, call IT to come and pick up your ancient desktop. There are still several of the older precincts that haven't signed on, so there might be some residual travel, but we're working on getting them on board."

Sebastian grinned. "You're a miracle worker, Cap. You won't regret this."

"Yeah, well, you might. You know what this means, right? Those police departments that have been mostly out of reach of your services will now be able to make use of you."

Sebastian shrugged. "I can get a lot more done this way. It's been a long time coming. We've been quite antiquated from that standpoint, for my job, anyway. And, I'm happy to help as much as my schedule allows. You know that, Sir."

His captain nodded and clapped him on the back. "I know. We have the technology where it's most beneficial according to the higher ups. But someone finally paid attention, so I'll consider us lucky. Let me know how it goes. Thanks, Sebastian."

"Thank you, Cap."

As his boss left, he practically dove into the brand-new laptop box he'd be using for video conferencing with other police departments in the state, meaning much less travel. Less travel meant the possibility of more time with Gideon, and as far as he was concerned, that was the best news he could have possibly gotten that day. He settled in, humming to himself as he began to set up his new toy.

Chapter 22

GIDEON

The Sunday before Thanksgiving marked their third week in contract. Gideon felt they'd settled into a comfortable rhythm and were seeing to each other's needs quite well. His boy seemed to be flourishing under his domination, and Gideon was quite satisfied by his submissive's progress. Sebastian seemed to be coming out of his shell. There was less of the shyness around him for sure, less of the hiding or glancing away to avoid scrutiny, and less of the self-deprecating comments. He hoped it meant the boy's confidence was growing, as that was one of Gideon's biggest goals with his sub.

He couldn't believe his luck, really. The boy was a natural and never seemed inclined to say no to trying something new. His behavior was impeccable, his submission absolute. He'd yet to have to punish the boy for breaking a rule. He wondered if it would be a different story if they were in a committed D/s relationship, not just a committed short-term D/s contract.

Admittedly, they didn't spend enough time together, and as much as he wanted to change that, he'd agreed to the stipulation that Sebastian retain the control of their schedule. It was constantly in flux as a result of his work, and as a business owner, Gideon had the ability to adjust his schedule at will. Though he knew it was best to keep their schedule as is because he was already in danger of getting too emotionally attached.

He had a feeling his boy had many secrets, and they'd agreed to that damn rule about keeping out of each other's personal business. At first, he'd thought it would benefit *him* the most. He thought Sebastian had been exaggerating or denying his true nature when he'd said he wasn't built for relationships, that it wasn't what he was looking for.

He'd been convinced Sebastian would be the one pushing for a more personal connection. But damned if his boy didn't avoid asking any personal questions. In fact, he was very careful not to ask anything at all. He let Gideon steer their conversations, always, as if that was a part of his submission.

Gideon didn't know what it meant. Did he not want to know more about his Dom? Did he not care? Or, more likely, did he think if he asked questions of Gideon he'd be asked questions in return? If that was his assumption, Gideon had to admit it was probably true. The more he got to know the boy, the more he wanted to know, which, to his mind, was a trap he needed to steer clear of if only to save the boy confusion and himself heartache. But the more he tried to deny himself what he knew he wanted deep down, the more he found it impossible not to ask Sebastian the probing personal questions they'd promised to avoid.

With the holidays coming up, he wanted to know his sub's plans. They wouldn't be spending them together—he'd stipulated that before they even signed the contract. He wanted, needed, to maintain those lines. Blurring them would be no good for either one of them. But he still couldn't help thinking, would Sebastian have his family visit him or would he travel to visit them? He knew from the tiny bit he'd been able to glean, in a moment when his sub's defenses were down, he didn't get along that well with his parents, so he knew the visits would be short which was fine by him as he wouldn't have to be too long without his boy.

He needed to enjoy his sub while he had him. He could see them signing one more contract for a second six months. A good solid year with Sebastian should be enough. It would have to be. Any longer and he feared he'd be in too deep, any shorter and he was sure he wouldn't feel like it was enough. But after only a handful of weeks, the beautiful boy was twisting him up inside. When he wasn't with Sebastian, he thought of him, and when he was with him, he wanted to learn everything there was to know about him.

He knew their contract was benefitting his sub, but with Sebastian not sharing any of his thoughts and feelings freely, he didn't know how much. He wanted to be able to make an impact on the boy's life and ensure he got what he needed. Later, Sebastian would be free to find the perfect Dom to replace him. One that was good enough for Sebastian and would treat him as he deserved to be treated. He knew his boy was made for long-term relationships even if he wouldn't admit it.

He glanced at Sebastian on the video feed playing on the computer monitor in his office and marveled at the stillness of his beautiful sub. That ass of his was a thing of beauty, and the first time he'd been able to slip deep inside of his welcoming heat without a condom had practically been a religious experience.

His beautiful boy was trussed up to a small spanking bench he'd had made. Sebastian was in what used to be his spare bedroom that he'd turned into a sort of makeshift playroom for his sub while he was in his office watching him on his computer monitor. He'd told the boy he had important things to take care of, and that he wanted Sebastian to be fully occupied so he didn't get bored.

The scene played with his sub's desire to feel vulnerable and powerless. He'd admitted to his Dom that the helpless feeling of being tied up and not knowing when he'd be let go or what would happen to him scared him but turned him on in equal measure, so Gideon had trussed him up and told him he'd be back when he was back.

The truth of the matter was: he was watching every second of the scene as it played out, keeping an eye out for any issues. The cameras Custos had installed in his place were state of the art, and he would have heard a pin drop, but he wasn't going to take his eyes off his boy. He'd already been back into the room a couple times. Once to drip hot wax on his shoulders and back, and once to remove it and flog his beautiful skin.

He was on edge, and Gideon knew he needed to play his last hand before he let his sub free. Knowing he was about to disturb his boy's calm, he brought up the new app on his phone, tapped a few buttons, waited and watched. Sebastian was tilted at a slight angle in a kneeling position. His ass was stuffed full of a long vibrating butt plug that promised prostate stimulation. He hadn't put it on its highest setting, but it was a close thing. He knew the stimulation would send his boy into a frenzy of lust.

And he couldn't believe his ears or eyes when he heard the telltale signs of Sebastian having an orgasm without permission. But that wasn't even what shocked him most. His boy was trussed up in such a way that he couldn't stimulate himself in any way, and on top of that, his cock was fucking caged, so he couldn't get an erection even if he wanted to.

But those noises, coupled with the spurts of cum that had now slowed to several slow drips, were proof that his boy didn't need an erection to have an orgasm. He smiled to himself as he realized this was the first time he'd have a reason to punish his sweet sub. But that smile vanished as he heard a whine, a hitched breath, and then a sobbed word that had his heart jumping into his throat.

"Red."

Sebastian's stop safeword had never been uttered during a scene. He fumbled with his phone, turning off the vibrator immediately, and ran to his boy. Wondering what the hell had gone wrong and if Sebastian was hurt had his heart racing. Rounding the corner, he ran into the room to Sebastian's desperate contrition. "I'm so sorry. I'm so sorry. I didn't mean to, Sir."

When Gideon got to him, he slid his hand over his boy's throat, clasping him there gently. It was where he placed his hand while they were dabbling in light breath play, something Sebastian enjoyed, but it was also a reminder of Gideon's total domination over him and always served to calm his sub down like little else could. "Are you hurt?"

When Sebastian only shook his head, he repeated himself more sternly. "Answer me, Sebastian. Are you hurt?"

Another head shake and a soft sob followed finally by an answer, "No. No, Sir. I'm okay. I'm so sorry."

"Shhh, boy. It's all right. I'm here. I'm gonna remove the plug, okay? Relax for me, baby."

He eased the plug slowly out of the boy's ass, whispering reassuringly to him, and tossed it on the towel that was lying on the table by the wall and pulled his emergency shears out of the back pocket of his jeans, cutting the ropes tying Sebastian's wrists and chest to the bench, and his ankles to the padded knee rests.

Gideon scooped him up, hugged him to his chest, and carried him over to the massage table, setting him down on the edge, legs spread. He yanked off the chain he wore around his neck that held his military ID tags and Sebastian's cock cage key and crouched down as he proceeded to slowly and gently removed the cage from his boy's soft cock.

The panic had nearly subsided, but the uneven breaths continued in between Sebastian's litany of apologies. "I wasn't holding back like I should. I didn't think it was possible. I safeworded. I'm sorry. I shouldn't have. . . I didn't even. . . And your ropes. You cut your ropes. They're your favorite ropes."

"Bastian, goddammit!"

When his sub jumped at his outburst, eyes wide, Gideon cursed himself for snapping at him. "Fuck. I'm sorry. Boy, don't you know? I don't give a fuck about my ropes. You are what matters to me. Just you. I'm sorry I yelled. Come here."

He drew his boy against his chest and hugged him tight. He felt the pressure of Sebastian's legs squeezing his hips, his feet crossing at Gideon's lower back. His boy, never one to half-ass anything, was hugging him from the top of his head, which was resting against his heart, to the bottom of his toes. He tilted his head down and kissed Sebastian's hair.

"Tell me what happened. You weren't hurt? I need to know so it doesn't happen again. Were your restraints too tight? Did you get a cramp?"

Sebastian shook his head and took a deep breath. "No, Sir. I just. . . I broke your rule, and I failed you, and all I could think of was stopping everything before I continued to fail you."

Incredulous, Gideon asked, "How did you fail me?"

"When you started the vibrator, it felt so good. It was hitting my prostate, and I wasn't paying enough attention. I just assumed I couldn't have an orgasm because I couldn't get an erection in the cage." His voice got high with incredulity. "Who the fuck orgasms in a cock cage? How is that even possible? I wasn't even hard so it never occurred to me to try to hold it back."

Still not understanding, Gideon dug deeper, "But how does that equate to failing me?"

"Because I can't come without permission!"

"You broke a rule, Sebastian. It isn't the end of the world, and you didn't do it on purpose."

"But. . . I failed, and it was too much. You told me to safeword when it became too much. I don't want to ever fail you. I can't. . . I don't want you to end our contract!"

What? He tried to pull the boy away from his chest, but he clung harder. "Bastian. . ."

Sebastian shook his head. "Please, don't!"

Gideon ran his hands up and down Sebastian's back, soothingly. "First, you did exactly what I wanted you to do. You safeworded when it became too much. Second, you didn't fail me. You broke a rule, but not on purpose. You're human, boy. All that happens if you break a rule is you get punished. The punishment fits the crime, and you'd have to fuck up monumentally for me to cancel our contract. This was nothing. A minor infraction."

"I never want to disappoint you. I feel like a failure."

"I'm not disappointed, and you are far from a failure. I'm damn proud of you for safewording. And now I know that I can trust you to do so again in the future."

"The future?"

"Yes, boy. You're not going anywhere. You signed yourself over to me for six months. You're stuck with me."

"I don't mind."

Gideon chuckled. "Good thing. Come on, let's get you more comfortable."

Gideon slid his hands beneath his ass and picked him up off the table, carrying him into his bedroom. He went to place Sebastian on the bed, but his boy wouldn't release his hold. He clung to him like a limpet and still didn't release him when Gideon climbed on the bed on his hands and knees and slowly lay them both down. The only thing Sebastian did was release his locked ankles and hook them loosely around the back of Gideon's thighs. Holding some of his weight off his boy, he leaned on his side, peering down at his gorgeous sub.

Sebastian closed his eyes and shook his head. "I'm—"

Gideon growled and grated out, "If you apologize one more time, Bastian, I'm gonna lose my shit."

Sebastian's eyes got wide as saucers. Gideon had never talked to him like that, and he nodded, remaining mute. His sad eyes had Gideon leaning in and offering his lips to the boy, the sweet kiss he received in return melting his heart. Gideon kissed along his cheek and licked just behind his ear, making Sebastian squirm.

He whispered, "You could never be a failure in your submission to me, Bastian. You have a desire to please me like no one else I've ever been with. I can see it in your eyes, in the way you allow yourself to be vulnerable, and the way you completely let go, trusting that I'll be there to take care of your needs. I couldn't be more pleased with you, boy."

Sebastian bit his lip, a hopeful smile on his face. "Yeah?"

Gideon brushed the hair off Sebastian's forehead, nodding. "Yeah."

Still worrying his lip between his teeth, this time in apprehension, he asked, "What's my punishment for breaking your rule?"

Gideon quirked a brow. "Did you enjoy what just happened in there, Bastian?"

Sebastian paled and shook his head. "No, Sir."

Gideon kissed his neck and mumbled against his sweet skin, "Then that's enough punishment, I think."

The sigh of relief relaxed Sebastian's frame within the circle of his arms, and his boy began to caress his back and nuzzle into him, a sure sign that he was feeling a bit better. Gideon's first thought after making sure Sebastian was okay was that he was so goddamn proud of him. He'd had too much and he'd safeworded, and he was going to continue to be sure Sebastian knew how much he appreciated it, appreciated his bravery.

Sebastian didn't seem inclined to let him leave, so he handed him his half empty water cup then proceeded to massage out any kinks his boy might have from being tethered to the bench. Afterward, they lay there for a while, kissing and caressing one another. When Sebastian's stomach growled, Gideon laughed and asked, "Anything specific you want for dinner?"

"No. We can order in, or I can cook something."

Gideon shook his head. "Why don't you take a bath, and I'll whip something up?"

Sebastian snorted. "You're gonna '*whip*' something up?"

Gideon rolled his eyes and pinched Sebastian's side, tickling him and enjoying the boy's carefree giggle that he'd deny he let burst from his mouth. "I'll whip you, brat."

Sebastian grew serious and whispered, "Anything you want, Sir."

Gideon growled and rolled them over so Sebastian was lying across his larger frame. "Don't tempt me. I mean it, go ahead and grab a bath, I'll put something together for dinner."

Sebastian frowned. "I should be serving you, not the other way around."

Gideon tilted his head. "There you go again. Remember, we serve each other, and I've given you an order."

"Yes, Sir."

Sebastian hopped up, mumbling to himself about silly Doms and their quirks, Gideon smacked his ass and got up to see what he could do for them for dinner. He had a hankering for some breakfast for dinner, and checking his fridge, he discovered he had everything he needed. He pulled out his griddle and started cooking. By the time he was done, Sebastian was walking into the kitchen, barefoot and wearing a tight, worn Ramones concert tee and some pajama bottoms. He set both their plates on the bar along with some freshly brewed coffee.

They made quick work of their meals and cleaned up the kitchen together. He ordered Sebastian into the living room to strip and present on the middle of the ottoman facing the leather sectional. Gathering up what he needed, he sat, still fully clothed, in the middle of his sectional, facing his boy. He turned the TV on and used his phone to launch his iTunes app on the Apple TV micro-console. Once it was up, he toggled through the app and clicked on what he wanted to bring up.

"Climb up on my lap, face the TV."

Sebastian scrambled to do his bidding, seeming quite eager to see what was in store for him. After a second or two of moving his body this way and that, trying to figure out how to climb on, Gideon smiled and picked the boy up, depositing him on his lap, Sebastian's back against his chest. He put his hand on his boy's throat, gently squeezing until he heard a hitch in his breathing. He leaned back, and Sebastian, submission so complete his body melded to his, automatically moved with him, head leaning in the crook of Gideon's neck and shoulder.

He squeezed a bit tighter on the boy's throat and got a moan for his trouble. "You'll watch the video I turn on. You won't turn your head or close your eyes. Is that understood?"

"Yes, Sir."

Gideon whispered in his ear, his voice impossibly deep, "That's my good boy."

He licked just under Sebastian's earlobe when the boy shivered in his arms at the sound and feel of his voice in his ear. Sliding a hand down Sebastian's smooth chest, tweaking his nipples as he went, his hands skated lower, rubbing back and forth on his beautiful treasure trail. He softly gripped his boy's hard cock and ever so gently drew the foreskin down his shaft, revealing his cockhead, and then slowly back up. He moved on to the boy's sack and lightly squeezed him, tugging on the delicate skin until he drew out a whimper.

He slowly released the boy's throat, wending that hand down the boy's chest, sliding a thumb over the peaked nipples, and then going straight for his sub's foreskin again. This time he tugged on it, pulling it completely over his cockhead, he rubbed the soft skin together, just over the boy's slit as he continued to tug lightly at his scrotum. When Sebastian began to pump his hips in conjunction with Gideon's ministrations, he removed his hands and placed both on Sebastian's inner thighs, calming his movements immediately.

Slouching a bit, he raised one of his feet and placed it on the edge of the ottoman and then raised his other foot to do the same. He smoothed his hands down his boy's thighs and then moved Sebastian's legs on the outside of his, helping him plant his feet on the edge of the sofa so his knees were raised a bit and he was splayed open.

He slowly slid his hands over Sebastian's body, up his thighs, over his hard cock, up his stomach to his pecs and then slowly down his arms until he clasped his boy's hands in his. Drawing them up, he placed them behind both of their heads. With his face beside Sebastian's, he had a good view of his boy's spread open thighs, cock already glistening at the tip.

Turning his head to the side, he bit his boy's earlobe and growled, "You won't move your legs from that position or your hands from behind our heads. Is that clear?"

Sebastian let out a soft moan, and Gideon watched as goose bumps skittered across his thighs as his whole body stiffened then shivered. His boy finally whispered, "Yes, Sir."

Chapter 23

SEBASTIAN

Getting himself dressed for the club's Black Friday event, Sebastian felt his nerves taking hold. Remembering the last time he'd gotten himself ready for a trip to Catharsis, he shivered as his confidence took a nosedive. He'd purchased all new clothes since the incident that had drawn him and his Dom together, tossing everything he was wearing that night except his Docs.

The harness he wore was similar to the last one he'd had, but he'd felt brave enough when purchasing it to forgo the mesh shirt, hoping his Dom wouldn't be embarrassed by his surprise appearance. But as the time approached to get himself out the door, his legs didn't seem to want to carry him there. His Lyft ride would be arriving any second, and he felt as if he was going to be sick.

The Monday before Thanksgiving he'd gotten a call from Braden. He and Zavier had agreed to visit Catharsis together for the first time on the night of the Black Friday event. He'd sounded nervous and had called to ask Sebastian if he'd be willing to meet them there to show them around a bit from a sub's perspective. They'd get the full tour from Gideon of course, but as his Dom had to work that night, Braden wanted another perspective on it.

He'd been happy that Braden had called but had felt strange about not talking to Gideon about it first. They hadn't talked about him visiting the club, but as Gideon hadn't forbade it, he thought it would be okay. He told himself that if Gideon called him before the party, he'd mention it, but if not, he didn't want to bother him. He knew his Dom would be busy before the holiday then would be spending Thanksgiving with his family, so he didn't want to interrupt him or distract him from what he needed to get done before the event.

The day before had been like any other day, except it was a Thursday and he had been off work for the holiday. Not knowing what to do with himself, he'd cleaned his place from top to bottom. When dinner time rolled around, as was his normal Thanksgiving habit, he'd microwaved a frozen "Thanksgiving Dinner" entree and hunkered down to binge-watch a few shows he'd missed recently.

Friday he'd gone to work, preferring to exchange that day off for another of his choosing and not wanting to sit around at home and worry himself sick about the event that evening. Midway through his day, he'd had one of his episodes in the station's bathroom in front of an officer who'd been shocked to learn that Sebastian experienced seizures. When it was over, he'd had a rattled beat cop on his knees beside him that he'd had to assure he was fine in order to avoid a trip to the hospital.

He'd gone back to his office, sent an email to his boss, and headed home for the rest of the day, cancelling his last appointment. He'd slept the rest of the day and evening, trying his best to ignore the panic building inside of him that his meds were no longer keeping the episodes at bay. But nothing was going to deter him from keeping his commitment to Braden, so he'd forced himself to get up and eat something before getting ready for the party.

Knowing he couldn't let the panic take over, he threw on a tight black t-shirt over his harness, figuring if he didn't have the guts when it came down to it, he could take off the harness and just wear the shirt. Tossing on his hoodie, he made his way outside just in time for his ride. He put his buds in and sat back, ignoring his stress level increasing exponentially the closer he got to the club. Instead, he cast his mind back to their scene Sunday night, the moment he'd given himself over to Gideon and had been splayed wide on the man's lap, at his mercy.

Gideon used the remote to turn on the video. When Sebastian saw what came up on the huge flat screen TV that was mounted above the stone fireplace, his whole body went rigid. He'd signed the contract and knew it said that Gideon could tape their scenes as long as he didn't share them, but he'd forgotten about it. He was about to turn away when he remembered Gideon's order and he sighed, wanting more than anything not to have to look at himself.

He shivered when Gideon whispered in his ear. "Don't look away, boy. Detach yourself from it for a minute and just look at your lines. Your arms, shackled to my headboard above your head, your long, slender back arched so perfectly for me. That perfect bubble butt raised up in the air, legs tucked under you and spread by the bar. Your pose is perfect, and when I ask you to stay in position, you can last for hours if I need you to."

He shook his head, and Gideon wrapped his arm around his chest and put his hand against his throat. That move never failed to jack up his heart rate yet make him feel so. . . owned which strangely calmed him. And god, he wanted to be owned by the man.

"You're fucking stunning. Look at you. All soft dewy skin, beautifully reddened by my tawse. You always take the pain I give you so well."

Sebastian watched as Gideon, naked from the waist up, tawse in his hand, walked around to the other side of the bed. His lips were moving, but Sebastian couldn't hear it. He kneeled there beside Sebastian's ass, and Sebastian made a frustrated noise.

"What, Bastian?"

"I can't hear it."

Gideon growled and turned on the volume. "That's my good boy. Watch yourself, listen to us."

Sebastian saw Gideon place his palm on his ass and squeeze. He heard him say, "Your ass is hot from my marks, boy."

Sebastian couldn't help but be turned on by watching his Dom in this way. Being able to see what Gideon did to him had his cock dripping. His Dom raised his hand and brought it down on his ass, his handprint left behind. Suddenly, Gideon's hand was on his cock, stroking it. He glanced down, but as soon as he did that, Gideon let go.

"Don't look at your cock. Eyes on the TV."

His head shot up again and he watched and listened as his Dom reached between his legs, running his fingers over his hole, caressed over his sac, and then grabbed hold of his leaking cock, jacking it hard and fast a couple times.

He never knew what he looked like in submission. Honestly, he'd be happy to never have to look at himself, but being forced to, he had to admit the scene was hot. He heard his Dom speaking to him on the video, and he saw his own body's reaction, heard his whimpers. He was embarrassed by them. He'd never known what he sounded like.

He shook his head, and when Gideon asked why, he whispered, "I didn't know I made so much noise. It's embarrassing. I sound feminine."

Gideon paused the video and reached to get something beside him. Next thing Sebastian knew, he had a clothespin attached to each nipple, on his foreskin on the underside of his cock, and then another and another for good measure. It hurt like a son of a bitch. He cried out, not having had that type of CBT before and not sure he ever wanted to feel it again.

Gideon's low menacing tone, full of what Sebastian had assumed was disappointment, had his stomach dropping. "You don't sound feminine. You sound like every gay man's wet dream. You're so vocal and so honest in your reactions. You don't hold back, and I know that every time I do something you love...or hate... I'll be able to tell where you're at in your head by the noises you make. It's a turn-on."

"It is?"

"Fuck yes, boy. I could come just from listening to you moan, whimper, and gasp. And fuck, the panting and the way your breath catches when I pound you gets me so hot, so fucking turned on. Listen to me when I start it up again. Every time I hear you react, I respond to it. Whether it's encouragement from me or a touch of my hands on you, or I touch myself. It's one of the things that turns me on most about you. Never curb your reactions from me, it's the biggest high I get from dominating you."

Sebastian was floored. He had no idea Gideon got that much from his reactions. The fact that he had that type of power never even occurred to him. He always assumed the turn-on for Gideon was in the dominating, not in his sub's reactions to being dominated. It flipped what he thought he knew about their dynamic on its head and he asked, "Can we watch more?"

"Yes."

Gideon pushed play and took the clothespins off his nipples and cock, painstakingly slow. It was excruciating, but before he knew it, Gideon's freshly slicked-up palm was gripping him and stroking him and he forgot all about the torture to his foreskin. Sure enough, every single time he whimpered, moaned, or said something to his Dom, the lust in Gideon's body amped up. Without fail, when Sebastian let Gideon know what he was feeling with noises, Gideon reacted positively in some way. It was beautiful to watch, in a way.

"It's like a dance."

Gideon's grip on his cock tightened, and he gave him several tight strokes, amping up Sebastian's arousal levels. He bit down on Sebastian's earlobe then licked it. "It is."

"A give and take."

"Yes. Tell me what else you see."

Sebastian took a deep breath and watched as Gideon took hold of the spreader bar and did some type of fancy maneuver which flipped him over onto his back. He got a look at his own face then, saw how flushed with arousal it was. Watched and tracked his video-self, watching his Dom unbuttoning his jeans and slowly taking his long, fat cock out and stroking it while his sub watched. He heard the desire in his own voice when he begged Gideon for a taste, when he pleaded with his Sir.

He was breathless when he said, "I sound so needy. You always make me a quivering needy mess."

Gideon removed his hand from Sebastian's cock. "Is that good or bad?"

Sebastian groaned when that hand went away. "Good, Sir. I've never reacted with anyone the way I react with you."

Gideon growled in his ear at the same time his video-self growled when he leaned over and shoved his cock in Sebastian's mouth and held him there while Sebastian choked on it. He gripped Sebastian's cock again and continued his mind-blowing ministrations. Sebastian's eyes were drawn back to the video in time to watch as Gideon pushed on the backs of his thighs and rimmed him.

Gideon squeezed his cock and played with his balls, alternating from soft to hard but keeping Sebastian on the knife's edge of orgasm. Again, Gideon bit his earlobe and whispered, "This is my favorite part. Watch yourself closely and listen."

Sebastian quieted his breathing, needing desperately to know what he sounded like, what he looked like that made Gideon declare it his favorite part of the video. Sure enough, he watched as he threw back his head at Gideon's rimming, arched his back, and panted. He moaned and thrashed around in his bindings then slowly, quietly began to beg. "Please. Please. Please, Sir. I need... I need..."

His Dom removed his tongue from his hole, growling up at him, watching him between his barred legs. "What do you need, boy?"

His voice got louder, faster. "More. Please, more... Oh, yes, yes, yes, yes. Oh god, Sir. Oh fuck, so good. So good. Please don't stop. Please..."

As Sebastian watched himself lose all control in the video, his cock wept onto his abdomen, and he shivered when Gideon whispered, "I love it when you beg. Such a good boy for your Dom." Fuck if that wasn't the hottest thing he'd ever heard. "And you are my good boy, aren't you?"

He couldn't hold back a gasp and a frantic nod, and now that he knew how much his Sir enjoyed it, he didn't try. "Yes, Sir."

"Keep watching."

Sebastian kept his gaze trained on himself on the TV, the discomfort of watching now set aside, he could see how open and honest his reactions were, how hedonistic he became under his Dom's ministrations. As he watched, Gideon edged him near orgasm. If he said something negative, Gideon stopped. If he said something positive, Gideon gave him more of what he so desperately needed. His whole body was tense with a bone-deep desire to come.

His muscles, held tight, were shaking. Gideon gripped his cock in one hand, jacking him off then reached under his sac with his other hand and prodded softly at his entrance. Sebastian pushed back against Gideon's finger and at last, he was inside, slowly sliding in deeper while his jacking became faster on Sebastian's cock.

When they reached the video's crescendo, Gideon asked, "How do we look together, Bastian?"

He responded immediately without thinking, "Beautiful, Sir."

"That's right." Gideon found his prostate, tapped his finger against it, and whispered, "Hold your breath for me."

Sebastian groaned then sucked in a breath. The hand that had been wrapped around his cock was unceremoniously clamped down over his mouth and partially over his nose, tilting his head back with its force. He could tell by the placement of Gideon's fingers that if he needed a breath, he'd be able to pull one in through his nose. But he'd do just about anything not to have to do that.

Gideon's finger nudged his prostate again and he bucked against it, wanting more. Pretty soon his hips were rolling, pumping into Gideon's hand to feel more, while Gideon held his finger still. His prostate was pegged with every thrust of his hips, and the hand over his mouth got tighter. He needed to come so badly it hurt. Holding it at bay by the skin of his teeth, he moaned behind Gideon's still lubed fingers over his mouth. He bucked in Sir's arms, needy for a breath, needy for an orgasm.

So. Fucking. Needy.

At the last moment, when he thought he could take no more, he heard the growling order, "Come for me, boy," and could do nothing but obey.

He didn't think, he just let go before Gideon was even done speaking. He didn't even realized nothing was touching his cock until he went to breathe in and realized Gideon's hand was still over his mouth. Not able to wait, he breathed in through his nose, which had Gideon releasing his face as Sebastian shot rope after rope of cum against his stomach, chest, and neck. His breath sawed in and out of him, and his body shook in the aftermath. He vaguely heard the words, "My beautiful boy," as his mind drifted and he was floating. And when he finally came back into himself—

"Sir? Sir, we're here."

Sebastian started at the driver's near shout, and he apologized for having spaced out on the ride over. He stepped out of the car to stand in the line at the club's door. The event had brought a big crowd and it took him a while to get inside. When the crowds were big, Khaleo had to individually scan people in by their personal QR codes. When it was his turn, Khaleo frowned at him.

"Master G didn't tell me you were coming. Next time, come in the side entrance." He hitched his thumb back toward a darkened hall behind him. "As his boy, you don't need to wait, Sebastian."

Feeling hot all over at the attention he was garnering from those still in the lobby entrance and those still behind him waiting to get coded in, he mumbled, "It's fine. I'm happy to wait."

Khaleo lifted a brow. "But Master G wouldn't be happy."

A stern voice behind him made him jump, and he was nudged aside by what he assumed was a Dom, the move so unexpected he nearly fell and caught himself on the edge of the tall reception desk. "You're keeping everyone waiting. Get a move on."

Sebastian's heart raced at the annoyed tone of the man's voice, and he muttered a quick "Thank you" to Khaleo before he shuffled off towards the subs' locker room. The challenging look on Khaleo's face as he stared the dominating man down made him want to run in the opposite direction. And he wondered again at Khaleo's status of sub versus Dom when he had the balls to talk down to the impatient man.

"You're not permitted entry, Mr. Forrester. You were banned from Catharsis and any other fet club in the state. You're the slimy bastard that brought a visitor that assaulted one of our subs. Kindly leave the premises before I'm forced to call the authorities."

Sebastian heard the man bluster and begin a ranting list of threats as he ran the rest of the way to the locker room toilets, barely making it in time to lose the meager contents of his stomach. He flushed, put the seat back down, and sat on it, head in his hands. He didn't even get a good look at the man that had been behind him, but to know he was the one that had brought the visitor to the club that had assaulted him nearly stole Sebastian's breath. And he had no doubts that's exactly who the man was.

He had no idea how long he'd been there when he finally felt well enough to get up, rinse out his mouth, toss a mint in for good measure, and lock his belongings away, including his harness which he'd had to get nearly completely undressed to remove. He no longer had an inkling of the energy needed to pretend he had the confidence to wear it without a shirt of some kind. Feeling cold and utterly exhausted but knowing he had to get out there so Braden didn't worry, he cast one more look in the mirror at his sallow reflection and shrugged as he headed for the door. It was fairly dark in the club, so he hoped it wouldn't be noticeable.

He rounded the corner into the Tranquility Room and scanned the crowd. He figured he'd be looking for a while because of the amount of people there, but he saw Zavier immediately as he was the tallest man there and was standing at the bar, Braden sitting on the barstool in front of him. He rounded the bar and headed towards them, grinning at the death glare Zavier sent a man that had the audacity to look at Braden. As he got closer, he saw that they both had the visitor cords on their wrists and Braden was collared for the occasion.

He smiled to himself, knowing Braden never wore a collar, and he'd be willing to bet Zavier was so protective of his boy that he wanted the extra layer of protection while they were at the club. He approached them, feeling suddenly nervous, and sat down next to Braden when the man Zavier had just given the death glare had quickly picked up his drink and left. When he realized Zavier might have wanted to take the seat, he stood again, eyes cast down. "I'm sorry, Sir. I wasn't thinking. You can sit by your boy."

He saw Zavier's hand rise and that big paw, so reminiscent of his Dom's, landed softly on his shoulder. "Look at me, Sebastian."

When he did, he saw only kindness in Zavier's eyes. He smiled shyly and said, "Hi, Sir," and then glanced at Braden whose hair was up in some kind of sexy man bun thingie so that his collar was obvious to all onlookers. He gave him a smile. "Hi, Braden."

Zavier squeezed his shoulder. "You don't need to call me Sir. Please, call me Zavier. And have a seat."

"Yes, Sir," Sebastian blushed and looked down again, "I mean, Zavier."

He sat next to Braden, and they did a weird little side hug, but instead of it feeling awkward, it felt good, and they laughed away any discomfort. "Are you nervous? Do you like it so far?"

Braden nodded, a bit wide-eyed. "Yeah. I love it. I thought I'd feel uncomfortable, but it's more relaxed than I expected and with him here," he tilted his head to his massive husband, "I don't feel as nervous as I expected I would. How are you? You look kinda tired."

Damn. And he thought it would be dark enough in the bar. "Yeah, I'm okay. Just feeling a bit run-down. Been really busy lately," he hedged. "I'll be fine. Did Gideon take you on a tour yet?"

Zavier shook his head. "No. He sent me a quick text. He's busy with last-minute event stuff and a demo he's got to do. He'll show us around after that."

Sebastian tensed, a sick feeling setting up shop in the pit of his stomach. Doing his best not to show a reaction, he nodded as if the fact that his Dom, his contracted Dom, was going to do a demonstration scene with another sub was no big deal. In reality, he felt like he'd been sucker-punched and immediately the urge to flee spread from his head to his feet, and he had to use the former to control the latter to keep him right where he was.

Squaring his shoulders, he knew he had a job to do, and when he was done with it, he'd escape as fast as he possibly could. If he was lucky, he'd be able to miss the scene altogether and do his best to forget he'd heard Zavier mention it at all. Because really, what choice did he have?

He had right around five months left in their contract, if he was lucky and didn't do something to fuck it up. He wasn't about to rock the boat. He'd take what he was given and enjoy it while it lasted because he wasn't likely to get another chance like this again. Taking a deep breath, he put it out of his mind and did what he'd come to do; show his new friends the club he loved and hope it helped them to make a decision.

They settled in, and Sebastian told them all about the club, showed them the app and what it could do. He then walked them around the main floor to let them see everything for themselves. They wound themselves through the crowd back to the elevator, Sebastian glad to have avoided seeing Gideon on stage with another sub.

Crossing his arms over his chest, protecting himself the only way he knew how, he got himself mentally ready to see his Dom, knowing it was inevitable. Unease unfurled in his stomach when he realized the reason Gideon didn't invite him was because he didn't want to be seen with him.

Jesus, how obvious could it be? They didn't go out together, they never scened at the club when it was open, in fact Gideon had never once mentioned it. And really, it wasn't like he could blame the man. Not that Sebastian wanted to scene in public, even the thought of it spiked his blood pressure, but not having Gideon ask him to do so seemed strange suddenly. His face grew hot with embarrassment at not having realized all of this before that moment.

They took the elevator down to the Liberation Room, Braden and Zavier chatting about the club, neither noticing his upset. Quickly he pulled his phone out of his pocket and opened his Lyft app, scheduling a pick-up as soon as someone could get there. Knowing on a Saturday he'd have to wait twenty minutes or so, he figured he had enough time to show them around before he left.

Looking up, he was glad to see the excitement on their faces the minute the doors slid open, and they got a look at the atmosphere of the room. The bass was thumping and the crowd was one big huge mass of moving bodies, tuned to the same rhythm, moving as one. The undulation of the crowd appearing to emulate the movement of the ocean.

The music switched over to something a little faster and as one, the crowd began to jump and writhe, no longer a wave but a mass of bodies moving with no discernable pattern except for the beat of the music. He usually avoided the room. That many people in one space made him nervous. He looked over at Braden and Zavier and smiled when he realized they wanted to join in the melee.

He quickly took them around to look at the voyeur rooms, enjoying Braden's blushing cheeks. They asked a few questions and walked back towards the Liberation Room. He hugged them both then pushed them out onto the dance floor and told them he'd maybe see them later and to take their time and have fun.

Knowing that wasn't true, he made his way back upstairs and was about to leave when he heard Gideon's voice coming over the speakers in the Tranquility Room. His voice, as always, drew him near and instead of going out the front door, his body refused to listen to his mind and walked closer and closer to the stage where he saw a girl tied up to a St. Andrew's Cross at the far end of the long stage.

When he drew closer he saw the single tail bullwhip held coiled loosely in his Dom's hand. As Gideon spoke into the ear mic, to the crowd that had gathered around the three sides of the stage facing the girl, Sebastian could do nothing but watch, feet rooted to the floor as if held by an invisible force.

Sebastian watched in morbid fascination as Gideon warmed up with the whip and then gave the first lash. It was like he felt the lash himself, and it was the only thing that allowed him to get his feet moving. He was in and out of the locker room in seconds and walking towards the front door, smiling for Khaleo as he approached the door.

"I'm gonna head home. I gave Zavier and Braden the tour for Gideon. They seem to really like the place, so I think they'll probably submit their applications."

A surprised look crossed Khaleo's face. "It was nice of you to come down and do that. I could have arranged something. Do you want to stay until he's done?"

Sebastian shook his head. "No. It's okay, I'm getting pretty tired. Long week."

"All right, Sebastian. Do you need a cab?"

He held up his phone and was happy to see the Lyft notification that his driver had arrived. "Nope. My ride just pulled around. Thanks. Goodnight!"

He was out of there with a softly spoken "night" from Khaleo trailing behind him. The trip home was uneventful. As he let himself into his place, he tried not to think too hard on the evening. He didn't know quite what he felt. Strangely, seeing a woman strapped naked to the cross had made him feel less upset.

If it had been a male sub, he probably would have felt worse. But as he couldn't blame Gideon for doing his job, and he knew Gideon wouldn't be sexually stimulated by the scene with a woman, he didn't feel so worked up about it. He also felt a strange jealousy at the fact that she'd been whipped with a single tail by his Dom when he hadn't yet. He'd always wanted to feel the bite of a single tail wielded by someone that truly knew what they were doing, and clearly, Gideon did.

It was more the shame of being an embarrassment to Gideon, of being the type of sub he had to keep hidden that he felt awful about, but yet again, he couldn't place any blame there. When it came down to it, he had no control over his Dom and how his Dom felt. All he could do was control how he reacted. He needed to think about what his feelings were. For that, he'd give himself time.

He locked up behind himself, fed the little monsters, turned out the lights, and made his way towards the stairs. Almost to the top, he got the tingling sensation in his fingertips that sometimes warned him of an impending seizure. It wasn't early enough, and before he could sit himself down to try to mitigate the damage, he was seizing and falling down the stairs as it happened, knocking himself out in the process.

Chapter 24

GIDEON

Gideon let himself into Sebastian's home feeling like a complete asshole. The event was a huge success, but an event that large took a lot of work and there had been several issues throughout the night that had required his attention. One of the scheduled demos was going to be cancelled because the Dom had a neck injury from a car accident and wouldn't be able to perform. As Gideon was the only available Dom that was skilled enough with the single tail, he'd agreed to scene with the sub so she wouldn't have to miss it.

He hadn't scened with anyone since he'd signed Sebastian, and he felt uneasy about it, but as they'd never discussed it and he felt it was his job, he'd made the decision to do the scene. Making that last-minute decision, and dealing with the other issues that had cropped up during the night, calling Sebastian had slipped his mind. He'd fucked up.

He'd been pulled away to deal with an equipment malfunction that thankfully hadn't hurt anyone, and a panicked sub that needed help who'd been abused by his Dom. Turns out the Dom was none other than the man that had recently submitted a membership request that he'd been holding back pending a deeper background check, so he'd mentally marked it off his to do list.

He'd texted a well-respected Dom through the club's app. Dr. Gabriel Price was a mild-mannered psychologist who Gideon knew was a softie when it came to troubled subs. They'd talked several times about having him work at the club to give the subs someone to go to if they needed help. They hadn't ironed out the details yet, but he had some ideas brewing that he wanted to discuss with the soft-spoken Dom.

He'd left the panicked sub in Gabe's capable hands and had texted Zavier again to let him know he'd try to find them later. When Zavier had responded that they'd arranged a tour with a friend, Gideon had assumed he meant

Braden's barista and had put it out of his mind to check up on stock for each of the bars.

Only when he was done with his demo was he able to find Braden and his brother. They'd both greeted him, smiling and looking like they'd been enjoying themselves. He wanted them both to feel comfortable at his place and knew their joining it was contingent on whether Braden felt safe and content in his surroundings. He placed his hand on Braden's shoulder and squeezed gently.

"You look like you're having fun."

Braden hugged him as usual, something he'd had to get used to. "We were just downstairs dancing in the Liberation Room. So wild. You have a great place here, Gideon."

"Thanks. I hope you feel comfortable enough to join. Do you guys want a tour? I'm sorry it's taken so damn long for me to join you."

"No, we're good. Sebastian showed us around. He left us downstairs and said he'd see us later. Did he find you?"

His heart took a dive. His boy was there? "No. When was that?"

"I don't know, probably thirty minutes ago now."

"Fuck."

He jogged to the entrance and could see Khaleo's disappointment in him immediately. "He tried to hide it, but he couldn't get out of here fast enough and didn't look well when he left. On top of that, when he arrived, Mr. Forrester came in behind him, nearly shoving him off his feet to get him out of his way and tried to intimidate and threaten his way into the club."

"Was he hurt?"

"No, but it was a close thing."

Anger seethed just under the surface, everything Khaleo had just said making his mind hum like there was a hive of bees up there. "You didn't try to stop him?"

Khaleo raised a brow at him, not intimidated by his anger. "I don't make it a habit of accosting our members and refusing to let them leave. He said someone was pulling around the front to get him."

Incredulous, Gideon asked, "He was here with someone?"

Before he had time to think about how irrationally jealous that thought made him, Zavier gripped him by the back of his neck and squeezed. Hard. Hard enough that he couldn't ignore it. He tried to shrug him off but in the end, the palm gently placed on his shoulder that came just before the gentle words of his brother-in-law calmed him like nothing else could have. "Gideon, talk to us. What happened?"

"He left. I didn't know he was coming tonight. Had no idea he was here. . ."

His voice trailed off and he scrubbed his face in frustration. He shouldn't have yelled at Khaleo. He was angry at himself. He looked up to apologize and the man shook his head, but he said it anyway. "I'm sorry. It's not your fault."

"I know, Sir."

Braden, still confused, asked, "What do you mean, you didn't invite him to tonight's event? That's the only reason I asked him to give us a tour. So, what? He came here just to walk us around? I assumed he'd be here with you. Aren't you guys seeing each other?"

Taking a deep breath, he let it out slowly. He'd never take his anger out on Braden or any other submissive. And if, for some reason, he lost his mind and did so, his brother would have killed him regardless and though their fights were always evenly matched, he wouldn't fight back if it came to that.

"No, I didn't invite him. It didn't occur to me, honestly. Fridays are not our nights."

"Your *nights*?"

Sighing, he gripped the back of his neck in his hand and squeezed at the tension there. "Yes. Our nights. We're not seeing each other in the sense you mean. We're in a six-month contract. We're Dom and sub, only."

"But—" Braden was cut off by his husband who drew him into an embrace.

Gideon looked at Zavier in thanks and got a stern stare in return. Zavier had always been able to read him and this time wasn't any different. "So, you didn't invite him and when he came at Braden's request, I'm guessing the fact that you were demonstrating with another sub was news to him as well."

Gideon clenched his jaw then his shoulders slumped when he heard Braden's gasp. Nothing could have prepared him for the quick right jab to his ribs that Braden shocked him with. The punch was pulled, but he could tell that Zavier had been practicing with his boy. He rubbed the sore area.

"You better go fix it, you big jerk."

He laughed, incredulous. Did he really just... "Big jerk?" Jesus, the kid was priceless.

Braden wasn't laughing, however, and his arms were crossed over his chest in anger. "Yes! Go find him and make it right."

Gideon sighed, knowing that's exactly what he should do. "He's working tomorrow. He's probably already asl—"

"So you go and wake him up! Gideon, he'll be thinking about it all day tomorrow and feeling like shit. Not to mention, if you don't talk to him, he might not show up at your next 'scheduled' time."

Gideon growled at that thought but couldn't deny it. He looked at Khaleo who nodded at him. "I've got it. Go find your boy."

He nodded and made his goodbyes to Braden and Zavier. Making his way across town, he parked as close to Sebastian's house as he could and jogged the rest of the way. As he locked Sebastian's door behind him, Slap and Tickle came to greet him. He spent a moment scratching them under their chins.

He made his way up the stairs, the little fur balls nipping at his heels. Leaving the hall light on, he walked into Sebastian's room and saw him curled there in a tight ball, asleep. Not wanting to wake him but knowing he had to, he sat down on the bed and rubbed his shoulder.

"Sebastian, can you wake up for me?"

Gideon could feel when he woke because his body tensed up. He gently rubbed his hand up and down Sebastian's arm, but his boy stayed where he was, facing away from him when he whispered, "Can we talk tomorrow night? I'm exhausted, Gideon, and I don't feel well."

Gideon remembered that Khaleo had mentioned he didn't look well. Worrying he was getting sick, Gideon turned on the light next to the bed and glanced at him. There was an old-fashioned ice bag in Sebastian's hand, and when he glanced up at Sebastian's face he was shocked to see a huge lump just above his temple that was swollen and bruised, the skin broken. Out of his mind with worry, he spoke louder than he'd meant to. "Jesus Christ. Baby, what happened? Who the fuck did this to you?"

Sebastian winced then groaned and covered the lump with the ice pack. "I fell. It's nothing. I'm just tired, Gideon. Please, can we talk later?"

Gideon didn't believe it was nothing for a second, but he sighed and said, "We can talk about what happened at the club later, yes. But I need to know what happened to you. Are you hurt anywhere else?"

"I'm fine. I slipped on the stairs. Slap and Tickle got underfoot and I missed a step. I'll be okay. I just want to sleep."

Something in his gut told him that explanation wasn't the whole truth, but he didn't want to push. "Did you lose consciousness?"

Sebastian sighed but still didn't move. "I don't know. Yeah, I think so."

"Bastian, you probably have a concussion. We need to take you—"

"I'm not going to the hospital for a bump on the head. I'm fine. What I need is sleep."

Still worried and not wanting to take any chances, Gideon pushed, "Let me—"

"Gideon, please. Please, don't make me safeword right now. I'm tired. I need sleep. You can stay or go, but I'm not going anywhere, and I need you to let me sleep."

Safeword? His gut churned, knowing that Sebastian was feeling so upset, so utterly without defenses that he felt he might need to use it. Everything in him wanted to push, to order Sebastian to go with him, but he didn't want to force a safeword, and he knew that's what would happen. He sighed and softly rubbed Sebastian's arm again, up and down and whispered, "Okay, baby. But I'm gonna stay if that's really all right with you."

Sebastian gave the briefest nod and sleep slurred his words when he responded, "S'all right."

Sebastian was asleep before Gideon even got off the bed. He placed a call to Finn and got some advice on what to do and how to help, and then he got ready for bed himself, stripping down to his boxer briefs and getting in bed beside his boy. He wanted to hold him but knew he shouldn't move him. He got as close as he could without disturbing him, moved the ice bag to the nightstand, and held Sebastian's hand against his chest.

He couldn't help but let his mind wander, allowing himself to imagine what it would be like if Sebastian was truly his. To imagine how that conversation would go between them. Because the longer he was with him, the more he felt, and the more he felt, the more he wanted to claim his boy's mind, body, and heart. He didn't have any desire for a slave, and God knows he'd never presume to call himself a Master, but he admitted to himself that's what he was craving.

As his possessiveness took over, his desire for permanent ownership did its best to take control as well. It was like a burning ember at his core that seemed to be growing by the day. He was afraid that ember, which had started as a simple spark the second the boy had slapped him across the face that first morning, would eventually turn into a fiery inferno he wouldn't be able to contain.

Sebastian's past, his present, his future desires were a gift he wanted to be offered, one that he would treasure. Every nuance, every emotion, every thought in that gorgeous brain of his, freely given. He was the light to Gideon's darkness.

There was an inherent sweetness and innocence that exuded from the boy in waves, and he wanted to help him keep it and do everything he could to encourage it to continue. But he couldn't. None of that could happen and that heartbreaking thought was his last before he drifted off into a fitful sleep.

Throughout the night, he'd woken Sebastian up every couple hours to make sure he was doing all right. His phone's alarm went off marking another two hours gone, and Gideon roused quickly, ready to wake Sebastian up again at the designated time, but he found himself alone in bed. He got up and checked the bathroom and found a note that said Sebastian had gone to work. He read it twice and still couldn't believe his eyes.

Work? After a concussion? What the actual fuck? Pissed off that his boy wasn't taking care of himself as he should be and having the discomfiting feeling that he was quickly losing control, he took a two-minute shower and got himself dressed and out the door in five. He drove across town to the Mission Station to search for Sebastian.

He wandered around the north side of the building then made his way over to the south side when a uniformed cop asked if he needed help. Gideon knew what he really wanted to do was ask what the hell he was doing wandering around. When he mentioned Sebastian's name, Officer Henson directed him further back into the bullpen and along a bank of offices. It appeared his boy had his own cubbyhole office which was empty.

He was approached again by a plainclothes detective who didn't look nearly as helpful as the uniform had, even if he'd been faking it. "Can I help you?"

He decided to wing it and pulled out his phone, pasting on a confused look as he checked it as if looking for something that could help. "I have an appointment with a Sebastian Phillips for a composite sketch."

The stern lines around the man's eyes loosened, and he became more cordial immediately, though he now appeared confused. "Uh, Sebastian doesn't work weekends."

Gideon tensed at that bit of news, anger at possibly being deceived by his sub burning through his last bit of control. "Hmm. I guess I—"

"Hang on a minute."

The guy held up a finger and walked a couple doors down, knocking on a doorframe. Gideon could hear part of the conversation. "Cap, there's a guy out here saying he's. . ."

A beefy older man with more muscular bulk than fat came to the door. Though he was probably shy of six feet, he had a commanding presence and, after he got a good look at Gideon, didn't look like he believed the story the detective had given him. "Why don't you step into my office, sir."

Gideon's affable and confused act vanished as he did just that. The man sat behind a desk that was cluttered with a mountain of paperwork and files, contained three coffee mugs, all containing dregs of what he assumed was some really bad brew, and a calendar blotter that had seen better days.

The man, whose name plate read Captain Jon Conway, steepled his fingers as he stared at Gideon. "We both know you don't have an appointment with Sebastian. I know that because I know his schedule which has never included Saturdays. So, why don't we cut the bullshit, and you can tell me why you're really here."

Gideon couldn't help the tiny smirk that passed over his lips. The man saw a lot which was probably the reason he'd made captain. Gideon settled back in the chair and responded in kind. "Look, Sebastian's a close friend. He said he was working today, and I need to see him immediately, so if you know where he might be, I need to know."

All he got was a raised brow. "What's your name, sir?"

Gideon stared at the captain for several long, drawn-out seconds and finally answered, "Gideon McCade."

That got a reaction. The man unconsciously gripped his wrist and asked, "McCade as in…"

"Yes."

Both brows winged up at his response and the man sat up a little straighter. "Mr. McCade, I don't make it a habit to discuss my employees' personal lives and whereabouts."

Gideon leaned forward, elbows on his knees, and prepared to maneuver his way into finding out what he wanted, even if he was giving too much information to the man. "Look, Captain Conway, Sebastian fell down his stairs last night and knocked himself out. He shouldn't be working in those conditions. If he's not working as he said, I need to track him down. If you know anything, please, I'm worried he's going to hurt himself if he doesn't take it easy."

The man's countenance changed completely, and the protective boss came through. "Shit. Kid can't catch a break. All I know is that he has an art studio somewhere. And I only know that much because he accidentally mentioned it once when I asked him about some travel he needed to do. He's pretty close-lipped about his personal life."

Gideon clenched his teeth and stood. "Tell me about it. Thank you. I think I can work with that information."

"Look, I don't know what kind of friends you are, but I care about my people. You tell him to call me if he needs some time."

"Will do. Thanks."

Gideon made his way back out onto the street before he pulled out his phone and dialed. "Zavier, I need your help. Can you use whatever means you have at your disposal in your fancy security offices to figure out where Sebastian has some kind of art studio?"

"I don't need to."

"Brother, don't fuck with me right now. He fell down the stairs at his place and got a concussion. I woke up this morning, and he was gone. He left me a note that he was working. With a fucking concussion, Zavier! I came down to the police station and talked to his captain who said he never works weekends, and yet, every single goddamned weekend since we've been together, he's said he has to work every Saturday!"

"Fuck. That kid pushes himself too hard. He *does* work every Saturday at his studio. Braden and I have been there. I'll text you the address. Call if you need anything."

They hung up, and all he could think was that his brother and brother-in-law had been to his boy's studio and he hadn't even known he had one. His anger at himself and his boy was mounting, and he was glad he had some time to get himself under control before he got there so he didn't lose his shit. Moments later, he had an address. And after that another text from Zavier's phone.

The text read, *"This is Braden. Don't yell at him. He's already hurting enough. Just take care of him, please. I get the feeling nobody does."* And fuck if that didn't just take the wind out of his sails. Literally. He was in the middle of the sidewalk and stopped when he read it, and he had to wonder how true it really was. Something told him it was truer than he'd ever know, and that didn't sit well with him at all. He ached, literally ached, to be the one that did, and yet, he knew he couldn't be.

The realization that he had a contracted sub whom he only knew topically and from a sexual preferences standpoint twisted him up inside. He'd known more about Boone within their first contracted week, and he'd never had feelings for Boone. What was he supposed to do with that?

One thing was for damn sure, while they were still in contract, he would do his goddamn level best to ensure his boy was taken care of in any way he could do so, without crossing the lines he'd drawn. And when their time ended, he'd do his best to find Sebastian a Dom worthy of him.

By the time he reached the art co-op, he'd calmed considerably. Taking the elevator to the second floor of the office-like building, he knocked softly on the door marked two fifteen, not wanting to interrupt or alarm Sebastian as he had no idea what was going on behind the closed door. When he didn't get a response, he tried the door and was frustrated to learn it wasn't locked. Didn't he know he could get robbed or worse leaving his door unlocked?

He opened it a bit and was confused to see what looked a little like a really large dentist chair. Beside it was a large rolling shelf with a lot of supplies on it. There was an L-shaped span of white cabinets mostly covering two walls. At the end of the cabinets was a massive, black-framed, standing mirror leaning against the wall, beside which was a set of cubes, plain white and plain black about chair height, with nothing on them. As the back wall came into view, Gideon sucked in a breath when he saw a huge array of black-framed photographs ranging in sizes from huge to postcard size in an artistic pattern that radiated from the centermost photograph.

He walked farther into the room, glanced to the right and found his boy sleeping on a couch, covered in a bright red, crocheted blanket. His heart ached at the depth of exhaustion he knew Sebastian must be feeling if he was sleeping in his studio between clients.

Giving in to a desire to know more about the boy who had intrigued him from the start, he let Sebastian sleep so he had time to really look at his sub's talent. Somehow, he knew that if he asked questions about what he was seeing, Sebastian would play it down and make excuses for them to leave. Attention paid to his sub for any reason other than a scene made the boy twitch. Some of the photos were very intimate and those that were didn't contain faces.

It was a wall of color in an otherwise black and white room. The picture that drew him in was the large center one of a nearly naked, muscular man that was sitting on the white cube wearing only black cotton briefs. The photo was from the chest down, the man at a slight angle, his muscular arms were wrapped around one leg that was drawn up on the edge of the cube, but the thing that drew the eye to the center of the photo was the colorful tattoo done over the man's partial leg amputation scars. The artwork was amazing and depicted a tattooed battle scene containing Roman warriors with intricate armor and realistic looking weapons.

Moving on, he looked at some of the best art he'd ever seen, inked into strangers' skin. Not all of them were done on scars, but most of them were. One that touched him deeply was of an older woman whose right arm was bent and draped over her face for anonymity, clasping onto her left hand, her left arm bent to cover her left breast for modesty. Her hair was long, curly, and steel gray, and it rioted about her head in a halo effect. Her right mastectomy scars covered with a starburst of color, depicting a phoenix rising from the ashes.

So moved by the image, he was reminded of his own mother's battle with breast cancer. He'd been a child at the time, and she'd been a survivor, with the scars to prove it. The mastectomy of her left breast something she'd never been embarrassed about. He moved closer to see the detail of the wings, the lines of each feather. The vibrancy of the colors was amazing and covered the range of the rainbow.

Like the woman in the picture, his mom had never wanted an augmentation. She used to say her husband loved her just the way she was, and she never wanted to go under the knife again, unless she was forced to. She wore a breast prosthetic that she laughingly called her chicken cutlet. While other people's mothers would say they were going to take their eyes out, and remove their contacts, his mother would say she was going to go take her boob off and get comfortable.

He continued to look at every single photo in detail. He couldn't believe his boy had been hiding this kind of talent. And then it hit him. His boy wasn't hiding this kind of talent from anyone except him. There'd been numerous times he could have told his Dom what he was doing on Saturdays, but he'd chosen not to.

As much as he felt frustrated, maybe even angry at his sub for keeping it from him, he realized maybe he was only doing it for the same exact reasons Gideon wasn't sharing more of himself. It would be too hard in the end to say goodbye the more they got embedded in each other's lives. The other option; that Sebastian believed Gideon didn't give a shit, he couldn't believe was true. *Could he?*

His boy had to know he'd want to know everything about him. *Didn't he? Fuck, he probably didn't.* What had Gideon given him to show that he was interested in knowing him like that? *Nothing. Not. One. Fucking. Thing.* But he did. He wanted to know everything he could possibly learn about his beautiful sub.

The fact that he couldn't ask, that he'd made it impossible to do so, pissed him off. But it was an impotent rage and a self-inflicted one that he'd have to bear for his boy's sake. He just knew he couldn't share more of himself because if he did, Sebastian would start to believe they could have more, and his boy didn't deserve to be crushed like that.

When he was finally done looking at the photos, he turned and realized with a jolt that Sebastian had woken up and was watching him warily. He softened his features as he approached, not wanting him to feel stressed about his presence there. He crouched down in front of his boy and rubbed his thumb along his cheek then up near his still swollen, bruised forehead. "Worried about you."

The wariness dissolved at that, and Sebastian let out a slow breath, as if he'd been holding it but didn't want him to know it. He nodded and admitted, "Worried about me, too."

He looked around the room, still awed by his surroundings "This is... Sebastian, it's so unexpected, but goddamn, you're so fucking talented." He sighed and shook his head, continuing, "Look, I can't tell you what to do in this part of your life. But, I don't think you should be working today or tomorrow. I think you should be taking it easy."

Sebastian nodded. "I worked on one client, just a few touch ups for no more than an hour, but I knew after that I couldn't work all day. My head is killing me. I cancelled the rest of my clients today. I just didn't have the energy, so I figured I'd take a little nap first then work on getting myself home."

Gideon clamped his mouth shut, his jaw aching with the need to hold in a frustrated growl. The fact that his own sub never thought once of calling him for help just about did him in. *Was he such a monster?* He let out a calming breath, ignoring his own reaction and focusing on what needed to be done. "Okay, what do you need to do to shut down here?"

"Nothing. It's all taken care of, I just didn't have any juice left after I cleaned up. I figured after I rested I could call a driver to come get me."

Unable to help himself, Gideon said, "You could have called *me* to come get you."

The confused vulnerability on Sebastian's face made Gideon's heart ache. His boy shook his head and whispered, "I wouldn't bother you with that. I'd have called for a Lyft ride."

Bother him? Jesus. Fucking. Christ. Was he not the boy's Dom? Was he not supposed to take care of Sebastian's needs? His sub was plunging that knife in deeper with every comment, and then twisting it for good measure. Why would he assume that he was being a bother? Why would. . . And then he realized why. He'd specified it before they signed the contract. He'd made it very clear that theirs wasn't a relationship, that they weren't dating, they were merely contracted. *He'd* done it. *Him.*

Fuck.

He found it telling that he'd spent so much time angry at himself for the last several days. He took a deep breath and did what he needed to do. He helped Sebastian up. They slowly made their way down to Gideon's SUV and headed to Sebastian's home. When he pulled up as close as he could to Sebastian's place, he put a hand on his boy's leg to stay him. "I'm gonna go get Slap and Tickle. You're coming to my place."

Sebastian shook his head, looking wary and sad. "I'm sorry, Sir. I don't think I'm up for that. I know we have our scheduled time the next two nights, but I... I'm sorry, I don't think I can."

Killing. Him. . . Was he for real? "What?"

Sebastian rubbed his hands back and forth on his thighs, the nervous gesture making Gideon's guilt spike. And then Sebastian twisted the knife again. "I know I'm cutting out two overnights. If you need me to make up for it, I can try an extra weeknight this week and next."

"Make up for... What? No! That's not... Jesus Christ, Sebastian. What kind of man do you think I am? What kind of Dom?"

Sebastian rubbed his hands over his face. He shook his head then rubbed his fingertips over his brow. The fact that he was so obviously in pain just sucked the energy right out of Gideon. Sebastian murmured, "You're a good man, Gideon. A great Dom. I don't want to disappoint you. I know I'm taking a lot of our scheduled time away because I hurt myself. I—"

"Jesus, baby, stop. Please, stop. You're killing me. I'm not asking for that."

Sebastian let out a pained whisper, "I don't understand."

"You're hurting. I want to keep an eye on you. To make sure you're all right. You're coming to my place to rest, that's all. Nothing more, nothing less. I just need to make sure you're okay."

Sebastian shook his head. "I'll be okay. I'm not your responsibility."

Yes, you are! Gideon grunted and replied, "You need help right now, and I'm not taking no for an answer, Bastian. And, besides, all you have is a shower. Wouldn't a bath feel good on your sore body?"

Sebastian huffed. "You fight dirty."

"Always. Please, Bastian, let me take care of you."

When he finally got a nod from his boy, he was in and out with the little monsters in minutes but had to wait for Sebastian, who'd gotten out of the SUV to grab what looked like a pill bottle from his own car that he was tucking surreptitiously into his pocket. That made him pause, and then his mind was churning, his thoughts combatting each other.

Check his pockets later because you're worried about him. Don't check his pockets later, it's a violation. Fuck, he'd never felt so on edge in a contract before, never so off balance.

Once Sebastian was settled back in his SUV, face pink with embarrassment, Gideon handed the furballs over. Having purchased a litter box and food for them to keep at his house—not to mention a ridiculously large, five level cat tree, a cat bed that they had yet to sleep on, and a myriad of cat toys that he was always stepping on—he'd made it much easier for them to travel back and forth with the little monsters.

Once he got Sebastian home, he helped him to the bed while he went to fill up the tub with scorching hot water and some bath salts he liked. When that was done, he went back in where Sebastian was sitting on the edge of the bed.

He looked a bit dazed, and when Gideon moved to help him up, he stood up shakily on his own.

"The bath's ready. Let's get you in there."

"I can do it. Thank you for running it for me. I'll be out in a little while."

Knowing an evasive maneuver when he saw one, he shook his head. "I'm helping you. Let's go."

Confused by his boy's reticence, he ushered Sebastian in and began to help him get undressed, finally understanding why he'd wanted to do it himself. His boy had bruises all over his body, making it obvious that he'd not just slipped on the stairs but had slipped and fallen down them, hitting every body part on the way to the bottom.

Fuck.

"Jesus, Bastian," he whispered as he took in his boy's battered body. He was damn lucky he didn't break anything, including his neck. He took a deep breath and asked, "What type of pain meds are you taking and when was the last time you took any? I might have something I can give you that's a bit stronger."

"I took some acetaminophen when I woke up. I don't want to take anything stronger."

Gideon narrowed his eyes at him but knew that tone of voice from his boy. It wasn't a negotiation, and he wasn't budging. There were very few things in which Sebastian was immovable, but when Gideon hit on one, Sebastian's spine got straight, his voice got stronger, and he looked him dead in the eyes and held his gaze without blinking, something he rarely did. "Okay, well, it's been long enough for you to take some ibuprofen. You can alternate them safely."

Sebastian shook his head, this time avoiding his gaze. Curious. "I can't take ibuprofen. Don't react well to it, so I need to stick with acetaminophen. If you don't have any, I'll be okay without. You don't need to worry about it."

Christ, didn't the boy know he'd go get some if it came to that rather than allow him to be in pain? "No, I have some. You'll be safe to take some in about an hour, I think. I'll dig them out, and we'll keep you on a good schedule so you can get ahead of the pain."

Sebastian nodded, and Gideon helped him into the bath. Just like with the kitten supplies, he'd purchased things for Sebastian so he didn't have to pack much, if anything, when he came over. He gathered some pajamas so Sebastian would be comfortable and took them into the bathroom, leaving them on the counter and grabbing Sebastian's clothes from earlier to toss in the hamper.

Walking out of his closet, Gideon realized the pill bottle Sebastian had tucked in his pocket had fallen out of his pants and landed by the bed. He picked it up and examined the translucent orange bottle, sitting down on the edge of the bed when he realized the sticker had been taken off. Knowing he'd seen the label on the bottle when he'd watched it being shoved in Sebastian's pocket, his shoulders tensed, and he grew frustrated when he realized he didn't have the right to ask.

He'd made sure of that with the contract stipulations. Not to mention he'd specifically asked if Sebastian had any serious medical issues that would impact or be affected by their play, and the boy had said no. Remembering that moment, he had to admit to himself that Sebastian had paused before answering and thought about it, but when he'd said no, he'd been speaking the truth, so he'd let it go. But faced with this goddamn pill bottle that had been stripped clean, he had to wonder.

Unable to stop himself, he opened the bottle and looked at the pills. There were six and he was itching to spill them out onto his palm, check to see if there were any identifiers. He even went so far as to wonder if he could take a picture and ask Finn to figure it out for him, but the disgust he felt for himself, even if he was doing it because he was worried about the boy, was too much.

He put the cap back on the bottle and placed it on the nightstand on Sebastian's side of the bed. He wouldn't mention it, no matter how much he wanted to order Sebastian to give him an explanation. But he knew Sebastian wouldn't mention it either, and that just summed up their relationship right there, didn't it? And he had no one to blame but himself.

Fuck.

Knowing he still had a while, he went to the kitchen, heated some soup, and made a few paninis. He knew Sebastian was hurting, and he wanted to keep an eye on him, ensure he was all right for the next couple days. Maybe they'd binge-watch some awful TV or watch some bad movies. He'd do his best to ensure Sebastian got a lot of rest and was feeling much better by Monday when he had to return to work.

He knew it probably wasn't smart. Taking care of him in this way was not part of their contract, and in the end, would only begin to—or, maybe more accurately, continue to—blur those goddamn lines that were quickly becoming the bane of his existence. But as much as he could distance himself mentally and emotionally from most everyone else in the world besides his family, he was beginning to realize that doing so with Sebastian was becoming downright impossible.

Later, he helped Sebastian out of the tub, they ate lunch, and he led Sebastian to the couch so they could talk about the night before. He could see the reticence in his boy's expression, but he asked that Sebastian give him a chance to explain. The sad look in Sebastian's eyes prompting his apology. "I'm sorry, boy. I normally wouldn't have done it, but I didn't want to let down the other submissive and would have struggled to find a replacement last minute."

Sebastian shrugged. "It wasn't sexual, and it wasn't stipulated in the contract. I don't really have the right to be upset, Sir."

"But you do. And you are. And rightfully so. We'll amend the contract to spell that out. I don't want to be scening with anyone else, and I for damn sure don't want you scening with anyone else."

Just the thought of Sebastian scening with another Dom had his blood boiling. And the reality was that it had felt wrong when he'd done it. He'd pulled the contract up on his computer, added the addendum, and brought it out for them to sign. Afterward, he'd clasped Sebastian's hand, murmuring, "I'm sorry, Bastian. I didn't mean to hurt you. Going forward, if someone needs a last-minute stand-in and we don't have someone available, I'll reschedule it."

Sebastian nodded, and he leaned in and kissed the boy's soft lips. Sebastian sighed into his kiss and went limp, his features softening, his body relaxing, much more at ease with that settled and out of the way. Sebastian's eyes were drooping, and he apologized for being so tired. Gideon gently eased him up from the couch and led him towards the bedroom to rest.

When they got there, he saw Sebastian's whole body tense up when he spotted the medication on the nightstand. He didn't move for several moments and Gideon ignored the voice in his head prompting him to question, to push, to dig for those details he so wanted to know.

He pulled back the duvet and urged Sebastian to rest. The relieved look on the boy's face, the fact that Sebastian avoided eye contact completely, barely acknowledging his presence after seeing his pills, told Gideon he'd been right. Sebastian wasn't going to share any details, and as much as he didn't want to, Gideon admitted it was probably for the best. He watched as Sebastian lay down and stared blankly into space. He couldn't help but think that the headway they'd just made regarding exclusivity had just been mowed down by that goddamn, tiny pill bottle.

He couldn't miss the desolation that was in Sebastian's eyes, the hopelessness in their depths before he closed them and turned away from Gideon. It was like a punch to the gut, and he stood there and watched Sebastian pretend to sleep, finally walking away when he realized his presence would just stress the boy out more and probably keep him awake. As Gideon went back into the kitchen to clean up after their lunch, he couldn't deny the uneasy feeling that he was losing something that was never supposed to be his in the first place.

Chapter 25

SEBASTIAN

It had been a long month. Christmas was right around the corner, and Sebastian was exhausted. His neurologist was doing his level best to find an anticonvulsant that worked. In the last four weeks, he'd tried two new medications with mixed results.

Dilantin was the first one that seemed to help him a bit with minimal side effects, but it wasn't enough, so they'd added a second to the mix. The Keppra had sunken him into a depression so deep he'd called in sick from work for a solid week, prompting not only his doctor, but also his captain, to worry. It was the first time he'd called in sick for more than one day in a week for the entirety of his employment.

He'd thought about trying to take some short-term medical leave, but he'd been put on another drug when his doctor had seen what the Keppra had done to him. In addition to the depression, he'd been dizzy and weak, had fevers, nausea, and had lost seven pounds in just nine days. He'd easily been able to convince Gideon he'd had the flu without saying a word when the fevers and nausea had hit on a Tuesday evening, one of their weeknights. Gideon had asked him to stay so that he could take care of him, but he'd begged off under the guise of not wanting to make him sick.

He'd been put on Trileptal which had the same list of possible side effects but the crippling depression slowly lifted, and the worst side effect he had was nausea, a hives breakout that had gone away after the first week, and continued weight loss. The seizures had slowed, but not stopped. So far, so good. He hoped it would work, but he had a feeling it wouldn't. There was talk of surgery, and he wanted to avoid it at all costs for obvious reasons. He asked the doctor to give him more time before that prognosis was made, thus the new medication.

The muscle weakness that he'd been lucky to mostly avoid prior to then had begun to make an appearance. Stairs were a bit harder to climb, the tattoo gun was harder to grip. He was never more thankful that he'd trained himself to be ambidextrous. He could still tattoo with both hands but he wasn't able to last very long, and his once dominant left hand had been swapped for his right.

He counted himself lucky he'd had no new issues with his eyesight. At his neurologist's request, he'd been to see an ophthalmologist that specialized in glaucoma. There was no change with his sight, and he was thankful for small favors. He knew the probability that he'd eventually lose his eyesight in one eye because of the ocular disease was high, but there was nothing he could do to prevent it.

The only bright spots in the last month were his tattooing days and his sessions with his Dom. He'd had to cancel multiple meet-ups with Gideon and was thankful that he was understanding. He'd expressed concern numerous times regarding Sebastian's weight loss and lower energy levels. Sebastian could tell he was doing his best not to pry and push for more information. All Sebastian had given him was that he was having tests done to see what was going on, and that he'd let Gideon know if he needed anything or more time to deal with it.

He did his best to keep their scheduled sessions because they were mostly what was keeping him going. After his fall down the stairs a month ago, their relationship had changed. He couldn't pinpoint it exactly. When he'd seen the pill bottle on Gideon's nightstand, he'd nearly gotten sick, thinking Gideon would start asking questions, and when he didn't, Sebastian was confused by his feelings of both relief *and* disappointment.

He was angry that the pills weren't doing their job, but that was then followed by more rational thoughts that he'd always known this would most likely happen and he'd prepared himself for it, both mentally and physically, for years. He knew the anger stemmed from the fact that for the first time, things in his personal life were going well. He'd finally found a gorgeous, equally kinky, but nurturing Dom whom he cared very deeply for, but he knew, deep down that theirs was never a love match. At least not on his Dom's side.

He was pretty sure love was exactly what he was feeling, and he felt cheated that the meds, and everything they stood for, were a huge part of the reason Gideon would never want to permanently tie himself to a sub like him, let alone *love* a man like him. All that fell on Sebastian. He'd never blame

Gideon for his own shortcomings. But those shortcomings were so immense, he felt a sort of quiet despair, his self-blame akin to a self-flagellation.

Though they were still having intense scenes, he'd eventually realized that Gideon had reduced some of the rougher play they'd participated in previously. He didn't know what to feel about that. He supposed he felt both frustrated at Gideon's high handedness and taken care of at the same time. He couldn't very well fault his Dom for making the decisions regarding their play, but he also didn't want to be considered weak and unable to handle their scenes.

He was still wearing the cock cage on a regular basis, but Gideon had given him a key in case he needed to remove it for a doctor's appointment. That too had filled him with mixed emotions, the biggest of which was feeling as if he wasn't keeping up his end of the bargain. But as much as he wanted to throw his hands in the air and ask what the point of wearing one was in the first place, he felt grateful for that key multiple times over the last several weeks when he'd needed to remove it for various medical reasons, not the least of which was an MRI.

He'd explained everything to his boss, and the captain was being enormously supportive regarding his schedule. If he had long doctor's appointments, he could delay sketch appointments until later in the day and sometimes evenings. He was given free rein regarding his schedule and was told that if a solid work week was too much, they could work on the paperwork for short-term disability.

Knowing disability leave was inevitable for him, the more it looked like the meds were no longer going to be enough, he wanted to delay it if possible so he didn't use too much of it. As he never used much vacation, he had enough accrued that he was able to use that for medical appointments and, if he was honest, rest time when he had pushed himself to his limits. But with the schedule changes in his job, the medical appointments, the continued tattoo appointments he maintained, and doing his best to keep his scheduled sessions with his Dom going, Sebastian was at his wit's end.

His exhaustion was such that he'd decided to use a couple days vacation after the holiday leave he was given. He'd gotten the idea from Braden when he mentioned in a text that he was looking forward to taking several days off over the coming holidays. He'd stayed in close contact with his new friend though they hadn't seen each other much since he'd visited Catharsis on Black

Friday. They'd texted and talked over the phone many times, but he didn't have the time to spare to get together with him that often.

He'd also belatedly realized that Braden was the protective sort, and when the questions began about him being sick or not looking well, he'd told his friend he had a couple doctors' appointments, and that he'd be pretty busy during the time leading up to the holiday before he could take a few days' holiday vacation. If he'd made it sound like he had big holiday plans, all the better. He liked to avoid those questions, and he figured the fact that he was using the time to rest was plan enough for him not to be lying.

The day before Christmas Eve and halfway through his last work day before vacation, Braden had called. He grinned as he answered, "Hey, you! What's up?"

He could hear the answering grin in Braden's voice when he replied, "Not much, but I know you're about to go on vacation yourself, and I wasn't sure if you were headed out of town to see your family or if your family was coming to see you, so I didn't want to interrupt."

Sebastian deftly avoided answering that by trying to joke and distract his friend. "You're so damn nosy. Get to the point already."

Braden snorted out a laugh. "Will you be family free on New Year's Eve?"

Evasive as ever, Sebastian replied, "Hmm, I might be able to shake myself loose, what's going on?"

"There's a big New Year's Eve party I was invited to, and I'm allowed to invite whoever I want. Will you come with me?"

A New Year's Eve party? He'd never been to one before and his heart rate picked up at the prospect. "Really?!"

After a pause, Braden's incredulous voice came over the line. "What do you mean, really? Yes! I want to see you. I've missed you."

He grinned wide at that, knowing it was the truth and he felt the same way. "I've missed you, too. Yeah, I can probably make it. What time?"

"Yay! Okay, I think it starts around seven or eight p.m., not sure. I'll get back to you with the time and location."

"All right, sounds good. Talk to you soon and Merry Christmas."

"You too, bye!"

"Bye!"

He hung up the phone and stared at it for several beats. He jumped in his chair when his captain's voice called out from his office door. "What're you still doing here? And what's put that smile on your face?"

"Uh, working? And nothing, really. A friend just called, that's all."

"Well, knock it off. There's no smiling around here near the holidays, Sebastian, especially when I tell you to leave early. You have no more appointments today, and there's no need for you to stay. Have a good week off. Get the rest you need and we'll sort everything else out when you get back."

"Really?"

"Yes, really. Get outta here. I don't wanna see your face until next year."

Sebastian laughed at his boss's faux anger and nodded. "Yes, sir. Thanks so much and Merry Christmas."

"You too, son."

It was a Friday and as Christmas Eve was the next day, he didn't schedule any tattoos for Saturday, and he wasn't scheduled with Gideon either because it was the holiday. He had time on his hands, but no energy in which to do anything, so he went home.

After a bit of rest and binge-watching some really awful television, he decided to get out his little miniature Christmas tree and set it up in his bedroom on top of the dresser that was just below his wide window at the back of his house. It was his only foray into Christmas decorating, and it didn't come out every year. It depended on his mood, but since he had some time off, he figured he could be a bit festive and get into the holiday spirit.

He baked half a batch of snickerdoodles, knowing he'd never eat enough of them before they went stale, and watched a movie on Netflix. It was Friday night. What the fuck was he going to do for a week? There was only so much sleeping he could do, no matter how exhausted he was. He thought about showing up for work on Monday, or scheduling some tattoos, but he had a barrage of medical tests spread out later in the week that would keep him fairly busy after he was able to get plenty of rest.

He was getting increasingly nervous going outside of his home as the seizures increased in frequency and length. Having them in public was about as mortifying as you can get. Rather than helping and making him feel productive, going to work, tattooing, and especially going to see Gideon, were now an extreme source of anxiety. And the more anxiety he felt, the more becoming a recluse sounded like a good plan. He could have anything he wanted delivered, so he decided he'd order in and even get his groceries delivered.

Sitting around and eating sounded like a good idea. He was down a solid fifteen pounds, and he hadn't had any to spare in the first place. The mirror showed a gaunt, grayed-out version of himself, and he knew that come Tuesday night, if he kept his appointment with Gideon, he'd be asking more about what was going on. Sebastian didn't look forward to that, as he never made a habit of lying. He'd just have to be vague and tell Gideon he didn't want to talk about it.

When Christmas Day rolled around, he wasn't feeling well, but he passed that off as feeling cooped up and needing to get out. He made himself a breakfast sandwich he had no hopes of finishing and filled his to-go mug with coffee. He bundled himself up and packed his supplies so he could head to the park and sit at a picnic table and draw.

It was fifty degrees out, and on a normal day he'd feel chilled at that temperature, he ran cold anyway, but being down fifteen pounds had him bundling up in long johns, a beanie, and a scarf with his heavy coat. He picked a table that was in the sun and just closed his eyes, enjoying the warmth on his face. He ate a couple bites of his sandwich, drank his coffee, and then pulled out his sketchpad. It had been a long time since he'd drawn for fun and anytime he could practice with both hands and come up with new designs was a bonus.

He'd been there a good hour before his energy started to flag. He gathered his things into his messenger bag, hooked his empty coffee mug onto a carabiner, and stood to throw the rest of his sandwich in the trash. The pain in his chest hit hard and fast and he gasped for breath, turning the heads of those few that had gathered at the other picnic benches to enjoy the sun. Clutching his chest, he took deep breaths, and the panic set in when the tightness was so great he couldn't breathe in deep enough. When he reached the bench and tried to sit down, his weakened arm wouldn't hold him, and he fell on the ground.

The edges of his vision were getting blurry, and he was too panicked to try to calm himself down to help with his breathing. The more he thought about his chest tightness and breathlessness, the harder it was to get any air. He was dimly aware of voices around him and the words nine-one-one and ambulance, but he couldn't concentrate then everything went black.

The next thing he knew he was being strapped to a wheeled stretcher. Someone off to the side said, "Don't forget his bag."

He felt the bag being placed between his legs on the stretcher, and he was being bumped and jostled all the way back to the ambulance which had pulled onto the walking path relatively close to the picnic benches. Blackness consumed him again until he felt someone pulling on his arm and heard, "Medical alert bracelet lists epilepsy. Sir? Sir, can you hear me?"

He turned to look at the woman and realized she was talking to him. He blinked when his vision became blurry and blinked again. She spoke a little louder. "Sir? Can you tell us if you're on any anticonvulsants?"

He closed his eyes, rolling the question around and around in his head. He had an answer, and then it went away. Another one popped in, and that one faded as well. A vision of the bottle he'd held in his hand that morning floated by, and he grasped at it, bringing it back. "Di…" clearing his throat, he tried again, "Dilantin."

"Very good, sir. We're almost there, just try. . ." That was all he heard before he blacked out again.

Coming to, he was in a brightly lit emergency room bay and just that fact alone had his heart racing, nausea roiling, and a cold sweat breaking out over his whole body. A beautiful woman was approaching the side of his bed with an iPad in her hand, her white coat had Nisha Patel, M.D. and under that Emergency Medicine embroidered on it. She looked up from the tablet and frowned in concern. "Sebastian? I'm Dr. Patel, you look a bit panicked. Are you all right?"

He was confused and angry at his constantly recurring reactions to all things hospital related. He shook his head. "No. I… Um, how did I get here? When can I be released?"

"Not for a while yet, I'm afraid. An ambulance picked you up from the park, do you remember that? Glad your medical alert bracelet was a USB. We love it when that happens. Got all your information at our fingertips. We've placed a call into our on-call neurologist."

Sebastian's brows drew together in frustration. So much for getting the hell out of there. "I… I think I couldn't breathe. My chest hurt. Did I pass out because I didn't have enough oxygen?"

"No. They got you stabilized in the ambulance. Most anticonvulsants have fainting as a side effect, but couple that with the chest tightness and trouble breathing side effects, and it was the perfect storm for you to lose consciousness. Looks like that new medication isn't your best option."

Sebastian nodded, feeling moderately better but just being in the hospital had his stress levels skyrocketing by the minute, instead of calming down. "When can I be released?"

"You already asked that, Sebastian. We need to hear back from the neurologist to see what the next steps are with your meds. Keaton is going to be your nurse, he'll be here in just a moment. I'll be back when I've spoken with neuro."

He nodded, blushing at having asked the same question twice. He was so goddamn confused. The day was going down as his worst Christmas ever. He glanced around the room and was relieved to see his messenger bag. He threw back the blanket to get it, but realized he was wearing a hospital gown and pulled that blanket back over him. A cute, slightly chubby nurse came in, smiling so big he couldn't help but answer it with a small smile of his own. "Sebastian, hi! I'm Keaton, your nurse." He leaned in conspiratorially and whispered, "I've seen you at Catharsis before, right? I'm a fairly new sub there, but I know I've seen you."

Sebastian blushed and nodded. Feeling reassured when the nurse continued, "Don't worry, I won't say a word, I just wanted to introduce myself. Maybe we can hang out at the club together next time you're there. Unless you're collared and can't."

Sebastian blushed again and reached up to pull his necklace out. "I am, but it's just a short-term contract."

Keaton smiled sheepishly. "Of course, you are. You're too gorgeous not to be." He shrugged. "Well, if you're allowed to, maybe we can chat next time. Um, what was I... Oh yeah, you were getting up to get your bag? Here, let me."

Feeling completely out of his element with the nurse's comments, he just nodded his thanks as he took the bag. He looked up again when Keaton asked, "Do you need us to call anyone?"

When Keaton glanced down at his collar, the thought of him calling Gideon had him feeling sick to his stomach. He shook his head and, more loudly than he'd intended, said, "No!"

Keaton's eyes popped wide. "All right."

"I'm sorry. It's just... It's not like that with us. We just have scenes together, mostly."

"Okay, I understand. Anyone else? Friends or family?"

Sebastian shook his head and busied himself with opening his bag. When

Keaton got the hint, he said he needed to check his vitals and went about doing his job. As he was leaving, Sebastian murmured, "Thank you, Keaton. Next time I'm at the club, I'll look for you."

The smile he got in response made him happy that he'd said it, but he wasn't sure when he'd be back to the club. With what had happened the last time he went, he didn't have any desire to go there unless Gideon invited him to go, and he doubted that would happen. He pulled out his sketch pad and began to work on the last drawing he'd been working on.

He was there for an hour before Dr. Patel returned. "Sebastian, Dr. Chen, the on-call neuro, is a partner at your neurologist's office and was able to look at your files. He'd like to keep you here for observation and to give you IV anticonvulsants to stabilize you. They want to run a battery of tests, including an MRI, with contrast medium this time, to get a better look at the angioma. They've ordered a head CT, and PET and SPECT images as well. He also wants to do an EEG to determine the focus of your seizure area and evaluate your brain function. We'll work to schedule those but you might be here several days."

"But, I have all of those scheduled for later in the week. Can't I just go home and go in for the tests at the scheduled time?"

"I'm afraid not. Your reactions to the last several drugs have not been good. They're running out of options and don't feel it's safe for you to go unobserved. For several of the tests, you need to be twelve hours from your last convulsion, so while we'll do our best to get as many tests done as soon as possible, some of them have stipulations. The faster we can get some answers with the scans, the sooner we'll have some solutions for you."

Sebastian's shoulders slumped, and he nodded. God how he hated being in the hospital. His mother had been a hypochondriac. The fact that he'd had a whole lot of health issues only made it worse, and he was constantly in the hospital emergency room or his doctor's office for whatever it was she was convinced he had. He'd had an aversion to doctor's offices and hospitals ever since, and being forced to stay in one was a nightmare he hadn't been prepared for.

He'd been moved up to the ICU after having the head CT. Everyone was being so nice to him while he waited, nurses stopping in to check on him off and on. He'd even been brought a couple Christmas cookies after he'd had the MRI later that afternoon. He felt bad for the staff having to work on Christmas.

The night was uneventful after that, and Monday rolled around before he realized he was the worst pet owner ever.

Slap and Tickle. Fuck. What the hell was he supposed to do about getting them fed? He'd never call Gideon and couldn't put Braden in any situation that he couldn't tell his husband who would then tell his brother. The only person he had left was Zoe. He knew she'd do it. He just hated what he'd have to ask of her. Knowing there was nothing for it, he dug in his bag for his phone.

Keaton had come in and given him his number before he'd been taken up to ICU, so he'd put yet another number into his phone. Another new possible friend perhaps? Where were they all coming from, and why now? He thought it strange that he'd basically been without anyone for most of his life, and now he was plugging in more numbers than he'd added in years. It was disconcerting to say the least. And also made him paranoid the other shoe was gonna drop when his health got worse and worse.

Pulling his phone out of his bag, he realized it was dead. Chuckling to himself, he picked up the phone beside his hospital bed and dialed her number. There was a benefit to having hardly any friends, he guessed. He didn't have many numbers to remember, so he was able to recall them all fairly easily.

"Hello?"

"Zoe, it's Sebastian."

"Hey, Sebastian. How was your Christmas?"

"Um, okay. How was yours?"

"It was great. I spent it with my sister, as usual. Hey, I'm just about to go on the clock here at the café. What's up?"

Sebastian cleared his throat nervously and dove right in. "I need a huge favor from you. But I can't have you asking me questions right now, and I can't have you telling anyone what's going on."

"Sebastian, are you a government spook?"

Sebastian couldn't help but laugh at her ridiculousness. "I just might be. And listen, I'd owe you big. It's gonna be a pain in the ass, and I really do mean it about no asking and no telling."

"Okay, on one condition."

"Name it."

"Will you tell me all about it later?"

Sebastian paused and thought about that. The thought of it made his stomach plummet, but at the same time, it might be good to have someone know what was going on with him in case he needed help again. Not that he'd make a habit out of asking for it. God knows being a burden was anathema to him. He'd been a burden to his parents, and he'd had it pointed out to him from a very young age. It was the last thing he wanted to be to a friend. Finally, he answered her, "Yeah. I'll tell you."

"Okay then. Tell me what you need from me."

"When you're done with your shift at the café, are you free?"

"Yeah, I don't have any plans tonight."

"Could you come by the hospital to—"

"WHAT?!"

"...get my house key, and go by and feed Slap and Tickle?"

"Sebastian!"

He sighed. "No questions, remember?"

"Jesus. Are your parents there at least?"

He paused for a fraction too long, and she said his name again. Finally, he said, "No."

"No? What do you mean, no?"

"I haven't seen my parents in about nine years, Zoe."

"But... What did you do for Christmas? I thought you took some time off."

"I took some time off for the reasons I'm in the hospital. Listen, I—"

"And for Christmas?"

"Uh, I went to the park for a while and— "

"Sebastian, are you telling me you were alone on Christmas?"

He cleared his throat and admitted, "I'm alone every holiday, Zoe. It's not a big deal. Look—"

She made a sound of frustration and asked, "But, why didn't you call me? You could have spent Thanksgiving and Christmas with me!"

"Zoe. You gotta stop interrupting me. I said no questions, and you've already asked a gazillion."

"A gazillion?"

He chuckled. "At least. I'm in the ICU, room three forty-nine. Let me give you the phone number. My phone's dead." He rattled off the number and continued, "I don't know when I'll be in and out of the room for more tests yet, so you can call if you need to, but I'll leave my house key at the nurses' station closest to my room if I'm gonna be gone later. Okay?"

He heard her sigh. "Sebastian, I'm worried about you."

Warmth filled him at that unexpected response. "That's. . . that's really nice, Zoe. Thank you. I'm sure everything will be just fine. See you later, all right?"

"All right, Sebastian. Bye."

"Bye."

But he wasn't sure. In fact, as the days went by, he was becoming less and less sure of anything. Later that morning, he was taken to radiology for the PET and SPECT scans, and after that, there was a lot more waiting. Strangely enough, he was feeling a bit better and was hopeful the anticonvulsants they had him on in the hospital were the right kind to allow him to leave sooner rather than later.

When Zoe arrived later in the day, she'd taken one look at him and burst into tears. Not having a lot of experience with females crying for him—hell *anyone* crying for him for that matter—he didn't know how to react, so he apologized in general hoping that would help.

Sobbing, she approached him and hugged him tight. "Why are you apologizing?"

"Because you burst into tears when you looked at me?"

"You don't look well, Sebastian."

"I know. I'm sorry."

She huffed. "Stop apologizing. Why didn't you call me before it got this bad?"

She was still crying. Why was she still crying? That wasn't what he'd expected at all. He had no control over his automatic response. "I didn't want to bother you."

She gave him a withering look. Christ almighty, he'd botched it up. Those tears hit some sort of internal panic button that was completely out of his control, and he found himself reaching out to her so she could continue to cry on his shoulder.

"This is why I didn't call you. I don't like making you so upset."

"I'm just upset because you're sick, Sebastian."

"I know. I'm sorry."

She rolled her eyes and proceeded to ask him more questions, and he told her what he felt comfortable with. He was grateful she'd stopped by because she was doing him a huge favor, and she'd even brought her extra charger to leave for him to charge his phone. Not to mention, she drove back to his house, fed the cats, leaving enough for a couple days, and brought him back a change of clothes and some dinner, which he technically just picked at but was able to get down a small portion.

The next morning, he was transferred to a step-down unit which made him feel like he was getting closer and closer to being sent home until his own neurologist walked in, a frown creasing his brow. "Good morning. How are you feeling, Sebastian?"

Sebastian shrugged, knowing his frown meant he didn't have good news. "As good as can be expected, I guess, with everything going on."

His doctor nodded and continued, "Unfortunately, we can't get you in for the EEG over on the neurology floor until tomorrow morning. So, we'll be keeping you here for one more night for observation then releasing you after that final test if you're stable. We've got you on a different anticonvulsant, and so far, so good, according to your nurses."

When he nodded his understanding, the doctor continued, "Sebastian, even if these meds are helpful in slowing down your seizures, I don't think you'll ever go back to the time where they were being controlled nearly completely. We have very few viable options left for you, and the ones we do have are all surgical in nature. I'll be working with the partners in my practice to come up with our best plan of attack once we have all your test results, and we'll go from there. As soon as we decide what's best, we'll talk to you about your options. We'll want to move fast once the decision is made."

Sebastian took a deep breath. "What do you mean by fast?"

"I'd prefer to move within the next month, but I know you'll need to arrange time off and work with our insurance manager to get the approvals. We'll get your EEG results tomorrow after the tests then I'll come and see you before you're released."

They finished talking, and his doctor left. That afternoon he slept for several hours then had a short visit from Zoe. As they chatted, he had to hand it to her, she didn't ask too many questions and had kept his confidence. After she left, his nurse brought him a tray for dinner, and he moved it aside, knowing he couldn't put off making the call he'd been dreading since he woke up.

Unplugging his phone from the charger, he dialed.

"Bastian."

His Dom's low rumble when he said his name sent a shiver throughout his body. "Sir."

"How are you, boy? How was your Christmas?"

"All right, Sir. Yours?"

"Great. Thank you. I'm looking forward to spending time with you later. I've missed seeing you."

Overwhelmed by those words, Sebastian fell silent, not knowing how to respond.

"Boy?"

He cleared his throat, utterly wrecked. "Thank you, Sir. I've missed seeing you as well. But, um, I'm…I'm calling to cancel tonight. I'm really sorry. I'm still pretty sick and am going to see a specialist tomorrow morning."

"Jesus, Bastian. Do you know what's wrong yet?"

"Yeah. They're pinpointing what's going on. I'm just exhausted and am not feeling up to it tonight. I'm sorry."

"Why don't I come over? I can bring dinner and see you, make sure you're okay."

His shoulders slumped, and he glanced at the tray of plastic hospital food. "I've got dinner right here. I'm just going to go ahead and eat and go to sleep early. I'm really sorry, Sir."

"It's all right, boy. I just want you to get better."

A tear escaped, and he hoped his voice wasn't too wobbly when he whispered, "Me too, Sir."

"Bastian? You okay?"

He pasted on a smile, hoping it came through on the line. "Yes. I'm fine. I'll call if I'm going to be unable to make it on Thursday. I'm hoping I'll be feeling a bit better. Less run-down."

"Okay, Bastian. Sleep well. Goodnight."

"Goodnight, Sir."

He hung up and sat, staring at the wall in front of him, emotion overwhelming him. He knew he'd have to end their contract early. There was no way around it. Things kept getting worse, and he'd need time for his surgical recovery, or at least, he hoped he'd get the chance to recover. It was probably for the best. He knew he was in love with his Dom, and those feelings would never be returned. He'd been warned from the beginning. He needed to end it before the pain of losing him became unbearable.

The next morning finally rolled around, the EEG was taken care of, and a vague conversation concluded with his doctor as well. He had a new appointment to discuss his surgical options in his doctor's office on Thursday. He got dressed in fresh clothes after taking a shower in the en suite, gently pulled his messenger bag over his head and waited in the chair by his bed until a nurse came in with the dreaded wheelchair. Though, in all honesty, his legs were a bit shaky, and even with the days in the hospital bed, he was exhausted.

Sitting in the wheelchair in front of the elevator to go down to the lobby, he heard a familiar voice and his whole body tensed. He surreptitiously tugged up his hood and kept his eyes on his bag. The nurse pushed him into the elevator and turned him around to face the open door. The voices stopped, and he saw a pair of feet stop just outside of the elevator door. Not now, please. Not now. He cringed when he heard the confused tone of voice, "Sebastian?"

Looking up, knowing he couldn't avoid it, he met Dr. McCade's gaze then looked quickly down at his bag again. Things went from bad to worse when Finn said, "Jessie, I've got this. I'll get him down to the lobby for you."

"Okay, Doc. Thanks. Bye, Sebastian. Good luck with your surgery!"

Traitor, he thought, as she walked out of the elevator. And of course, she'd mentioned the surgery. Fuck. He waved halfheartedly at her and glanced at Finn, not knowing what to say. The steady, concerned gaze ripped at something in his chest, and he looked away. Finn hit the lobby button and down they went, not saying a word. But instead of wheeling him out of the automatic doors, he wheeled him over to a small, secluded seating area, partially hidden by several potted ficus trees. He turned Sebastian's wheelchair to face an upholstered loveseat and sat opposite him, elbows on his knees, eyes kind, patient as could be.

He looked away again and finally spoke. "I know you can look up my chart and find out why I've been here. I hope you won't."

"Even if it wasn't against hospital policy to check patients' charts for your own gain, I wouldn't do it. It's only my business if you make it so. I'm worried about you, that's all. You don't look well, Sebastian."

He shook his head and looked down at his lap, picking at a loose string on his bag. "I don't want to talk about it yet. If..." He gulped and tried again, finally looking at Finn again. "If I pay you a dollar and ask you to be my doctor, can I ask you to respect doctor/patient confidentiality?"

The sad look in Finn's face only made him feel worse. Finn shook his head, and Sebastian's stomach dropped. But the man said, "Sebastian, you don't need to do that. If you're asking me not to tell anyone that I saw you, I wouldn't—"

"That's what I'm asking," he said so forcefully he had to look away in embarrassment as his cheeks flamed.

"Okay. I won't tell anyone, Sebastian."

He nodded and began to stand. Nearly tripping over the foot rests, his legs wobbly from disuse, Finn caught him easily and helped him gain his footing. He gently extricated himself from the doctor's hold and made his way around the seating area. He looked back at Finn and said thank you, continuing on his way. He thought he was free until he felt a gentle hand on his shoulder by the automatic doors. As he turned, Finn held out his hand, a business card in it.

"Please, call me if you need anything, all right? No questions asked. Truly. If you need help, I'll be there."

He nodded quickly, took the card, and turned away before Finn could see the raw emotion on his face. As he walked outside toward the waiting Lyft car he'd ordered, he tucked the card into his pocket, realizing belatedly that his contact list was growing fuller. But instead of feeling happy about that, it just made him feel empty and, ironically, more alone.

Chapter 26

GIDEON

Hanging up the phone, Gideon looked at it in his hand for several minutes. He decided right then to ignore his boy's wishes and go visit him to see for himself if Sebastian was okay. He knew it wasn't smart. He knew getting in even deeper with his sub was a recipe for disaster, but over the last several weeks, he'd been pulled from opposite ends of the spectrum so many times he felt like he was experiencing emotional whiplash.

There was the overwhelming need for him to take care of Sebastian: mentally, physically, and emotionally. And every day that need grew stronger. But there was also a growing desire to keep himself emotionally isolated, knowing he could never offer Sebastian everything he so desperately needed and deserved. He grew increasingly frustrated with the situation, an out of control feeling that he didn't enjoy one bit. Control was something he maintained in all things, and his lack of it where Sebastian was concerned grew alarming in its breadth.

But none of that frustration, none of that desire for distance could have convinced him to stop himself going over to check on his sick boy. Something told him this sickness wasn't a surprise to Sebastian. The bone-deep weariness, the sadness in his eyes, pointed to him being sidelined by an eventuality he'd seen coming, had expected, in fact. But he couldn't back that up with fact, it was just a feeling.

His heart ached for the sweet sub he'd fallen for. He'd had to watch—with barely any information to go on and ever increasing apprehension—his boy's light slowly dim. His beautiful skin had grown pale, the brightness in his eyes had dulled, the smiles that always lit up his face had decreased ten-fold. He tried to hide it every day, but those fake smiles were miles apart from the genuine grins of happiness he'd gotten at the beginning of their contract.

He'd decreased their hard and rough play. They still did most of what they'd done before, but he was undoubtedly gentler and less willing to push his boy's limits, no longer sure where they were anymore and not willing to chance it. His sub still flew, and he was still able to reach his own high, but the energy at which they'd played had flagged. It took much longer to give Sebastian aftercare, and he often rested longer afterwards.

He felt like their scenes had regressed as they would had they both aged twenty years. He literally had to stop himself from asking the boy personal questions; questions about his health, his life, his family and friends. He had to stop himself from telling him what to do, from calling on his own family doctor, from dialing Finn every goddamn time he visited.

Was he losing his sub, not only mentally, but physically? It seemed like things started going downhill right around the time of Sebastian's fall. But he couldn't be sure of that. Pulling up outside Sebastian's house, he walked up the steps and knocked on the door. His self-reflection on the drive over having distracted him from what he was doing so much he didn't even remember the drive.

When no one answered the door, he pulled out his key and opened it. The house smelled a bit stale. The kittens, once so tiny, came running. They were still much smaller than they'd be full grown, but they'd filled out quite a bit, so much so that Gideon laughed as they tumbled over each other, their round bellies showing as they fell over for belly rubs.

The light was on in the kitchen so he walked that way. There was a plate still out, and a bit of a mess left there, which confused him. Sebastian was fairly tidy and had always picked up after himself immediately. Walking back towards the front of the house, he walked quietly up the stairs, not wanting to scare Sebastian, but not wanting to wake him, either. His bedroom, however, was empty. The cat's food dishes in the bathroom filled with three times the food Sebastian normally left out.

A growing unease took the form of anger, rather than frustration or worry. If he was angry, he wouldn't be scared for his sub's wellbeing. If he was angry, he wouldn't be hurt that his boy had lied to him. If he was angry, he wouldn't be letting his uncertainty in his standing in Sebastian's life make him feel out of control. He checked the other bedroom just to be sure he wasn't going off halfcocked, and then got himself the hell out of there, too angry to think clearly, too frustrated to make the call that would clear up any confusion.

What he wanted to do was drive to the club, find an available sub, and get out his frustrations with a hard pounding until they both came screaming, if only to prove that he could. He scoffed at himself, knowing he'd never do something like that; not to an innocent, unsuspecting sub, and definitely not while he was in a contract. Instead, he forced himself to drive home, slowly, and go about his day, his week.

When Thursday rolled around, as he suspected, Sebastian called and begged off their plans, claiming he was still sick. And damned if he didn't sound it, and deep down, Gideon knew that he was, but the fact that he had to wonder if the boy would be home if he went to visit him that night frustrated him to no end. Their trust in each other was paramount, and he was losing that.

He wanted, no needed, to give Sebastian the benefit of the doubt, but having him go MIA when he said he was sick and couldn't come see him was weighing on his mind. Not to mention the fact that he wouldn't see the boy until the following Tuesday because it was a holiday weekend and they spent those apart.

He had to slow down and think about his reasons for feeling angry. The only time Boone and any of his other past subs had made him angry was when they were outside of any Dom/sub context. He normally didn't have that level of emotional involvement with a sub, and he knew he'd gotten in too deep. And if *he* had, what could be said about Sebastian? The boy had been adamant that he wasn't made for long-term relationships, but if anyone was made for something, that boy was made for someone to love him, deeply, and take care of him.

He had to remind himself on a regular basis—lest he forget he'd never be the kind of man Sebastian deserved—that he was a killer. For a huge portion of his life, he'd been trained and used to kill. It didn't matter that it was for the government. It didn't matter that the men—always men, never women or children, his one stipulation—deserved it. It didn't matter that he'd been ordered to do it.

Those reasons didn't matter because when all was said and done, he didn't regret doing it, he didn't feel bad about the lives taken, and he didn't think of any of the dead men's family or friends. When it came down to it, he'd done his job, yes, but there was a part of him, deep down, that might have even begun to enjoy it. And a man that could so easily take a life wouldn't ever be the type of man that could settle down and make a life with someone else.

So, instead of spending that evening with his sub, he'd spent it working, and the following night, and a portion of the night after that, as well. And when Teddy Forrester had tried to slip past Khaleo again on New Year's Eve—perhaps assuming it would be so busy, he'd be able to enter unnoticed—he'd freely admit to being quite a bit rougher than it probably warranted.

Dragging him by the collar of his coat to an office just behind Khaleo's desk and throwing him up against the wall probably shouldn't have felt so good. But his nerves were raw and working out at Vaughn's gym, The Knockout, both Friday and Saturday afternoons, sparring with some top-level fighters, had apparently only taken the edge off.

"Sit down, Teddy."

"How dare y—"

"Stop right there. I don't want to hear your bullshit."

"Who do you think y—"

"How's your friend, Teddy? You know, the one that you brought in here? The one who drugged and beat my boy? How's he faring these days?"

When the man lost all color at the mention of his buddy that had lost everything in the span of roughly thirty days including his business, his home, and his wife, Gideon smiled and said, "That's who I think I am. I also think I'm the man that knows your home address where, right now, your pretty, young, pregnant wife most likely thinks you're at a business dinner, schmoozing a client. Or was it some other excuse you gave her? You're aware that the contract you signed here stipulates that it's my right as the owner to record anything and everything I deem appropriate to record, right?"

He let that sink in, and when it did, he nodded his head and continued, "That's right. Now it's coming to you, isn't it? And what happens if wife number two finds out about your predilections?" He watched as the man rubbed his shaking hand over his mouth. "Ah! There it is! Yes. That cushy job you have, working directly under her father, the one that allows you to keep her in the style to which she's accustomed, might not be there, come morning time."

"Please... Please don't... I'll never come back. I promise. You'll never see me again."

"I know that, Teddy. Believe me, I do. But the thing is, I'm angry that you brought that scum into my house. I'm angry that you felt the need to come back twice now to try to get back into a club that had banned you. And although I care a great deal about all the subs in my club, I'm *particularly* angry that of all the subs he could have drugged, it was MY boy he did it to. And make no mistake, Teddy, I think you're equally culpable. So, you gotta ask yourself, was it worth it?"

"Fuck. No. Look, I'll do anything. I have a lot of money, and if it's not enough, I have access to more. Please."

Gideon made a tsking sound and shook his head. "You're operating under the false assumption that I need money. You're also operating under the assumption that my boy is just a boy. But let me tell you who that boy is, he's *everything* to me, and you invited someone into *my* house to drug him, to beat him, and if he'd had time, to rape him. It would behoove you to get the fuck outta my club and to stay the hell away. And even if you do all that? I still might pull that trigger."

The man was sweating, pale as a ghost, and swallowing convulsively like he was gonna vomit on Gideon's clean floors. "If I were you, Teddy, I'd clean up my act. I'd stay faithful to your beautiful wife, I'd do my best to become best friends with her dad, I'd do everything I could to be a wonderful father to that baby you've got coming. I'd become an upstanding member of the community, one that donates his time and his money. That's what I'd do… If I were you. Because I'm gonna be watching, Teddy."

At that point, all the man could do was nod. After staring at him a minute longer, he grabbed him by the collar of his jacket, pulled him from the room and down the hall to the exit door, tossing him out on his ass, literally.

Seething, he slammed the door and paced back and forth in the hallway until his heart rate slowed, and his anger receded. Somewhat. Knowing he was going to be at least an hour late for his parents' New Year's Eve party, he made his way out to let Khaleo know he was leaving and was in his SUV less than five minutes later.

The drive to his parents' house in Sea Cliff was uneventful. His anger had abated, marginally, but he was still tense and quite honestly not looking forward to a festive holiday party. But it was his family, not to mention Zavier had sent a cryptic text earlier in the day about needing to talk to him at the party later that night, so he'd set it aside for a while and do his best to relax, or at least fake it well enough to avoid an inquisition.

The white Christmas lights were still up on the outside of the house, the trees, and the shrubs. In the huge bay window to the right of the front door, the

Christmas tree was still up as well. He parked on the street to avoid getting blocked in and got out of the SUV.

He thought about entering from the front door but decided against it. He'd ease his way in from the side, say hello to Buckley and Thor who were most likely playing together in the backyard. If he was honest with himself, he wished he could stay out back with the dogs and avoid being social altogether.

He made a kissy noise and both dogs made a beeline from the backyard. Buckley, the more boisterous of the two, planting his paws on Gideon's hips looking for the first hello. Thor hung back, tail wagging but much more contained, his training obvious. He gave them both some attention then made his way to the side entrance.

Hanging his jacket in the mudroom, he walked down the hall and entered his father's office. He texted his brother to meet him there and strolled toward his dad's antique liquor cabinet. Getting out two tumblers, he poured them both two fingers of the aged Macallan Sherry Oak Scotch that was his dad's favorite. He sat in one of the leather chairs in a seating area in the middle of the room in front of the large desk his dad sometimes used when he wasn't in the office.

He leisurely sipped the whisky, knowing his brother would extricate himself soon enough. One finger down and he heard the door open. Zavier walked in, a much too serious expression on his face for a holiday party, making him sit up and pay attention. He nudged the other tumbler towards his brother as he sat across from him.

"We think we've found him."

"You think?"

"Yeah. We're still working through the details, but it looks like he spent some time in the Philippines and later in Latin America, feeding munitions through to several guerrilla insurgent groups within Colombia. We lost him for a while but followed the money and finally picked him back up in Jordan which was a fucking mess last year with weapons stolen and funneled to arms merchants on the black market."

Gideon whistled low in surprise. "I think I read something about that. Guy gets around."

Zavier took a drink of his scotch. "He does. And, ironically enough, most recently, he blipped in the States, but it's not his normal MO so it may be just that, a blip, before he headed back out of the country."

Gideon tilted his head. "It's almost as if he has a death wish."

Zavier looked up from his glass, his gaze steady when he answered, "Perhaps you can help him with that."

Surprised by that sentiment coming from his brother, he raised a brow and replied, "Perhaps I can."

"We're trying to get his last location, and I've got several guys on that right now. He had people working for him in Latin America, but his network was relatively small. We believe he might be working *for* someone with a bigger reach this time around. Not exactly a runner, but not the leader by any means."

Gideon shrugged. "That might actually make things easier."

Zavier nodded. "My thoughts exactly. I wanted to give you a heads-up tonight because we're not looking at weeks or even days, we're looking at hours before we have the final pieces of the puzzle. I'm not sure how fast you wanna move on this, but knowing you, it'll be immediately, so be prepared to go wheels up when we've got what you need."

Zavier shared a few more salient details, and they finished their scotch. He told his brother to head back out to the party, he was going to do a little planning. What he really wanted was a moment alone to think. He had no idea how long the op would take. He could be gone for a week or three months. What he did know is that he wasn't going to let the chance to take the guy down slip through his fingers because more than likely, he wouldn't get another one.

He'd been the one to visit the family members of every single one of Lars's victims from his team. He'd had to see the devastated parents clutching onto each other's hands when he expressed his condolences, the tears on the children's faces as they watched their fathers' caskets get lowered into the ground, and he'd had to hug and console the grieving widows that were left behind.

Adrenaline and anger rolled through him like a tidal wave. The fact that he was going to be able to take the man down finally sinking in. He mentally warned himself to slow down and plan meticulously. Going off halfcocked wasn't going to get him anywhere. He'd need to scout a place like he always did.

As he left the office, someone opened the bathroom door and walked out into the dimly lit hallway, closing the door behind him and leaning on it slightly as if gearing himself up for something. That someone wasn't supposed to be there. That someone was supposed to be too sick to be at a party. Gideon stilled, not believing what he was seeing.

The first thing that hit him, surprising him with its ferocity, was warmth and happiness at seeing his boy after so long. He was then hit with an overwhelming sense of relief that he was all right. And then a feeling of rightness. This was where his boy belonged, at a family gathering in his parents' house. But then he remembered that couldn't happen, and those thoughts vanished, replaced by anger. Anger that it couldn't happen, anger that he'd gotten in too deep, anger that the trust he'd had in his boy was slipping away.

Because, what the actual fuck? He'd been stood up twice that week and here his submissive was, at his parents' house, rubbing shoulders with his family and friends. Hadn't they talked about this? Hadn't they agreed they wouldn't mix their personal lives? Sebastian had agreed, and he'd stuck to that agreement, until now. What the hell was he thinking coming here?

He knew his emotions were too close to the surface. He was being irrational and letting his feelings take over. He'd been stressed out, worried sick, and emotionally wrung out for what seemed like weeks now and being knocked off his feet with his greatest desire when it was literally the *last* thing he'd expected was akin to being hit by a Mack truck. He needed to back away and regroup. He didn't know how to react, but he knew, he *knew* if he talked to Sebastian right then, it wouldn't go well.

He was about to turn and head out the way he'd come in, however, Sebastian glanced his way, the soft, fake smile he'd pasted on slipping from his face. Looking unsteady, he kept a hand on the bathroom door as he faced Gideon. Gideon turned his back on the boy and headed outside through the mudroom entrance, knowing Sebastian would follow.

Once outside, he walked towards the front of the house and stopped. Sebastian stood more than a foot away, looking too scared to get any closer. Yet one more thing that pissed him off. His boy crossed his arms over his chest self-consciously and said, "Hello, Sir."

Gideon narrowed his eyes and was about to say hello to him, but instead blurted out, "What are you doing here?"

What the fuck, Gideon?

Sebastian flinched and Gideon very nearly reached out, but held himself still. "I'm sorry. Braden invited me. I didn't—"

"We agreed not to mix our contract with our personal lives. I don't appreciate being blindsided by you being in my parents' house." He wanted to stop the words, to call them back, but something, some uncontrollable thing, kept him from it.

Gideon watched as Sebastian gulped and nodded. "I understand. I'm sorry, Sir. I didn't realize it was your family's party. He just gave me the address. I wouldn't have—"

Again, his mouth ran without thought. "And when you found out? Why didn't you leave?"

Sebastian reacted like he'd received a physical blow, and Gideon's heart broke. *Goddammit, what was he doing?*

But true to form, Sebastian acquiesced, nodding. "You're right. I'm sorry, Sir. I don't know what I was thinking. I should've left as soon as I found out. I'll go now." As his boy turned to leave, Gideon moved to follow him but stopped when Sebastian held up a shaking hand. "It's okay. You don't need to. . . I can see myself to my car. I really am sorry, Sir. It won't happen again."

His mind was screaming at him. The boy had really done nothing wrong. *NOTHING*! He wanted to tell Sebastian that he was in love with him more than he wanted to take his next breath. So why did he treat him like that? Why not just hug him, tell him he was happy to see him, ask him if he was all right, tell him to stay, introduce him properly to his parents? Because all those things were true!

But so was the fact that his boy had lied to him. So was the fact that his boy had blindsided him at a family party. So was the fact that he couldn't stay with Sebastian in the long term. Because what the fuck had he just talked to Zavier about? His brother would have the information Gideon needed, in hours. Information he'd be using to kill a man.

To. Kill. A. Man.

And without remorse. Not to mention all the others he'd killed. How could he, for one minute, think he could be the kind of man Sebastian needed, the kind he deserved? He was a killer. That was who and what he was. And the evil he had in him that allowed him to do the things he'd done would eventually snuff out the beauty of his boy. He was darkness and he was tainted.

No. He had to stop this now. He had to end it before he lost more of himself to Sebastian. Or worse, before Sebastian lost more of himself to him. He had to do it for them both. Determined to do just that, he followed Sebastian to his car on the street. Everything in his body was pulling him in the opposite direction. Everything in his soul was telling him to let Sebastian go tonight and to go see him in the morning, explain himself and get them back on course. But his mind, his mind knew what had to be done.

And so he continued, regardless of the force pushing him back so hard it felt like a physical thing. He continued and saw Sebastian drop his keys. Saw him scramble nervously to pick them up, pause and then glance back. Saw him realize he was coming and practically run in the opposite direction. God. He'd done that. He'd made his boy afraid of him. Something in Gideon broke, but he'd grieve later. Clenching his teeth, holding himself rigid, he approached and placed a gentle palm on Sebastian's shoulder, before he could get into his car.

And when his boy turned, trepidation in his eyes, knowledge of what was to come, he did nothing to assuage those fears. No, he stood there and he broke that boy's heart and he watched as everything bright and beautiful in the boy's eyes shattered and died. He watched as those now dead eyes looked away from him, avoiding his gaze. And he listened as the boy took the blame for every goddamn thing. As he worked hard to make sure Gideon knew that he understood. As he did his best to convince Gideon to go back inside and enjoy his family and friends.

Just when he thought he couldn't take anymore, his boy turned, made to get in the car, paused, and then turned back around with a gift bag in his hand. A fucking gift? Jesus, he couldn't take this. His boy then proceeded to try his goddamned hardest to joke about what he'd gotten Gideon. And as Sebastian finally got in his car to drive away, Gideon stepped forward as the door was closing and said, "Sebastian, wait…"

But his boy didn't hear him or pretended he didn't. And as the love of his life drove away, Gideon shattered, gift bag falling from his hand. A billion pieces of pain, anger, self-disgust, and self-hatred falling around him like sharp shards of glass, just waiting to cut him open, to make him bleed. But to bleed, he'd have to have a heart, and he no longer did. It had just left in that little rat trap of a car, and he knew he'd never get it back.

He let out a gut-wrenching, primal roar. Fisted his hair in his hands and curled in on himself before jackknifing up, hands now gripped behind his head as he began to move, walking aimlessly. Towards the house, away from the house, he didn't know. At least, not until he heard Braden's dismayed voice say, "Why did he leave? What have you done?"

Gideon lowered his arms, fingers now lax, strength having left him. "I ended it."

"You. . . What?! Why?"

He turned towards Braden who was standing in front of Zavier at the top of the stairs to the front door. He had his arms crossed over his chest, and he looked just as devastated as Gideon himself felt. "I didn't expect... I didn't... He wasn't supposed to be here."

"So, you ended it, and sent him away because he wasn't supposed to be here? What the fuck does that even mean, Gideon? And he was! He WAS supposed to be here. I invited him. I wanted to spend the holiday with my newest friend. The friend that was fucking alone on Thanksgiving, and Christmas Eve, and Christmas Day."

He didn't think he could hurt anymore. He didn't think it possible. And yet, he could, he could hurt so, so badly. Almost feeling sick with it, he managed, "What?" He shook his head. "No."

"Yes. I heard Zoe talking to him on the phone at work." Braden shook his head in disgust and swiped at his tears, angrily. "What is wrong with you?"

Braden turned and walked into the house, slamming the door. Zavier stared him down, anger and disappointment like he'd never seen directed at him, blazing in his eyes. He shook his head and folded his huge arms across his chest, the dappled light around him illuminating his tattoos, which just reminded him of the man he'd just run off. "Look, I don't know what's going on with you. But from what I could see through the window, that wasn't you. That's not the older brother I've looked up to all my life. You crushed that boy. God, the love he had for you." He shook his head again. "Every time your name was mentioned his face would light up. If you didn't see it, you were blind, brother."

"I'm not good enough for him. He needs a good man, Zavier. That's not me."

"Well, you got one thing right, but only one. You're not good enough for him, just like I'll never be good enough for Braden, but you know what? I'm gonna bust my ass for the rest of my fucking life to be good enough for my boy, to deserve him. And if you're not willing to do the same thing for yours, you're not the man I thought you were."

Gideon's shoulders slumped, and he shook his head, turning away from his brother, hands on his hips. When he turned back around, he tried to say something, but couldn't. There was nothing he could say to make what he'd just done okay. Nothing he could do to make up for the pain he'd caused. He closed his eyes and tilted his head up to the sky. The quiet of the night surrounding them both.

When he opened his eyes and looked back toward Zavier, he was surprised to see his brother had approached him. "You need to sort your shit out, Gideon. Get the info from my guys, do what you need to do to set your mind at ease, free yourself from the past. But you get back here and you fix this."

His brother turned, walked up the steps and entered the house. Knowing he couldn't be around anyone right now, he walked out to the street, picking up the gift bag as he walked by it on the way to his car, and left for home. He had a lot of shit to do to get ready to go, and his brother was right. He needed to sort the shit out in his head, deal with the ghosts of his past, before he could move forward.

Chapter 27

SEBASTIAN

W hen Saturday evening rolled around, Sebastian was feeling a bit better. He hadn't had a seizure in a full week, and he'd gotten a lot of rest and a lot of drawing done in his downtime. He felt a bit like himself again. The meds they'd given him at the hospital had been working so far, but he didn't want to jinx it by assuming all was well. He'd just have to take it a day at a time. And that day had been good. So, he was feeling mostly well enough to go to the New Year's Eve party with Braden because the chance to spend a holiday with someone he cared about was so new and exciting, he wouldn't dream of giving up that chance.

He was nervous. Of course, he was nervous. But he was also excited. He might not get the chance again, so he was going to make the most of it even if he knew it would take every ounce of energy he possessed. He looked at himself in the mirror and frowned, shaking his head. He was three notches down on his belt, and his pants, once fitted, were loose and baggy. His shirts were the same. He'd put on a button-up and covered it with a sweater in the hopes that he'd be able to mask some of the weight loss with bulk. Instead he just looked like a waif with clothes that hung loosely on his frame.

There was nothing he could do at that point. He hadn't even thought of shopping for new clothes for the party. He'd had other things on his mind. He'd heard from his doctor the day before and he and his partners had come up with a plan of attack and wanted to meet with him on Monday. When Dr. Cabrera had asked, he'd agreed that he'd like to get the insurance pre-approvals process started so it wouldn't be delayed.

He slid on his shoes, grabbed his keys, phone, and a nice bottle of wine for the host and was on his way. He turned on his music full blast, gathering courage and getting more eager as he drove. But when he finally arrived at the location Braden had given him, he was completely intimidated at the sheer size and elegance of the home and its posh location. Jesus. Whoever they were, they had money. And a *lot* of it. Losing the confidence he'd gained on the way over, he parked on the street out of view of the house and sat gathering his courage for a minute.

He nearly jumped out of his skin when his phone buzzed in his pocket, but when he saw the text, he smiled wide.

Braden: Let me know when you're here. I'll come out to meet you.

Thank fuck. He texted back that he had just arrived and Braden had perfect timing. He got out of the car, wiped his sweaty palms on his pant legs, and walked up the driveway. He was met halfway by a grinning Braden and the same gorgeous dog he'd seen at the café a couple times now. Thor was his name, if he remembered correctly. He'd wondered whose dog it was, and now he knew. He was so well behaved he didn't move from Braden's side. He stopped, not knowing if he should shake Braden's hand or hug him, or what.

That problem was taken right out of his hands when Braden hugged him. He then got down on one knee and ruffled the dog's fur. He looked at Sebastian and asked him to put his hand out, palm down for the dog to sniff. "Thor, this is Sebastian. He's a friend."

The big dog's tail wagged at the last word, and he glanced at his owner then back at Sebastian, tongue lolling, and he could swear he could see the gorgeous dog's mind working. Braden said again, "Friend."

As Thor moved forward to sniff his hand, Braden assured him that he could pet him freely now. That Thor would recognize him in the future as his friend. When Sebastian raised his brows at Braden, his new friend answered, "I have diabetes, and you probably know some of the story of my stalker. From that situation, I have PTSD. Zavier got Thor from the shelter I volunteer with. He had him trained as a service dog for both my diabetes and my PTSD, not to mention as a guard dog. My husband is ridiculously protective. If he's not with me, he wants Thor with me, at all times."

Sebastian smiled. "Kinda nice to be loved that much though, right?"

Braden laughed and nodded. "Yeah. Yeah it is."

They turned and started walking towards the house, Thor between them. Sebastian offered, "I saw him at the café a few times. I wondered who he belonged to. He kinda seems like the unofficial mascot of the place."

Braden laughed again. "Oh, there's nothing unofficial about it. He's definitely become the Sugar n' Spice mascot. Maya even suggested getting him a vest that matched their aprons, but I put my foot down at that."

"Is he a German Shepherd?"

"No. He's a Belgian Malinois."

He gave a confused look to Braden who laughed in response and said, "Exactly. I had no idea what kind of dog that was either until Thor came along. Apparently, they're very popular military and police dogs. Take well to training of all kinds, really. Zavier knew that and surprised me with him." Braden looked over at him and looked like he was debating saying anything then finally asked, "Are you all right, Sebastian? I know you haven't been feeling great. You look like you've lost weight. I just...want to make sure you're okay."

Sebastian shrugged and nodded. "Yeah, I'm doing okay. I've been sick, and I've been seeing a specialist. They're working with me to get me healthy again."

"That's good. I'm glad. You know if you need anything, you can call me, right?"

Sebastian was surprised by that, and it must have showed because Braden looked sad and asked, "Will you call me if you need help?"

Sebastian smiled, thinking how nice of an offer that was and how he'd never take Braden up on it. He didn't want to be *that* guy. He'd never take advantage of a new friend like that. He'd had a hard enough time asking Zoe to feed his cats. But he nodded and said, "If I need help, I'll keep you in mind."

From the look on his face, Braden must not have loved that evasive answer, but he surprised Sebastian by leaning over his dog and giving Sebastian a one-armed hug. "I'm glad you came."

When Braden let him go, Sebastian was blushing, and he nodded and said, "Me too."

Braden leaned down and gave Thor a vigorous pet then patted him on the side and told him to go play with Buckley. Sebastian thought that must be another dog because Thor bounded off in the direction of the backyard and barked with excitement. Sebastian looked at Braden when another dog barked right back. Dog speak. They grinned at each other, and Sebastian was taken by surprise when Braden clasped his hand and tugged him towards the steps to the front door.

He couldn't help but feel a warm feeling at Braden's hand holding. It wasn't sexual in any way, it was... he didn't know what it was, but it felt amazing and right. Like maybe they'd been friends forever and were just reconnecting after years apart. He scoffed at himself internally. How fanciful that all sounded. But he couldn't shake the feeling that he and Braden were going to be the best of friends. And he hoped he was right.

He was so distracted by his thoughts he barely registered that Braden had opened the door and was in the process of pulling him inside. Sebastian nearly gasped as he looked at the grand foyer he'd just walked into. There was a gorgeous sculpted chandelier, dark variegated hardwoods, a sweeping staircase wrapped in what appeared to be very real garland, and lots of it, with twinkle lights throughout and small red ornaments attached to add a pop of color. There was a mini-tree—one that put his to shame—on the gorgeous hand-carved, wooden entry table.

There was a crowd in the room to the left of the staircase and a crowd in the room to the right, and if he wasn't mistaken, there was another crowd at the back of the house as well. Feeling stressed suddenly and grateful to be holding Braden's hand, he pasted a smile on his face.

He leaned closer to Braden and whispered loudly above the noise of the festive party goers, "This house is gorgeous and huge!"

Braden laughed and nodded. "I know, right? It's all that watch money! Geesh. It's intimidating at first, I know, but that's just the house, not the people. The people are the best."

Confused, Sebastian asked, "Watch money?"

Braden looked confused by his confusion and replied, "McCade Military Watches?"

"You mean those fancy smartwatch thingies?"

Braden snorted, "Smartwatch thingies." He laughed harder, snorted again, and nodded. "Yep, those. Didn't Gideon tell you?"

"Tell me wha... Wait, McCade. *That* McCade?"

Braden rolled his eyes. "That man, I swear! Yes, that McCade. It's their family business. Have you never noticed the watch he wears, religiously?"

Sebastian shrugged. "I've seen it. I just... I didn't know and had never seen a watch like it, really."

Braden hummed. "It's an Imperator McCade Military Watch. Only the family wears that model, and they're all connected so they can communicate through them. I thought you knew or would have been told. Sorry."

"No, I wasn't. So, like…they send bat signals to each other?"

As Braden laughed, reality was catching up with him. Cracking that joke and distracting his friend from his current OMG state of WTFuckery was his only saving grace. Because, oh hairy shitballs, he was at Gideon's parents' house. Fuck! Oh, fuckity, fuck, fuck, fuck. This was not good, this was not good. He whispered nervously, glancing around, planning his escape, "I shouldn't be here."

Braden looked at him, confused. "Wha—"

"Braden, who do we have here?" A beautiful, older, curvaceous woman in a gorgeous, deep burgundy sheath dress approached, hand outstretched. He took it automatically feeling hot and cold all at once. He shouldn't be here. He shouldn't be here. Was Gideon here? Shit. Shit, shit, shit.

"…is Sebastian Phillips. He's a police sketch artist which is how I met him, but more importantly, he's a brilliant tattoo artist who's done a tattoo for me and for Zavier. He's extremely talented. And Sebastian, this is Siobhan, my mother-in-law and Zavier and Gideon's mom."

Before he could say hello, she pounced on that last bit. "You know Gideon?"

He couldn't stop the blush if he tried. Shit. Fuck. "Um…" He shook his head, glanced at Braden, trying to mentally send him an SOS message, and then back at Siobhan and shook his head again for good measure. "Uh…it's not—"

"They're just dating right now, Mom."

She beamed and wrapped her arm around Braden. "Oh, I do love it when you call me that!" She glanced at Sebastian and grinned at him and shocked him with, "Well, you're perfect for him. Just gorgeous, and talented, and ambitious it sounds like. It's such a pleasure to meet you."

As Zavier approached, bringing Braden a drink of what looked like ice water, Sebastian wasn't sure he could blush even more than he had, but, yep, he could. "Thank you, ma'am." He handed her the bottle of wine he'd nearly forgotten he was holding. "And, thanks for letting me crash your party."

"Oh, aren't you sweet! Thank you so much. I'm so glad you came, and you're welcome anytime. When I hunt up my husband, I'll bring him over to meet you. Until then, enjoy. Braden will show you around, maybe give you a tour."

He nodded and she was off, approaching a small group that waved her over. He gulped, not knowing what the fuck to do and feeling so out of place. He realized Braden and Zavier were looking at him and tried to muster up a smile. He was about to say something when Zavier reached out his hand. Sebastian clasped it to shake and Zavier said, "I'm glad you could make it, Sebastian. Happy New Year. What can I get you to drink?"

He pasted on another smile and replied, "Happy New Year to you as well. Water is good for now, thank you."

As Zavier walked off, Braden whispered, "Why did you say you shouldn't be here?"

"Because Gideon and I agreed not to mix our contract with our personal lives. We're not dating, we're just Dom/sub. I should leave."

Braden looked horrified. "No, you shouldn't! I asked you to come. You're my guest. Plus, Gideon isn't even here. He's working tonight, and I don't know how late he'll be. Please, stay, I want you here."

The truth was, Sebastian wanted to stay. And if it wasn't for Gideon, he wouldn't dream of leaving. Sure, he felt nervous and out of place, but shit, he felt nervous and out of place basically everywhere he went. He wanted to spend time with friends. He wanted to spend a holiday with someone he enjoyed. And he didn't want to go home and sit in his empty house with his cats, no matter how much he loved them. So, he gave Braden a small smile and nodded, saying, "Okay, I'll stay for a little while at least."

The smile Braden gave him was worth it. He'd just have to hope and pray that he'd leave before Gideon arrived. He was playing with fire and would probably get burned, but he didn't want to disappoint his new friend. Braden clasped his hand just like before and tugged him towards the back of the house, saying, "Come on. Zavier's getting you a drink, but you need to try some of this food, it's to die for!"

And with that, he was tugged back into the most beautiful kitchen/dining room combination he'd ever seen. When Zavier approached, he self-consciously pulled his hand from Braden's. Braden glanced at him, confused, and must have seen him looking at Zavier because he looked at his husband, clasped his hand again, and said, "I'm holding his hand."

Zavier grinned at his husband, clasped the back of his neck in what Sebastian could see was a tight grip of ownership and kissed him on the head. "Good. Make him feel welcome. Sebastian, keep an eye on my boy here. Make sure he doesn't get in any trouble. I'm going to mingle and help my parents keep everyone well sauced. We've got drivers on call tonight to take anyone home who needs a ride. That goes for you too, Sebastian, so if you have a little too much to drink, don't worry about it. You boys have fun, all right?"

He gave his husband a heated kiss then popped him on the ass as he walked away. Braden grinned at him, and he couldn't help but grin back. They walked towards the table that was laden with an enormous spread of food of all kinds. He smiled and thought to himself that he might just gain a few pounds back tonight. Braden put a few select things on his plate but when he saw Sebastian do the same he said, "I've already eaten some of this, and I'm diabetic. You need food, and this stuff is amazing. Pile that plate high."

He did just that, and while he couldn't even come close to finishing what he'd taken, he did put quite a dent in it. They sat in a little secluded nook in the corner of the kitchen by the fireplace and chatted about inconsequential things. Sebastian could tell that his friend wanted to ask more personal questions but didn't want to put him on the spot. For that, he was grateful. They were just about to get up when a younger version of Siobhan approached them. He realized before they'd even been introduced that she was Gideon's sister. His face grew heated when she asked how long he'd been seeing Gideon, but Braden saved him by changing the subject.

Siobhan stopped back over with her husband next, and Sebastian met the clan's patriarch, Duncan McCade. Sebastian could see the kindness in his eyes first then the curiosity peeked through. He started sweating and feeling distinctly uncomfortable, but it looked as though a tacit agreement had been made, and they didn't press him for details.

When he realized that was the case, he relaxed a bit and found himself talking to Siobhan and Rowan about tattooing and handed over a card to them both against his better judgement. He had an impossible time trying to avoid it, and the twin, shrewd gazes coming from both beautiful women was more than he could take.

"There he is! Sebastian, I heard you were here."

Sebastian jumped at Clara Cross's unexpected but exuberant greeting. He smiled, remembering how great she'd been to him when he'd done the composite sketch of her assailant. Standing, he held his hand out to shake hers, and she waved it away as she pulled him in for a hug. She joined them for a bit then she excused herself when a man her age entered the room. Her face lit up, and she walked towards him, took his proffered arm, and they made their way to another room.

Braden got his attention, smirked in their direction and whispered, "Ira."

Sebastian grinned, remembering their conversation about the high-in-demand neighbor of Clara's. "Yeah?"

Braden nodded and continued, "Oh yeah. Apparently, he did bring flowers and wait on her hand and foot. They've been inseparable ever since which is unheard of for her. She liked to play the field."

They chuckled at that, and he was happy that Clara had found someone. He realized that Braden must have understood his social anxiety, at least in part, because they stayed there for the next hour, people approaching them, chatting for a bit, and then moving off. He talked with Braden's business partner, Maya, her brother and Zavier's business partner, Cooper, and several of the guys that worked for them both.

He hadn't planned on making a lot of new contacts for his tattooing, and frankly, he didn't have time to take them all on as clients. But he ran out of business cards after Siobhan and Rowan and just ended up giving his mobile number out to those that were interested. Which prompted a whole flurry of texts from them providing him with their name to go with the number that texted so he could add them to his ever-growing contacts list. It was kind of unreal, and as much as he enjoyed his time there, even just an hour of being "on" was enough to make him tired as hell.

He excused himself to use the restroom after being told where it was. He used the toilet and stayed in there longer than necessary to catch his breath. Jesus. It was a New Year's Eve party, and he wasn't even going to make it until midnight. That was pretty much the definition of pathetic. Taking a deep breath, he opened the door and exited the bathroom, pulling it shut behind him and leaning against it to give himself one more moment of quiet before heading back into the fray.

He saw someone out of the corner of his eye and pasted a smile on his face, turning to say hello. His stomach plummeted when he realized it was Gideon. Fuck. He'd known he wasn't going to be able to avoid seeing him, and still, he was surprised by it. The hallway was dim, but he could see confusion, a few other emotions he couldn't name, and then the one he'd expected. Anger.

Without a word, his Dom had turned and walked away from him, but the look he'd given Sebastian before doing so was one of warning. Palms sweating and hands shaking, he followed Gideon through a mudroom and out to the driveway at the side of the house. He didn't dare get too close. He was too raw for any sort of contact. He knew Gideon would never raise a hand in anger towards him. He wasn't that type of man. But the anger he saw reflected back at him wasn't an emotion he'd ever seen on his Dom's face, and quite honestly, he never wanted to see it again.

He crossed his arms over his chest, feeling self-conscious at the stare down he was getting. "Hello, Sir."

His Dom narrowed his eyes, not even trying to disguise his contempt. "What are you doing here?"

Sebastian couldn't help but flinch in reaction, garnering no reaction at all from Gideon. "I'm sorry. Braden invited me. I didn't—"

"We agreed not to mix our contract with our personal lives. I don't appreciate being blindsided by you being in my parents' house."

Sebastian nodded. "I understand. I'm sorry, Sir. I didn't know it would be here. He just gave me the address. I didn't know it was your family's party. I wouldn't have—"

Sebastian nearly wept at the anger he saw on Gideon's face. "And when you found out? Why didn't you leave?"

He didn't think rejection could hurt so much, like he'd been punched in the gut. This was a nightmare, but one he realized he'd brought upon himself, so all he did was nod. "You're right. I'm sorry, Sir. I don't know what I was thinking. I should've left as soon as I found out. I'll go now." He turned to leave and saw Gideon move as if to follow him. He turned back and held up his hand. "It's okay. You don't need to. . . I can see myself to my car. I really am sorry, Sir. It won't happen again."

Sebastian's hands were shaking when he turned to head down the driveway. As he walked past the cars parked there and out onto the street, his heart felt like it would beat right out of his chest. He wouldn't cry. He wouldn't. He just needed to get out of there. He needed to escape. He didn't think he could take anymore.

He dug in his pocket for his key ring; pulling it out, he fumbled for his car key. But he was shaking so badly he dropped them on the street. Sinking down to the ground, he picked them up and gripped them tight, not knowing if he had the strength to get up until he saw Gideon approaching out of the corner of his eye.

He bolted up, adrenaline spiking, and managed to get the key in the lock. His first instinct was to wrench the door open; his frustration, no, his anger at himself a palpable thing. But he didn't want to lose his composure and humiliate himself any more than he'd already done. He gently eased the creaky car door open and stepped into the V between the door and the car itself. He made a move to slide in but stopped when a gentle but firm hand on his shoulder had him turning to face what was coming.

Gideon looked at him, no warmth in his eyes. The emotions Sebastian was sometimes sure were there, just below the surface, had vanished as if they'd never existed. And, he admitted to himself, they probably had never been there in the first place. Gideon's hands—hands that were always quick to touch him, caress him, hold him—were in fists by his sides. Sebastian thought he might be sick. Looking at his Dom, he knew what was coming before it escaped those beautiful lips, and he took a shuddering breath and braced himself in preparation.

"Sebastian, we both agreed from the beginning that this might not work. That one of us might not want to continue through to the end of the contract terms. We agreed, there would be no questions asked, no blame placed. I think it's best for both of us that we end our contract tonight. It's obviously not working, and I don't think it's fair for either of us to draw it out. I'm sorry."

His preparations hadn't worked. The wall he'd hoped to erect hadn't had time to solidify and lay in ruins at his feet. His heart shattered in his chest at those words. No matter how hard he'd tried, he'd truly failed this time. Failed himself. And worse, failed his Dom. A scenario he would have done absolutely anything to avoid. A scenario he'd told himself from the onset of their contract would be the likely outcome. And still he'd hoped.

Why hadn't he made the connection that this was a family party? Why hadn't he assumed that Braden would always spend holidays with the people he loved and who loved him back? The notion of true family was so foreign a concept that it hadn't even occurred to him. Just the fact that he'd been invited had meant the world to him. Which was exactly why he should have known better.

Something in Sebastian died in that moment, causing a black void to crack open deep within him so vast he wasn't sure he'd ever be able to fill it. A pain, deeper than any he'd ever experienced, was pummeling him from every angle. He clenched his teeth as he felt the sting of tears and did his best to mentally will them away. Sebastian couldn't show Gideon the damage he'd done with his rejection. He couldn't let him see how much it hurt. It wasn't Gideon's fault. He didn't need to feel guilt.

Sebastian was the one at fault and breaking down in front of this strong, beautiful man would only make Gideon feel as if he was to blame. The onus was on Sebastian, so he needed to be strong. Slowly, piece by piece, he mentally stitched back the fabric of his armor. Thin as it may be, it only had to last him until he could get away from his Dom. His *former* Dom. A sense of calm settled over him when his armor was in place.

He lost his focus on Gideon. He was no longer seeing him, or anything else for that matter. He cleared his throat and managed to shake his head, remembering a conversation they'd had when he'd first used his safeword. "There's no reason for you to be sorry. I understand. You warned me before that I'd have to fuck up monumentally for you to end our contract. I was stupid. I really should have made the connection." He managed to focus on Gideon for one last moment and give him a tremulous smile. "I'm truly sorry to have shown up like this. I hope you can go back in and enjoy your family. Happy New Year, Gideon."

He turned as quickly as he could and was about to slide into his car when he saw the package on his passenger seat. The package he'd tossed there yesterday, knowing he was going to see Gideon the next day and not wanting to forget it. He leaned in, and when he did, his collar slipped from under his shirt and his heart stopped. He took a couple deep breaths, unclasped it, and put it in the bag. He turned around and handed the festive gift bag to Gideon.

Unable to meet his eyes, Sebastian patted the bag once it was in Gideon's hands and stared at it while he explained, "Um, you always said you'd never get me gifts. But I double checked the contract and it didn't say anything about *me* getting *you* gifts, sooo…"

Sebastian smiled sadly, remembering how tricky he'd felt, getting around that rule, and how happy he'd been to be able to get Gideon something useful for Christmas. "It's not much, really. I just…" He touched the bag again then tucked his hands in his pockets, embarrassed. "I know you never replaced the ropes you cut… Um, when I safeworded at your loft? Khaleo told me where I could find quality rope. They've already been pre-treated and the center lines are marked, just like you like them. The ends are finished properly as well. I got a few different lengths, because. . . Well, it doesn't matter, really... I hope you'll find them useful."

Tears filled his eyes as he realized he'd gotten the gifts in the hope they'd use them together. He kept his head down as he turned and slid into his car. As he was shutting the door he almost convinced himself he heard Gideon say, "Sebastian, wait—" but he knew he was mistaken. He shoved the key into the ignition and turned the car on.

The blaring of the music he'd listened to on his way over—when he'd been so excited to be going to his first holiday party—made him jump in his seat. He slapped at the dials until he was greeted with silence. Thinking only of getting away as fast as possible, he pulled out into the residential street and drove off, wiping his eyes, and only belatedly pulling on his seatbelt after he was well away from the house and his car dinged at him to do so.

The emptiness inside him grew as he got further away from the man he'd fallen so hopelessly and irrevocably in love with. He focused on getting himself home safely where he could allow himself to let his emotions free. The last thing he needed was to get in an accident on the way home.

He had no idea where they came from, but in that vast black void that had taken route deep inside of him, he began to see images of himself. Images of his never-ending laser surgeries, his medications that no longer worked as they should, images of himself having more and more episodes, of the face that he hated gazing back from the mirror, so tired and drawn.

He saw images of himself speaking with his doctor, and later his neurosurgeon, he saw images of what might happen during his brain surgery. He saw images of a future he wasn't sure he'd have in six months' time, of his arm weakened by the SWS, his eyesight getting weaker with glaucoma, a future devoid of the art he created with ink to skin or paper.

His future was bleak, and he'd known of that possibility from a ridiculously young age. His mom had dropped him off for hours at their local library starting when he was just nine years old. Instead of reading what normal nine-year-old's read, he'd done research. He'd heard his parents talking about Sturge-Weber Syndrome, about how different he was, how disappointed they were to be saddled with him.

He had known he was different, but he thought it had ended at his port-wine stain. His "episodes" were something else he knew most people didn't have, but he'd never had a name for what made him different. Never understood he was broken. He hadn't understood until he'd convinced his mother to drop him off at the library every time she went to her prayer group or volunteered at the church.

He'd spent hours and hours reading, researching, trying to make sense of it all. For years, he kept going back. The older he got, the more he understood. The more he understood, the more scared he got. He did the only things he could think of to do. The only things he felt he had the power to do. He'd worked diligently to ensure that when the muscle weakness came, he'd be ready. When he lost strength and eventually function on his dominant side, he'd be prepared. He'd trained himself to have no dominant arm or leg.

He'd taught himself to become ambidextrous on the off chance that if his situation followed most cases and he lost his strength on one side, he wouldn't be helpless. His other side would be able to take over, to take over the job of being the dominant side. But there were no guarantees.

There was the possibility he'd have muscle weakness on both sides and lose the ability to use his hands to work, to take care of himself, to create. If that time came, he didn't know what he'd do, or perhaps he didn't want to admit what he'd do. So, he prepared for the worst and hoped for the best. It was the only thing within his power that he could think of to do.

Driving down Geary Boulevard, he got the first inkling that he could be in real trouble. He slapped his blinker on and cut a couple people off to get across two lanes to the shoulder. He skidded to a stop in the bus lane, flipped on his hazards and turned off the car. He sat there for nearly a minute, staring at his left hand, thinking he'd just been ultra-paranoid and hadn't really felt the tingling sensation and had stopped for no reason. But it hit, and it hit hard, and he found himself in that hazy confused state, not knowing how long the episode lasted or how long he'd been sitting there.

He looked at the clock and then looked at it again what felt like only seconds later and found he'd been sitting there ten minutes since it happened. Still a little dazed, he grabbed the bottle of water he always kept with him and drank what was left. He sat until he'd fully calmed and felt steady enough to drive home.

As he was just about to turn onto his street, he saw the flashing lights of a couple police cruisers handling a fender bender. It dawned on him as he parked that his medical condition had him on a restricted medical license. If he had active seizures, he was supposed to report in and his license would be suspended temporarily until he had them under control. With everything going on: work, illness, medication issues, his contract with Gideon, hospitalization, the holidays, and the New Year's Eve party, it hadn't even crossed his mind. He hated driving and didn't do it often, preferring to use Lyft half the time anyway, so it really didn't surprise him that he'd failed to remember.

Guilt washed over him. What would have happened if he hadn't had any warning signs? He could have caused a huge accident with devastating, even fatal, results. Hurting himself was one thing, but hurting others because of his own irresponsibility was unforgivable. His stomach churned, and he collapsed forward in the driver's seat, letting his head hit the steering wheel. He'd been so wrapped up in his own bullshit that he hadn't stopped to think.

Feeling utterly broken, he hauled himself out of the car and got himself inside. He'd figure out what needed to happen with his license in the morning. He'd hit a wall and barely had enough energy to feed the kittens. And just as he'd expected, when he finally fell into bed, utterly exhausted from the night's events, the floodgates opened, and he let himself grieve. He had no idea how long he cried. No idea how late it was when he finally fell into a fitful sleep with Slap and Tickle lying curled up beside him, but he didn't wake for a solid fourteen hours.

Chapter 28

GIDEON

He'd gotten home from the party—having mentally derided himself on the entire drive back for the way he'd treated Sebastian—and had forced himself to turn his mind off his boy when he stepped into his loft. Compartmentalizing had never been such a struggle for him—which said a lot about his feelings for Sebastian—but he didn't have a choice in the matter. It was too much to deal with that and the Lars situation at the same time, he needed his head in the game. So, after forcing his mind to shut down, he'd slept a solid eight hours, knowing he'd need it. When he woke, he'd readied himself for his trip, not knowing how long he'd be gone or what to expect, nor how quickly he'd hear from Zavier's men.

The call came that afternoon. They'd found Lars in Texas of all places. But they'd also bumped up against some surveillance that was already on him which was going to make things more difficult for Gideon but not insurmountable. Unsure of what other agencies were surveilling him, Gideon knew he had to be very careful not to be seen. If the FBI or ATF was after the bastard, he'd need to slip in and slip back out. He didn't want to fuck with another investigation, and he'd do what he could to gather as much information as possible while the man was still alive, but nothing was going to keep him from doing what needed to be done.

He was in Texas later that evening, an old contact of Zavier's having provided him with everything he might need over the course of what could be a month-long op including a secluded cabin on the water with a docked boat.

When he'd left the CIA, he'd gotten rid of all his government issued aliases, but he'd never quite felt comfortable not having several of his own, should they be needed. He was glad to have a contact that could issue him a driver's license and credit cards on short notice because it had been several years since he'd gotten clean identification. Knowing he'd be needing a couple when the time came, he'd ordered them well over a month ago. He'd flown and rented his car with one, planning to use the other as needed.

Settling in for the night, he inspected everything he'd been given and had to admit the man was thorough. He didn't think he'd be needing everything he'd unpacked, but the surveillance equipment was top notch, and after he'd inspected and cleaned the two handguns he'd been provided, he tucked them away, knowing he'd carry them, but he'd only use them if he was in a pinch he couldn't get himself out of easily. His sat phone vibrated in his pocket, and he took it out to see an encrypted text from Zavier.

Zavier: I've got backup headed down to you from upstate.
Gideon: You know I don't play well with others.
Zavier: They're on vacation and will only be dispatched if you contact me.
Gideon: I won't. Don't have them follow me. The last thing I fucking need are witnesses.
Zavier: You do realize I know what I'm doing, right? And you must know I'm aware of what you used to do for a living.
Gideon: No witnesses, Zavier.
Zavier: You have my word. Only if you signal me.

Gideon didn't respond, but he knew his brother wouldn't fuck this up for him, so he put it out of his mind and focused on the task at hand. When everything was ready to go, he sat down and went through the dossier he'd gotten from Custos, wanting to learn all there was to learn about the man he was going to kill. When he was done, he felt like he had a good place to start and would begin his search in the morning.

He got ready for bed, absentmindedly thinking of which thread to pull first, but knowing he needed to shut his mind down from over-analyzing everything. He tried to ignore the nagging feeling that he wasn't going to get what he wanted out of this op, even when the man was dead.

Then he had to wonder if he'd ever get what he wanted which inevitably turned his thoughts to Sebastian. His shoulders slumped just thinking of the damage he'd done. Crawling under the covers of the cabin's too-soft mattress, he stretched out on his back, staring up at the ceiling, and let the memories he had of his boy run through his mind. It was a special kind of torture, but he knew he deserved no better.

Come daybreak, he'd flipped the switch again; Lars on his radar from the moment his eyes popped open. His day was spent following the leads Zavier's men had been able to find and pulling at each little thread to see what unraveled. It was a lot of footwork and a heavy amount of assumption with not a Lars sighting to be had. One thing about this whole situation bothered him though, he was entirely too close to the Corpus Christi military base, and that set his inner alarms to screaming. By the time evening rolled around, he'd done what he could do. He made some headway and would come at it from a fresh perspective in the morning.

That next day was more of the same. Tracking down leads, pulling loose threads, gathering more data on the man he was looking for. That night, after one of those threads pulled loose on a new lead, he waited until he could use the cover of darkness to his advantage and ended up at a local, outdoor storage facility a couple miles off base. He pulled up short when someone pulled onto the lot in an ancient Chevy pickup, driving to the end unit he was approaching. A man got out of the cab of the truck on the passenger's side, threw up the garage door on the last ten-by-thirty storage unit on that row and flipped on the lights, illuminating a pontoon boat, of all things.

Both men worked to hitch the boat to the truck. When that was completed and the garage door was closed, the passenger climbed in the cab of the truck. As they made to pull out, Gideon walked up behind the boat, placed a tracker on the back of the boat, and then backed up into the shadows as the truck pulled away. It was exactly the break he needed.

They led him back to what Gideon assumed was their home base, a run-down shipyard ten miles from the storage unit, surrounded by several huge piles of scrap metal and boat parts, and no fewer than fifteen rusted shipping containers. Upon closer inspection, he couldn't see any security measures on the perimeter fencing which struck him as strange. But when he thought he saw the other party the dossier had warned him about doing surveillance, he knew he had the right place and made sure to stay out of their way.

He watched as the bay doors of the dilapidated shipyard building opened automatically, the technology incongruent with the derelict surroundings. The truck reversed into the wide-open doors and the doors slid closed, but not before he saw a man carrying a semi-automatic rifle standing in the shadows.

An hour later, he watched as the men from earlier moored the boat to one of the docks by the launching ramp behind the shipyard. Hopping back into the truck, they drove around the building and out of the shipyard. Gideon stayed there for another couple hours, but nothing else happened.

The next morning, he headed back toward the shipyard on the boat from the cabin. He watched for a couple days, off and on, always able to track the pontoon with the tracer. But much to his consternation, all they did was head out into the gulf and go fishing. He knew it wasn't as innocent as that and eventually thought to drag the diving gear out of the little boathouse down by the dock which is when he finally got some answers.

Seemed there was a hatch underneath the boat running down its center, disguised as a third pontoon. Divers were moving boxes from the seabed and swimming them up to the pontoon. Gideon guessed the boxes were most likely filled with munitions and were just a small part of a much larger smuggling operation.

He spent well over a week watching the comings and goings of those in the shipyard, and out on the water, getting an enormous amount of footage, while he worked. Several times he caught a few other people doing the same thing, so he figured these boys were caught up in something that was about to blow wide open. If he could help with that, he would, but nothing was going to keep him from his end goal.

It wasn't until the ninth day that he saw his quarry. He'd known patience would pay off, but Christ, he'd been frustrated with the waiting. He'd known, absolutely known he was in the right place, but not seeing Lars for nine fucking days had almost convinced him otherwise. Lars came that day in a goddamn limo to a run-down shipyard, practically shining a light on the illegal activity for fuck's sake. Two men, who he treated with great respect, got out of the car with him.

Lars and company were there for hours. When they left, Gideon followed them to the airport where the two men shook hands with Lars and walked into the terminal. Gideon was only able to snap off a few photos before he had to pass the limo and pull over to the side and wait them out.

The limo finally dropped Lars at a condo complex and left. He watched as the man let himself into a two-story, corner unit. Gideon stayed there until the following morning when the condo's garage opened to reveal a new Mercedes which he followed and tagged on one of Lars's stops. After that, he took his own pit stop, used the bathroom and grabbed a huge breakfast, and then kept his eyes on the tracker as he headed back to the condo.

As he was doing his best to break into the place, he thought his issue would be a security system, but apparently, Lars didn't feel one was needed with the snarling Doberman at the top of the stairs. Never one to hurt women, children, or animals, Gideon turned to leave, knowing he'd need to find another way to deal with it.

It took another day, but he tracked down someone with animal tranqs. The trip was a long one, and more than once, the absurdity of his actions hit him. The irony that he was driving all over the damn state to avoid hurting a dog when he was doing so in order to kill its owner was ridiculous. He waited until 5 a.m. and got the door open, and the dog knocked out within minutes. Not hearing any indication Lars was awake, he walked up the steps into the main floor of the condo.

Seeing there were no bedrooms, he figured they were all on the third level. He heard Lars upstairs before the man's voice rang out in the silence, "Cujo! Where the fuck are you, you worthless piece of shit?"

Classy guy. And, Cujo? Really? Jesus Christ, what a douchebag. He shook his head, thinking that it took all kinds, as Lars made his way down the stairs. Tucked away as he was, in the little breakfast nook at the back of the kitchen, Lars didn't see him until he was right there in the middle of the room, wearing nothing but a white t-shirt and loose boxer shorts, scratching his balls and yawning. His eyes popped wide when he saw Gideon, who was holding a gun in his hand.

Gideon leaned back in his chair. "Lars. Just the man I wanted to see. So nice of you to join me. Cujo, was it? Cujo is taking a little nap in the garage. Why don't you sit down with me here." Jerking the gun towards the seat in front of him, he kicked the chair back to make room for the man to sit.

Sitting, but not happy about it, Lars' voice was calm when he finally asked, "Who are you?"

He watched closely when he finally answered, "Gideon McCade."

Lars looked at him, confusion clouding his eyes, and when Gideon said nothing more, he asked, "What are you doing here?"

"I came to kill you."

The man tensed then, and Gideon could see he was readying himself to move. Jesus, was the man a complete novice? As Lars went to stand, pushing up off the table, Gideon pulled out his tactical knife, stood, and slammed it through the back of the man's hand and clear into the wooden table.

The high pitch of the scream was a surprise, more than the scream itself, and Gideon's brows rose as he made himself comfortable again. But when the screaming continued, Gideon picked up the gun and tapped it hard against the side of the knife, repeatedly, until the man shouted for him to stop, face contorted in pain.

"Shhh shhh shhhh." Gideon smiled and placed his finger over his lips. "We can't have your neighbors getting too curious, now can we?"

"Get it out of my hand! Please!" The strangled whine escaped as the man tried to reach toward the knife's hilt to remove it.

Gideon tsked and shook his head. "Nah, can't have you doing that, Lars."

"I haven't done anything wrong!"

Gideon laughed, a hollow sound without a hint of amusement. "Come on now. You don't honestly expect me to believe that, do you? I mean, I'm a trained killer, Lars. Trained killers don't just show up at your house to drug your dog and knife your hand to your table for no reason, now do they?"

The man was blubbering now. "Please. Please."

Gideon reached into one of his cargo pockets, making Lars flinch, and pulled out the picture he had of his SEAL team, placing it on the table in front of the man who was fast becoming a whining and sniveling mess.

"These were the best men on my SEAL team. My brothers. You brokered a deal with some Ba'ath loyalists to attack a munitions bunker that was well-hidden and well-fortified, not to mention highly classified."

At Lars's hitched breath, he continued, "My team was on a counterinsurgency mission in Baghdad, but that day. . . That day *my* men were pulled from that mission to go babysit this bunker out in bumfuck Nasiriyah, three hundred sixty fucking klicks from our base of operations. Alan Lewis, remember him? He was quite forthcoming when push came to shove. They all are, eventually. But we've got time to figure out what you know."

The stunned look on the man's face was priceless. He'd probably thought someone was after him for his current illegal dealings. The fact that someone was coming at him for something he'd done more than ten years prior was probably the last thing he expected. He looked from the picture up to Gideon and down to the picture again and promptly lost the color in his face. Again, telegraphing his moves, the man stood and tried to yank the knife out of the table and himself.

Gideon stood, grabbed the butt of the gun, and slammed it into the side of the man's head, knocking him back into his chair, out cold. He searched the drawers for a kitchen towel and found that along with an extra garage opener, an extra car key, and a couple fresh garbage bags.

He pulled duct tape from another cargo pocket, removed the knife from the man's hand and proceeded to wrap the hand thoroughly in the towel to keep the blood from soaking into the carpet of the car. He taped his ankles together and his wrists behind his back, picked him up, and tossed him over his shoulder in a fireman's carry. He took the stairs to the garage where he put Lars on the floor while he placed the garbage bags down, wanting to make sure no blood was left behind, and tossed Lars none too gently on top. He taped his wrist and ankle ties together behind him and closed the trunk.

Gently picking up the dog, Gideon carried him upstairs, found his bed in the tiny laundry room, tucked away and out of sight. Gideon laid him down on it and saw the dog had timed food and water dishes because why put yourself out more than you had to. Jesus, the guy was a gem. Cleaning up the blood from the table and anything else he might have touched, he left the place as he'd found it, driving Lars's Mercedes to his home base where he could finish what he started without worrying about being caught.

His shoulders finally sagging with the knowledge that very soon, he'd be able to say a final goodbye to his past and focus only on his future. Not knowing what that would entail, he couldn't stop his mind wandering to Sebastian. He had to set aside the fact that Sebastian would never approve of what he was about to do.

He knew taking this last step toward laying his past to rest would also probably take the last bit of humanity he had. He wasn't proud of what he was doing, not by any means, but the weight of the men that died on his watch would always be heavier than the weight of the loss of his own humanity. His men had suffered, it was only fitting that he suffer along with them.

Pulling up to the cabin an hour before sunrise, it was still fairly dark out. He had plenty of time to get the information he wanted from the man, slowly, and with much pain. And after that, hours to get rid of the body under the cover of darkness. He'd already prepared the cabin's spare room for Lars and the wetwork to come. He'd chosen the pool table in the spare room. It was the perfect height.

He got out of the car, manually opening the garage door and then driving into it. Closing the garage behind him, he turned on the lights and opened the trunk. His prey was awake. Leaning down, hands resting on the lip of the trunk, he forced a grin and asked, "Nice trip?"

"Fuck you!" The words were spat out, angrily.

He chuckled and cut the tape connecting arms and legs together. "Come on. Up you go." Hefting the man into another fireman's carry, he walked into the cabin with the screaming, thrashing bundle of half-naked man. The more the man struggled, the more Gideon's adrenaline made itself known. He knew peace would never be his, but his men would have it if it was the last thing he did.

As he walked into the spare room and Lars saw the plastic, the thrashing and screaming which had abated began anew. When he roughly put the man on the table, he nearly rolled off the damn thing trying to get away. Gideon shook his head, wondering at the absurdity of the man's actions. "Where do you think you're going, Lars?"

"LET ME GO! I'm sorry. Whatever you think I did, I'm sorry!"

"I know what you did, Lars, and so do you. You're gonna have to stop fighting me, though. The more you fight, the longer this will take. The longer this takes, the more it will hurt. So really, it's in your best interest to calm the fuck down."

The man was quiet, but instead of arguing, which is what Gideon thought he'd do, the man nearly threw himself over the edge of the table again. Exasperated, Gideon shook his head and yanked the man back onto the center of the table before he could toss himself face first onto the floor. "What's your ultimate goal here? Your legs are duct taped. Your arms are duct taped behind your back. I've got you at a remote cabin where no one will hear you, no one will see you, and no one will find you. I'm gonna go out on a limb here and say you're fucked six ways from Sunday."

And then the blubbering began, and continued while Gideon set about tying the man to the table. When he was done, Gideon's stomach growled. Leaving the man alone in the spare room, he made himself a big breakfast to the sounds of Lars begging and screaming to be let go.

He took his time eating it, telling himself he wasn't avoiding what was to come, but knowing he was kidding himself. Cleaning everything up in the kitchen, he made himself a second cup of coffee and sat at the table with his iPad, making his flight arrangements for the following day.

Knowing there was no avoiding it, he donned some protective gear. Suited up, he brought his kill kit into the room and put it on the table in the corner, unravelling the rolled-up sleeve of knives and various other tools of the trade. He plugged in his phone and turned on the voice recorder, knowing he was going to need it, and got down to business.

He'd barely been one very deep cut in before the man sang like the proverbial canary. All the information he'd wanted, all the questions he'd had, answered, and more to boot. He got information on the op that killed his men, the op Gideon had discovered two weeks ago, and several others before the job was done.

Knowing the information would be inadmissible in court, Gideon figured it would still be helpful to many people closing open cases in whatever agencies were involved. He'd have to have Zavier's men splice the recording and remove his voice but the information recorded would provide a lot of details and leads for others to follow.

When Gideon had gotten everything he was going to get out of the man, he didn't have it in him to drag it out. The man had been weak in every way, and Gideon had hardly done any damage, by his standards anyway. The killing was enough. He couldn't help but feel a sense of relief at that fact.

When all was said and done, he was exhausted. He looked down at his protective gear and realized with surprise that he hardly had any blood on him. He cut the ropes that had been rendered useless, and taking off his gear, he tossed it on top of the body and wrapped the first layer of plastic around it. He cleaned his knives and got everything of his out of the room.

He realized it hadn't been like Alan. With Alan he'd still gotten the kill high as he had when he'd done it for a living. The man had done enough in his lifetime to warrant a painful bloody death ten times over, but he hadn't felt anything but a sense of finality, an obligation fulfilled.

A couple of hours later, it was finally dark outside, making things much easier. Wanting to get the body down to the boat before rigor mortis set in, he made quick work of cleaning all traces of the man away.

He carried the body down to the boat, having already prepared what he'd need on board to weigh the body down, he turned on the ignition and headed out to the spot he'd scoped out earlier in the week miles away from shore. Afterward, he steered the boat back to the cabin and dealt with swapping the cars while it was still dark.

His flight didn't leave until noon, so he had enough time to get up with the sun, double-check there wasn't a trace of what had been done in the cabin or the boat, and pack up the rental.

The following morning, he realized he couldn't leave until he dealt with one final detail. Departing from his usual MO, he sent Zavier an encrypted text from his sat phone, knowing his brother wouldn't have been able to leave the situation as is either, he felt justified.

Gideon: Your men still here?
Zavier: Yes.
Gideon: Might as well make them earn their pay.
Zavier: Might as well.
Gideon: Think they can handle a dog situation?
Zavier: Dog?
Gideon: Call me.

He explained he didn't want to leave a dog to die in an empty condo, vicious or not. "I'll leave the tranq gun with the second dose, along with the garage door opener in a box in the mailbox of the cabin. There's a no kill shelter on Caldwell Street that has good ratings."

"It'll be taken care of."

"Thanks."

"You all right?"

Knowing Zavier could feel the tension across the scrambled phone line, he sighed and replied honestly, "I will be."

"Come home."

"Will do."

"Be at dinner tonight."

After a few moments of silence, Zavier repeated the demand. "Be there, Gideon."

Gideon sighed and nodded, even knowing Zavier couldn't see him. "Yeah. Yeah, okay."

His brother hung up without another word. He thought he should feel lighter. Freer. His men finally got the vengeance he'd promised them years ago. He knew his obligation had been fulfilled, but he couldn't shake the sense that while he'd laid his past to rest, his future was completely unclear. He wasn't sure he liked the feeling. It left him unsettled. And he could think of one thing, and one thing only.

Sebastian.

Chapter 29

SEBASTIAN

Sebastian hung up the phone with his bank. The transfer was complete. Half of his surgery was paid for. The other half would come from the proceeds of the sale of his house which would close in three weeks, after the surgery. The hospital AR department said if half of it was paid for, he could make payment arrangements for the second half. Why they were all right making arrangements for seventy-five thousand dollars, he'd never know, but the issue was dealt with. The house was in escrow, and he had a rental lined up already.

Movers were scheduled the following week, the week after that he'd be in surgery, and yet another week after that he'd have the funds from closing on the house. He'd made a tidy sum; it was a sellers' market after all. Even with the surgery, he would have enough for a down payment on another house which is why he was going month to month. He had the option of signing a lease later. He'd just have to see what surgical recovery would be like, realistically.

His boss had been great. The Monday after New Year's, he'd called to give his boss the news that his doctor didn't want him working any longer, let alone tattooing, or driving. His boss had assured him they'd survive without him. They had a computer software backup that everyone hated to use and never produced the quality sketches that an artist could do, but they'd deal with it while he was gone. He was on medical leave that same day and had contacted any tattoo clients he'd needed to cancel so he could focus on packing up his house and tying up loose ends.

And though his surgeon had argued against it, he had a laser surgery scheduled for the following morning. He didn't know how long it would be before he felt up to another one so he wanted to get it out of the way so he didn't get too far off schedule. He wasn't working, so there wasn't really a reason not to do it. He just had to hope he wouldn't have an episode while he was there, but his laser surgeon was aware of his health issues, so if it happened, it happened.

He finished packing up the box he was working on and heard the doorbell as he dragged the packing tape over the top of the box. Not expecting anyone, he made his way downstairs and smiled when he saw Zoe holding up a box from the café and a couple coffee cups. He'd never been more grateful for a friend than he was for her the last couple weeks. She'd hated it, but she'd kept his confidence.

She hugged him gently, treating him with kid gloves. He couldn't blame her really. Hell, he was about to have surgery on his brain for fuck's sake. Not to mention his meds kept him pretty nauseous, so he'd lost another six pounds. He'd noticed he got tired more quickly and didn't have the energy to keep going throughout the day without taking several short rests. He had no interest in food but found himself forcing a spoonful of peanut butter at least once a day, just to get himself some calories and protein.

They sat on his sofa and she handed him his mocha and grinned when he peeked in the box she'd brought. So many pastries. "You're taking these with you when you go, right?"

She made some kind of a pfft noise before answering, "No. I work there. These are for you."

"You know I can't eat even a quarter of these."

She grew serious and patted his knee. "All of them are freezable. Pull them out when you need a treat."

He set the box aside and nodded, unable to express his thanks just yet. Clearing his throat he managed, "Thank you."

"You're welcome. How are you feeling?"

"Meh. More of the same. I have a little bit of torture scheduled tomorrow, but after that, it'll just be packing and waiting for D-Day."

Her brow furrowed prettily. "What's going on tomorrow?"

"Laser surgery."

"What the hell are you talking about? I'm sure they'll let you cancel."

"I just scheduled it. I don't want to cancel. I want to stay on schedule. I already delayed it around the holidays."

"Sebastian, it's too much."

He shook his head. "It'll be fine."

"I'm coming with you. What time is it at?"

"Nine in the morning. No, you're not."

"I'll just call in sick."

"You're not calling in sick for me and putting them in a tough spot."

"Sebastian, why do you insist on being alone for everything? Why won't you let me talk to Braden about what you're going through? I'm sure he could ask Zavier not to tell Gideon. You need your people around you."

Sebastian tilted his head then shook it slowly. "I don't have people, Zoe. Not like that."

She crossed her arms, defensive, and his heart broke a little when a tear slid down her cheek. "What am I, then?"

"Don't cry! You're my friend. Of course, you are." He leaned forward and hugged her and then pulled back. "But we haven't been close that long. You're being so good to me and for that I'm so grateful. But, Zoe, I'm used to relying on myself. It's literally all I've ever known. I'm not going to be the friend that was an acquaintance three months ago and as soon as he needs something, he starts abusing that new friendship. I won't be a burden."

Confusion furrowed her brow. "But it's not a burden, and Braden wouldn't think it is either. I want to help you, Sebastian. You mean a lot to me. Please let me come tomorrow."

He shook his head, and when she was about to say something else, he asked, "When do you get off?"

"Noon."

"Perfect. Why don't you just come by for a little bit when you get off work? It's right around the time I'll get home."

Her shoulders sagged, and she nodded. "Okay, fine. But, Sebastian?"

"Yeah?"

"What if I was having a scary surgery and I needed help with some stuff? Would you help me?"

His mouth fell open. "Of course! You know I would."

Her smile was small, but it was there and she nodded. "Then you're one of my people."

"I—"

"And I'd like to be one of yours if you'd let me."

Knowing this was monumental only for him, he looked her in the eyes and did his best not to blubber when he nodded and said, "All right."

Like he'd been the one to do her a favor, she bounced happily and leaned in to hug him. When she pulled back she looked at him seriously and said, "You know, if you just gave him half a chance, Braden would be one of your people in a heartbeat."

He knew the truth of that down to his bones, but he shook his head none-theless. "I won't put him in that position. I'm not going to ask him not to tell his husband, and I'd never expect his husband to keep that from his brother. It's too much. It's best this way."

"He's asked about you. I haven't told him I'm coming to see you, but I'm pretty sure he knows. He said you weren't answering his calls, and that you sent him a text saying you just needed some time. But, that'll only hold him for so long."

Sebastian had been afraid of that, but he'd been doing his best to just get through each day. Stressing about Braden was paramount to stressing about Gideon, and he couldn't go down that road. He'd given himself a couple days to mourn what he'd never really had to begin with, but he'd had to lock it away in a box so he could function day to day, which was no exaggeration.

Between getting a medical leave of absence scheduled, getting his surgery scheduled, his laser treatment scheduled, his house market ready, put on the market, leaving the house for showings, hoping that he didn't have an episode while he was walking around the block, packing up his house, arranging to view apartments, choosing one that would take Slap and Tickle and would go month to month, scheduling his movers, meeting with his lawyer, and so much more, he just didn't have it in him. He was just lucky his house had sold nearly immediately.

Everything he'd been dealing with would have been hard when he was at his most healthy, but he was at his weakest point: mentally, physically, and emotionally. The fact that he got through every day felt like a colossal task. To say he was exhausted was a ridiculous understatement.

He didn't have much left in him, and he was holding on by the thinnest of threads. Actually realizing that had his shoulders slumping. He never let himself think about it. Never let himself stop to take a breather because too much noise filled his mind, and if he let that happen, all the balls he was juggling would drop. And who was going to have to pick them up? He was.

He must have telegraphed his defeat because Zoe was patting him on the arm then hugging him. "I'm not telling you this to worry or upset you. He won't wait long before he takes things into his own hands. If you want to keep him away until you're through the worst of it, you're going to have to call him and tell him that you need time, that you'll contact him when you are ready, but you need him to respect your wishes."

Knowing she was right, he nodded and thanked her. They chatted for a long while after that, and he was exhausted afterwards. When she could see his energy flagging, she let herself out, and he sat on the couch, unable to move. Feeling every emotion bombarding him, he lay down and curled up and slept for several hours.

When he woke up, he made the call he'd been dreading. He was vague, but he got his point across, and when he hung up, he knew that Braden had been hurt, but he also knew that his new friend wouldn't push and would give him the time he needed. Sebastian had promised he wouldn't let their friendship end, that he just needed more time, and he needed it to be on his terms. That, more than anything, is what had done it.

He slept fitfully that night, and the laser surgery was one of the hardest he'd ever dealt with. Suda, his favorite nurse, had been off that day, and for that he'd been grateful. She'd have been worried about him, and he didn't have the energy to deal with the gentle woman, no matter how well meaning and genuine. When he was dropped off in front of his house, Zoe was sitting on his front stoop. She hopped up when she saw him and helped him inside.

He tried to do what he normally did but she shooed him to the couch and proceeded to take care of him. It was nice. He was iced, his kittens were lying on him, and he'd fallen asleep. He was shocked when he woke up hours later to find that Zoe had cooked him dinner, washed several loads of his laundry, and packed up half of his kitchen. He was so grateful and touched that she would even bother.

She'd smiled and hugged him tight, murmuring, "I'm one of your people."

He'd finally agreed, nodding. "You are. And I'm so grateful. Thank you. Would you like to stay for some of the dinner you made?"

"You're welcome and no. I should get going. But, can I come over tomorrow? I work most of the day, but—"

"No. Please. The second day is actually the worst day. I spend it sleeping and icing. That's it."

"You're sure?"

"Positive."

"All right. I work Sunday as well. But I'm coming to see you after work. No arguing. I'll bring you dinner. We can eat dinner and watch bad movies."

He grinned. "Not good movies?"

She scoffed. "What's the fun in that?"

He shrugged. "Good question. Sunday, dinner, bad movies."

She grinned and said, "It's a date."

With that, she was gone, and he sat, shocked. He'd never had anyone that would do what she'd done for him today. He'd been dreading the kitchen and getting up on the small step stool over and over and carrying heavy kitchen stuff. He'd been avoiding it like the plague, and he couldn't think of a better gift she could have given him.

Feeling content for the first time in nearly two weeks, he got up and checked the kitchen. So many boxes stacked against the back wall that he just stared at them for several long moments before he turned and realized that she'd made him chicken and dumplings which he actually loved. He ate more that night than he'd eaten at any one time in the last month.

Chapter 30

GIDEON

When Gideon finally walked into the loft, he immediately got undressed and showered off the grime of the last forty-eight hours, or more accurately, the past two weeks. After he showered, he pulled on some boxers and was walking towards his bed when he stepped on a plastic cat toy. He glanced in the corner and saw Slap and Tickle's bed he kept there.

Knowing he'd made the right decision to get out of the loft for dinner, he picked up the cat toy and tossed it into the cat bed. The longer he stayed in the penthouse alone, surrounded by memories, the more his thoughts drifted towards Sebastian, and the look on his face when he'd ended it all.

He got several hours of rack time, and feeling a bit more rested, he walked into the kitchen to grab his keys and noticed the bag he'd put on the kitchen table. The Christmas gift from Sebastian. Fuck. He dropped the keys on the countertop and made his way over to the table. Sitting down heavily, not wanting to open it but knowing he couldn't put it off any longer, he reached into the tissue paper and pulled out several professionally pre-treated lengths of rope, just as his boy had said.

His boy.

As much as he knew he needed to stop thinking of him that way, he just didn't see how that was possible. A part of him would always think of him that way. Setting the last length of rope down on the table he reached in and realized there was a card. Opening it up, he laughed at the silly rendition of a Santa on a sleigh whipping a reindeer that was telling Santa to do it again, but harder. The note from Sebastian was short and sweet.

Sir, Merry Christmas. I hope we get the chance to get a lot of use out of these. Your boy

Jesus. Shoulders slumped, he tossed the bag on the table in defeat and heard a thunk. Brow furrowed, he reached in, and his breath caught. Leaning forward, he pulled Sebastian's temporary collar out of the bag and stared at it, pooled in his palm. Running his finger over the links, he took a deep breath and squeezed the necklace in his hand.

He'd had the collar made specifically for Sebastian even though it was only meant to be a temporary collar for their temporary relationship. Contract. Fuck. Sure, he could have gotten him some cheap collar any Dom could give any sub, but giving a submissive a collar—whether temporary or permanent—was a serious thing, and even though it had been for the short term, he felt a collar should signify how a Dom saw his sub. And when he looked at his boy, he saw beauty, strength, and above all, worthiness. All things he wanted Sebastian to see in himself but knew he didn't.

He looked back down at the links of metal and shook his head; it was temporary, yes, so why did it hurt so much that Sebastian had given it back? He sat there for a while unable to move. He'd made the right decision, hadn't he? Sebastian needed someone good, someone that would love him the way he deserved to be loved. A niggling thought that no one could ever love Sebastian more than he did snuck in, but he pushed it out. Sighing, he stood up, put his boy's collar in his pocket and grabbed his keys again.

Thirty minutes later, he walked into his parents' house and was immediately enveloped by the sound of Adele crooning from the kitchen speakers and the aroma of his mother's perfectly prepared beef Wellington. It was his favorite of all of her culinary endeavors, and he couldn't help but smile when he realized his mom must have been missing him. He headed towards the kitchen.

He spotted Buckley lounging in front of the lit fireplace on his enormous dog bed. His ears perked up as Gideon walked in, and he stood to amble over for a nice rubdown which Gideon was happy to provide. His mother was at the main sink. She hummed along to the music, her back to him, oblivious of his arrival.

Gideon walked up behind his favorite woman on earth. When he slipped his arms around her and kissed her on the head, she squeaked and her kitchen shears clattered in the sink. She turned around to reprimand him. "Dammit, Gideon! You're too stealthy! You're gonna give me a heart attack one day!"

But even while she admonished him, she pulled him in for a tight embrace.

He swayed with her from side to side. "You look gorgeous, Ma. Always have, always will."

"Oh you! Stop that." She pulled him down so she could kiss him on both cheeks. "Gideon, you're looking tired and worn out. I don't like it when you're away for so long. I worry."

He hugged her to him again. "It wasn't that long. I'm okay, Mom."

His dad patted him on the back, and he turned and clasped his hand and pulled him in for a hug. "Hey, Dad. How are you?"

His dad pulled away enough to look into his eyes. "Good, now that you're here. Your mother worries."

Gideon gave his father a knowing smile. "There's no need for either of you to worry. As you can see, I'm good."

He could tell they didn't believe him when they both continued to scrutinize him. However, he was saved from further discussion as the front door slammed and Finn and Rowan came into the kitchen, chatting animatedly about something. He skirted around the side of the island and unwrapped the flowers he'd brought. While his mom was distracted with his siblings' arrival, he got out a vase, cut the stems, and arranged the bouquet of stargazer lilies, one of her favorites. His mom headed back to the sink, saw the flowers he'd arranged, and clasped her hands together over her heart. She hugged him and whispered, "Thank you, my sweet boy."

"Anything for you."

His father winked at him and moved the flowers to the sideboard that faced the dining table. As he finished and cleaned up, he heard Buckley bark and knew that Zavier and Braden had arrived with Braden's dog Thor, Buckley's best friend. Braden bent down to remove Thor's chest harness. Besides his tail wagging slightly, you wouldn't know Thor was excited about seeing Buckley. He was obviously working.

Buckley and Thor barked and ran through the open patio doors to frolic together in the backyard. Braden set the harness down by Buckley's bed and came back to greet him. They hugged and Gideon could see the strain in his eyes. "Thor's working? You all right?"

Braden's smile didn't reach his eyes when he nodded and said that he was. Zavier approached; having greeted everyone, he returned to his husband and wrapped him in his arms from behind. He whispered something in Braden's ear which prompted the smaller man to lean back against his husband and lift up to kiss the side of Zavier's face. Gideon knew his brother was overprotective of Braden, but seeing that the younger man wasn't at his best made his own protective instincts kick in. "What can I get him to drink?"

His brother helped Braden onto one of the counter stools. "If you could heat up some water, some herbal tea would be great. We couldn't prevent a migraine yesterday, so he's dealing with the hangover from that today."

The water boiled, and Gideon fixed Braden the tea, sliding it across the counter in front of Braden who thanked him. He wrapped his hands around the mug as if he was cold and needed the warmth. When dinner was ready, they moved to take their seats and passed around the food.

He watched his brother and Braden interact. Acknowledging that his reaction was jealousy, pure and simple. What they had with each other, he wanted for himself. He realized that he'd always wanted it in an offhand, someday sort of way, but someday wasn't going to cut it any longer. When would someday come? Was it just a trick he played on himself to believe he had a future to look forward to? Why the fuck did he leave the CIA to begin with if he wasn't going to get the fuck on with his life?

After Lars, he realized his thought process was slowly changing. The thoughts that he'd never let take hold slowly began to creep in, to take root. There was so much in his past that he wasn't proud of, but punishing himself for the rest of his life wasn't going to do him any good. It wouldn't right the wrongs he'd perpetrated. It wouldn't turn back time. When was enough going to be enough? He was the only one that could answer that, and the answer came clearly when he finally allowed himself to listen. He needed to allow himself to live.

He wanted someday, and he wanted someday to come immediately. And not only did he want it—with a fierceness that was nearly his undoing—but he wanted it with someone specific. He always kept himself from seeing what could be, and suddenly, that's all he could see.

He'd known he was in love with Sebastian, but that was all about how he felt about his boy. It was outwardly projected, something other. But thinking of it now in terms of him, in terms of them together, and what he could do and be for his boy was something altogether different. Without realizing it, he set his knife and fork down and moved his napkin from his lap to the table.

He was about to push his chair back when his father who sat at the head of the table to his left placed his hand over the back of Gideon's. He looked up into his father's eyes, startled that he'd been so out of it he hadn't realized that everyone at the table was looking at him. He cleared his throat. "Sorry, I must have checked out."

His father squeezed his hand gently and said, "Finn asked you a question."

Gideon turned to face his brother. "What?"

"I was just saying that I haven't seen you in a while. How is Sebastian feeling? Is he recovering from his illness?"

His mother piped in. "What's wrong with Sebastian?"

He ignored his mother's question and turned his confused gaze to his brother. "Illness? I... I don't know." He narrowed his eyes at his brother. "I ended it with him. How do you even know Sebastian was sick?"

"What do you mean you ended it with him? That boy was perfect for you!"

"Mom."

"Don't you 'Mom' me. That boy was the sweetest thing. And *so* talented. I'm going to call him for a tattoo appointment. You need someone like him. What happened?"

He closed his eyes and took a deep breath, praying to whatever deity would listen, for patience. "It wasn't working out. We set clear boundaries in our contract, he broke them. I was losing trust in him. He kept canceling on me. Finally, a few days before New Year's, I went to check on him after he cancelled again. He wasn't even home. I just—"

"Jesus, you're something."

Gideon's heart stopped at his brother's disgusted tone. He turned his head in Finn's direction, glaring. "Excuse me?"

Finn glared right back. "You're a piece of work, is all. Get off your goddamn high horse for a minute and think. How did he look the last time you saw him, Gideon?"

Thrown off by the question, he couldn't help but bring up an image in his mind of Sebastian on the night of the party. He'd dressed up, but now that Gideon thought about it, his boy had looked tired and drawn out. Pale and too thin. His pants had been too big, the sweater even bigger. Jesus. How could he have overlooked that?

He glanced back at his brother who was shaking his head. "Not good, right?"

No. It hadn't been good. Fuck. Was he so goddamn blinded by his own self-righteous indignation that he hadn't even bothered to really see his boy?

To really notice something wasn't right? But Finn hadn't even been there, he'd been working. He hadn't seen Finn since Christmas, and he hadn't asked about Sebastian at that time so why now?

"How do you know he was sick?"

Finn stood up from the table, grabbing his napkin before it fell to the floor. "I just know he hadn't been feeling well."

"But how, Finn?"

Finn wandered away, into the kitchen, all eyes on him. "What's your issue, Gideon? Why does it even ma—"

"It matters! What. Do. You. Know?"

Finn shook his head now. "I can't…"

He stood so swiftly, the chair he'd been sitting on skittered back and nearly tipped over. "You can't what? So help me god, Finnegan! Tell me what you know about my boy!"

"I can't talk to you about it, and I honestly don't know any details. I saw him, Gideon."

"Where?"

"I can't tell you anything more. One, because he asked me not to, and two because. I. CAN'T. Tell. You."

Sick dread made the dinner he'd consumed feel like lead in his stomach. If he couldn't, not wouldn't, but couldn't tell him, there was only one place he could have seen him. He shook his head in denial.

"Just please, remember how he looked the last time you saw him."

He did, and the more he did, the sicker he felt.

Braden's near whisper grabbed his attention. "He didn't look well on New Year's Eve. I didn't say anything because I could tell he was trying really hard to look and act like he was fine. He's been avoiding me since that night. Won't answer his phone. Texted once then finally just called and said he needed time and would call me when he was feeling up to it."

Gideon was dizzy with panic, gripping the back of his chair with one hand, he reached his other out, and it ended up tipping his plate off center and spilling some of his food onto the table. If Finn had seen him, presumably at the hospital, how sick was he? Why hadn't Sebastian told him? Why… But he knew why, didn't he? Self-loathing hit him at lightning speed. God, what kind of monster was he?

The worst fucking kind.

His boy had needed him, and what had he been doing? He regained his balance, ignored the outstretched hands on either side of him that tried to help him and stepped back, out of Finn's and his father's reach, and stood there for several moments, focused straight ahead of him, his family's words a muffled din in the background. All he could think about was getting to Sebastian.

He was on the front porch, unable to even remember getting there, when he felt a heavy hand clamp onto his shoulder. His instincts kicked in, and before he could stop himself, he turned and dislodged the unwanted hindrance and ended up glaring into Finn's eyes. His lips moved but Gideon couldn't hear above the chaos in his head. His brother finally clasped both hands on either side of his face and shouted his name which brought him back around.

"Gideon, you can't drive like this. Wherever you're going, I'll take you."

He realized Finn was right and tossed his keys at his brother as he slid into the passenger side of his Rover. He told Finn where to go then sat in silence and tried desperately to gain some semblance of control. His mind was moving a hundred miles a minute. The only thing keeping him from completely losing it was his own self-defense mechanism of shutting down all of the myriad possibilities that would send him into that mental tailspin.

"Fuck, Gideon. I shouldn't have said anything."

"Oh, hell yes you should have. We were together, we'd signed a contract. He damned well should have told me."

"BDSM contracts stipulate that kind of thing?"

"Yes. It calls out medical issues that would impact or be affected by any play outlined in the contract. Fuck, Finn. I didn't think I was good enough for him, and it didn't matter that I was in love with him. Nothing would convince me to give us a try outside of our six-month contract. I was looking for excuses to end it so I wouldn't hurt either one of us further by allowing it to continue. I'm a monster and a coward."

Finn pulled up to a stoplight and looked over at him. "You're neither. You can fix this."

"I don't know if I can. I devastated him."

"So you'll just have to try harder and not take no for an answer. You do what you have to do for forgiveness."

"God, why didn't I see it? How fucking selfish am I? Why didn't I ask more questions? The last month, he was never interested in food, and he was losing weight! He knew something from the beginning. I don't know how I know, I just do. From the beginning, he said he wasn't made for relationships. I thought, how perfect, neither am I. Jesus Christ."

"Look, let's not borrow trouble. It could be anything from the flu to heart surgery. Thinking the worst now isn't helping."

He felt more and more guilt weigh him down the more he thought back on their time together. There had been signs. "From the beginning, he said he had a very demanding schedule, and he would have to let me know if his availability changed, but maybe he was just too sick, or seeing specialists. I went along with it because in my mind, that would make it easier to keep my emotions out of the picture. God, I'm an asshole."

"Gideon, you need to stop castigating yourself for not knowing he was sick. He obviously didn't want you to know and took some painstaking precautions to ensure you remained in the dark. Let's just wait until we see him."

They drove in silence the rest of the way. Gideon pointed out the yellowish green row house where Sebastian lived and had him pull in front just behind Sebastian's beater. He sat and stared in disbelief at the huge for sale sign outside of his house that had a "SOLD" sticker slapped over it.

His hands shook when he opened the car door. Jesus, was he even here? If not here, where? He'd have to have Zavier track him down. He'd have to... Fuck. He was just about to slam the door when he remembered Finn and said absentmindedly, "You can take the Rover. I'll call a car service."

"I'm not going anywhere. I'll let you go in and have some time with him, but if you need me, I can come in and check on him, or you can text me that you'll be staying and you don't need me. I can entertain myself in the car with my phone for a while to be sure you don't need anything before I take off. But, Gideon, don't go into attack mode. He may have kept secrets, but in the end, he was probably protecting you rather than him. Keep that in mind when you talk to him."

Gideon nodded and headed up the stairs to Sebastian's front door. He pulled out his key and unlocked the door, hopeful that meant Sebastian was still there. There were boxes everywhere, and he wasn't sure his boy was home until he saw Slap and Tickle using the moving boxes as scratching posts. They headed his way when he crouched down. He petted them both then stood when he heard voices and headed in the direction of the back of the house.

The front room facing the street was dim, only a table lamp turned on to fend off the oncoming darkness. The voices were clearer now as he headed through the dining nook that housed a round table piled with paperwork, towards the kitchen. "I can open up my own goddamn can of soup, Zoe. It's even got a pop top. Stop hovering. We need to talk about this. You can't keep ignoring me every time I bring it up."

Gideon paused just outside of the kitchen and out of view of its occupants. He did his best to settle his racing heart at not only hearing Sebastian's voice, a voice he'd missed so much and hadn't even realized it until that moment, but also, the utter weariness that was obvious in his words. His thoughts were interrupted by Zoe's response. "I'm not discussing it, Sebastian. I'll worry about it if the time comes."

"If the time comes, I won't be here. That's why we need to talk about this now. I just want to make sure you'll take care of them, and that you have my lawyer's number."

Gideon's breath hitched at that, knowing what Sebastian was saying, even though he didn't say the words. Zoe's response was soft when she replied, "We don't need to make any sort of plan, Sebastian. You'll be fine. Let's not jinx it, okay?"

"Zoe, I know it's hard, but we have to be practical."

"I'm not discussing this. I'm gonna go change my clothes. I came over straight away, and I smell like coffee and croissants. I worked it out to get some time off so I'll be here to help."

"You did what? Why would you do that?"

"It's just a few weeks, and you're gonna need help after the surgery. Maya and Braden were cool with it. Gave me a couple weeks off, more if I need it, and they have someone to take the hours, so it won't impact them."

Surgery? Fuck.

"You shouldn't have done that."

"Regardless, it's done. I'll be back in a few." She headed out of the kitchen just as Gideon heard the microwave turn on which stifled the gasp Zoe let out when she saw him. Her hand flew up to her racing heart as she gazed at him, wide-eyed. Tears pooled in her eyes, and she launched herself at him. Her hug was unexpected, but he returned it, nonetheless, and gripped her tighter when she whispered, "I'm so angry at you right now. But, don't let him push you away. He needs you."

He nodded as she walked off, presumably to go change. He heard the microwave ding and waited several seconds to avoid any accidents. When he heard the bowl touch down on the countertop, he walked in to see Sebastian get gingerly onto the counter stool at the kitchen's small island.

God, it had only been two weeks, and he'd obviously not really noticed on New Year's, so he guessed it was more like three and a half weeks. The time had ravaged his boy's body and sapped his strength. He must have made some noise because Sebastian looked up with startled eyes and made to straighten his body and appear stronger, more whole. Gideon couldn't help it, he growled out, "Don't. Don't fucking pretend with me. Not after all this time."

Sebastian's shoulders slumped, and he stared down into his bowl of soup and muttered, "When did you find out? How did you find out? Zoe?"

"Less than an hour ago, and no, Finn asked me how you were feeling. You just mentioned surgery. Did you have it already?" Gideon pointed to Sebastian's face.

Sebastian's face heated and shook his head, turning away to hide it from him. "No, this is just a laser treatment. It's nothing."

Gideon approached him and turned Sebastian on his stool. "Don't hide from me, boy. You have nothing to be ashamed of. You're beautiful—" Gideon stopped in shock when Sebastian raised his eyes to meet his. "Jesus, your eyes! What—"

He'd never seen anything so beautiful. He had one amber colored eye and one azure blue. He'd only ever seen him with two amber colored eyes, and they were gorgeous, but this. *Why?* When his boy looked away and tried to turn his face again, he clasped it gently. "Don't. I'm sorry. It just shocked me, that's all."

"I wear a colored contact to hide it."

"Why would you hide it? Your eyes are gorgeous. How many people can say they have different colored eyes? That's amazing."

When Sebastian shook his head and looked away again, he mumbled, "It's just one more thing to make me different. Anyway, it doesn't matter."

"It matters. Everything matters, Sebastian. You're sick, and I don't even know what's wrong. I thought you just had some kind of flu bug or mono or something."

Bastian sighed, lowered his head into his hands and rubbed them through his hair, his exhaustion evident. "What do you want me to say, Gideon?"

"How about you just tell me why you didn't think that sharing the fact that you're really sick was an important thing to do?"

Sebastian rubbed at his temples and sighed. "That's not how our arrangement worked."

Gideon's back went up, and he stood taller, his voice deepened to that pitch that had Sebastian's eyes lowering, and his hands moving to his lap, palms up. "Arrangement?!"

"Yes, Sir."

"You think of our relationship as an arrangement?"

Confusion passed across Sebastian's features, his eyebrows winging up in question. "Yes, Sir?"

"So, I've been operating under the assumption that we had been in a committed D/s relationship? Admittedly, it was to be short term, but you thought of it as an arrangement?"

"We had a contract. We never deviated from it. When I pushed those boundaries, you were always quick to keep us on course. So yes, I thought of it as an arrangement, Sir."

"Fucking hell, Sebastian."

"I'm sorry, Sir."

"Jesus fuck, boy, stop calling me Sir. We're not in a scene."

"You're using that voice. It's a reflex, Sir."

Gideon made his way to stand beside his boy. He sighed, relaxed his shoulders and calmed his tone. "You're right, I'm sorry, Bastian. I'm feeling out of my element right now. I'm worried about you."

Sebastian looked up into his eyes, a look of disbelief replacing the fatigue for a moment, which caused Gideon to close his eyes in self-disgust. "Was I so horrible to you, so heartless, that you can't fathom an apology?"

"Heartless? No, never that. You were always good to me. It was just a surprise, that's all."

"Seems like I'm going to be doing a lot of apologizing then. I'm sorry that I was so closed off. I'll work on that."

Again, confusion clouded Sebastian's eyes. "Gideon, I appreciate you stopping by, but I guess I'm a little confused as to why you're here. I'm sorry I didn't tell you that I was sick, but now that you know, I don't know what else there is for us to discuss."

Confused himself, Gideon responded, "I'm here for a lot of reasons. But most of all, right now, I'm here to help. Where are your parents?"

Sebastian seemed speechless by this line of questioning and there were several drawn-out seconds before he asked, "Where are my parents, right now?"

"Yes."

He shook his head and looked at the clock on the wall. "Well, it's past dinner time for them, so they're probably sitting in their living room. My mom is either doing needlepoint or reading the Bible, and my dad is in his recliner watching one of his Gospel programs."

"At their home?"

"Yes?"

"I thought you said they live in San Diego."

"They do."

"So, they're coming up for your surgery?"

"No. They won't be coming up for anything. I told you, we don't get along."

"What are you talking about, Sebastian? Who's been taking care of you?"

"I've done just fine taking care of myself."

Gideon lost all color and felt sick to his stomach and remembered Braden telling him he'd spent the holidays alone. How had he forgotten that? "You've done just fine? You had no one? What about Zoe?"

Just as Gideon had lost all color, heat infused Sebastian's face as he admitted, "I told her about three weeks ago. I had to visit the hospital unexpectedly. I had to call her to take care of Slap and Tickle."

"That week I couldn't see you because you were sick? Wait. Unexpectedly, as in via ambulance?"

Sebastian's face grew even more red, and he looked down at his now cold soup. "Yes, Sir."

Gideon blew out a breath. He couldn't believe what he'd just heard. He brought his hands up behind his head, took another deep breath, and turned away from Sebastian. He'd been through a lot in his life. He'd been shot, he'd been attacked, tortured, chased, hunted, and he'd lost men that were like brothers to him, but he couldn't ever remember feeling this much anguish, this much devastation, and that was saying something.

He'd been off doing fuck all, while his boy was sick, in pain, and hospitalized. God, he was never going to forgive himself. What kind of man did that? He shook his head, knowing going down that road wouldn't help here. This wasn't about him. He wasn't the one that mattered right now, so he sucked it up, set it aside to deal with later, and turned back toward Sebastian who looked nearly as devastated as he was. He softened his expression and asked, "Okay, so when is your surgery?"

Sebastian shifted his eyes up to Gideon's chest and whispered, "A little over a week."

"Okay, so do you have a bunch of appointments beforehand with your doctors this week for whatever's going on?"

"No. I'm moving."

"Why did you sell your house?"

Sebastian just shook his head and looked down again. "It doesn't really matter. I have to be packed and out of here soon."

Gideon wanted to push on that but figured he'd come back to it later. "Will they have everything packed in time?"

"I should have everything packed for them on Wednesday."

"You?"

"Yes, Sir. I don't have that much left to pack."

Gideon knew his face registered his shock. "You've done all the packing?"

"Well, Zoe has helped. She did most of the kitchen and a few other things."

"But, you're sick. You should be resting. You've packed the rest of your house by yourself?"

"Well, it's not quite done like I said but almost. I've been on medical leave for a few weeks, so I've used that time to get it sold and packed up."

Gideon rubbed his hands over his face, at a loss. "Jesus, boy."

"Sir?"

Dazed, he met Sebastian's eyes. "Yeah?"

"You did the right thing."

Gideon, afraid he knew what Sebastian meant, shook his head. "No."

Sebastian continued, undaunted. "You did what was best for us. I was planning on doing it myself. We always knew this wasn't going to last. Neither of us are made for long term."

"Sebastian, I was a coward and an asshole."

Gideon's heart wrenched when he saw such resigned sadness in Sebastian's eyes. His boy gave a little chuckle though and said, "Well, I admit, you could have been a little gentler. But, in the end—"

"Don't. Don't say it."

"You did what I couldn't do. You stepped up and did what was right."

"I don't agree."

Sebastian stood, gripping the edge of the island to steady himself. Gideon moved forward to help, but Sebastian pulled back from him raising his hand up to stop him from getting closer, breaking his heart. "Be that as it may, that's how I see it. I think you've got a misplaced sense of guilt, but there's really no need." He walked toward Gideon and ran a gentle hand down his arm. "We're right where we were meant to be. Truly. Now, I'm getting a little tired, so you'll have to excuse me. I'm going to go rest."

"Sebastian."

Sebastian was already walking away when he replied, "Thank you for coming, Sir, but I think you should leave. It's easier that way."

Gideon, unable to fathom how things went south so fast, just stood there in shock. When he finally got his wits about him, he turned to find Sebastian gone, most likely on his way upstairs.

Chapter 31

GIDEON

Gideon walked out the front door to see his brother on the landing at the top of the stairs, chatting with Zoe. He was in a daze and had never felt so utterly broken. He glanced up to see his brother watching him, concerned. He was about to tell him to head on home that he'd be staying, but a crying Zoe was headed towards him.

"You're just giving up? You weren't even in there thirty minutes!" She shoved him in the chest, not moving him an inch. "He needs someone who's going to be strong for him, not leave at the first opportunity. He needs help, Gideon. I'm doing my best, but it's not enough."

He was so shocked by her outburst and so completely wrecked that he didn't try to stop her tirade, he just hugged her. Kissing her on her head, he pulled away. "Your best was enough to get him here. I'm so grateful to you. I'm not going anywhere, he just went upstairs to rest. I came out to tell Finn that he could take my car home."

Her eyes turned up to him as if afraid to believe what he was saying. "Really?"

"Yeah. I don't know what's going on. He told me I made the right decision for us, and he asked me to leave." When she opened her mouth to argue he held up his hand. "I'm not listening to him. I'm here to stay."

She began to tell him just some of what he'd missed, emotion obvious, in her voice. "He's sick as a dog, Gideon. And so tired. His meds have really bad side effects, but that's better than the alternative. His insurance denied the preauthorization request that his doctor had fast-tracked."

"Wait. His insurance won't pay for treatment?"

"Some treatment, yes. This surgery? No. They think he has viable alternatives. He's been on the phone talking to his insurance, calling the hospital, other doctors. This is the only option unless he wants to live like he's been living for the last few months. But they'll just continue getting worse, and he'll have no quality of life, this is his only option to be free of them."

He had no idea what she was talking about. "Slow down. What keeps getting worse? What does he need to be free of?"

The stunned look on her face didn't make him feel better. Her voice shook when she finally managed, "His seizures."

Seizures were so far from anything he would have guessed that he didn't know what to do with it. He was reeling, and he didn't even know the implications of what she was saying. He shook his head and tried to say something but he had no words.

All Gideon could think was he'd been doing it all without any help. Zoe had done her best, but she wasn't available to Sebastian like he would have been.

But instead…

Instead he'd been going on some fucked-up revenge mission. He glanced away from Zoe, his eye catching the sign in front of Sebastian's house.

"That's why he's selling his place."

"Yeah, but that's only for the second half of the surgical costs. He couldn't get the money fast enough. He had to pay for part of the first half out of his retirement account and lost a lot in taxes. The rest wiped out his savings. He's been appealing his insurance's decision, but all of his requests have been rejected."

He ran his hands through his hair in frustration. "All of this could have been avoided if he'd just told me that he was really sick in the first place. He's giving me nothing to go on, and he asked me to leave.

Obviously, that's not happening, but I don't want to be digging for every scrap of information. I don't even know what kind of surgery he's having. I'm going in blind."

Zoe crossed her arms over her chest as if to ward off a chill and whispered, "I can't pronounce it. It's an extratemcortal recession, something like that."

Gideon looked over at Finn and saw him close his eyes and take a deep breath before he met Gideon's gaze. "Extratemporal cortical resection. It's a craniotomy, Gideon."

His knees gave out, and he slumped back against the front door and slid down its surface until he was on his ass, looking up at his brother in shock.

Finn approached and squatted down in front of him. "We'll make sure he's got the best surgeon. I know of several I'd pick to be on his case, but we'll check and see who it is and go from there. You won't be alone in this. We'll deal with it."

Gideon shook his head and fisted his hands in anger aimed only at himself. "He's been doing it alone this whole time, and I don't even know how long 'this whole time' is. He told me his parents are down in San Diego. He didn't admit anything to Zoe until just three weeks ago. It makes me fucking sick to know that he's been struggling and feeling as if he has no one to turn to. He was alone for Thanksgiving and Christmas, and I ended it and asked him to leave our family on New Years. I chased him away, for fuck's sake!"

Zoe whispered something he didn't hear, and he had to ask her to repeat it. "He's never really had anyone. His family is awful. I'm one of his first real friends, Gideon. And I only know what he's felt comfortable telling me over the last couple weeks. We weren't that close before. He never seemed to want to let anyone get too close, or I don't know. Maybe he didn't know how?"

He needed to see his boy, hold him. "I'm gonna go be with him."

His heart hurt. Standing up, he grabbed the door handle and opened it, ushering Zoe inside. She put a hand on his arm and whispered, "You need to see something."

She walked towards the dining nook and shuffled through some of the paperwork until she found an envelope in the pile and handed it to him. Finn stood beside him as he opened it up.

She crossed her arms over her chest again and nodded to the paper he pulled out. "He hasn't given up. I want you to know that. But he's prepared for the worst. He wrote his parents a letter, letting them know what was going on, telling them that he loved them and that he was sorry things were so strained between them; this was their response."

Gideon looked down at the paper and began reading.

Sebastian,

Leviticus 20:13:

If a man also lie with mankind, as he lieth with a woman, both of them have committed an abomination: they shall surely be put to death; their blood shall be upon them.

We did not raise you to be an abomination in the eyes of God, and yet, that is exactly what you have become. God's work is being done, as was inevitable, as is just. If this sickness is to be the death of you, it is the punishment you must bear for such atrocities against The Lord Our God. Only by His hands, upon your death, will you truly learn about everlasting damnation.

Colossians 3:25:

For the wrongdoer will be paid back for the wrong he has done, and there is no partiality.

You get what you deserve in this life, Sebastian, God makes it so.

Beatrice and Harold Phillips

Gideon's hands shook as he handed the letter over to Finn. He stood, his hands fisted at his sides. He wanted to punch a hole in the wall, find Sebastian's parents, and make them suffer, as they'd made him suffer. Zoe gently placed a hand on his shoulder as she stood in front of him which pulled him out of his livid thoughts. "Do you love him, Gideon? I know you care. You wouldn't be here otherwise, but if you're going to help him, if you're going to be what he needs right now, he won't truly lean on you unless he knows that it isn't pity, that it's love."

Gideon hugged her to him, his whole body still vibrating with anger. "He couldn't have done better in choosing you. When I tell him how I feel, I want him to be the first to hear it. I'll be taking over, going forward. He's had enough on his plate, and the stress can't be helping. I want him to focus on getting well."

He pulled away and smiled gently at her. "Is that mountain of paperwork all related to everything going on?"

She nodded, and he looked at Finn, his eyes beseeching, knowing he was asking a lot of his brother. When he received an immediate nod, he continued, "Gather it all up and hand it over to Finn. He'll work with our financial advisors to ensure it's dealt with. Provide him with anything you can find regarding his treatment plan, surgery, and prognosis, and he can let us know his thoughts on next steps."

She clung to Finn when he pulled her to him. Gideon headed towards the stairs but turned back to look at his brother. He knew it was asking a lot, but what Finn couldn't do, he'd hand over to someone else in their family.

"Find his bank account info and make sure to make a sizable deposit. I need him to have what he needs. Also, get our lawyers involved with his insurance regarding any appeals he's been working on and to go over everything with a fine-tooth comb. There's got to be a way to get his surgery approved. I'll pay for whatever's not covered, but he's been paying for insurance for a fucking reason, so we need to make sure they're doing right by him."

Finn nodded and said, "I'll get everyone over here to finish his packing and anything else he needs done starting tomorrow. He could probably use some peace and quiet tonight."

Gideon nodded and thanked his brother. He was about to climb the stairs when another thought occurred to him. "Also, I want them to draw up a medical power of attorney. It needs to be clear that I'm legally responsible for him and will provide advanced directive with any health care proxies, and his living will, in case he is incapacitated for any reason and I need to make his medical decisions."

Zoe spoke up, "He has a lawyer. I'm sure his information is here somewhere. We'll figure it out."

Gideon looked at Finn. "His parents are to have no visitation rights, let alone be able to make medical decisions, on his behalf. Oh, and, Finn, destroy that fucking letter. The paper is worn. He's been reading it, most likely, over and over again on a daily basis, taking those words to heart. I want no evidence of it left."

Finn nodded and continued to hold Zoe, rocking her back and forth as her crying slowed. Gideon took the stairs two at a time and found Sebastian in bed, bundled in his duvet with only the top of his head showing. Gideon removed his shoes, emptied his pockets, and got into bed with his boy who was warm with a fever. When Sebastian stirred, and turned his body toward Gideon's, he kissed his head. Sebastian looked up, his bleary eyes red-rimmed from crying nearly broke Gideon's heart.

He smiled a soft, dreamy smile and whispered, "I'm dreaming, aren't I?"

Gideon replied just as softly, "No, baby, I'm here. Rest now." But Sebastian's eyes were closed again, and he was out.

Gideon woke a short while later when the bed shook. Disoriented, he pushed himself up on his elbow to check on Sebastian and realized his boy was in the throes of a seizure. Scared to death and not sure what he should be doing, he didn't try to intervene except to keep Sebastian's head from hitting his nightstand. He didn't want to try to do any more than that and harm him accidentally. He watched and he waited what was probably less than a minute but felt like the longest moments of his life, his heart shattering into a million pieces.

Sebastian settled right back into a deep sleep without waking. Gideon drew him near, tucking him into his body again. His boy had endured so much pain, and there was still so much he didn't know. As he thought about how alone he'd been for so long, he made a promise to himself and Sebastian that he'd never be alone again. He'd have more love, more family, more friends, and more happiness than he could imagine. He wouldn't want for anything.

A calmness settled over him, and his attention refocused on the man in his arms. He let his hands roam gently over his boy's small, gaunt frame. He'd always thought of Sebastian as being so tough and resilient. Small, yes, but still so full of strength. The fragility of the boy's body in his arms brought home, as nothing else had, his vulnerability. It belied the strength Gideon had attributed to him physically, and he had to admit it was more a mental and emotional toughness that made his boy seem stronger physically than he really was.

His mind took a while to shut down. He made a mental list of all the things he needed to do to ensure he was able to be away from the club for an extended amount of time. He wasn't worried about it and knew his family would step up if something happened that his management team couldn't deal with. Another list was made for the various things he needed to do for Sebastian. It seemed never ending, the lists he was making, but he worked best under pressure, and he wouldn't fail his boy ever again. With that knowledge, he let himself drift, his boy safely ensconced in his arms.

Gideon woke several hours later feeling uncomfortable and overheated and realized that Sebastian was in the midst of a fairly high fever. He eased himself out from underneath him and went in search of a thermometer. When he didn't find it in Sebastian's bedroom or bathroom, he headed downstairs to try to find one and get a cold compress and some water.

What he saw there made him stop in his tracks. Finn and Zoe were on the floor on the living room rug. The coffee table had been moved, and they were organizing the paperwork in small piles, trying to put like pages together and make heads or tails of the still huge pile. There was a pizza box on the floor between them, and they were murmuring while placing papers here and there in some organized fashion that Gideon was glad he didn't have to figure out.

They must have realized they had an audience because they both looked up at him, and she asked, "How is he?"

Gideon sat on the coffee table and scrubbed his hands over his face. Glancing from her to his brother, he said, "He had a seizure but never really fully woke up. He slept two solid hours afterwards. I didn't know what the fuck to do to help him, Finn. What do I do?"

"There's not much you can do. Wait for it to pass. Never hold him down, but if you can keep him from getting hurt, that's good. Turn him on his side if you can, during or afterward to prevent choking. If he's not on the floor, try to get him there. People get injured most when they don't feel one coming on, and they can't get to a safe place."

Gideon glanced over at the stairs. "Fuck. Fuck me. He didn't trip, he had a seizure. I knew he wasn't telling me everything. Goddammit."

"What happened?"

"He fell down the steps. He was fucking bruised from head to toe. Jesus." He lowered his head into his hands and pushed them back into his hair. "Fuck. Why didn't he just tell me?"

Zoe sat beside him and put her arm around his back. "I asked him the same thing. It's not a reflection on you. He's always been alone. He doesn't know any different. His parents did a number on him, telling him flat out he was a burden to them. He never wanted to put anyone in a position to have to take care of him."

He glanced over at her, incredulous. "He'd never be a burden. Jesus, they're monsters."

She nodded. "Yeah. They are. But we're here now. He's finally got people in his corner."

Gideon patted her knee, standing up. "He does. He's got a pretty high fever from what I can tell. Does he have a thermometer? I'm gonna get a cold compress and some water. Maybe some acetaminophen for when he wakes."

She got up and headed into the kitchen, leaving Finn to continue with the paperwork. Gideon sighed, knowing he was asking a lot of his brother. "Thank you, Finnegan. I know this isn't what you had in mind for today."

Finn looked up and gave him a look he couldn't discern. "Gideon, I don't think you've ever asked me for help with something this important to you my whole life. If I can do anything to help you or your young man up there, I'll be doing it. I've talked to Mom, filled her in. She'll fill the rest of the family in. I'm sure you have several texts on your phone. I know I did. You'll probably have visitors tomorrow if Sebastian is up for it."

Gideon nodded his head. "Yeah. I think that's good even if they only stay for a short time. He needs to know he's got family now. I'm going to lean on you a lot to get me the information I need. I want the best surgeon, whatever the cost."

Finn smiled. "That goes without saying. I've texted Camden at Connelly, Taylor, and Bennett. They're aware we need their help with the legal aspects of his case. He said first thing tomorrow morning, he'd draw up the papers you need and bring them by before noon with a notary so you can get them signed as soon as possible which will make dealing with the rest of this stuff much easier. They'll have a nice little skirmish with the health insurance people, but I'm sure they'll have it dealt with fairly quickly."

Finn continued to shuffle papers around, adding more from the bigger pile onto the smaller piles surrounding him and held up a paper. "His receipt for the first half of the surgical costs."

"How much?"

"Seventy-five grand."

"Jesus Christ. All right. We'll have to find out how much of that was from his retirement and see if it can be paid back. There's no reason for his insurance to reject the surgery if his doctor says it's medically necessary, so I'm counting on Camden to work that out."

"I've talked to his doctor as well. He can't give any specifics, obviously, without Sebastian's consent, but we spoke in generalities. He doesn't think a surgery like this should be delayed too long, but if we get another doctor to come in to perform it or travel to another hospital, he recommends it gets done within a month."

"Okay, well hopefully Sebastian will sign the necessary paperwork. I'm not going to force anything on him, but I hope he's willing to look at other options if you feel it's necessary. I'm assuming you need his medical records?"

Finn nodded. "Yeah, the sooner the better. I've got a couple people in mind, depending on his specific circumstances."

Gideon was about to comment further when Zoe approached him with her hands full. He reached out and pulled everything he'd asked for out of her hands, thanked them both again with a promise to talk to his brother more later, and headed upstairs to tend to Sebastian.

When he got back to the room, Sebastian was buried completely under the blankets again, his whole body shivering and covered in sweat. He set down the items he had in his hands and went to gather some fresh clothing and bedding. He came back to the bed with what he needed and went about waking Sebastian. He got him to sit up and was able to remove his soaked shirt and replace it, but his boy was still out of it.

When their eyes met, Sebastian blinked at him sleepily, a sweet smile on his face. "Hi."

Gideon couldn't help but smile in return. "Hey, baby."

He laid him back down, pulled off his sweatpants and briefs and replaced those as well, his boy barely stirring. He pulled the new blanket from the pile of bedding, wrapped him in it, and carried him over to his big upholstered chair.

Gideon made quick work of making the bed up again and tossed all the linens and clothes in Sebastian's hamper. He picked him back up and slid him under the covers again. Sebastian curled in on himself and seemed to be asleep again. Gideon looked around, trying to figure out what he could do to help while Sebastian continued to rest. His heart stopped in his chest when he heard a whispered, "I love you, Sir."

His knees grew weak, and he sat beside Sebastian as he slept, running his big hand over Sebastian's tiny frame. Gideon knew he was asleep and didn't know what he was saying, but he took the words to heart, knowing Sebastian wouldn't have said them in sleep unless they were true. Gideon leaned over him and kissed his head, murmuring, "I love you, too, baby."

He knew he was probably imagining it, but he thought he heard a happy sigh as he stood up again. Glad that the worst of the fever was gone for now, he went about getting a load of laundry together and started it. He wandered the rooms of the house, making a mental list of what still needed packing.

There was still so much to do, he had no idea how Sebastian would have gotten it done on his own, but knew somehow, he'd have found a way. It seemed his boy always found a way. He grabbed his phone off the nightstand to get some of the stuff down so he wouldn't forget it and saw half a dozen texts had come in. Ignoring them, he made several lists in an email and sent them out to his family asking for help and knowing he'd get it, no questions asked.

He ignored the new texts coming in, and the vibrating alerts of his email box. As he went to work packing up what seemed to be Sebastian's combined office and guest room, he couldn't help making plans for their future, regardless of how uncertain that future seemed.

Chapter 32

SEBASTIAN

Sebastian woke disoriented. His head rested in the crook of what could only be Gideon's enormous bicep, his fingers curled protectively in Gideon's huge palm. His Dom's other arm was wrapped snugly around Sebastian's waist, holding him tight against his broad chest. He thought perhaps he might be dreaming, but his lack of energy and the constant dull ache in his head made him realize he wasn't. He looked at the clock and saw it was 3:33 a.m. He slowly removed his hand from Gideon's and turned in his arms.

Assuming Gideon would be asleep, he was surprised to find him wide awake and gazing back at him. He felt Gideon's arm wrap around his back and pull him closer. He reached up and touched his Dom's soft, scruffy beard, almost not believing he was there. His Dom. He should really start thinking of him only as Gideon. He was no longer his Dom, but damned if he could force his mind to make that mental switch. Gideon would forever be his Dom even if the man no longer had the desire to own the title.

"Sir?"

"I'm here, baby. I'm not going anywhere. Close your eyes and rest."

"Why?"

"Why what, boy?"

"I thought you left."

"I'm never leaving you again. Please, just rest. I'll still be here when you wake up."

That was all it took for the floodgates to open. The firm grip he had on control slipped an infinitesimal amount, and no matter what he tried to do, he was too weak to clench it tight again.

Too exhausted to be embarrassed, his sobs wracked his small frame, and he felt himself being drawn inexorably closer until every inch of his body was touching Gideon's. Gideon's lips were in his hair, kissing, and then that deep voice he'd missed so much was whispering to him. The "I've got yous" blended in with the "I'm here nows," and finally taking over were the "You're gonna be all rights."

When the maelstrom of emotion finally abated, he tried to catch his breath. He lay in the tight embrace of his Dom, so many confusing, mixed feelings not allowing him to voice his thoughts. He pulled back just enough to look into Gideon's eyes, but Gideon pulled him in again, tucking his head under his chin, running his hand up and down his back, and kissing his head again. "I hate that you've been so alone and in so much pain. I'm so sorry, Bastian. I'm here now. You'll never be alone again."

"I don't understand. You can't… What—"

"Shhh." Gideon pulled away, and Sebastian tilted his head up, their eyes meeting. "I'll explain everything. I promise you, I will. But right now, you're too exhausted. We have plenty of time to talk in the morning. Please, close your eyes for me and sleep."

Sebastian's energy was flagging, so he nodded, burrowed himself deeper into Gideon's arms, and closed his eyes. He'd take the comfort offered for now, he didn't have it in him to argue. He placed his palm on Gideon's chest, and feeling the rise and fall, attuned his breathing to his Dom's. Drawing strength from the solid beat of Gideon's heart, he used that as the metronome to lure him back into sleep.

When he woke again, sunlight was streaming through his curtains, and he was cold and alone in bed. Not knowing what it meant and half believing maybe he had been dreaming the night before, he lay there a while longer, taking stock of how he felt. The ache in his head had abated somewhat. He wasn't as tired, but his body ached, and he didn't have much energy. Knowing he needed to get himself something to eat, he sat up and pushed the blankets to the side.

The door to his bedroom opened, and his heart stopped at the tousled hair and heavy-lidded eyes of his Dom. He held two stainless steel travel mugs and a box from the Sugar n' Spice Café that he set down on the nightstand. Sebastian's mouth watered.

"I wanted to be here when you woke. I'm sorry. I had to let my family in."

That last bit had Sebastian's heart rate ratcheting up and confusion and nervousness taking over. Gripping the bedding in his hand, he twisted it and asked, "Why is your family here?"

"To get your packing done and do anything else that needs doing for your move on Wednesday."

Feeling like he'd missed a huge conversation he should have been privy to, he rubbed his hands over his face. Shaking his head, he looked up at Gideon, confused. "Why? What's going on?" Almost afraid to ask, he forced his last question out. "Why are you here?"

"We're all here to help. You need people in your corner, and we all want to be here for you. You're not alone anymore."

Remembering some of Gideon's words in the middle of the night and his own emotional reaction, Sebastian suddenly couldn't catch his breath. This didn't feel right. This was the last thing he wanted and was exactly why he'd not told anyone what was going on. Shaking his head, he looked at Gideon, his eyes beseeching. "They can't be here, Gideon. Please. Tell them thank you, but I'll handle everything. I need to handle everything."

"You don't, Bastian."

"I do. Please. It's important to me. I don't want to be rude. Your family is amazing, but I can't have them here. I can't."

"Sebastian…"

Feeling lightheaded, his breathing was coming in short bursts. "I can't have you here. You all need to leave." He was shaking his head, and his hands were shaking. He couldn't breathe, his chest felt tight, and his vision was fuzzy. He slumped back onto his pillows against the headboard as he tried to breathe again and the blackness set in. The next thing he knew, he felt hands rubbing his arms up and down and then clasping his face.

"Jesus. Bastian. Hey, come on. Open your eyes. There you go. Deep breath. Take a deep breath with me. That's it. Another. And again. Good."

Humiliated beyond belief, he avoided looking at the larger than life man now sitting in front of him on the bed, hands cradling his face. He shook his head and pulled back, dislodging the grip Gideon had on him. How long had it been since he'd eaten? Every time he did, he felt sick, and he was never very hungry to begin with, but obviously, he'd have to force the issue. He had too much shit to do to be passing the fuck out. He had to get them gone. He couldn't have them in his house.

"Gideon, please listen to what I'm saying. I need to deal with this on my own. Please."

"You don't, Sebastian."

"I DO!" Angry suddenly, he didn't have the energy to temper his reaction. "Don't you get it? I can't lean on anyone because I don't have anyone to lean on! I won't be a charity case!"

"Jesus, Bastian, you're not a charity case. What are you even—"

"That's exactly what I am. And I won't stand for it. I won't be a burden ever again!"

"You're not a burden!"

"I won't be, if you leave. Please go."

"I can't."

Tears rolled down his face, and he whispered, brokenly, "Jesus, Gideon. All I've got left is my pride. Can't you give me that at least?"

Gideon's large palms clasped his face again and forced his eyes to his. "Listen to me, Bastian."

"No! Please, just…"

Frantic, he shook his head and was about to continue when a dark look passed over Gideon's face and his voice took on his Dom tone when he snapped out, "Settle, boy!"

Just like that the noise taking up too much space in his head stopped, and his body stilled. Goddammit. Why did his body still have to react so completely to the man? Why did his mind betray him and calm when there was nothing to be calm about? Why did his heartbeat slow its cadence in his chest as they stared at each other?

Gideon shook his head. "I'm sorry. I know I don't have the right to call you boy after what I did."

Sebastian sighed, defeated. "I'll always be your boy, Gideon. Don't you get it? That's the problem. It doesn't matter what you did. It doesn't matter that we're over. That's why I need you to go. All of you, just go."

The firm, deep tone continued when Gideon responded, "I can't do that. And we aren't over, Sebastian."

"We are. We have to be."

Gideon shook his head again. "I don't believe that. And I need you to stop pushing me away for just a minute while I ask you something really important. All right? And no matter what, I need you to tell me the truth. Can you do that, Bastian?"

Sebastian glanced away, unable to hold his gaze when the question had him wanting to say no. He shook his head ineffectually and earned a growl in response. His eyes flicked immediately back to his Dom, and he couldn't stop his sigh. "Yes, Sir."

Gideon nodded, loosening his grip on Sebastian's face and caressed his hands down his arms and clasped Sebastian's hands in his. "I don't know exactly what's going on with your health. We'll talk about that later. Right now, I need to know if we set aside your illness, whatever it is, and set aside our contract and our Dom/sub relationship—if none of that existed—what would you want from me? What would you want from us?"

No. Why would he ask that? How could he not know the answer already? He had to know. He shook his head and looked down. He wasn't strong enough for this. Pulling his hands free of Gideon's, he pulled his knees up to his chest to bury his face in.

"Baby?"

"Don't."

"Sebastian!"

He jerked his head up at his Dom's commanding tone and sucked in a startled breath. Angry at what he was being forced to say, he tried to refuse again with another shake of his head.

"Answer—"

"Everything! I'd want everything from you! None of which I can have, Gideon! Jesus. Did you think I misunderstood you at the party? What is this? Punishment? Bring your family over to tease me with a world I'll never belong to? Hold my hand because you feel sorry for me, and then leave when reality hits? I'm a strong person. I've had to be. But a person can only take so much before they break."

"I love you, Sebastian."

"Is that what you want? Do you want me to br…" A gasp escaped when he finally realized what Gideon had said. That wasn't possible. "What? What did you say?"

"I'm in love with you, Sebastian."

"NO! You can't be!" He scrambled off the side of the bed when Gideon tried to reach for him. "You can't, Gideon. I'm a bad bet. You *have* to see that! Please. Please just go. Take your family and go."

"Sebastian, what are you talking about? I'm not going anywhere."

"You have to. Don't you get it? This," he gestured between them, "can't work. I told you that I wasn't made for long term. You made the right decision for us. You don't know what you're saying. You don't have all the facts."

"So, tell me! Because I'm not going anywhere."

"I have a surgery next week. Brain surgery, Gideon. There's a very real chance I won't make it, but if I do, I've got a long road of recovery ahead. And even if I recover fully, I'll always have problems. My port-wine stain will always be an issue. I'll constantly have laser treatments and other problems as a result."

"I don't give a shit about that!"

As if Gideon hadn't spoken, he continued, "I'm losing strength in my arm and may not be able to use it years from now. My leg could be the same in the future. Glaucoma could be next. I'm high risk for strokes, paralysis, and blindness. It's never ending, Gideon!"

"It doesn't matter. None of that matters!"

"Of course, it matters! Everything matters. Christ, I barely have the energy to deal with it. I would never put that on anyone else. You deserve someone whole. Someone who can keep up with you. Someone who will be as healthy as you. Someone who won't be a burden for the rest of your life. Because that's all I'll be in the end, and I won't be the one to do that to you."

"You don't get to make that choice for me!"

"I do, though. I have to. Don't you see? Because I love you, too, Sir. Enough to never put you through it. Enough to let you go."

"Jesus, Sebastian. You're killing me. I'm not leaving you."

"You don't have a choice. I'll ask your family to leave myself if it comes to that."

"You can ask them to leave, but the likelihood that they'll do as you ask is slim to none. They know what you mean to me. They know that you need help."

"I don't need help," he said stubbornly.

Gideon approached him and squeezed his shoulders, gently. "Jesus, Bastian. Everybody needs help. And that's all they need to know. You've got a real mom down there that's waiting to lavish you with love and help take care of you because that's what real mothers do. You've got a father organizing everything in the house so that everything runs smoothly on Wednesday."

Overwhelmed, all he could get out was a, "But," before Gideon ignored him and continued, drawing him near.

"You've got your two closest friends down there, doing whatever my dad says to do. You've got a brother doing the heavy lifting and a sister filling all the holes in your wall with toothpaste and painting over them. And you've got Finn working with our lawyers and your medical paperwork to find a way to get your surgery approved. My other brother would be here, too, if he wasn't overseas with his SEAL team. You have a whole family down there, Bastian."

He shook his head and crossed his arms, rejecting Gideon's words. "I don't have family. They—"

Gideon pulled him against his chest and wrapped his arms around him. "Yeah. I know what your mom had to say to you. Something is deeply broken in them to reject a son like you which makes them your birth parents, but not your family. Your family is here, in your house, taking care of what needs to be done so that you can finally rest."

He pulled back. "It's not right, Gideon. I can't accept it."

"It's already done. There's nothing to accept. They love you because I love you. It's as simple as that."

Shaking his head, he extricated himself and backed away, isolating himself from Gideon's words and touch. "Nothing's that simple. And that doesn't change the fact that they're wasting their time on someone who may very well not be here next week."

He watched, devastated as his words shattered Gideon before his eyes.

"It's not a waste of time. You've gotta stop talking like that."

He backed away and faced his window. "That's my reality, Gideon. Denying it won't make it go away."

"It's not going to happen."

He turned around again, frustration seeping through. "It could! Anything could happen. I can't ask you—"

"You're not asking! And Christ, Bastian, I could get hit by a bus tomorrow."

He crossed his arms over his chest and shook his head. "Don't be ridiculous. Nothing's going to happen to you."

Gideon reached out and slowly unfolded his arms, clasping his hands. "You can't say that for sure. Sebastian, my grandfather died of colon cancer. My mother had breast cancer. What if I get cancer or some other disease? Would you leave me when I needed you most?"

He tried to pull away, but Gideon held fast. "Let me go."

"No. Are you going to leave me if I get sick or hurt, Sebastian?"

"You won't."

"You don't know that! I'm not invincible!"

He shook his head at the absurdity of this conversation. "Stop."

"No. Answer the goddamn question, Bastian. Would you leave me if I got cancer?"

"NO! You know I wouldn't!"

"But cancer would put a burden on you."

"Don't twist my words. It's not the same."

"It's exactly the same! It's exactly the fucking same, Sebastian. Put yourself in my position for a minute. Answer me truthfully. If you were me and I was you, would you walk away from me? If I lost my eyesight and lost use of an arm or a leg, if I had seizures and needed surgery to stop them. Where would you be, Sebastian?"

"Gideon…"

"WHERE WOULD YOU BE?!"

"I'D BE WITH YOU!" A sob escaped, and he admitted again, brokenly, "I'd be with you."

Gideon crushed him in a hug and swayed with him as he whispered, "I know you would, baby. We love each other, and that's what you do for someone that you love. I won't leave no matter what you say or do and neither will your family downstairs. It's okay to accept help, Sebastian. It doesn't make you weak."

His family. Could it really be as simple as that? He didn't think so, but then again, Gideon wasn't prone to lying. He couldn't wrap his mind around it. If his parents could essentially tell him he deserved what he got, how could these strangers accept him and love him so easily? And then he remembered the people he'd met at the New Year's party, and suddenly, it didn't seem so farfetched.

He'd been accepted immediately and most of them didn't even know he was with Gideon. He'd be willing to bet he met more good people that night than he had the whole of his life so far. It was a pretty shitty thing to have to admit to himself. But he realized if they were going to give him a chance, what kind of man would he be if he didn't do the same for them?

He took a deep shuddering breath, and Gideon lifted him up effortlessly and carried him back to the bed. The ice that had seeped into his bones weeks ago began to melt. He was safe. Safe to be himself. Safe to express his emotions any way he needed to. And safe to be who he was without trying to hide any part of himself.

He didn't know what was to come. He knew they still had so much to talk about, but right then, sitting in Gideon's lap and holding onto him as tightly as he could felt right. Hearing Gideon tell him over and over again that he loved him went a long way in convincing him he wasn't being weak accepting the help so freely given. It took strength to admit help was needed, didn't it?

Gideon was being so persistent and Sebastian was so goddamn tired. So mentally, physically, and emotionally wrecked he didn't have the energy to push back any longer. Hell, he didn't even know for sure if he wanted to push back at all because what would it hurt to try? Things couldn't get much worse than not having Gideon in his life, so what harm could come of him trying to make it work? And if his days were numbered, and it was what Gideon wanted, why not take a little happy for himself? He decided if it came, he'd deal with the fallout later and jumped off the ledge, grabbing onto Gideon's lifeline.

He pulled back and gazed at his Dom. Gideon clasped his face and asked, "Will you accept our help?"

Sebastian smiled tiredly. "Yes, I'll accept your help. Thank you, Sir."

When he saw the relief and love in Gideon's eyes, he knew he'd done the right thing. "You're welcome, baby. I love you so much."

"I love you, too," Sebastian said. A tired sigh escaping.

He smiled and buried his face in Gideon's neck, holding on for dear life. Saying those words to Gideon was life changing, so he said them again and again. He'd never thought he'd ever be able to say them to someone. He never thought anyone would ever want to hear them. And they felt better and better, every single time he said them.

Chapter 33

GIDEON

Gideon held Sebastian in a tight embrace, realizing he had a lot to make up for and he meant to make things right. When Sebastian finally whispered his "I love yous," Gideon knew he'd never been happier, regardless of the uphill battle they were about to face.

He made a promise to himself that come hell or high water, he'd do what needed to be done to see his boy well. They had a long life to live together, and he wasn't going to compromise where the love of his life was concerned. When he went to pull back a bit and look in Sebastian's eyes, the grip on his neck tightened. He closed his eyes and smiled, loving the feel of his boy in his arms.

When Sebastian finally allowed him to pull back enough to clasp his face gently, he kissed his boy's cheeks, forehead, nose, and lips. "Braden brought over some breakfast. Let's get some food in you. Are you vomiting?"

Sebastian shook his head. "No. Just feeling nauseous and uninterested in eating."

"I need you to get some calories down. I asked him to bring pastries and your favorite drink."

Sebastian curled his lips between his teeth, trying to keep from laughing, a twinkle in his eyes that Gideon hadn't seen in a couple months. "You had Braden bring me chocolate milk?"

Gideon smirked. "I did."

Sebastian let a giggle escape before he could stop it, and Gideon couldn't have been happier. He lifted Sebastian off his lap and put him gently down on the bed beside him. Reaching for the goodies on the nightstand, he placed the box on Sebastian's lap and handed Sebastian the cold travel mug, keeping the hot one for himself. He leaned back against the headboard and drew his boy into the crook of his arm as he took his first sip of the Americano he'd had Braden bring him.

He watched as Sebastian took a slow drink as if testing the waters to see how his stomach would take it. Several more sips followed and Sebastian smiled shyly back at him. Gideon rubbed his hand up and down Sebastian's arm and watched as his boy opened the box and leaned over it for several long drawn-out seconds before he leaned back and sighed. He reached in and pulled out what looked like a lemon ginger scone. He pinched off a little corner of it and again sampled it slowly before making the smallest of whimpers before taking a bit bigger bite.

His heart broke just a little bit that a couple sips of chocolate milk and a few bites of scone was akin to success in Sebastian's book. Every time he thought things couldn't look worse, he got one more reality check of what Sebastian's current world was like. He took a couple more sips of the milk and another couple bites of the scone before he slumped back into Gideon's arms.

"That's all I can do for now. I'll keep trying though, Sir."

"I'm just glad you could take a few bites. You've lost so much weight, and you didn't have any to spare."

The fact that his boy was still calling him Sir made him give Sebastian an extra hug before he moved the box from his lap and took the mug. He placed them both on the nightstand, settled down into the pillows, and Sebastian curled into his side, placing his small hand on Gideon's chest, gliding it up and down in an absentminded way. He'd so missed his boy's touch.

"Can you talk to me about what's going on? I only know bits and pieces. Not enough to understand the whole."

Sebastian nodded and continued to move his hand across Gideon's chest and stomach. "The port-wine stain, PWS, is a vascular malformation. It's basically an overabundance of capillaries just under the skin. But for me, it's part of an underlying disorder. I have what's called Sturge-Weber Syndrome. It affects lots of people differently and I'm lucky in a lot of ways…"

When Gideon sucked in a breath at that and hugged him tighter, Sebastian looked up and smiled sadly, continuing, "It's true. My PWS reacts well to laser treatments which diminish the dark color and also help slow or stop the bleeding that occasionally happens for me."

"Jesus. It bleeds? Finn said it's not painful."

"It's not really. Well, I mean, not usually. Um, it's hard to explain. In cold weather, it sometimes aches and sometimes there's a tingling numbness when that happens. I don't really know if that's normal for everyone, it's just what happens for me. It's also extra sensitive, and I have to be really gentle with it when I wash my face or if I scrub my hands over my face too hard to avoid bleeding when my skin is dry. But overall, no, it's not painful."

"Do you have to get laser surgery? Why not just leave it alone?"

"Well, I could, but as you get older and don't treat it, they tend to thicken, darken, and get bumpy. If it's prone to bleeding that would get worse as well, so it's better to treat it fairly often."

"So, this Sturge-Weber Syndrome causes the PWS?"

"It's part of it for me, not for everyone. For me, it presents as a PWS, but also as a sort of stain, I guess you could say, on my brain which causes epileptic seizures. It has since I was little. And until recently, my medications worked just fine to keep them mostly at bay. I rarely had them then the meds just stopped doing their job."

Sebastian went on to tell him that for the last several months he'd been trying many new combinations of medications and nothing was working. The side effects were making him sick and tired which is what he'd been dealing with while Gideon was none the wiser, thinking he just had mono or something. Jesus. It hurt him to know that he'd been no help while his boy had been suffering.

Sebastian explained that he'd been in the hospital, and they'd basically found a combo of drugs that kept him from having as many seizures as he'd been plagued with, but those side effects were getting worse by the day which was why it was imperative for him to have the surgery. Eventually, they'd stop working too and his quality of life would diminish further.

"So the seizures will stop after the surgery?"

"They probably won't stop completely for another year or two after the surgery, maybe never. But they will, supposedly, be more manageable with meds so I don't have any, or at least as many, seizures. There's no guarantee, and the location of my seizures in the frontal lobe makes it hard to find the seizure foci which I think is why my insurance won't pay for the surgery. This type of craniotomy is risky, and the success rate isn't as high as other areas of the brain where seizures may occur."

The more Sebastian spoke, the more he knew he had to convince Sebastian to take Finn's advice on the doctor he would choose to do the procedure. He didn't want to broach the subject so early, but he knew he couldn't wait. They needed to make their move and get the best possible surgeon which meant possible travel and working to get the money back from the hospital for the surgery if they indeed did need to cancel with his current surgeon.

Not knowing how else to approach it, he simply asked, "Are you open to finding a different doctor?"

Sebastian sat up to look at him, but he didn't like not having his boy in his arms, so he pulled him back down to lie across his chest so they could look at each other while they talked. He waited to hear what Sebastian had to say, rather than pushing for an answer.

"I don't think I have a lot of time. The side effects are pretty hard for me to deal with for any longer than the scheduled date of the procedure. If I had to find another doctor, that could take a long time. I've already paid for half of the surgery. I just…I don't think that's the best move to make at this point."

"But if we could find the best possible doctor that performs this procedure with the highest success rate, and they were willing to take you quickly, would you be willing?"

Sebastian buried his face in Gideon's chest and shook his head, making Gideon nearly panic that he wouldn't be willing to make the change. "I don't know. It's expensive here, I can't imagine what a better hospital with a better doctor would cost. And my doctor has been great. I don't know what kind of difference it would really make. I'm getting a pretty good return on the sale of the house, so I can see what another location would do, but if there's a delay or it's out of my price range, I just can't imagine how I'd be able to make it work."

"That's where Finn comes in. That's where our lawyers come in. And that's where my money comes in."

Sebastian was sitting up again, putting distance between them at his last comment. "No. Absolutely not. Please don't make this about money. I have enough for the surgery. I don't want or need your help."

The defensive posture was back, and Gideon hated that he had to have this discussion with him, but he wasn't going to bulldoze or try to order Sebastian to do what he said even if that's what he wanted to do. No, this was something they had to agree on, and something he needed to work at framing just right so that he could sell it.

"I've tasked Finn with using his contacts in the medical community to find you the best doctor for the surgery and to get your medical file to the doctor so that a surgery can be scheduled as soon as humanly possible. In addition to that, we'll have our lawyers working night and day to figure out a way to get your insurance to approve the surgery so you won't have to pay more than your out of pocket cap. But if all that fails, we'll use my money to pay for it."

"No. I'm not okay with that, Gideon. And nothing you say will change that. I won't allow you to pay for this surgery. I'll accept the help with my insurance company because I've been fighting them myself, so I'd love help there. And all right, I'm not going to cut off my nose to spite my face. If you find the best doctor, and they can take me quickly, I'm in. But I can't wait much longer. I don't think my body can take much more."

Gideon knew the truth of that, so he didn't argue the point. He took those two wins and decided he'd deal with the money conversation later. He looked at his watch and realized the lawyer and notary would arrive within the next thirty minutes, and they needed to get all the paperwork signed as soon as possible. He didn't want to delay anything, so he explained as much as he could at that point.

"We have some paperwork you'll need to sign with our lawyers and with Finn so that he can have access to your medical files and have permission to speak with your doctor on your behalf. Are you all right with all of that?"

Sebastian hesitated for a moment before he nodded, but then he said, "Gideon, I love you, but I need you to respect my wishes about the money. I'm willing to learn more about a different doctor, I'd be stupid to turn down the best. And I'm immensely grateful for any help with the insurance, but the money is a sticking point with me."

"That's your hard limit."

Sebastian gave him a sad smile and nodded. "Yeah. That's my hard limit."

Gideon figured he had the rest of his life to take care of his boy financially, so he wouldn't push. "Okay, I'll work with that. Let's get you up, and I'll help you shower. Camden will be here soon."

He stood and helped Sebastian to his feet and helped him get his clothes off. When he got them in the shower, he washed them both quickly, not wanting to keep Sebastian on his feet for long. Everything seemed to be a monumental effort for him at this point, and he just wanted to get the paperwork dealt with and get him resting again.

Gideon helped him down the stairs and realized from the smell that bagels and coffee had been made. Braden looked up from the box he was packing, and Gideon's heart clenched when he saw the tears start to fall as he ran across the room and gently clasped Sebastian in a hug.

Zavier was in the middle of removing the flat screen from the wall mount and leaning it against the wall. When his brother turned to see his husband hugging Sebastian, he smiled sadly at them and then nodded solemnly at Gideon, sending a clear message that he understood what the moment between their boys meant.

Braden had been a wreck when he'd heard about his friend. He glanced back at Sebastian and saw his boy still caught up in the hug Braden didn't seem to want to end. Confusion and sorrow etched Sebastian's features as if he didn't understand why Braden was so upset.

Gideon rubbed Sebastian's back and knew he'd just have to learn for himself that he had friends and family that loved him and were heartbroken that he hadn't reached out. When Braden pulled back, he wiped his eyes and then scowled. Zavier approached and clasped Braden's shoulders. Braden crossed his arms over his chest and turned his glare on Gideon. He couldn't help but smile at Braden's fierce protective streak.

Braden glanced back at Sebastian and asked, "How could you keep this a secret from me? Why wouldn't you lean on your friends? Do you know how hurt I was that you didn't tell me what was going on?"

Sebastian looked down at the floor and said, "I'm sorry."

Braden continued as if his friend hadn't spoken. "I thought you were just avoiding me because this bozo here," he pointed at Gideon, "was too blind to see how perfect you guys are together. If I'd had any idea you were this sick, I'd have gone with you to every doctor's appointment. I'd have stayed with you at the hospital. I'd have made sure you were eating okay. That's what friends do!"

Tears slid down Sebastian's face at Braden's words, and he shook his head. "I didn't know."

"You didn't know what?"

"I didn't know that's what friends do."

"What are you talking about, you didn't know?"

"I didn't know." Zoe walked in the room, and Sebastian glanced over at her as he continued, "You and Zoe are my first real friends. When I needed help when I was little, my parents told me I was a burden to them, so I thought if I asked for help that's what I'd be."

Braden pulled in a shaky breath, and he whispered brokenly, "Well you wouldn't be. You could never be."

Sebastian nodded as he replied, "Okay. I'm sorry."

"You're forgiven but don't do that ever again."

Sebastian shook his head. "I won't. I promise."

Braden hugged him again, rocking back and forth. Finn walked in the room and put his arm around Zoe's shoulders and handed her a handkerchief from his pocket which had her laughing as she dabbed her eyes with it. Braden and Sebastian looked at her and held their hands out to her. A little sob escaped her, and she fell into their arms, all three of them hugging and crying, the brothers looking on.

Finn rocked back on his heels and cleared his throat. "I don't want to break up the hugs, I really don't. But I have some paperwork for you to sign, Sebastian, and our lawyer, Camden Connelly, will arrive shortly."

The three parted but continued their whispered conversation for another few moments. When they were done, Sebastian clasped his hand and looked up to him. Gideon drew him in and kissed him, walking them towards the dining room. Sebastian stopped in his tracks when he saw Rowan and his parents.

His mom opened her arms, and Gideon watched, heart in his throat, as his mom gathered his boy into her arms. Ever the pillar of strength, emotion showed on her face but she refused to let the tears fall. Gideon knew she felt it was her duty to be the strong one. Later, she'd probably have a good cry on his dad's shoulder.

Gideon didn't know what she said, but Sebastian was nodding, and when they pulled apart, his father tugged him gently into a hug as well, his mom unable to let go completely, rubbing his back. When his parents relinquished their hold, Rowan hugged him quickly, murmuring to him, and then drew him further into the dining room and had him sit down. She placed a pink frothy drink in front of him with a straw.

"It's a protein shake with berries and bananas. I thought you might see if you could keep it down."

He looked up at her and gave her a tremulous smile and replied, "Thank you all so much. You don't have to be here, but it means a lot that you are."

Gideon watched as his mom murmured to Sebastian again as she passed him and gave him a kiss on his cheek. She wandered into the kitchen, followed by Rowan and his dad. Gideon sat by Sebastian and watched as he drank about a quarter of the shake and looked as though he'd enjoyed it.

Finn joined them with a form for Sebastian to fill out and soon after, Camden arrived. Finn excused himself and left to meet with Dr. Cabrera in person. Gideon and Sebastian spent the next hour signing paperwork and discussing next steps with Camden as the others continued to pack up Sebastian's belongings.

Another hour later, Finn called Gideon's phone, and Sebastian spoke with Finn and Dr. Cabrera about two possible surgeons that could fit him in within the next couple weeks. It would involve travel and testing on the other end, but Sebastian didn't have a problem with that. In the end, he left it up to Finn to work it out with his doctor to pick the best surgeon.

When Gideon realized Sebastian's energy was flagging, he helped him back upstairs to rest. When he came back down, he pulled Zavier aside. "Can you work with Killian to track down a service dog for Sebastian? Killian can train him to be a guard dog as well, but I want him to find a seizure alert dog that's already trained for that. I know Thor has been a tremendous help to Braden, and I've done the research and think it's a good idea."

"Yeah, I can do that. I'll call him today and get him on it. But I thought the surgery was going to fix the seizures."

"I did too. It sounds like a controlling measure, not a permanent solution, so I need to talk more to Finn about it. I'm sure he's been researching his ass off because it's not his specialty."

"I'd hoped it would solve the problem."

"Yeah, me too. We'll see. It may not be as bad as that. Sebastian seemed resigned to it not working to solve the issue, as long as it helps with seizure management."

Zavier nodded and pulled out his phone. "Let me give him a call right now to get the ball rolling."

"Thanks."

Gideon scooped Slap and Tickle up in his arms and headed up the stairs. He figured his boy could use some time with his little fur balls. He knew his family had everything under control, and he didn't want to be away from Sebastian for too long. Knowing he could have a seizure at any moment and might need help, he didn't want to take any chances at not being there if he was needed.

Chapter 34

SEBASTIAN

Sebastian rested his head on Gideon's shoulder, drifting in and out, thinking about the last stressful couple of weeks. Thanks to the McCade family, his move went off without a hitch. His new apartment felt cramped compared to his house, but he wasn't going to complain. He'd put half of his stuff in storage but consoled himself with the fact that he considered it a stopgap measure to finding another house for himself in the next several months after his surgery. He was paying through the nose to go month to month, but he hadn't had another solution.

Gideon had let his feelings be known regarding his living situation. He'd asked Sebastian to move in with him, permanently, but Sebastian had refused. It was too early. Everything still felt so new, and he was too sick to really think that far ahead. He wanted to take one day at a time and told Gideon as much. He hadn't been happy, but he hadn't pushed either.

Once he'd been moved, he'd felt too cramped in his new apartment with his six foot five hulking brute of a man making his apartment walls shrink to what felt like a broom closet with all the boxes, so he'd suggested staying at Gideon's until the surgery. That had started another conversation on where he'd recover from his surgery. Gideon made it clear that he'd be by his side the whole time, so Sebastian had eventually agreed with his Dom that they'd both be better off at Gideon's place.

Gideon had been ridiculously accommodating about pretty much every-thing. Sebastian found himself surprised he hadn't pushed about the money thing, but figured it was because it was looking more and more like the McCades' lawyers were going to have his insurance company caving and paying. The reputation of his new doctor might have had something to do with that. Camden had even worked with the hospital to refund his down payment more quickly than they'd have done so otherwise. They'd learn the outcome of the insurance dispute the next day.

Finn and Dr. Cabrera had narrowed it down to two doctors that had equally impressive success rates with the same type of surgery. But they'd also let him know that the edge was with his new neurosurgeon, Dr. Naomi Cook, whose hospital was the Mayo Clinic in Rochester, Minnesota and was the best neuro-surgery hospital in the country. She'd been able to fit him into her schedule in just over two weeks, so Sebastian had been sold on her fairly quickly.

He was scared to death, not to mention humiliated. Gideon hadn't left his side, and he'd had three episodes over the course of the last two weeks. Nope, make that four because Gideon had admitted to witnessing one the night he'd first stayed with him. His fear of the unknown was growing by the day, and having never met his surgeon, he didn't have anything to go on but what he'd been told. Not that he doubted the veracity of her stellar reputation, he just felt strange going into the situation blind.

Gideon had made all the flight and hotel arrangements through his travel agent when Sebastian had been distracted by a visit from Braden, so of course he'd refused to let Sebastian reimburse him, and their flight, car rental, and hotel were apparently as luxurious as one could get in Rochester, Minnesota. They'd have to have a conversation later about it. Extravagance wasn't some-thing he needed or wanted in his life, but simplicity was, so they'd have to come to some sort of compromise going forward.

They arrived early enough to have room service brought up to them and went to bed early as he had a long series of pre-op tests at the hospital and the neurologist's office. He'd gone through most of the tests nearly a month ago, but they wanted current testing as well as new blood work, a chest x-ray, and an EKG.

He thought it was overkill and was feeling nervous as they lay in bed the night before. "They have copies of all of my previous tests and nothing is wrong with my heart. I don't understand why I had to get here three days before the surgery and spend all day tomorrow getting tested for everything under the sun."

Gideon pulled him closer and kissed him on the head and effectively shut down his complaints when he said, "Well, I for one would like them to do whatever tests they feel are necessary so they know everything they need to know before they drill and saw a big hole in your skull. You're not having your tonsils out for Christ's sake, you're having a craniotomy."

Sebastian lay in Gideon's arms contemplating his words, and the longer he did the funnier they seemed and a laugh bubbled out before he could stop it. Soon he couldn't control himself, and he was laughing so hard he had tears streaming down his face. When his head started bouncing up and down with Gideon's laughter, he lost it completely. Because really, why was he complaining about them being over prepared for brain surgery? Jesus.

When Sebastian's laughter finally died down, he propped himself up on his elbow, gazed down at Gideon and said, "So, a little bit of gallows humor as therapy for my whining?"

Gideon scrubbed his hands over his face and sighed. "Shit, I'm sorry. You weren't whining. I just... Goddamn, you're having brain surgery, Sebastian. Fuck. Nothing about that is simple. Let them do all the tests they need to do. Please."

Sebastian chuckled again and nodded, putting his head back down on Gideon's chest. "Don't be sorry. You're exactly right. I'm being ridiculous. I think I was feeling a little sorry for myself and scared."

"You'd be stupid not to be scared, and if that's what you call feeling sorry for yourself, I think you're entitled. I don't want you to be stressed about tomorrow though. They're covering their bases and learning everything they can about you before going in. I think it's a good thing. And I'll be with you as much as they'll let me."

Sebastian nodded again and sighed. "Yeah. I know. Shit. I just want to use the DeLorean to take me to the future when I'm done with the surgery and the recovery. I don't like being weak."

"You're the furthest thing from weak I've ever seen. But I don't think a fictitious time machine is needed. We have everything going for us here. You've got the best doctor and the best hospital for this surgery. You've got the time you need off work to recover, and you've got family and friends to help you the whole way through."

Sebastian wrapped his arm around Gideon's chest and hugged him tight. "You're right. I know you're right. Okay, no more pity parties. Maybe we should watch some hotel porn."

Gideon chuckled and said, "I don't think they've got gay porn. I've got my laptop though. We can check out some kink.com if you need your engines revved."

Sebastian snorted which prompted Gideon to ask if he'd actually snorted, and then they laughed together again. He couldn't have explained it if he tried, but their shared laughter did a lot to make the burdens of the days to come not seem so dire. He'd take what he could get. He leaned back and looked up at Gideon with a grateful smile. Gideon rolled onto his side and pulled him close, kissing him softly and cradling his body so gently it made Sebastian grateful and so very hopeful for the best outcome over the next several days.

It turned out that Monday's tests, though they made for a long day, weren't so bad. He'd met his new doctor first thing, and as soon as he had, he'd been put at ease. She was older and had a gentle but no-nonsense way about her that made her discussion of his surgery not seem so frightening. Though the fact that he'd essentially be awake for the whole thing was nerve wracking.

It was surgery day. Finn had shown up the day before so he could be there with Gideon during the surgery. Sebastian was so grateful he'd come because the closer they got, the more Sebastian could tell the stress was wearing him down. Gideon's demeanor hadn't changed, he'd been a rock for Sebastian, but Sebastian had learned to read his Dom well, so when he saw it happening, he nudged Finn in his direction.

His own stress levels were beyond high. The IV and the catheter weren't fun and set his heart to racing with the knowledge that he was minutes away from having his skull opened up. Before they could take him, Gideon asked for a moment alone with him.

He watched as Gideon moved closer and sat on the edge of his hospital bed. Leaning down, Gideon put his forehead to his, and they sat there in silence, eyes closed, as they gave and took strength from each other. When Gideon pulled away, the emotion in his eyes matched Sebastian's, and his Dom's voice was gruff when he said, "Everything's going to go perfectly. You're in good hands. I'll be by your side as soon as they'll let me."

Sebastian nodded and whispered, "I love you."

Gideon smiled and rubbed his thumb over Sebastian's lower lip. "I love you too, baby. We're going to have a good, long, happy life together."

God, how he wanted that. Knowing he shouldn't but unable to help himself, he asked, "You promise?"

When Gideon's smile grew and he answered, "I promise," without a hint of hesitation, Sebastian's confidence was bolstered. Gideon was still leaning over him when the knock came on the door. When Gideon told whoever it was to enter, Dr. Cook walked in, a wide smile on her face.

"Good morning, you two. Sebastian, you ready to do this?"

Sebastian nodded, albeit a bit less enthusiastically, and said, "Yeah."

Her smile didn't diminish as she looked back and forth between them. "Let's get you as close to seizure free as we can, shall we?"

Sebastian's smile bloomed at that. "Yeah. That sounds like a plan, Doc."

"All right. I'm gonna get scrubbed in, and I'll see you in the OR. We've got an amazing team assembled to help things move like clockwork."

They both thanked her as she exited as quickly and confidently as she'd entered. Gideon kissed him softly as the nurses walked in. He held his hand as long as he could as they moved his bed out the door and down the hall. He looked back and the last thing he saw was Gideon's gorgeous smile. Several turns later, he was being pushed into a large room with medical staff, machines, and tools that overwhelmed him.

A doctor approached and introduced himself as Dr. Chase, his anesthesiologist. He explained what he'd be doing during the surgery, but all Sebastian could do was nod in response. He was quickly and efficiently moved to the operating table and positioned properly; the nurse helping him explained why he was moving him this way and that as they turned him to the side and put a wedge pillow under half of his body so that he was lying on a bit of a tilt.

As he was prepped further, he sucked in a breath when they parted his hair, clipped some of it back and out of the way, and began to cut the section they'd exposed. Suddenly, reality kicked in, and his breathing ramped up along with his heart rate. Fuck. What if it didn't go well? What if it did nothing to help him and he had to deal with the seizures impacting him for the rest of his life? What if he had an aneurysm in the middle of it and died? Jesus, to never see Gideon again would kill him.

He'd never had anything or anyone to lose, and now he had so much to lose he felt paralyzed. Knowing that he was loved was all well and good when he was healthy, but to know he'd be hurting people if things didn't work out, that he'd be leaving a hole in people's lives, stole his breath.

His panic must have shown because the anesthesiologist leaned down and began to talk to him in low soothing tones, explaining what everyone was doing and why they were doing it. His voice and his demeanor were relaxed which went a long way toward calming Sebastian. And before he knew it, the air on his newly shaved scalp felt cool as the antiseptic they used made him shiver. He relaxed degree by degree, willing himself to get into a better headspace.

When he'd calmed enough to force himself to think positively again, he was able to focus back on the words the doctor was saying. He was apparently going to be put under what was called twilight anesthesia for the portion of the surgery that required his input. He'd be sedated but not unconscious, making it unlikely that he'd remember much, if any, of the procedure. His head would be put in a sort of vise grip to keep it in place during surgery.

Dr. Cook took it from there, explaining that they'd be covering his head to keep the area sterile. She wanted to warn him so he wouldn't be alarmed. She continued, telling him she'd use several incisions to expose the section of the skull they'd be operating on then perform the craniotomy by making burr holes in his skull with a drill. A saw would then be used to cut the section of the bone away, and they'd cut through the dura mater to expose his brain.

When the actual cortical resection was underway, they'd essentially wake him into twilight sedation where he'd be able to assist them during the surgery. They'd be able to ask him questions which would help them avoid damaging areas of the brain responsible for motor function and speech, and target the area of the brain with seizures.

Several minutes later, the anesthesiologist had him counting down and he was drifting off. Sometime later, he heard murmured voices and someone softly calling his name.

He saw a nurse step into his line of sight and ask, "Sebastian? Are you with us?"

"Y… Yes."

"How are you feeling?"

"I don't know. Strange but good."

"That's good. We're just going to have you answer some questions, all right?"

"Okay."

He heard Dr. Cook's voice from behind him. "Sebastian, can you count to ten?"

When he did, there was a pause and some murmuring he couldn't decipher. Next thing he knew he heard someone calling his name again, and he opened his eyes to see a nurse leaning over him. The lighting was different, and so was the smell. He glanced around and realized he was out of the OR. He glanced at the nurse again, confused. He'd just been in the OR, and they'd been asking him some questions.

"What happened?"

"You're in the recovery room and about to be transferred to the neuro-science intensive care unit where they'll monitor you closely."

"Where is Gideon?"

"Is he a friend or family member?"

"My...partner?"

She smiled at that and winked. "You'll be allowed visitors once we move you."

"All right. Did... Am I okay?"

"I'll let you speak to your surgeon about the specifics, but what I do know is that you've had a successful operation. Go ahead and rest. We'll be moving you in about ten minutes."

He might have responded. He didn't know. What he did know was that he was still out of it, and he didn't remember anything except being asked to count to ten. He heard some more voices and opened his eyes. Gideon was hovering over him, concern etched over his features. Sebastian was gonna have to get better quickly and stop worrying his Dom. He didn't like making him upset. He smiled and whispered, "Sir."

Gideon smiled. "Hey, baby. How do you feel?"

"All right. Tired. Throat hurts."

Gideon glanced over when another voice said, "That's normal. The breathing tube usually causes some pain when it's put in and taken out. It will pass."

Sebastian turned his head to see a nurse standing beside his bed, looking at the computer monitor. When she glanced his way, she smiled and said, "Hi, Sebastian. My name is Megan. I'll be one of your nurses while you're in the NSICU."

"Hi. I'm thirsty."

"I know you are, but we can't give you anything except ice chips for now, or you'll get sick. I'll bring you some in a few minutes, all right? Your surgeon should be here in the next hour or so to talk to you about your surgery."

All he could do was nod. He glanced back to Gideon and might have been able to get out an "I love you," before he was out again.

Sometime later, he pulled himself out of a fog and opened his eyes. The room was dim, and he could hear voices off to the left. "Gideon?"

"Hey. Yeah, I'm here, sweetheart. How are you feeling?" He approached the side of Sebastian's hospital bed and ran his hand up and down Sebastian's arm.

He was just about to answer when he heard a light knock on the door. Dr. Cook walked in, her smile as wide as the one she'd had before the surgery. Any tension he had eased at the look on her face. He gave her a tentative smile as she approached the bed.

"How are you feeling?"

He wondered how many times a day he'd be asked that question, but answered anyway. "All right. Tired. Thirsty."

She looked around and reached for something at the foot of his bed. Handing Gideon a cup, she said, "Gideon is going to give you some ice chips. Let them melt on your tongue or chew them slowly so you won't get sick. I'm going to run a few tests while I'm here, but first things first. We were able to find and remove three seizure foci which is great news and means that your surgery was a success. We won't know for some time how successful, but I couldn't be happier with how it went."

He smiled and glanced up at Gideon whose grin had gotten even bigger at hearing that. The doctor took something out of her lab coat pocket and approached him. She used her flashlight to see if his pupils reacted properly.

"Can you tell me your name?"

Confused, he answered, "Sebastian Phillips."

She smiled then asked him to move his fingers, his toes, his arms, and his legs. "You'll experience some nausea and headaches. We've already planned for that and given you pain medications and anti-nausea meds, but they may not be able to stop both from causing issues for you, so let us know if they do. We've also got you on some steroids for the swelling in your brain and an anti-convulsant."

Sebastian's eyes grew heavy, and he tried to think of what he wanted to ask. Finally, all he could come up with was, "Will I always have to take anti-convulsants?"

The doctor shrugged and answered, "We're not sure. Some people are able to get off of them completely. Some take them for a year or two and then are weaned off of them. Others have to take them for the rest of their lives. Seizure activity should hopefully be reduced significantly or completely."

When all Sebastian did was offer a small nod, she continued, "If you have any strange symptoms or anything feels off, you need to let the nursing staff know, immediately. No suffering in silence. You'll be here for about four days. You'll be monitored closely and put through tests repeatedly. We just want to make sure everything is functioning as it should be. And remember you'll need to stay in Rochester for two weeks before you can fly home, and we'll have to clear you as safe to travel the day before. All right?"

Overwhelmed, all he could say was, "Okay," and he looked up at Gideon when he felt Gideon's hand clasp his. They both looked at the doctor then, and Gideon asked, "I'd like to stay overnight while he's here. Will that be an issue?"

Dr. Cook shook her head. "No. They should have cots or some kind of convertible chair. All other visitors will have to leave when visiting hours are over."

"Doc?"

"Yes?"

"Um, I remember counting to ten during the surgery. Am I making that up in my head?"

A surprised look passed across her features, and she shook her head. "No. Most people don't remember anything that goes on while under twilight seda-tion. We asked you to count to ten, identify some pictures, raise your arms, and wiggle your fingers and toes. You did great."

"Do I have a hole in my skull?"

"Well, we had to drill small burr holes to be able to use the saw, so those are there still, but very small. After the surgery was done, we sutured the dura mater back together, reattached your skull bone with titanium plates and screws, and then sutured your muscles and skin back together."

Sebastian's eyes popped wide, and he asked, "Will the plates and screws be removed later?"

She shook her head. "No. You'll have those permanently. We've also got a small tube inserted in a burr hole to drain any blood and fluids over the next day or so."

Sebastian glanced back and forth between Gideon and the doctor. Gideon finally asked, "What is it?"

Sebastian blushed when he asked, "Am I going to set off the security at the airport?"

Dr. Cook laughed and shrugged. "You don't have that much metal, but you might, as there's not a lot of muscle and skin on top of your head to hide it. It won't be an issue. You'll be one of many they deal with daily."

Feeling silly for asking, he nodded and thanked her. They spoke for a couple more minutes then she said her goodbyes and Gideon sat down on the side of his bed. He gazed up at Gideon, his eyelids feeling like they weighed a ton. He smiled when Gideon leaned down to kiss him, and he admitted, "Tired."

"Go to sleep, baby. I'll be right here when you wake up."

Sebastian mumbled, "I love you," before he was down for the count.

He woke sometime later; the room was dim, and he heard murmuring again. He opened his eyes and smiled, glancing Finn and Gideon's way. His eyes popped wide, and he sucked in a breath when, instead of seeing Finn, he saw Braden in a recliner across the room. Gideon was resting in his same recliner beside his hospital bed.

Looking back at his friend, disbelief in his voice, he asked, "What are you doing here?"

Braden tilted his head like he couldn't understand the question. "What do you mean what am I doing here? Where else would I be?"

Sebastian shook his head. He could be a million other places. He couldn't wrap his mind around the fact he'd flown to be with him. "When did you get here?"

"Late last night. We arrived at the hospital while you were being prepped for surgery. We didn't want to distract you or cause any stress beforehand, so we waited in the waiting room."

He glanced at Gideon. "Wait, we? Who's here?"

Gideon gently placed his hand on top of Sebastian's. "Everyone. But only two people can be in the ICU with you, so they're swapping out while I stay with you."

Sebastian didn't know how to process any of that. It was all too much, so he focused on Gideon instead. "Wait, was that all the texting you were doing yesterday and last night?"

Gideon smiled and nodded. "Yeah."

Sebastian turned his hand over in Gideon's and gripped it like a lifeline, overwhelmed. He glanced over to Braden and smiled. "Thank you for coming."

Braden grinned. "You're welcome. Go ahead and rest, Bastian. You don't need to try and stay awake."

"No. I was just asleep for hours, right? I'm good for a while."

Famous last words. He wasn't awake more than another five minutes before he was out again. He woke in the middle of the night with pain in his head and nausea roiling in his stomach. Gideon was asleep in the nearby recliner which he'd pulled as close as possible to Sebastian's bed so that he could hold his hand. God, how had Sebastian been lucky enough to deserve him? He wasn't sure he actually did, but he couldn't seem to let him go.

He turned when he heard the door open. A nurse he'd never met walked in. He was African American, skinny as a rail, and nearly as tall as Gideon.

Sebastian heard the leather of the recliner squeak, and he looked over at Gideon, who'd just woken up. "Hey, baby."

"Hi." He turned to greet the nurse and grimaced. "Hello. I'm hoping you can help me with the pain in my head. And I'm feeling nauseous, is there something…"

"Yeah." The nurse reached over to the counter on the wall by the door and got him a deep pan, in case he threw up. "There you go. My name is Will and I'll be one of your night nurses while you're here in the NSICU. You're gonna feel nauseous for several days, most likely, and you won't feel hungry much at all which is probably for the best. We'll increase your dose of the anti-nausea meds. You've got pain meds coming through your IV right now, but if you've got breakthrough pain, go ahead and push that button on the cord beside you. That'll administer some pain meds if you're able to have more."

Sebastian reached for the cord and pressed the button, hoping he'd get a dose. "I can't seem to stay awake to save my life, is that normal?"

Will smiled and nodded. "Yeah. You'll basically be sleeping while you're here. Tomorrow, we'll get you ambulatory, and you'll have a CT and MRI to check and see how you're progressing. If you're doing well, you'll be moved to a step down unit."

"All right. I—"

That was all he got out before he was sick into the pan he'd just been handed. His whole body did its best to expel anything and everything he'd had left in there, which wasn't much, but his body sure wasn't convinced of that as he continued retching. He realized that Gideon had stood and was rubbing his back.

Will brought him a cup of water. "Rinse your mouth if you think you're done, but don't swallow. It'll just set you off again."

Sebastian nodded and raised his other hand to his head where the pressure of the vomiting had sent shooting pain into his skull. Gideon clasped his hand before it could make contact with anything. He swished the water in his mouth a couple times, spitting it into the pan. Will took the pan and set it on the counter behind him, and Sebastian rested back into his pillows.

He looked at Gideon and asked, "Can you lay my bed all the way back?"

Will typed a few commands into the computer and said, "It's not good for you to be lying flat, yet. You can tilt it back a bit more, but that's it, and keep those pillows behind you to stay elevated. We want to keep your head above your heart at this point. I've ordered your meds and I'm going to bring you some ice chips in a minute or two, all right? But don't eat too many or you'll be sick again."

Sebastian nodded his understanding, feeling slightly better, the meds kicking in fast. He closed his eyes to rest, but the nurse had other ideas and had him go through several tests like the doctor had done when she'd been in and then took his vitals. Afterward, Gideon kissed him and murmured, "I love you. Get some rest."

He woke up the next morning and though he shouldn't have been, he was still surprised to see Siobhan sitting at the table. Gideon, as always, was reclining in the chair beside him, looking up at the muted television while some sports team or other was playing a game. He told her thank you for coming then was out again.

The following three days were more of the same, but the tube was removed and after several hours without any issues he was moved to a step down unit where he was allowed more visitors. His heart was full even if his skull felt like a jackhammer had taken up residence in there. His new family was there, every one of them, and he couldn't have been more grateful even if he did sleep through most of it.

What they thought would be four days turned into five then six. There were no complications, thankfully, but the doctor was being extra cautious and wanted him to stay those two extra days so he could be monitored before being let go. On the sixth day, he was allowed to leave. Gideon's family had already left two days prior after he'd been declared stable enough to move out of the NSICU. But Zoe, Zavier, and Braden had remained behind. It still amazed Sebastian they'd come at all, let alone stayed for that length of time.

The final three would be leaving the following day after he'd been settled into their hotel suite. The hotel was comfortable, and he had all the amenities they'd need, but he'd still much rather be at home. Zavier and Braden had gone grocery shopping for them. They had a full kitchen in their suite, and Gideon didn't want them to have to order room service or other takeout for every single meal.

Even when he was in the hotel, he was still sleeping through most of his days and nights. His doctor assured him it was normal. He was sick to death of the bed, but Dr. Cook said no sofa sleeping or recliner sleeping, so the bed it was. And though the bed didn't incline, Gideon had called down to the front desk and had what probably amounted to every single pillow in the place brought up so that he was ensconced in a mound of fluffiness reminiscent of what he assumed clouds would feel like.

Every day, he was able to get up and move about a bit more, but he felt almost like he had the flu. He was exhausted, mentally and physically, he didn't want to eat, didn't have energy, slept all the time, and his whole body seemed achy. But, he hadn't had even a bit of a tremor or warning of an impending seizure, and he couldn't help but mentally cross his fingers, and even his toes, that he would eventually be completely free of them.

The following Friday, twelve days post-op, he had his final appointment with Dr. Cook to get signed off on air travel so they could head home. Finn was waiting for the go ahead, and then he'd be flying back to Rochester so that he could travel home with them in case he was needed. Sebastian had been embarrassed when Gideon had told him that and had tried to tell Finn he didn't need to come. But Gideon had asked Finn, not wanting to take any chances with Sebastian's health, so nothing was going to deter him.

When he'd gotten the all clear and an encouraging final checkup with his doctor, he'd finally relaxed and started to think that things could finally be turning in his favor. When Sunday's flight went off without a hitch and he finally went to sleep in Gideon's bed after such a long time, he couldn't help but feel even more hopeful. He didn't know how he was going to put up with six to eight more weeks of convalescence, but he'd get through it. He fell asleep that night curled up close to Gideon, Slap and Tickle asleep at his feet, unwilling to sleep in their bed for fear he might disappear on them again.

Chapter 35

GIDEON

They were two weeks into what would probably be at least six of Sebastian recuperating at Gideon's loft. Sebastian had spent most of it sleeping, as his doctor had warned him he'd be doing. It annoyed the hell out of his boy, but Gideon could see the improvement in his coloring as the days went by. And Gideon couldn't be happier that Sebastian had settled right back into his home like he was meant to be there as Gideon knew he was.

When they'd walked in the door that first night back, Slap and Tickle had both tripped over themselves in their rush to get to Sebastian. His boy had sucked in a breath and turned toward him with a gorgeous smile and a thank you. Maya had watched the cats while Zoe had been visiting the hospital, but as soon as Zoe had gotten back, she'd taken over. Gideon had asked her to bring them to his loft that day, hoping it would make Sebastian happy. And as he'd watched the reunion, he'd been glad he had.

Sebastian had gone down on his knees and then he'd sat down, right by the elevator doors. He'd laughed softly and tried to pet them as they climbed on him, wound themselves around him, kneading his legs and chest. They'd both rubbed their faces on Sebastian's, sniffed him, and licked his face.

Sometimes they acted more like dogs than cats, and Gideon laughed as Sebastian held Tickle in his arms and the little monster had batted his paw at the turban-like length of gauze wrapped around his head. Gideon hadn't put a stop to it, only because the little monster was batting at the opposite side of the surgical wound and seemed to only be pointing out that he didn't like it, not trying to claw it off.

In addition to the little fur balls, also unbeknownst to Sebastian, Gideon had taken several of Sebastian's boxes, including two with art supplies, from the house to his loft before the move. He'd been happy he'd thought of it when they discovered Sebastian wasn't even able to do simple things like watch TV or read a book because his concentration was shot. He'd discovered he could draw because it was easily set down and picked back up again. He wanted Sebastian to have anything he might need at his place while he was recovering.

If he was honest with himself, he'd also done it in the hopes that it might help convince Sebastian to move in. When he'd found out, however, Sebastian had gotten frustrated that he'd done so. The only thing that had saved him from a fight over it was the fact that Sebastian couldn't keep himself awake.

Thankfully, when he'd pointed that out to Sebastian—with a smile on his face like he'd gotten away with something—his boy couldn't keep a straight face and finally laughed with him. It could have all gone tits up for him at that point, but Sebastian made sure to make it clear to him that Gideon was the one that would pack it all up to move it back to Sebastian's apartment. He'd readily agreed because it wasn't as if, in a million years, Gideon would ever make his brain surgery-recouping submissive pack and lift a bunch of boxes, but he didn't point that out.

They'd discovered there were other things Sebastian couldn't do as well. It brought home to Gideon how self-sufficient and independent Sebastian had had to be his whole life because he was annoyed and impatient as fuck to have to rely on Gideon. He wouldn't let his boy lift anything heavier than the cats, and even that he'd tried to discourage. Gideon drove them daily to a little local park, and they walked around the little pond several times before Sebastian would get tired. Inevitably, they'd get back home and Sebastian would annoy the hell out of himself again when he fell asleep.

Gideon had to push him to continue with his pain meds, but after the first real headache hit as soon as he'd tried to go without them, he'd caved when all he could do was lie in one position in the dark and not move, talk, or do anything at all. Sebastian had also taken to wearing Gideon's beanies at all times because his head always felt cold and the pressure of the hat soothed his nerve endings which seemed to be firing at all cylinders as they began to regrow.

The more time passed, the grumpier Sebastian got with him. They knew to expect it because the steroids Sebastian had to take for the swelling in his brain were known to cause irritability. He had a feeling Sebastian didn't remember what the doctor had told them about the meds, but Gideon watched his boy's temper get sparked at the simplest things. He'd let him grouse and grumble and even snap at him a few times, but when Sebastian had yelled, Gideon finally put an end to it.

He knew Sebastian needed to get out of the loft. Being cooped up too long made his boy's frustration simmer until it became anger. He walked into their bedroom and stood by the bed an hour after he'd first suggested a walk and said, "Why don't we take that walk now?"

Sebastian looked up from his drawing, glaring at him. "No."

"Bastian."

"Don't Bastian me with that scolding tone of voice. I'm not a fucking child, Gideon! I'm not. Going. On. A. Walk!"

Gideon immediately squatted beside the bed, reached out and clasped his hand around Sebastian's throat, gripping tight enough to get his attention. "Is that any way to talk to me, boy?"

It was the first time he'd called him that since they'd gotten back from the surgery and seeing his boy's reaction had his dick shifting in his pants. Sebastian's eyes went wide, and his pupils dilated. Gideon felt him gulp under his palm. He shook his head a bit and answered in a choked voice, "No, Sir. I'm sorry."

"I've let this attitude of yours go unpunished. And I'm not going to punish you now because we haven't talked about it. The meds are helping you physically, but not mentally, and being cooped up here hasn't done you any favors. Regardless, I won't have you speaking to me like that. Are we clear?"

Shame made Sebastian's face flame, and he nodded and tried to look down at his lap. When Gideon tightened his grip, he looked back up. "We're clear, Sir. I'm so sorry. You can punish me."

"You know better than that. We aren't in a scene and haven't even talked about that portion of our relationship yet. But as far as I'm concerned, I'm still your Dom and you, boy, are still my sub. Am I wrong in that assumption?"

"No, Sir."

"Good. Now, we're gonna go out for a while and take a walk, maybe grab some dinner and bring it back. I want you showered and ready to leave in twenty minutes. Understood?"

"Yes, Sir."

"Good boy."

He'd had to force himself to get up and walk away. They weren't cleared to resume having any sexual activity yet, and the blown pupils and hitched breaths would do him in if he had to be there a moment longer. It seemed, no matter how hard he tried, Gideon couldn't get their Dominant/submissive dynamic out of his mind. It meant a lot to him, hell, it was what had brought them together, but he'd give it up if Sebastian didn't want it going forward.

Being a boyfriend—god he hated that word—no, a partner, was something altogether different. Gideon knew their relationship was different than anything he'd ever had with anyone. He'd had several long-term relationships, and though he'd had a connection with them, he'd never felt a love like he did for Sebastian. That was altogether new and for his boy only. He also didn't want to rush the issue. Sebastian had agreed to spend his time recouping at Gideon's place and he'd hold him to that. They'd take their time.

Or at least he thought they would until they were walking and Sebastian said, "I'm able to take care of myself now, Gideon. I think it's time I went back home. I don't want to overstay my welcome."

Gideon stopped in his tracks, crossed his arms over his chest and asked, "What the fuck does that even mean? I asked you to move in with me, Sebastian. If that's not a sign that you *are* at home and could *never* overstay your welcome, I don't know what is. As far as I'm concerned, that offer is still on the table and still something we need to consider."

Gideon saw a runner coming their way and gently maneuvered Sebastian and himself off of the path and onto the grass. His boy glanced at the runner as he went by then looked down and away, turning his face and scar away from the stranger. Gideon bit down on his need for Sebastian to end that behavior and waited for his boy's response.

Sebastian shook his head. "It's too soon. We just decided to be together outside of the contract. We need to take things slowly and figure out how this is going to work. Moving in with you isn't the answer right now. I'm going to need space and time."

"We can put it on the backburner, but it's what I want, and I'm going to keep coming back around to it until I fully understand your reasoning. You've told me you'll spend your recovery here. We came to the agreement that you'd be here until you were cleared to go back to work full time."

Sebastian put his hands in his pockets and hunched his shoulders, the gesture all too familiar. He finally said, "I don't think that's going to be necessary. It seems like overkill. I just think I should start to settle in at home. I have so much unpacking to do."

"Are you yanking my chain? You're not allowed to lift anything yet. I'm keeping you as far away from your boxes as humanly possible. What's really going on?"

"You're babying me too much."

Incredulous, Gideon's eyes popped wide and then narrowed, dangerously, and he asked, "I'm…what now?"

Sebastian shook his head taking an unconscious step back. "You're treating me like a baby, like I can't do anything myself, like you have to make my decisions for me. Look, I'm glad I came out to take a walk, but really, just let me do my thing."

Gideon tilted his head to the side and regarded his boy like a specimen in a petri dish, "I'm gonna continue to treat you exactly the way your behavior warrants."

Sebastian huffed out an annoyed laugh and crossed his arms over his chest. "What the hell does that mean? I'm an adult. Treat me like one!"

"Your behavior is that of a selfish brat not getting his way."

Gideon nearly laughed when he saw Sebastian just barely keep from stomping his foot, but kept his face straight as he watched the anger vibrate through his boy's small frame.

"That's bullshit, and you know it! Stop acting like a father and start acting like a partner!"

"Jesus, Sebastian. Listen to yourself. You nearly stomped your foot at me like a teenager being grounded."

Sebastian let out a growl and turned to walk away from him. To fucking walk away. He very nearly told his boy to present, but he wouldn't humiliate him that way in public even if there was barely anyone in the park. Instead he took a different tack and whispered, "Do you know how hard it was to wait for you to come out of surgery? Do you even know how long you were gone?"

Sebastian stopped in his tracks and turned around, his eyes wide and haunted. Gideon continued, "You were in surgery for over six hours. Six fucking hours, Sebastian. Seven when you add in your time in the recovery room. I couldn't have gotten to you if I'd tried. I didn't know where the OR was, where they'd taken you."

Sebastian uncrossed his arms and stepped closer, but didn't say a word.

"Did you know I watched your surgery?"

Sebastian, looking pained, whispered, "What? No."

Gideon nodded. "They have rooms for families who want to watch. Viewing rooms is what they call them. They're little more than closets with chairs and a TV to watch the surgeries on camera. I sat there with Zavier and with Finn, who explained everything they were doing."

Sebastian moaned and his hand flew up to cover his mouth. He shook his head at Gideon, but Gideon continued, "It was like déjà vu, because I'd watched another surgery once with Zavier. Live, from a surgical theater above the OR. Braden died, and they had to bring him back. My brother lost his fucking mind. Finn was performing the surgery, and I was in there with Cooper, Zavier's business partner. It took both of us to hold him down, to keep him from going to Braden when he flatlined."

Sebastian whispered, "Oh god."

"It's so different watching something like that when it's the love of your life. I thought I understood how Zavier felt." Gideon shook his head and closed his eyes. "I didn't know. I couldn't know. Not until you were wheeled away from me that day. And all I could think was that same thing could easily happen to you, and maybe you wouldn't recover like Braden did. That's all I kept thinking for six goddamn hours."

Sebastian leaned his forehead on Gideon's chest. Gideon couldn't help but reach up to grip the back of his boy's neck. "I saw them shave your head, I saw them clean it and draw on it, make the incision, pull your skin back. I saw them drill holes into your fucking head, Sebastian. I watched them take a fucking saw and cut out a portion of your skull and set it aside. I saw your brain through a microscope. Your brain, for fuck's sake. I saw her start to poke at it with a bunch of instruments."

He had to pause and look away, gathering himself to continue. He felt Sebastian's palm cover his heart then reach up and wrap around Gideon's neck. He looked back down and continued, "They did something to wake you, or, I don't even know, but next thing I knew, you were answering questions for them, talking to them as they fucking prodded your brain. They used scissors, some kind of laser, a ridiculously long needle and some other things I hope to never see again."

Sebastian breathed out, shakily, and whispered, "I'm sorry."

"I'm not. I had to know. I needed to know. God, I'm so thankful we found Dr. Cook. She did an amazing job, and it went off without a hitch. But those were the seven longest and worst hours of my life, Bastian. You could have died. I had to go to your room and wait for you to be brought in. You were so goddamn pale, your head covered with gauze."

Sebastian finally wrapped himself fully around Gideon and hugged him tight. "I've never been so fucking scared in all my life, and I've been through a shit ton of scary moments. I know you're having a hard time with this recovery shit. These steroids are making you angry and short tempered. I'm doing my best to be patient, but I need your help. I'm trying not to go all domineering Dom when you lash out, but it's a close thing, Bastian."

Gideon felt him suck in a breath and let it slowly back out then Sebastian was looking up into his eyes. "Don't."

Gideon closed his eyes. "Don't what?"

Sebastian scratched the back of Gideon's neck making him open his eyes. "Don't keep from going all domineering Dom."

"Sebastian…"

"No, listen. I don't know which way is up with these goddamn pills. I'm finally off the pain meds which were keeping me loopy and unable to focus for more than a hot minute."

Gideon laughed. He couldn't help it because it was so true. Sebastian had been like water on a hot griddle, his attention pinging around, unable to settle. He still couldn't focus completely on anything for longer than thirty minutes at a time.

Sebastian continued, "These anticonvulsants are different than the ones I've been on in the past, so my body is still a bit wonky and unsure how to react. The steroids are making me hungry constantly, but the anticonvulsants are sending weird nauseous signals. The meds have me eating a shit ton of food, which I've never done my whole life, and then feeling sick afterwards."

"Why didn't you tell me that? We should talk to the doctor about it."

"Because if I have to go to the hospital or see my doctor one more time, I'm gonna go crazy. And speaking of going crazy, I'm just always so fucking irritated at every damn thing, and I can't make sense out of it. I never seem to know why, or what set me off. Half the time I don't even know I've snapped at you until I see the disappointment on your face which just makes me disappointed in myself and makes me angrier. It's a vicious cycle."

"Baby, you need to talk to me about this stuff. We'll talk to your doctor. We'll figure something out."

"I don't like making all these decisions. I'm stressed all the time. I hate not being able to do everything for myself, so I either do too much or nothing at all. I think that's part of what's making me so annoyed. I don't have a schedule and making one stresses me out. I feel helpless when I make myself too tired and when I've slept too much. I've never felt that way, so it makes me feel angry and out of control."

Gideon thought he knew where Sebastian was going, but he needed to make sure. "What do you need from me, boy?"

Sebastian took a deep breath and looked up at him with pleading eyes. "I need you to do it for me."

"Bastian," Gideon said, warningly.

Sebastian nodded and explained himself more fully. "I need to hand over control to you. Until this is over and I'm able to go back to work full time with no restrictions, I need you to be fully in control of everything, to help me feel less out of control. Please, Sir."

Gideon narrowed his eyes. He wanted this more than he was willing to admit. Hell, he wanted this even after Sebastian could go back to work, but he needed to make sure that he wasn't making this decision. It had to be Sebastian's. "You want to be under my full control twenty-four seven? I make your schedule, you do what I say, every moment of every day until you're able to go back to work?"

Sebastian nodded but then bit his lip, concern shining through. "I don't want to be…I don't…"

"We aren't going to do this if you don't want it, Sebastian. You know that's not how it works."

Sebastian shook his head. "No. That's not it. I want to be your submissive twenty-four seven, but, not…not…"

Sebastian sighed in annoyance at himself, and Gideon finally understood. "But not my slave."

Sebastian's shoulders relaxed, and he let out a deep breath. "Yes. Is that… Can we do that?"

Gideon drew him in and held him. "Bastian, I've never possessed nor do I want to possess a slave. I want my boy to be able to safeword, and set limits, to feel safe enough to know I'll never color outside of the lines he draws. I want to own a submissive, but I want my submissive to want to be owned by me. You'll always maintain your autonomy with me insofar as you stipulate in our contract. I only want as much control as you willingly give me. All right?"

Sebastian nodded and answered, "Yes, Sir. Thank you."

"Good. Since we never technically ripped up our contract and it was for six months, are you okay with keeping it as is, but stipulating that it will now be a twenty-four seven arrangement until that time when your doctor has cleared you for full-time work?"

Sebastian's smile grew wider at that. "Yes, Sir."

"Good boy. Let's head back."

Gideon kissed the top of his head and turned them towards the path, intent on getting them back to the car before his boy lost every ounce of energy he had. As they walked back, Gideon could tell everything that had happened during their time out of the loft had done wonders for his boy's mood. Gideon saw Sebastian's surreptitious glances and grinned, waiting for him to speak. When he did, he couldn't have been more surprised.

"I want a super burger and garlic fries, and a double chocolate super shake."

Gideon chuckled and replied, "That sounds really specific."

"Super Duper Burgers, it's not too far. I can call it in and run in and pick it up."

"We can go in together, but you won't be paying. Go ahead and call when we get to the car."

Sebastian huffed, like Gideon knew he would. "I'm the one that suggested it. I should pay."

"You don't pay when you're with me."

"My insurance has agreed to pay for the surgery. Your lawyers did the trick. I have plenty of money."

Gideon guided him around the SUV and opened the car door for him. When Sebastian got in, Gideon leaned in and kissed those soft lips before responding, "It's not about how much money you have. It's about me taking care of my boy."

Gideon could see Sebastian's frustration, but this particular topic was not up for negotiation. They'd talk it out, and Sebastian could have his say, but in the end, it's how it would be. Sebastian sucked in a breath as if gearing up for an argument. "I don't need that, and I don't need you thinking I do. I can take care of myself financially."

"I have no doubts about that. But it's not about what I think *you* need, it's about *my* need to provide for you. If you had more money than me, my need would be the same."

Gideon smiled when Sebastian glared at him and growled. He slumped back in the seat then rubbed his stomach when it growled right back. Narrowing his eyes, Sebastian said, "We're going to talk about this later. But right now, I need food. These stupid steroids make me a starving, acne-faced, rage monster."

Gideon chuckled, annoying his boy even more he was sure, and shut the door to round the hood to his side. The acne Sebastian was talking about was one pimple in his hairline and one on his chin. He'd groused about them off and on for the last couple days because apparently, he hadn't had acne when he was going through puberty. Gideon hopped in the car and made his way to Sebastian's choice of restaurant. His stomach let him know he was quite happy with his boy's decision; he hadn't had a good burger in ages.

When they'd both walked into the burger joint to pick up their food, they'd gotten a few guarded glances. Gideon was used to people looking at him warily and supposed he couldn't blame them. He was tall and broad, so he took up a lot of space. He knew he looked fierce most of the time because he didn't smile much and rarely spoke more than was necessary.

He figured the less approachable he was, the better. He didn't have much use for most people. And while his goal wasn't to scare anyone, he was also never looking to attract them. He supposed they might also be curious about his possessive grip on the back of his boy's neck. Gideon wasn't much for holding hands in public. It had never been his thing. But he wanted others to know Sebastian was his and his boy seemed to need that reassurance as well.

He'd realized that when they'd walked in to see his doctor that first day in Rochester. Sebastian's head was bowed, his hair falling over his face to hide it, and his hands were in his pockets, causing his shoulders to hunch. When he'd placed his firm grip on the back of his boy's neck, Sebastian had straightened, his shoulders had relaxed, and he'd lifted his head. He'd still concealed himself a bit behind his hair and his hands stayed in his pockets, but he looked much less like he was hiding.

Since the surgery, he hadn't been able to hide behind his hair because most of it had been shaved. Gideon had some ideas about how best to deal with Sebastian's insecurities, but they were all wrapped up in their BDSM dynamic, and as they weren't exactly sure footed in that area yet from a permanence perspective, he wanted to wait until they settled into this new twenty-four seven dynamic Sebastian had asked for. He knew what he was going to propose would terrify Sebastian, and he wanted to ease him into it.

When they got back to the loft, Sebastian took their food out of the big bag they'd been given and got them both a glass of water, extra napkins, and plates. Gideon went and typed up the addendum to their contract in a matter of minutes, printing it out to sign. Once they did, they both tucked into their meals ravenously. They'd ordered the same thing, but Gideon had ordered an extra burger and a large shake to Sebastian's small. The food hit the spot, and they ended up watching a movie in the bedroom afterwards.

When the movie ended, Gideon maneuvered Sebastian to straddle his lap and leaned back against the mountain of pillows with his hands clasped behind his head. He looked his boy over, enjoying that he'd begun to put on some weight in the last few weeks. When his roaming eyes met Sebastian's, his eyes had dilated, and he wore a scowl that startled a chuckle out of Gideon.

Smirking and knowing the answer to his question, he asked it anyway. "Why are you glowering at me?"

Sebastian thumped him on the chest and said, "Because you're looking at me like you want to eat me as a second dessert, and we can't do anything because *you* won't let me do anything for you."

"If you're not getting anything out of it, we're not doing it."

"I enjoy making you come. That's what I'm getting out of it."

Gideon shook his head. "That's not enough for me. I take my pleasure with you, or not at all."

"But what about orgasm denial?"

"Orgasm denial is my decision, this sexual moratorium is the doctor's decision."

Sebastian huffed and curled into his chest, laying his forehead in the hollow where Gideon's neck and shoulder met. He shook his head and kissed Gideon's neck, and whispered, "You're just being stubborn."

Gideon pushed him back so they were looking at each other again. "And if I'd just had a craniotomy?"

"That's not the same thing."

Gideon barked out a laugh. "What? That's the *definition* of the same thing."

Sebastian's mouth twitched. "No. You're the Dom. You get what you want, and I get what you want me to have."

Gideon sobered at that and frowned. "Did I not always see to your needs? I very rarely use denial as a form of punishment because it gets me off getting you off. I mean, I won't say never, and there's always edging you within an inch of your life, but I always tip you over, don't I?"

Sebastian's eyes went wide, and he nodded quickly and said, "Yeah." He cleared his throat. "Yes, Sir. Um. I just meant there's a hierarchy. You're top, I'm bottom."

"Those are our sexual preferences, not a pecking order. But, we're equals in all things, Sebastian. Did you not feel like my equal? Did I make you feel less important?"

"No." Sebastian shook his head, slowly, as if trying to figure out what he wanted to say. Finally, he continued, "It's just, you have all the control in what we do."

"We've had this conversation before and you know that's absolutely not true. I only have the control you give me. I wouldn't do it otherwise. I assume control because that's what you need, as a submissive. That's what it means to be the Dominant. You know that. I know you know that, so where is this insecurity coming from?"

"I don't know." Sebastian shrugged. "I just… I mean, earlier, you wouldn't even let me pay for dinner. Do you really think I'm your equal?"

"Yes, I do. We can negotiate the money thing later, but I'm warning you now, it's something I feel very strongly about. Money is just money, and I have a ridiculous amount of it. It has nothing to do with how I view you as my partner."

Sebastian still looked unsure. "That doesn't make sense to me. How can I be your equal in this if you control everything, including that?"

"Because I can't do what I do to you, with you, unless you allow it. I control what we do, but only to your limits, which is where the control lies. It's a give and take. We seem to come back to this when you're not feeling confident. If I make you feel less than, I'm doing everything wrong."

Sebastian shook his head again, a frustrated look on his face. "No. You've never made me feel less important. I've never had a better Dom. Maybe I'm just having a hard time combining the two in my mind. The contract and the relationship." He huffed out a sigh and distractedly shoved his hand through his hair and yelped. "Ow! Fuck me! Goddamn, shit!"

Gideon sat up and moved Sebastian's hands from around his surgical scar. He pulled a hand free and went to touch it again, but Gideon pulled it away again and grumbled, "Don't. Hands down by your sides, boy. Let me take a look."

Sebastian mumbled, obviously in pain. He'd gotten the staples removed the week prior and everything was still extremely sensitive to touch, so Gideon knew he was in pain. It looked like he'd scraped his nails over the large scar which started just to the left of his small widow's peak, arced back, and hooked back around to end just above his ear.

Gideon thought it looked like a curving question mark and was in constant awe of his boy for being able to withstand the surgery and the recovery like he was. It was redder than usual after Sebastian's absentminded gesture, but the hair stubble surrounding the bright red scar had probably kept it from getting too roughed up. He blew cold air on it, and Sebastian shivered. "Still hurt?"

"Mmhmm."

"All right. Here." Gideon moved Sebastian off his lap. "Massage the scar gently like your doctor showed you to break down the scar tissue."

Gideon got up and grabbed a couple of the prescription pain pills still left over and a glass of water from the bathroom and handed them to Sebastian who was on his knees on the middle of the bed still rubbing the scar. "Hurts like a son of a bitch."

"I know, baby. I'm sorry." He handed Sebastian the pills, and before he could argue, Gideon said, "You haven't taken the real drugs in several days, and you just hurt yourself. Acetaminophen won't be enough for the inevitable headache to come."

"But, we haven't finished talking."

"We have plenty of time. There's no rush. You need to do as I say now. Let me worry about the rest. I won't forget your concerns, boy."

Sebastian nodded and sighed like Gideon had just taken a huge burden off his shoulders. He tossed back the pills. They got ready for bed, and Gideon did his best to distract Sebastian until he went to sleep. Since it was still early for him, Gideon got up and went down to the club, putting in an earpiece. He did a walk-through of the place, making sure he was seen and heard, not just by his people, but by the club regulars. He went by their security room and perused the cameras of the owned rooms he sold at ridiculous prices to the rich men who wouldn't deign to lower themselves to use a public room.

There wasn't an inch of the club that was off-limits to his safety cameras. The men who paid an arm and a leg to own their rooms were all smart enough to use their retained lawyers to go through the contract, so they all knew about the cameras, and every single one of them had tried to push back, but in the end, they caved.

They knew he didn't need their money and didn't give a shit if they bought a room, so the power was always squarely on him which is the way he liked it in all things. And when they caved, they paid handsomely for their rooms and everything in them. So handsomely, in fact, that Gideon still would be running financially in the black if that was the only thing his club contained.

When he was sure everything was running as it should, he retired to his office and worked his way through some paperwork. His people had kept the club running like a fine-tuned machine while he was gone, and he hadn't had too much to come back to. He'd known that would be the case because he only hired the best, but he'd never been away that long, so it enabled him to spend as much time with Sebastian as he could.

He didn't need half the sleep Sebastian did on a regular day, let alone when he was in recovery mode, so when Sebastian was resting or wanting time alone, he was able to get work done and make appearances downstairs. It worked for them, and Gideon put a reminder on his calendar to give his staff a bonus after all was said and done. They'd earned it. After he was done with everything that needed to be done that day, he headed back upstairs to climb into bed with his boy.

⸺

Two weeks later, he woke up to his boy giving him head underneath the covers of their bed. He didn't bother to open his eyes, he just gripped the back of Sebastian's head lightly, pushing him down the length of his cock until Gideon felt and heard him gag on his long, thick length. He bent his knees a little, grinding his heels into the bed as he held the back of Sebastian's head in place and fucked up into his boy's mouth.

He was so close, his boy so talented, and was about to let go when he heard a weird choked laugh coming from Sebastian. Confused, his eyes popped open and he looked down to see Slap and Tickle climbing on the bed and batting their paws at the blanket-covered Sebastian. *Fucking cats.* He lost it at that point; his control over his laughter, his near orgasm buzz, and most of his erection as he continued to chuckle at the absurdity of the situation.

Gideon gripped Sebastian under his arms and dragged him up so that he was sprawled, a laughing heap, on top of his body. They both continued to laugh until Sebastian looked up into Gideon's eyes, and he sucked in a breath when he saw the love and happiness reflected on Sebastian's face.

"Goddamn, you're beautiful. I can't get enough of you. I'll never get enough of you. Move in with me. We'll make it work."

Sebastian sobered immediately. He shook his head and lowered his gaze, allowing what was left of the long length of his bangs to hang over his face. Hiding, again. Gideon had avoided it so far, but it was the right time. Finally, the right time.

"I want you to take off the rest of your clothes and present yourself to me on the floor of the bathroom, facing the toilet."

Sebastian's eyes went wide and he scrambled to obey. Gideon went into his playroom and grabbed a blindfold. Returning to the bathroom, he sat on the toilet, legs spread, Sebastian kneeling between them. He put the blindfold on his boy's head and heard the little hitch in his breath.

"Can you see anything?"

"No, Sir."

"Good. This is going to test your limits, boy. I've made a decision for you that I feel is a very important step for you. Do you trust me with your mind and your body?"

"Yes, Sir." The words were spoken without hesitation.

Gideon stood and pulled out one of the drawers just to the left of his sink. Quietly, he pulled out the box he needed and went about readying everything for this scene. He knew it was going to take its toll on his boy, and he knew aftercare would be what truly mattered in the long run. He sat down on the toilet again.

"Scoot forward a couple inches."

Sebastian did, and Gideon praised him and then asked, "What are your safewords, boy?"

"Green for go, yellow for slow down, red for stop."

"Use them, if you need them."

"Yes, Sir."

"Bastian?"

"Yes, Sir?"

"I will not be upset with you if you safeword during this scene. Do you understand me?"

Sebastian exhaled quickly and nodded. "Yes, Sir."

"Let's begin."

Gideon flipped a switch and the buzzing started. Immediately, his boy tensed, and even over the buzz of the clippers, he heard Sebastian's whimper. "Check in, boy."

Sebastian sat quietly and tipped his head as if to marinate in the sound of the constant buzz. Gideon was just about to ask again when Sebastian choked out, "Yellow, Sir."

"Granted. Do you need a moment to settle, or do you wish to talk about it?"

Sebastian sucked in a deep breath, and Gideon's heart broke. He nearly wanted to call it off, but he felt it was important, so he stood his ground. "I just need a moment, Sir."

"Take all the time you need."

He kept the clippers buzzing, knowing it was important for Sebastian to hear it, to let it guide him into making the correct decision for himself, whatever it may be. After a few long moments, Sebastian took a deep breath and said, "Green, Sir."

Gideon had never been prouder of his boy. He placed the clippers to Sebastian's head and began to shave it with the size three guard, which was closest to the length of the already shaved portion of Sebastian's head. As he made his first solid swipe of his hair, he heard Sebastian whimper and pull in a deep breath.

"You're all right, boy. I'm so damn proud of you. Check in with me, please."

Sebastian pulled in another deep breath and said, "Green, Sir."

He moved the blindfold up and then down in the back, making sure he got everything. Finally, when he was done, he carefully removed it. Sebastian's palms were no longer face up, but face down on his thighs, gripping them hard enough to turn his knuckles white. Gideon ran his hands over the soft stubble, the palms of both of his big hands wrapped around his whole head.

Gideon leaned down and kissed his head, over and over, everywhere he could reach, paying particular attention to the raised, bumpy edges of his scar. His boy's sobs were wracking his whole body at that point, and Gideon's heart was breaking.

"You're so good, baby. So strong. Let it out. I'm so fucking proud of you. So proud. You're the bravest man I know."

Gideon touched and stroked Sebastian's face, his head, his shoulders, and his neck, telling him how beautiful he was, how he'd never been more attracted to anyone in his life, how proud he was to be with him, and finally how lucky he knew he was that Sebastian had chosen him. When Gideon was sure Sebastian was calming down, he asked, "Do you want to go straight to bed, or are you up for me cleaning you up in the shower?"

Finally, Sebastian opened his eyes and nodded, "Shower, Sir."

"Good boy." With no hair in the way, Gideon found himself mesmerized by his boy's eyes and long lashes. His multi-hued irises so luminous and breathtaking he barely let himself blink, afraid he was some apparition that would disappear if he did so.

Finally, he whispered, "I love you, Bastian."

Sebastian replied, "I love you too, Sir."

Gideon made quick work of their shower, ridding them of any remnants of Sebastian's hair. He led him back to their bed and was finally able to give him the aftercare he so desperately needed. Afterward, they both fell asleep, emotionally and physically exhausted.

Chapter 36

SEBASTIAN

Sebastian stared at himself in the mirror in Gideon's bathroom. He looked so different, and he still couldn't wrap his mind around it enough to figure out if he hated it or was okay with it. He couldn't say he was happy about it, not yet anyway. He thought back to their conversation the morning after and knew Gideon was right and he'd done the best thing for him even if Sebastian wasn't comfortable with it yet, a week later.

When he raised his eyes to look at Gideon, his heart thudded hard in his chest at the realization that Gideon was watching him. He cleared his throat and said, "Good morning, Sir."

"Good morning. How are you feeling?"

"Fine, I guess. I'm not sure, really."

"Mixed feelings?"

Sebastian nodded. "Yes, Sir."

"I guess that's to be expected. Our aftercare last night was to settle you mentally and physically after the scene. It wasn't the time to discuss the reasons behind it, but I'd like to talk about it this morning."

"All right."

"I've been up for a while now. Gotten a workout in and showered. Why don't you get a shower, and I'll make us some breakfast? When you're done, come into the kitchen."

"Yes, Sir."

Sebastian couldn't help but be disappointed they didn't get to shower together, but his stomach growled, so he hurried to get himself cleaned. Gideon made quite a spread and they both sat in silence as they ate, knowing a heavy conversation was coming, but neither of them wanted to have it over food.

Once things were cleaned up, they took their coffee into the family room

SAVING SEBASTIAN: A CATHARSIS NOVEL

and sat facing each other on the couch. They always dealt with their difficult conversations while close enough to touch each other and when they could talk without any distractions. Gideon reached over and clasped his hand on the back of the couch, squeezing it gently. "Do you know why I shaved your head?"

Sebastian shrugged and ventured, "It gets in my face a lot, and... I guess... I guess I started using it to hide behind."

"That's right. You use it as a shield to hide what you think are your flaws. Sometimes you even use sunglasses and your hoodie to conceal your face completely. Your beard is thicker for the same reasons. Am I right?"

Sebastian looked down at his lap and nodded. "Yes, Sir."

"You know what that means, right?"

Sebastian scratched at his beard with both hands then rubbed his face and nodded. "Yes, Sir."

"All right. I can shave it for you later. For now, I'm going to lay out my expectations for you going forward."

When Sebastian merely nodded at him, Gideon continued, "From now on, I want you to work on your posture. Back straight, shoulders squared, chin up, facing forward. You do this already when we scene. I want you to do this at all times. I'd like you to make a concerted effort to meet people's eyes when you pass strangers on the street or when you are speaking with someone."

Inwardly, Sebastian groaned; outwardly, he crossed his arms over his chest. "I don't always realize I'm doing it. Sometimes, I do it on purpose; other times, it's just an automatic reflex."

"I don't doubt that's true. Which is why you're going to have to work at being more conscious of your behavior and your surroundings. It's my prefer-ence that you work with a psychologist as well. I think along with your self-consciousness about your appearance, your PWS has made you less confident in other ways like making connections with people and working at cultivating friendships."

Sebastian couldn't deny any of that, but he didn't think he needed a psychologist for shitty self-esteem, and he said as much to Gideon, who replied, "Poor self-esteem affects your mental health as does a lack of people in your life which leads to loneliness. Both of those things contribute to depression."

"Well you have everything figured out, don't you?"

Sebastian had looked up into his Dom's eyes and seen disappointment coupled with patience. He didn't know whether to be chagrined that he'd snapped at Gideon or annoyed with Gideon's never-ending supply of patience. He waited for Gideon to say something, but when he didn't, Sebastian asked, "Can I think about it?"

"About seeking help? Yes. If you decide to, I have the name of someone I trust implicitly. He lives our lifestyle, so you'd be able to be completely open and honest with him. However, you can choose whomever you like. Regarding the other, there's nothing to think about. You'll need to practice keeping your head up, meeting people's eyes, walking proud. Is that understood?"

"Yes, Sir."

In the end, Sebastian knew he was right, and even though Gideon shaved his face the following day, he only asked Sebastian to keep it at a one or two guard length. He didn't require his face to be devoid of hair completely. Sebastian knew, looking in the mirror in the bathroom, he was being let off easy, so he vowed to do better and eventually start shaving with a razor rather than clippers.

He looked so much younger already. He had a hard time looking at himself without picking apart his features one by one and examining them in a negative light which just annoyed the hell out of him when he realized what he was doing. He realized it probably wouldn't hurt to make an appointment with that psychologist. It wasn't like he enjoyed finding fault in everything he saw.

He was slowly getting better, the pain in his head subsiding more and more each week. He was going to the doctor the next day to see if he was going to be able to go back to work the next week or if he'd need to stay out for more than six weeks. He knew from some of the issues he was having, it wasn't likely he'd be going back to work, but he could hope.

He was having mixed feelings about the situation because he'd be able to work again, but also, he'd be moving to his apartment. He knew it was for the best, but he couldn't help but feel like the last thing he wanted to do was leave his Dom and his home. His Dom's home, rather. He was a jumbled mess of emotions, and that more than anything had him pulling out his phone and dialing the number Gideon had given him.

Three days later, he thought he'd had a good first session, and when he walked out of the appointment and saw the pride in Gideon's eyes at having done it, he knew he'd made the right decision. "How did it go?"

Sebastian smiled and looked up into Gideon's earnest eyes. "It went well. Thank you, Sir."

Gideon guided him out to his SUV and helped him into the car. He didn't want to admit to the fact that he was tired and his head hurt, but he supposed he wasn't very good at masking his emotions because when Gideon got in on his side, he leaned forward and opened the glove box, pulling out a bottle of acetaminophen and his sunglasses. As Sebastian put his glasses on, Gideon handed him two pills and a bottle of water he had in the cup holder.

Gideon's tone was low when he asked, "Did you feel good about Dr. Price?"

"Yes. We talked about—"

"I don't need to know." Gideon held up a hand and shook his head. "I just wanted to be here to support you. I'm happy to listen if you want to talk about it, but please don't feel as if I'm asking you to tell me the details. You're entitled to your privacy."

Sebastian looked at him for a long moment and nodded his head, taking him at his word. He did want to think about some things for a while before he talked to Gideon. He had no doubt he'd open up to him, eventually, but being given the time to figure out what he wanted to say was good. Gideon reached over the console with his palm up.

Sebastian put his hand in his Dom's bigger one and watched as he pulled it up to his lips and kissed it, gazing at Sebastian as he said, "Proud of you."

"Thank you, Sir."

"Let's get you home so you can rest."

"I'm okay."

"Boy, you're squinting even with your glasses on. Your doctor said to listen to your body and not to push yourself."

Sebastian sighed but agreed, saying, "All right. It's just driving me crazy. I can't seem to rid myself of these headaches, and I get tired so damned easily."

"Well, shit, you've got a gigantic scar on the right side of your head. Part of your goddamn skull was removed and put in a metal tray. I still can't wrap my mind around that. Frankly, I'm surprised you're improving as quickly as you are."

Sebastian chuckled then closed his eyes to relieve some of the ache in his head. Next thing he knew, Gideon was leaning over and undoing his seatbelt, kissing him awake. They made their way up to the loft, and Sebastian slept another hour. When he woke, he heard Gideon on the phone, just outside their room.

The door was open just enough to hear him, and he didn't dare move in case he missed something. What he heard surprised him. He didn't know Gideon had that much venom in him. The tone he was using wasn't his Dom tone. It wasn't even the tone he'd used when he'd called an end to their contract at the party. No, this tone held an anger Sebastian didn't even know Gideon was capable of. He wasn't for a second nervous for his own sake, but he sure as shit never wanted to make his Dom truly angry because the menace in his voice made goosebumps skitter up his arms and the hair on his body stand up.

"I assume that you're calling me because things with you and Connell aren't working out. Is that assumption correct, pet?"

Pet? What the fuck? An inkling of jealousy creeped in, but if that was how Gideon spoke to someone he called pet, he didn't think the jealousy was warranted. Frankly, he hoped for the other person's sake that Gideon's assumption was correct because it didn't sound like any other option was going to have a good outcome for anyone.

Sebastian shivered at the calm, even tone Gideon's voice took on. "I believe I made my feelings clear the last time we spoke." A pause, and then, "Stop talking, Boone. I don't like repeating myself, but I'll do it once more so that it will sink in. I'm out. End of story."

There was another pause then a menacing growl. "When have I ever played by your rules? Even when you paid me, besides providing me with dossiers, I was left to my own devices. So, explain to me why you think you can control me now?"

Another pause. "I heard nothing from you. Do you seriously think I'd put all my eggs in your fucking basket? Your loyalties aren't with me, they're to the job. Of course, I had someone else checking for me. They moved faster. End of story. This is the end of this discussion, Boone. Do not call me again, is that clear?"

A pause then a quiet, deadly whispered, "Is. That. Clear?" Another pause. "Good."

Thankfully, Sebastian had closed his eyes, perhaps thinking it helped him to hear the quiet but lethal conversation. The bedroom door opened and all was quiet, no movement that he could hear. He waited several drawn-out beats before he cracked one of his eyelids, afraid he'd been caught. But Gideon wasn't there and there was the telltale sound of his Dom's treadmill and the rhythmic, fast paced thumping of his feet on the rolling rubber mat as Gideon worked off what sounded like an enormous amount of anger on the machine.

As much as he wanted to stay awake to offer any help he could give him, the sound of the treadmill lulled him back to sleep, and he only woke when he heard the shower come on in the bathroom some time later. Throwing back the covers, he shed his clothes and walked into the bathroom, his mouth watering at the sight of his Dom, huge palms braced against the wall as the water pelted on his lowered head.

He quietly opened the door but should have known Gideon would hear him. His head turned quickly his way and he exhaled loudly, never taking his eyes off of Sebastian. He shook his head and nearly growled out, "Don't."

Sebastian was emboldened when he saw his Dom's huge erection. He walked into the huge glass enclosure and shut the large door behind him. "Why not?"

Gideon shook his head again and said, "Because I can't be gentle with you right now, Bastian."

His heart rate sped up, and he gulped. "I don't need gentle. You've given me nothing but tenderness since my surgery, and while I've loved every sweet kiss and soft touch, that's not us, Sir. You don't scare me."

"I can see your pulse pounding in your neck. Go back to bed."

"No, Sir."

"Are you defying me, boy?"

"Yes, Sir."

"Are you looking to be punished?"

Sebastian let out an unsteady breath, excitement thrumming through his veins, his skin going hot from the steam but also from his intense burning desire to be what his Dom needed in that moment. He whispered, "If that's what you need, Sir."

A deep rumble came from his Dom's chest, and he said, "On your knees. Worship my cock with your mouth."

Sebastian stepped toward Gideon into the spray of the shower, and in one smooth move that felt like coming home, he was on his knees. He raised his hands to touch Sir's thick, powerful thighs and looked up into his eyes. Water sluiced off his Dom's nose and chin and Sebastian was drenched, blinking water out of his eyes. So entranced by his Sir's fierce gaze, he almost missed the rough whisper, "I didn't say you could touch me. Put those hands behind your back and don't even think about touching me again until you're granted permission."

"Yes, Sir."

"Less talking, more sucking, boy."

Sebastian nodded and stuck out his tongue. Gideon spread his legs to lower himself to Sebastian's level and grabbed his cock, slapping it against his tongue and his cheek several times. He kept his mouth open, patient, knowing his Sir wouldn't waste time on the preliminaries for long.

He was right, Gideon slid his cock deep in his mouth until it hit his throat. Pulling it out, he shoved it back in again and again, never breaching his throat, just bumping up against it, triggering his gag reflex several times, and from the look on Sir's face, enjoying that response immensely. Sebastian gripped each opposite forearm behind his back so he wouldn't be tempted to use his hands.

Sir pulled his cock out of his mouth and stood there gazing down at him, a hungry look in his eyes. "Show me how much you love my dick."

Sebastian, wanting nothing more, did his best to prove just that to his Dom. He kissed, licked, nibbled, sucked, and even bit the shaft, eliciting a growl from Sir. In warning, in pleasure, he didn't know. He just kept going. He sucked on Sir's full balls, tugging on the wrinkled, soft skin with his teeth. He used his nose to lift Sir's sack just enough to lick his taint, and when he was rewarded with a deep groan, he took Gideon's cock deep in his throat as far as he could take it without help and only came up when he had no more air.

He pulled off just enough to fill his lungs and dove back down on that long, thick, cut cock, sliding his tongue down those sexy as fuck veins along its length. Running out of air again and lost in what he was doing, he didn't realize Gideon had taken half a step back until he was searching out his cock again with his eyes closed and it wasn't there. His eyes popped open, and he looked up at his Dom, seeing a look of pure carnal pleasure in his eyes.

Sir didn't get closer though, he stayed just out of reach. Sebastian nearly followed him, but thought better of it and was glad he did when he heard a snarling, "Tilt your head back." When Sebastian followed orders, he hummed, "Mmm, that's it. What do I want to hear?"

Fuck, his own cock was dripping. It was all he could do to answer him. "You want to hear me beg, Sir."

Snarling, Gideon grated out, "That's right. I wanna hear you beg for it. Beg for my cock like a good boy."

Sebastian whimpered, knowing if Sir kept talking like that he'd come without permission and without touching his cock once. "Please. Please, Sir. May I have your cock?"

Gideon slapped his dick against Sebastian's face again. "I'm not convinced you're a good boy. Convince me, Bastian."

Oh god. He let out a whimper and, horrified by his lack of control, he whined before his voice took on a higher, more desperate pitch as he whispered, "Please. Please, Sir. I need it. I want to taste it, feel it on my tongue. I'm begging you, please!"

"That's it. That's my good boy. Open up, now."

Sebastian closed his eyes and did as Sir bid. The next thing he knew, Gideon was surprising him by sticking two fingers down his throat instead of his cock. It was so fast, he gagged.

Making an annoyed noise in the back of his throat as if he was just so disgusted with Sebastian's poor attempts, Gideon ground out, "If you're gagging on my fingers, perhaps this is too much for you. Is that the case?"

He shook his head quickly. "No, Sir. Please. Let me try again. Please."

Gideon just grunted and shoved those same two fingers down his throat again. He kept himself from gagging, but only just. He looked into his Sir's eyes and swallowed around those digits until he saw the flair of desire burning bright again. He removed his fingers and stepped in again, only this time he didn't spread his legs and he growled for Sebastian to keep his head tilted up for a clear shot straight down his throat.

Gideon leaned one hand against the shower wall, and grabbed his cock with the other, pushing it down into Sebastian's waiting mouth. He didn't pause, he didn't give Sebastian any time to adjust, he shoved it as far as he could down Sebastian's throat and, ignoring the gagging around his cock, gripped the back of Sebastian's head and held it still as he pushed still farther. Sebastian swallowed convulsively, which pulled the head deeper still. He was running out of air, had tears rolling down his cheeks from the strain, water from Gideon's chin dripping on his forehead, and drool dripping down his neck.

He hadn't felt this alive since their last good scene before the holidays. This. Just this, felt so right even as his vision got hazy at the edges and dimmed when he convulsively tried to gasp for air. He heard a muffled curse then another growl before Gideon groaned out, "Holy fuck!"

He was close to passing out, and just as he felt his eyes about to roll back in his head, Gideon pulled his cock out and Sebastian sucked in a deep breath and coughed, gasping for another. He bent over double, unable to help but use a hand to catch himself on the wet tile floor and hold himself up. He coughed some more and gasped for another breath, sweet oxygen flowing through him and making his body shake in recovery.

It wasn't until he felt Gideon slide his hand under his chin and tilt his head up that Sebastian realized he had squatted down to check on him. He kneeled back again and put his hand behind him, "Sor—" Turning his head away from Sir, he coughed again. His voice raspy when he said, "Sorry, Sir."

Gideon's breath sawed in and out of him, and his eyes devoured Sebastian. His expression serious, he whispered, "Check in."

Sebastian held his gaze without wavering and rasped out, "Green, Sir."

Gideon scrutinized him to be sure he was telling the truth. Hand still gripping Sebastian's chin, he slid his thumb in his mouth, and Sebastian took great pains to worship it, just like Sir's cock. "Goddamn, boy."

When Gideon removed his finger, Sebastian gazed at Sir and whispered, "Thank you, Sir."

Surprise registered on Gideon's face, and he asked, "What are you thanking me for?"

"For using me, Sir."

Gideon growled, "Do you like being used by your Dom?"

Sebastian let out a shaky breath and nodded. "Yes."

"That's good because I plan on using your ass to make me come then denying you for defying me."

"If it pleases you."

"Oh, it will, I assure you. Grab the lube and prep us both."

"Yes, Sir."

He stood as fluidly as possible and walked to the cubby built into the wall of the shower and pumped some lube into his palm. He knew Gideon loved watching him move. He'd said so many times. It was something as a sub he'd always been aware of and tried to perfect. Moving into position as they were ordered to carry out specific tasks, subs were often watched closely. Sebastian, always feeling like he didn't have much to offer, knew he had to perfect everything he'd learned about serving and being pleasing to the eye while doing so.

He moved languidly, knowing he was probably driving Gideon nuts, but hopefully in a good way. When he was standing in front of Sir again, hot water cascading over his body, he slid gracefully down to his knees and rubbed his hands together. He wrapped one hand around the base of Gideon's thick shaft and his other above it, squeezing the rigid length in both hands and twisting them in opposite directions, coating it with slick.

When he was done, he kept his grip and looked up into his Dom's eyes. He looked so fierce as if he was barely able to hold on to his control. Sebastian hoped that meant he'd be deliciously sore in the morning with a few bruises, if he was lucky. He saw when Gideon narrowed his eyes at him, and his heart took up a hard, staccato rhythm in his chest.

"Do you enjoy teasing me, boy?"

"Yes, Sir."

Gideon raised a brow and ordered, "Prep yourself."

Sebastian smiled, eyes half-mast, and licked his lips. He turned around on his knees and leaned forward, bracing his forehead on his forearm on the floor of the shower, ass as high as he could raise it and still remain on his knees, he slid his other hand between his legs and used the remainder of the lube coating his hand to coat his crease.

He closed his eyes and enjoyed his own ministrations. Slowly, knowing Sir was watching, he rubbed his fingers up and down his crack, sliding one finger in, up and down again, and then two fingers in. He pumped them in and out several times then added a third and moaned at the stretch, smiling to himself when he heard a muttered curse and a groan.

He gasped when he felt Sir's palms spread his cheeks. He opened his eyes and lifted his head enough to look over his shoulder. Gideon had taken a knee and was staring at his fingers still lodged in his tight hole. He pumped them in and out again, enjoying the look on Gideon's face, loving the stretch of his ass being held wide open by those huge hands. He turned back around and leaned his head on his arm again and simply took pleasure in being watched and pleasing him.

He let out a guttural moan and nearly shouted, "Oh god, Sir!" When he felt teeth on his left ass cheek and then his right. These weren't gentle love nips, no, these were full-on painful bites that would leave teeth marks and bruises in the morning. His cock jumped and more precum dripped from the tip. The bites were followed by hard spanks on both cheeks, right on top of the bite marks, and if he hadn't anticipated it, he'd have come then and there.

"Turn around and face me."

He slid his fingers from his ass and slowly turned around, kneeled and waited for further instruction. Gideon lowered his other knee and kneeled himself, spreading his legs apart. "Wrap yourself around me."

Giddy, Sebastian scrambled up, wrapping his arms around his neck and hitching his legs up, he wrapped them around his waist, trapping their cocks between them. Gideon gripped his ass cheeks then stood and pressed them against the wall, Sebastian's back making contact with the cold tiles.

He gasped when Gideon turned on the other showerhead and turned both directly on them. Sebastian warmed immediately. Sir leaned down to kiss him, and he lost all rational thought. Seconds ticked into minutes and he lost track of time and self until he felt the bulb of Gideon's cockhead at his entrance. There was no teasing, no prepping, making him glad he'd prepped himself. He went from zero to sixty in two seconds and was balls deep, the momentum moving Sebastian up the wall another inch.

Sir pulled back and looked into his eyes, the look on his face one of barely controlled violence. Sebastian shivered but didn't break eye contact. He needed Sir to know that he wanted to be what he needed. This wasn't for him, this was for Sir. The phone call had fucked up their equilibrium, and if he had to be pounded through the bathroom wall to bring his Dom back down, he'd enjoy the ride.

Sir leaned in and whispered menacingly, "I'm gonna take your breath away."

Sebastian sucked in a breath, knowing he meant it literally and not in any figurative romantic sense. He whispered right back, "Take what you need from me, Sir."

Gideon growled, "Fuck." He pulled nearly all the way out and slammed his cock home again. "If you need to safeword, tap-out on the wall."

"Yes, Sir, but I won't need to. I need this as much as you do."

Gideon's gaze narrowed, and he nodded. "You do not have permission to come. Deep breath."

Sebastian closed his eyes feeling strangely peaceful. They'd been cleared for their regular sexual activities, but he knew, no matter his current state of mind, Gideon was too concerned with his well being after the surgery to push breath play into dangerous territory.

He opened his eyes and met Gideon's turbulent gaze, gave him a slight nod, leaned his head against the shower wall, and did as he was told, sucking in as much air as he could. Gideon gently placed his palm over Sebastian's mouth and nose, wrapping his fingers around the side of his face, almost cradling it, then Sebastian was closing his eyes as Gideon gripped his ass with his other hand and set a brutal pace, letting the high build. He was crushed between the wall and Gideon's equally unforgiving, muscular chest. Feeling more alive than he'd felt since the surgery, a dizzying euphoria stole his conscious thought as his greedy hole was drilled.

Gideon groaned as he pounded into him without reprieve, an animal acting on instinct without thought. Sir bit down hard on the juncture between his neck and shoulder and Sebastian gasped and bucked, nearly coming. Gideon bit higher on his neck, never slowing the pace of his pistoning hips. Finally, his teeth clamped down on his earlobe before he pulled back and glared, snarling, "Why'd you force my hand? You weren't ready for this."

Sebastian glared and nodded his head then his eyes went wide. Gideon changed his grip and allowed Sebastian to suck in much needed air. He resumed his hold over his nose and mouth, and Sebastian reveled in the fact that he wouldn't take a breath again until Sir made it possible. That was what he'd needed. He didn't want control. He'd needed so desperately to hand it over to Gideon, not just in the everyday things, but in this, and for his every breath.

They were so tuned to each other, Gideon loosened his grip again, Sebastian sucked in air and his head spun when that hand cut off his last desperate gulp, and he was lost to every point of pain and pleasure. His head was a whirlwind of feelings, thoughts, emotions. His hole clamped down convulsively on the thick, meaty length of Sir's cock as it slammed in and out of him. His prostate was getting a workout, and he didn't know if he could take much more without letting go.

A deep, animalistic growl roared out of his Dom, and he pulled back, removing his hand from his nose and mouth. He nodded and Sebastian sucked air back in then Sir's huge hand was on his throat, squeezing, and he was moaning, keening, bucking back into Gideon's thrusts. He tightened his grip around Gideon's waist with his legs and loosed his grip from around his neck, both hands clutching at Gideon's forearm as his hand clamped even harder down on his throat.

He heard a guttural groan then Sir's powerful hips lost their rhythm and Sebastian felt the pulsing heat of Sir's cum coat his insides, making him moan as he tried and failed to pull in a breath. Sir must have felt it because his grip loosened but stayed in place as he gulped desperately for the air he so needed.

Gideon leaned his forehead against Sebastian's, both of his hands now gripping Sebastian's ass, eyes closed as his chest rose and fell, his need for oxygen obviously matching that of Sebastian's. They both recovered in silence —Gideon from his orgasm, Sebastian from the breath play and merciless pounding. He was still floating a couple minutes later when Gideon reached for something, and Sebastian wrapped both arms around his neck, holding on, never wanting to let go. Sir's grip tightened on his ass cheek, and his other hand was reaching under him to touch his cock where it entered Sebastian's ass.

Hoping he knew what was coming, he gripped Sir harder and groaned when he felt Gideon's cock slip slowly almost all the way out of his ass. Quickly, Gideon pulled out fully and slid in the fat plug Sebastian had been hoping for deep into his ass, catching the cum before it could escape. The gesture made Sebastian shudder, and he buried his face in Gideon's neck and kissed him there.

"That what you needed, boy?"

Sebastian hummed and nodded into his neck. "Yes, Sir. Thank you."

Gideon bent down and placed Sebastian on the bench seat and kissed him. He was still being hit by enough of the spray to feel warm, but Gideon adjusted the showerhead so that it rained down on his shoulders and back. He glanced up, absentmindedly. "How in the hell is it still hot?"

Gideon chuckled as he grabbed the bar of soap and began to lather himself up to wash the sweat of his double workouts off. "The benefits of owning the building and installing a commercial-sized water heater for the whole thing."

Sebastian hummed, swaying a bit on the bench. The showerhead Gideon was using turned off then his as well, and a warm bath sheet was wrapped around his shoulders. Next thing he knew, he was leaning against a mound of pillows on the bed, a bottle of water in his hand, Gideon stretched out beside him. He was still floating a bit and was lying there exposed and still in need of relief.

Gideon traced the outlines of the tattoos on his skin. "They're beautiful. So vibrant. I can see your artistry in them. What made you choose where to put them?"

Sebastian chuckled. "Because the locations are so random?"

Gideon shrugged and smiled down at him. "There's gotta be a method to the madness. It's unlike you to do things without thought."

Sebastian hummed in agreement and added, "If I can reach it, I'll tattoo it."

"Wait. You did all these? How? Shit, I haven't even paid attention enough to know if you're left- or right-handed."

"Ambidextrous. Had to teach myself to be, but it helps a tremendous amount with tattooing. Others, and myself."

"Yeah, I can see how it would. How does one go about teaching themselves to use both hands?"

"Uh, well…" He touched his palm to his PWS and continued, "When I was a kid and my parents told me what was wrong with me, I started going to the library to read everything on the subject. When I found out weakness in the limbs, or even paralysis on the side of the body opposite the PWS, is really common, I started to train myself to use my right hand just as well as I could use my left."

"And you've got some weakness there, right?"

"Yeah. I think it was brought on as the seizures got worse. I wanted to be able to do whatever it was I wanted to do with my other hand if my left was paralyzed." He glanced into Gideon's eyes. "It could still happen. The surgery isn't going to be a miracle cure for everything."

Gideon slid his hand up Sebastian's chest to cup his cheek, rubbing his thumb over his cheek. "I know that. You aren't the only one who's done research."

Sebastian's eyes filled. "Really?"

"Of course, I started just after you told me. But let's not talk about that. I wanna know more about your past. How you got into art and became a tattoo artist, how you became a submissive."

Sebastian snorted, laughing at the absurdity of it. "We're so backwards. We're in love and committed to being with each other, and we haven't even learned about each other's pasts. It's a bit topsy turvy, isn't it?"

Gideon chuckled and admitted, "Yeah, I guess it is. But I still wanna know."

Sebastian nodded. "Well, I knew I wanted to be an artist of some kind when I was a kid. My homelife left a lot to be desired, so I spent a lot of time in my room or outside drawing. I had this great art teacher in high school who really helped me. I got bullied a lot, and she always let me come to her class during my free period and at lunch. But in the end, that bullying is what sent me to school and eventually got me my house, so I guess I can't complain too much."

"How's that?" Gideon questioned, eyebrows raised in confusion.

"A legal settlement." Sebastian glanced down and then back up again. "It's a long story."

Gideon shrugged. "We have time."

Sebastian sighed and then proceeded to share his past with the man who would be his future.

He was a senior in high school and lived with his parents in their house, but it had never been a home. His parents had long since divested themselves of him except to make sure he understood he was a burden, an embarrassment, and a disappointment, and that was before he told them he was gay. There was no question he'd be tossed out the door the second he graduated.

Bullying had been his constant companion from the moment he entered middle school and on through high school. Being different and considered weak was a death sentence for fitting in. One of his worst tormentors was a popular rich kid named Jeremiah Broderick. He picked on Sebastian every chance he got. Teachers usually intervened on his behalf, except the gym teacher, Mr. Terry.

Mr. Terry was an older, poorer, and less attractive version of Jeremiah. A man who had told Sebastian on more than one occasion—each time Sebastian went to him to ask him to help him stop the bullying, "Buck up and take it like a man. You need to toughen up and not be such a pussy."

It had been rugby day in gym class. He'd already had a run-in with Jeremiah and his crew. His knees were bruised from the numerous times he'd been tripped running laps. Teams were picked and the game had begun. The ball had been thrown to Sebastian, he'd done his best to pass it to a teammate, but everyone had conveniently looked away.

Jeremiah had grabbed him, wrenched his arm behind his back at an impossible angle, and landed on top of him. From there, the huddle of boys all converged and landed on top of them. Everyone's combined weight had dislocated his elbow and caused a spiral fracture.

The bell rang, and Mr. Terry was nowhere to be seen. The boys got up, each and every one of them kicking him before leaving him broken and crying in pain. Ten minutes passed before the groundskeeper found him. Kneeling down beside Sebastian, he asked, "What happened here? Do you need help?"

Sebastian nodded. "Some boys in gym class attacked me. I think my arm is broken."

The man placed his hand on Sebastian's shoulder, muttering, "Damn bullies get worse every year. Hang in there, okay? I'll go get the nurse."

She arrived and called nine-one-one, and he was transported to the hospital where the police and his parents were waiting. He was stabilized and had a temporary cast put on until the surgery was scheduled, and he had to stay overnight because of a concussion caused by several kicks to the head.

The police questioned him, and he was forced to relate the whole embarrassing story in front of his parents. One of the officers asked, "Do you want to press charges?"

He started to say no, but his parents interrupted, "Yes. The people who hurt our son need to be punished."

The officers took a few more pieces of information and left soon thereafter, finally allowing him to rest.

He awoke to his parents speaking with their pastor. He pretended he was still asleep while he listened to Pastor Gregory and his parents making plans that made him sick. They all seemed gleeful that he was finally proving useful. The church had many needs and perhaps his little accident would be just the thing to help their little fledgling house of worship. They decided he'd sue the school, teacher, Jeremiah, and perhaps even the school board, for good measure.

Pretending he was still asleep, he waited until his parents and the pastor finally left. He thought about what they'd planned. He didn't disagree with the idea completely, but he didn't find anyone at fault, except Mr. Terry and Jeremiah, and decided to press charges against them. He lay there and made plans of his own. He had some money stashed away from doing work throughout the neighborhood. His parents had no idea how much he had set aside. They also had no idea he'd been accepted to art school and was awarded a partial scholarship and a few grants.

All that remained was room and board, and if he sued and won, it might be exactly what he needed to begin a life far away from his parents. He went home the next day and started to research. He knew he needed to avoid his parents and their pastor providing their own lawyer, so he found what sounded like a good lawyer online and made an appointment. When he walked out of the law office the next day, he'd retained his own lawyer.

At dinner that night, his parents told him Pastor Gregory was contacting his lawyer for them but he explained, "There's no need. I already found one with an excellent reputation. He's won a lot of cases like mine."

While they were skeptical, they got excited when he told them how successful his lawyer was. The gleam in their eyes was unmistakable. His father patted him on the back and said, "We're glad you've finally done something useful."

They assumed he'd just fall in line with what they decided for him, allowing them to have the money, no questions asked. They never even gave a thought to the fact that he was eighteen years old, so any and all of the money would go to him.

It took months of evidence gathering, arbitration, and mediation for an alternative dispute resolution, but when the other parties realized he wasn't going to give an inch and the courts could do a lot more damage, they settled out of court. The settlement was for two hundred thousand dollars plus legal fees and was deposited in his account several days before graduation.

With the help of his lawyer, he'd purchased a used car and parked it in the parking lot of the law office. The night before he left, he stuffed it full of everything he owned and was off the day of his graduation, leaving his parents a long letter telling them how he'd felt for years living under their roof and many other things, including the fact he was gay and what really happened with the legal settlement.

He was halfway through his first year of school for a degree in fine arts, when he felt the need to seek part-time work. He applied all over town and was offered a position as a barista and as a front desk clerk at a tattoo studio. He took a chance on the tattoo studio and never looked back.

One day, about three months into his new job, he was caught by his boss drawing when there was a lull in business, but instead of getting in trouble, his job was upgraded to clerk/apprentice and he was given a slight raise.

It made for a ridiculously hard year where he worked and studied himself into exhaustion. He was so busy he didn't have time for a social life and remained isolated from others. As a result, he ended up in a pseudo-relationship with his boss and owner of the tattoo studio, only finding out after they slept together that he was a Dom. He explained to Sebastian that he thought he was naturally submissive, and if he wanted a relationship with him, he'd need to be trained as a proper sub.

And though he wasn't sure it was the right thing for him at first, he soon realized that being a submissive felt like coming home. His boss ultimately rejected him, but Sebastian was still grateful that he helped him discover his true nature. No longer wanting to work for his boss and dealing with some medical issues, he needed to find a new job with good medical insurance. Being a newly licensed tattoo artist, he searched for openings at other local studios but none of them offered it.

When he'd seen the ad for a police sketch artist and realized he could tailor his schooling and get the credits he needed to get the job, he applied for the position, got the job, and changed his coursework. Around the same time, he joined another local club called The Dungeon, where he met Zoe and they bonded over their common love of ink.

He smiled at Gideon and said, "So that's my life, in a nutshell."

"While you were sleeping in the hospital, Braden told me you were in high demand and don't have enough time to do as many tattoos as you'd like. How did that happen?"

"For a long time, I thought about trying to tattoo over my birthmark and sometimes you can do so successfully, but with the type I have, it wouldn't work. The changes that occur over time, like the blebs that grow or the bumpiness and thickness that takes over, would distort the tattoo anyway."

"What made you think to do scars?"

"Well, I thought about how much better I'd feel if I could cover it, how others with PWSs would feel. Then I got to thinking about other ways people get disfigured and would be self-conscious, and how tattoos might work to help them feel confident again. So I started on my own scars. It's really different tattooing over scars. So, I played at it for a while and tried to learn on myself. Then, I placed an ad in several local papers and on various social media outlets, asking for people that had scars they'd like to cover with a tattoo."

"And you got a lot of traction?"

Sebastian chuckled. "Well, I offered steep discounts because I couldn't guarantee it would work for everyone's scars, and I was just beginning to learn the differences of working over scar tissue versus regular skin. Eventually, I was confident enough that I started to advertise it as my specialty, and that's when things got kind of crazy."

Gideon ran his hand over Sebastian's shorn scalp, something Sebastian had learned to love the feeling of, and asked, "How's that?"

"Well, I worked on a woman's breast cancer scars. She knew someone else who had the same scars she had and asked me if she could give my card to her friend but wanted to be sure I would be very discreet. I assured her that I would. Her friend called and turned out to be a pretty popular actress who felt so much more confident after the tattoos, she posted them on Instagram, Twitter, and Facebook."

"Holy shit. I bet that was crazy."

"Yeah. She was nice enough to warn me, at least, so I was able to somewhat prepare." Sebastian laughed, remembering. "But, I seriously had no idea what it would do, and it took a while to figure out a system. My phone was blowing up. I finally created a form people had to fill out. I'm still booked solid, and I can't help as many people as I'd like."

"So, you want to be able to help more people, but you don't have the time?"

Sebastian nodded, knowing that's exactly how he felt. "Yeah. It's frustrating, but I do it as often as I can, and do my best to get to as many people as I can."

"Why don't you do it full time?"

"I need good insurance. That's why I took the police sketch job, and I'm really good at it."

"You're great at it, but is it your passion?"

Sebastian shrugged. "No, but it pays the bills, and I have the kind of coverage I need for my health issues."

"There are other options for health insurance these days. It sounds like you can set your own pricing for your tattoos, and if you could do them full time, you'd be making enough to be able to pay for it. I might be able to add you to mine as my domestic partner."

Sebastian gaped at Gideon. "But... How would that work? We're not even living together."

Gideon raised a brow. "We could be. I want to be."

Sebastian shook his head. "It's too soon. You know it is."

"I know nothing of the sort. You're scared. I understand that. You want to trust me, but I don't think you feel like you can, yet."

"I trust you!"

"I think you trust me with your body and for the most part with your mind. You trust me within our Dom/sub context, but I don't think you trust me with your heart. I hurt you too badly for that."

Sebastian shook his head. "No, I—"

"Yes, Bastian. And I can't blame you for it. I'll regret the way I treated you, the way I ended it and left, for the rest of my life. All I can do is work to prove myself to you. I'll wait until you're ready, but I will keep asking you because I want to start our life together, all right?"

He nodded, and replied, "Yes, Sir. I'll keep thinking about it."

"Think about giving your boss notice and going out on your own. I'll do everything I can to support you. Life is too fragile, too short to not be doing what you love when you know exactly what it is you were meant to do."

Sebastian knew he was right, but he was scared. "I'll think about it."

Gideon nodded. "Do that. I know it's scary. But you're immensely success-ful, you'd have enough work and would be able to help so many more people just by doing what you love."

"Yeah. I know. I'll think about it."

"All right. Let's get ready for bed and get some sleep."

Sebastian nodded, and they got up to brush their teeth. It's funny how someone else pointing something out made it literally all you could think about. He spent the time getting ready for bed thinking about Gideon's words. Then he thought about it as he lay in bed trying to sleep. He even dreamed about it that night. He realized the next day he'd been thinking along those lines for a long time but had refused to give it too much credence. As soon as Gideon mentioned it, it was as though he started something that couldn't be stopped.

He sat on it for another week, thinking of all the ways it couldn't work then realized he was just making excuses. Next thing he knew, and without even talking to Gideon, he was taking a Lyft ride to his office after setting up a meeting with his boss. He was nervous as hell and felt like shit. He'd been on paid medical leave, and he felt like he'd taken advantage of the situation.

Captain Conway steepled his fingers and stared at Sebastian across his desk after they'd caught up on what had happened over the last couple months. "You're quitting."

"I…" Sebastian's jaw dropped, and he scowled. "How the hell do you do that?"

"I'm a cop. And you look nervous and guilty. I knew I wouldn't be able to keep you indefinitely. You're too talented to wanna draw criminals' faces for the rest of your life. I even have a job requisition approved for whenever it happens."

"But… What if I never quit?"

His boss shrugged. "I'd have probably asked you what you wanted to do for the rest of your life then pushed you to do it."

"I feel awful."

Captain Conway frowned in confusion. "Why would you feel awful?"

"Because I took medical leave. Honestly, Cap, I had no idea I'd be doing this before I went out on leave."

"I know that, but even if you had known, you have a right to go out on medical. You've been paying into your short-term disability for years. You aren't doing anything wrong, Sebastian."

"But I don't want to leave you in the lurch. I want to make sure you have time to hire someone once I come back so I can train them before I leave. I'll give you as much time as you need when I get back."

"That's fine. Hopefully, I'll find someone before you come back. If I don't, that's on me, and you'll leave two weeks after your return. You'll just have to spend those two weeks giving extra training to whatever cop is going to take over until we do hire someone."

"Okay. I'll let you know as soon as my doctor clears me to return to work."

"Sounds good. And, Sebastian? I'm glad everything went well. You look better now than you did when you left."

"Thank you, sir."

He walked out of the station feeling lighter than he'd felt in a long time. He didn't know how it would feel not having his backup plan to provide for what he needed. He got into the Lyft car he'd scheduled and headed back to Gideon's place. He thought about telling Gideon when he got home but decided against it.

He knew he'd tell him eventually but wanted to be moved home first. He was worried that Gideon would feel like him being without a job and guaranteed money coming in, would mean he couldn't take care of himself and stay on his own. He didn't want to be pressured to move in with Gideon.

Pushing those feelings aside, he made a mental checklist of what he needed to do. The biggest of which would be to start researching insurance companies and plans. He had a lot to do, and he push himself to do quite a bit of it after he got home and rested. As much as he didn't want to admit it, he had another headache brewing and needed to be in a dark, quiet place with some acetaminophen before he could take on any other tasks.

Chapter 37

GIDEON

Sebastian was in the shower, so when the bell rang, Gideon was happy he'd timed everything right. He'd met with Killian several days prior to make sure everything was set, and that he'd made a good decision. He couldn't be happier with Killian's pick and hoped he hadn't overstepped. The last thing he wanted was for Sebastian to be insulted or angered by his gift.

He'd already made sure everything Sebastian would need was set up at his apartment, and that he had double of everything at his place as well. He buzzed Killian up and chatted with him about the beautiful golden retriever sitting calmly by his side. When they'd exhausted that subject, Gideon was about to ask him about his history with Custos when Killian broke eye contact and glanced down at the floor, scuffing his feet, suddenly nervous, his voice quiet when he said, "So, Zavier told me about Catharsis."

Huh, interesting.

Killian was a few scant inches shorter than his own six foot five and built along the same muscular lines. He'd met plenty of sizeable submissives in his day. But it was the shyness of his tone that surprised Gideon. Killian wasn't a young man to be embarrassed by the topic, but there was an air of wonder and newness to him like he was afraid to ask about the club. But, if his instincts were right, there was also a wounded boy inside the strong man. He'd gone from confident Custos guardian and dog trainer to timid and submissive in seconds.

His tone was gentle when he handed him one of his business cards and replied, "Are you interested in a tour? I can arrange one for you with either a Dom or a sub."

Killian ducked his head again, rubbing the back of his neck with his big palm. When he glanced back up, Gideon was again taken aback by the timidity. "I… Yeah, I think I'd like that. Thank you, Sir."

"You're welcome. I'll put someone in touch with you to schedule it but feel free to contact me with any questions."

"Thank you." Killian tucked the card in his pocket and stood a bit taller.

He'd have to have Khaleo give him a call and give Roarke a heads-up that he'd like Killian to receive the full submissive training—or if his instincts were wrong, the full Dominant training—for free for so generously helping him find the perfect service dog for Sebastian. When they'd spoken of payment, Killian had refused, only accepting payment for the dog itself.

Just as he was about to mention that to Killian, Sebastian made his way out of their bedroom, pulling a sweatshirt over his head and walking towards the kitchen, half blinded by the shirt. He opened the freezer, talking to Gideon still unaware they had company. Not paying attention, he took some grapes out and popped a few in his mouth as he turned around, his eyes popping wide when he realized they weren't alone.

Gideon watched as discomfort at a stranger being in his space registered quickly on Sebastian's face, making him take a step back. Gideon watched him mentally square his shoulders, set the grapes down, and approach with much more confidence than Gideon knew he felt. He loved his boy more every day, especially when he proved how brave he was. His boy was strong when Gideon knew he felt weak.

He walked around the bar, approaching them, a hand held out to shake Killian's, greeting him warmly. "Hello, I'm Sebastian." When he could see around Gideon, he looked down and gasped. "Oh! Who's this beauty?"

Gideon watched as he pulled his hand from Killian's before he could even respond in kind with his name and was about to touch the dog when he pulled back and glanced back up at Gideon as if remembering his place. He stood again, a sheepish look on his face as he glanced back at Killian. "I'm sorry. That was rude. I didn't even get your name." He gave Killian an embarrassed grin. "Your dog is so beautiful, I got distracted."

The flush on his boy's face made him want to toss him over his shoulder and take him to the bedroom to redden his ass to match before fucking him into the mattress. He cleared his throat, knowing that would have to wait and introduced the man. "This is Killian, he's a dog trainer and a guardian at Custos. This is Lola."

Confusion set in, but Sebastian masked it quickly. "Oh. Well, it's nice to meet you, Killian. Lola is gorgeous. May I pet her?"

Killian looked about to say something but looked to Gideon to see if he should. Gideon shook his head quickly, and Killian nodded imperceptibly. He looked back to Lola and bent down beside her. Her soulful eyes looked at him adoringly and her body straightened when he said, "Lola, this is Sebastian."

Lola's tail wagged, the name obviously familiar. She stood, Killian gave her a hand gesture, and she beelined it to Sebastian who'd squatted down to pet the gorgeous animal. Gideon grinned at Sebastian as he lavished Lola with attention, speaking sweetly to her, having a whole conversation with her about how beautiful she was and how well behaved and sweet. When Sebastian sat down and crossed his legs, Lola practically collapsed in his lap which made Sebastian laugh and continue to praise and pet the gorgeous dog.

Gideon kneeled beside Sebastian, and his breath caught in his throat at the love Sebastian already felt for the dog. He hoped he didn't lose that look of pure happiness when he learned what he'd done. He put his hand on the back of Sebastian's neck, squeezing to get his attention. Gideon knew the only reason he didn't present in a kneeling position for Gideon was because the dog was in his lap. His back straightened though, and he gave his full attention to his Dom.

Lola, sensing the new emotions coming from Sebastian, pulled herself out of Sebastian's lap and sat in front of him, patiently waiting for instruction. Just like Gideon thought he would, his boy kneeled and presented, hands on his knees, Gideon's hand still on the back of his neck. Gideon reached out to put his other on Lola's head, scratching her behind the ears. She sidled up to them both, wanting to be closer.

"Lola's yours."

Sebastian's mouth gaped comically. He looked from Killian to Lola to Gideon and back again. "What?"

"She's yours. I had Killian pick her out for you." Gideon cleared his throat, suddenly nervous. "She's a service dog. She's trained to detect seizure activity and give you warnings so that you won't get hurt if and when it happens. Killian picked her out from the best epilepsy dog training facility in the US. He trained her to be a guard dog as well. She's calm, good with strangers, and can accompany you most anywhere."

Still dumbfounded, Sebastian only repeated, "What?"

Killian squatted near them and spoke in a calming voice that Gideon realized did the trick to calm both Lola and Sebastian. "I'd like to let her get acclimated to you tonight. I know it's your last night here at Gideon's before you move back to your place. I find that it's best for there to be a 'getting to know you' stage before the owner training. I can come by tomorrow, to your new place, and we can go through your training so you know what to do and how to interact with her. She's just a big mushy sweetheart, really. I hope she's a good companion in addition to being useful."

Sebastian was so serious, Gideon felt a twinge of unease. He was about to speak when Killian continued, "If you'd hold your hands out."

Sebastian did, albeit in a daze. Killian stood behind them and introduced them again, putting his hand on Sebastian's shoulder. "Lola, this is Sebastian. Friend." He touched Gideon's shoulder. "Lola, this is Gideon. Friend."

Sebastian and Gideon both watched as she sniffed their hands and nuzzled them both, sitting facing them, wagging her tail. Killian crouched beside Lola. "I'm going to get going. Call me or text me tomorrow when you'd like me to come over and walk you through the training. I'm available as often as you need. You won't remember everything at first, and I've got a pdf file of instructions I can email you as well."

He gave a kissy noise, and Lola lifted her paw to him and he kissed it with a smile and told her how good she was and that she was home now. He stood, waved, and let himself out. Gideon and Sebastian watched him then Sebastian turned to Gideon, still kneeling, his face inscrutable. "You got me a service guard dog."

"I did."

"Why?"

"Because I worry about you. Because I love you. Because I can't be with you all the time, and we don't know if you'll still be plagued by these seizures. I don't want you to get hurt. And, because you're bound and determined to move out. I want to know you're safe and have help."

"In the form of a dog."

Gideon shrugged, knowing he'd find out the next day that Gideon had Custos install a security system as well. And that didn't even take into account the new car he'd gotten him. Fuck, he'd be piss—

Sebastian launched himself into Gideon's arms, interrupting his thoughts. Pulling his head down, Sebastian began to kiss his face all over. Gideon clasped his shoulders and held him back so he could look at him. Sebastian's smile set his heart to pounding and he whispered, "We're okay?"

Sebastian chuckled and nodded, whispering, "More than okay. Thank you. This is the best gift I've ever gotten. I've always wanted… Oh fuck, can I even have a dog at my place?"

"Yes. You can. I checked."

Sebastian touched his cheek, gently. "You thought of everything."

Gideon smiled and nodded. "I thought of everything."

Sebastian turned towards Lola and grinned, opening his arms. She made herself comfortable there again, wagging her tail, her tongue lolling out. They were both surprised by a hissing sound behind them, and when they turned, they saw Slap and Tickle had apparently awoken from a nap and were prancing sideways, their fur puffed out. Sebastian laughed and held his hand out to them. "Knock it off, you two. This is your sister, Lola. Make nice."

The cats prowled around, fur still sticking out, but the hissing had stopped. They'd wander close then run off, approach then skitter away again. This went on for a good five minutes until Slap, at least he thought it was Slap, approached and pawed at Lola's tail. When the dog responded by yawning, loudly, and wagging her tail, Slap jumped, fur puffing up again, backing up. When the tail kept thumping, Slap was back again, batting at it with his paws, trying to trap it under them.

Sebastian laughed when Lola reached her paw out and gently patted at Slap who batted at her paw. Tickle approached from the rear and suddenly he was on top of Lola's back. Lola lay down all the way on her side as if trying to make it easier for the cats to climb on, and they took advantage immediately. Sebastian and Gideon watched as felines and canine made friends. A friend-ship based on kittens jumping, pawing, gnawing, and rolling around on top of Lola, who just sat patiently and allowed it.

They spent the rest of the evening welcoming their newcomer to the family. The following morning, Sebastian seemed content, and much to Gideon's dismay, excited to get home. Deep down Gideon knew it wasn't because he was glad to be away from him, hell, he'd asked Gideon to stay with him the first night, it was that he was ready to get back to work and start living his life again, hopefully free of the seizures that plagued him for so long.

Gideon loaded his SUV with the repacked boxes of stuff Sebastian would be taking back home with him. He'd actually be leaving quite a bit at Gideon's as well so he wouldn't have to pack when he was over. They drove the twenty minutes to his new two-bedroom apartment.

When they pulled up to the building, Gideon handed Sebastian a wrapped box. Sebastian looked down at it and back up at him. "What's this?"

"A gift. Got it from my dad the other day. We wanted you to have it."

Sebastian tore off the wrapping and opened the box. Gideon watched as his boy's jaw dropped. "Sir."

Gideon smiled. "Boy."

Sebastian's head shot up then back down again as he pulled the Imperator McCade Military Watch from its box. Since Braden had demonstrated a while back that wide leather bands looked great with their watches, they'd come out with several options as add-ons to their watch lines, and he'd chosen one for Sebastian. The Imperator was only for direct family, so when his dad had handed it to him though it hadn't been too unexpected he'd been grateful for his family's official acceptance of Sebastian.

"It's gorgeous."

Gideon nodded, agreeing. "It's the line made only for direct family. And as you're now family, you needed to have one."

Sebastian just stared at him then back down to the watch. Seconds ticked by before Sebastian quickly leaned over and hugged him, kissing him thoroughly. Pulling back, he looked down at it again and shook his head. "I don't... I don't know what to say. This means so much. Thank you, Sir."

"You're welcome."

He put the watch on and admired it on his wrist. It looked great on him, like it had always been there. They looked at each other, kissed again, and opened their doors to step out of the SUV.

Sebastian looked around in confusion. Stared at the car in his parking spot and looked around again. "Shit. Shit, shit, shit. Someone stole my car!"

Gideon shoved his hands in his pockets and cleared his throat. "No. Your car was gonna fall apart. I know you can't drive for a while, but when you can, I want you to be safe."

"Gideon..."

"I got you a new one. You told me about the seizure you had on your way home from the party. Jesus, Sebastian, you could have died in that rat trap you called a car!"

Sebastian narrowed his eyes on his Dom. "If I hadn't told you that, would you have still gotten me a new car?"

The look of sheer stubbornness was his answer. Sebastian crossed his arms over his chest and said, "This makes me uncomfortable, Gideon."

Gideon shrugged. "I'm not sorry I did it. You need a safe and reliable car, Sebastian. I won't have my boy getting in an accident because he's driving a piece of junk. Not when I can so easily fix the issue."

"Where's my car?"

"I got it fixed up and donated it."

"If it could be fixed up, why not just fix it and let me keep it?"

"I saw something in the paper about a local women's shelter's car being stolen. Two birds, one stone."

Sebastian just stared at him for several drawn-out seconds. "Dammit, Gideon. You know I can't hold on to my anger when you do shit like that."

"That's what I was counting on."

Sebastian heaved a heavy sigh and shook his head. Hooking a finger into one of Gideon's belt loops, he stepped into him. Laying his head down on the arms Gideon had crossed over his chest prompted Gideon to loosen them and wrap them around him instead. "Are you taking care of your boy, Sir?"

Gideon's voice was gruff when he replied, "I am."

When Sebastian looked up at him, love and amusement in his smile, he said, "I suppose you can afford it, all that watch money you've got, and all."

Gideon smirked. "I suppose I can."

When Sebastian's face grew serious, so did Gideon's. He reached up to cup Gideon's cheek and whispered, "Thank you, Sir."

Gideon let out a sigh and nodded. "You're welcome."

Sebastian turned and looked at his assigned parking spot, his eyes popping wide at the BMW X1. "You got me a BMW?"

"It's a top safety pick."

Sebastian snickered, "Of course it is. You can take us for a drive later."

Gideon smiled, glad he'd made his boy happy. "Sounds like a plan. Uh, full disclosure, I have an app on my phone to locate the car. I just want to know where to find you if you have a seizure and need my help. The watch also has a button you can hit. It'll let me know you need help or are hurt."

Sebastian burst out laughing and apparently couldn't stop. His voice went high-pitched as he yelled out, "Help! I've fallen, and I can't get up!"

Gideon started laughing himself, realizing he wasn't far off. "How the fuck do you even know about Life Call? You're too young! And Jesus, now I feel old!"

Sebastian snorted and admitted, "I think I saw it on some funny commercial compilation, years ago."

Gideon shook his head. "All joking aside, I'm hoping we'll never need either, but I just need a way to try to see to your safety. I'm sorry it's a bit over the top."

Sebastian raised a brow. "A bit?"

Gideon shrugged, and Sebastian shook his head in response, let Lola out of the SUV, and grabbed the kittens in their travel crate. Gideon grabbed a few boxes, and they headed up to Sebastian's place. As he unlocked the door, there was a beep then a woman's mechanical voice telling them to enter the security code. Sebastian raised an eyebrow and snickered again. "You're out of control."

Gideon grumbled at his boy's apparent amusement at his safety precautions. "I protect and take care of what's mine."

Sebastian chuckled and maneuvered around him. "Oh, that's definitely sinking in. It's... What the... Gideon!"

But Gideon was busy turning off the alarm system, adding in his fingerprints, and grabbing Sebastian's hand to do the same. His boy's gaping mouth and dumbfounded expression at the state of his apartment remained on his face the whole time Gideon had his hand up against the security pad, putting a smile on his face.

Once he had their prints logged in, he went about setting the rest of it. He'd have to teach Sebastian later when he wasn't having an aneurysm over his family unpacking his place. When he turned around, he took it in. It looked great, and Sebastian's furnishings looked perfect in the space, his art already hung on the walls, the decorations put out.

The only things they'd left alone were his personal items that were left in boxes in his bedroom to unpack when he was ready. He turned back to look at Sebastian and saw him surveying the place, hands on his hips. "When did you get this done?"

"I didn't do it. My family did it with some help from Zoe. They said they can come over and change anything that doesn't work."

"I can never repay them for this. As much as I was looking forward to getting back to my daily life, I actually have been dreading unpacking."

"There's no repaying family. It's just what they do."

Sebastian looked up at him and Gideon saw that he was finally getting it. It would take a while for him to fully understand and be comfortable with it, but he was coming to grasp that he truly was no longer alone. When Sebastian wrapped his arms around him and held him tight, he relaxed as much as he could. They walked around the apartment, showing the animals around, and then went into the bedroom so that Sebastian could unpack the last few things.

When they were in bed that night, he pulled out the collar Sebastian had given back to him. He held it in his palm and asked, "Does it have too many bad memories?"

His boy tucked his face into Gideon's chest and shook his head. "No."

Gideon put the collar back on, murmuring apologies again for what he'd done. Sebastian shushed him, and they made love before falling asleep, exhausted from the day's events and the emotional toll they took.

They made plans to see each other Wednesday and then again Saturday evening when Sebastian was done with his tattoo appointments. The week seemed to drag by for him, and he began a more regimented workout schedule and began to consult at Custos on several cases to stay occupied and keep himself from stopping by and checking on his boy. He hated the separation.

When Saturday morning rolled around, he was downstairs taking care of some paperwork at the club while everything was quiet. Someone buzzed the front club entrance, and he got up to check the monitors behind the front desk. His hands immediately curled into fists as he hit the button to open the door. As it slid open, revealing Boone, he turned and headed towards his office without saying a word.

When he got to his office, he turned and faced the man down. "What the fuck are you doing here?"

Boone crossed his arms over his chest. "You know damn well what I'm doing here, Gideon."

"Actually, I don't, so why don't you spell it out?"

"You should have contacted me. We had a bead on him. We were waiting to contact you because he was under surveillance."

"Yeah, I saw the surveillance. It's dealt with."

Boone growled and strode forward, his anger bringing him within striking distance. "What the fuck does that even mean, dealt with?"

"It means those agencies got what they needed."

"That answer isn't good enough for my superiors."

"Boone, when is it going to sink in? All you can see is what your superiors need and want, but I'm not bound by that particular burden. I don't give a fuck what your superiors deem good enough. They are not my responsibility. And he wasn't even an official part of your investigation!"

"You can't be serious, Gideon. He's on our books, like you asked, he was part of the investigation because of you. And you fucking murdered him! A man who was under surveillance with ATF *and* the FBI! All for some vendetta from something so far in the past it's ridiculous!"

"You'll have a very hard time proving anything."

"I don't need to prove it, I know you! You fucking murdered the guy in cold blood. You didn't give a shit that he was part of a huge operation that he was being used to get the bigger fish."

"What the fuck do I care about the bigger fish? And why the fuck are you so worried about the kill? I did it on your payroll for years!"

"That's hardly the same thing! Jesus Christ, listen to yourself. Do you think you're the only one that matters in this goddamn world?"

Gideon huffed out an incredulous breath. "In the grand scheme of things, I don't matter at all. The agencies involved got what they needed and were very happy with the info provided. You don't need to worry about it."

"And I said my superiors don't give a fuck about that! They want to know where Lars went! What the hell am I supposed to tell them?"

"I don't give a fuck what you tell them. Tell them he left town, tell them he grew a conscience, hell, tell them he's chum."

"Chum? So, what... You dumped his fucking body in the ocean?"

Gideon was about to respond when he heard a noise in the hallway then saw Lola's tail and his heart plummeted. No! No, no, no, no, no. Fuck! He ran to the hallway and saw his worst nightmare. His boy, surrounded by spilled coffee and a box of pastries on the floor, Lola dancing around, doing her best to stay out of the mess. Sebastian had raised both hands to cover his mouth, and he shook his head frantically, as he slowly backed away.

All color leached from his face, and Gideon moved towards him, hoping to keep him from running. He gently but firmly clasped Sebastian around the wrist, but his boy pulled his arm back as if his grip scalded him. He couldn't let go though. He couldn't let him leave.

Sebastian's voice was full of panic when he cried out, "Let go! Let go of me, Gideon!"

Lola whined then growled, unhappy with Sebastian's anxiety. It was like his mind wasn't connected to his body, though, because no matter what it told him to do, he couldn't loosen his grip. "Sebastian, wait. Please. Let me ex—"

Sebastian was frantically yanking his arm hard, and finally he stopped completely, his gaze reflected how scared he was—of him, breaking Gideon's heart. Lola's growling continued, followed by a snap of her jaws in warning to Gideon, but he still couldn't bring himself to release his boy.

"Red! Red, red, red!"

Gideon let go immediately, raising his hands in the air and stepping back, his mind tuned to obey that word over all others. And it brought it all home as nothing else could, letting him know just how badly he'd fucked up. He watched as Sebastian backed away from him and backed into the wall in his frantic search for the exit door behind him. Gideon stepped forward to help, and Sebastian cried out no.

Lola had had enough by that point and stood in front of her charge, barking loudly and snapping her jaws. Gideon knew the only reason she hadn't attacked him already was because Killian had called him friend. He stepped back and away again, calming Lola, and watched, helpless, as Sebastian turned and ran out the exit door, Lola on his heels.

Gideon couldn't remember ever having been angrier than he was at that moment. He vibrated with it as he stalked back towards his office. When he entered and saw the object of his anger he stopped in his tracks. Boone looked like a frightened, trapped animal and the only thing keeping Gideon from beating him half to death was the fact that he was the one at fault for not coming clean to Sebastian to begin with.

Well, that and the fact that Boone was an analyst and not an operative. He couldn't have defended himself against Gideon if he'd tried, and as angry and soulless as he knew himself to be, Gideon wasn't cruel for cruelness sake, especially not to a submissive. That wasn't to say that he wouldn't put the fear of God in the man before he left, but in the end, more blame fell on him than on Boone.

He'd never wanted to admit the kind of man he was to his boy. Hell, he'd done his best to end it between them because of it, but in the end, what Sebastian needed from him and from their relationship outweighed what Gideon was trying to save him from. He'd have to come clean and share as much of his previous life with Sebastian as he could if he'd agree to see him. If he wanted to save what they had, for both their sakes, he had to tell him the truth and let the chips fall where they may.

He prowled threateningly over to Boone, who backed up so fast he nearly fell and didn't stop until he was backed up against the wall. Gideon gripped him by the throat and leaned in menacingly, growling in Boone's ear, "We're done, you and me. You've burned whatever bridges we may have had at one time. Do you understand me?"

Gideon pulled him away from the wall and then shoved his head back again, causing a satisfying thunk, bringing about a grimace from his quarry, who nodded desperately as his face began to turn a mottled red.

"I'm going to do your job for you and handle this situation, Boone, but understand that I don't ever want to see your fucking face again. Do you hear me? And if you've fucked up the best thing that ever happened to me in my entire fucking life because you can't seem to handle your professional responsibilities, I might still hunt you down and beat you within an inch of your fucking life."

After slamming his head back into the wall one more time for good measure, he growled and stalked to the phone, leaning over his desk and putting it on speaker, he dialed a number he never thought he'd have to call again. It rang twice before the man answered, "Hello?"

"There's an issue that needs to be dealt with."

After a long pause, the man said, "What can I do for you?"

"There's a case that certain people are holding on to. I've dealt with it, but there are a few who don't seem to want to let it go."

"I'll see that it's taken care of."

"Thank you. The case number is," he snapped his fingers at a wide-eyed Boone, which brought him back and he whispered the number, which Gideon repeated.

"Consider it done."

The man hung up before he could respond. He hit the speaker button and the dial tone was cut off. He glanced back over at Boone who looked shocked. He knew Boone would recognize Kepner's voice, it was the reason he'd put it on speakerphone to begin with. He waited for the inevitable reaction.

"What the fuck just happened? You have Deputy Director Kepner's phone number memorized?"

"I don't know what you're talking about. All I did was call a friend. The situation is handled, and with it, your need to ever contact me again. And you better hope that things with Sebastian work out, Boone, or so help me god…"

Boone rubbed a hand over his face, wiping the nervous sweat away. He nodded once and walked out the door without another word.

Gideon wanted to go after his boy, but that wouldn't help matters. He needed to give him some time. Gideon turned and headed to the stairs, taking them two at a time, he was up to his floor and dressing down for some heavy bag work and hard run, showering afterwards to clear his head. He checked the clock and realized it had been just shy of an hour since his boy had left. He sat down on his bed, tapped a few commands on his watch, and placed a call.

"Gideon."

"Zavier, I need you to get over to the café."

Gideon heard him moving around immediately, probably hearing the stress in his voice. He heard the elevator ding and then Zavier asked him to wait a minute. When Gideon heard street noises, he began speaking again. "Boone showed up again. He was pissed I never contacted him about Lars and was going off about it. Sebastian showed up and heard it all."

"Fuck."

"I've never seen him afraid of me. He safeworded to get me to let him go."

"Jesus."

Gideon heard Zavier start up his SUV. "I traced his location by his watch. He'll be talking to Braden."

"Let me check and see where Braden is, hang on."

Gideon waited, seeing the humor in the situation, both of them keeping tabs on their boys. He knew others on the outside would see that as control-ling, and he could admit they weren't far off. Hell, people would probably even call it obsessive, but the only reason they were doing it is to make sure they were safe, wherever they went.

Zavier came back on the line and said, "Braden's heading this way in his car, only a couple minutes out."

Gideon searched his boy's location again. "Sebastian's with him."

"Braden's in protective mode. He's got Sebastian and is bringing him here.

I'm gonna go back upstairs and wait for them. I'll talk to him if Braden will allow it, and if he doesn't at first, it'll only be a matter of time until he does."

Gideon nodded. "All right. I need you to be there for him. Take him in hand if you have to, he'll be feeling out of control, so if you can ground him by making him obey you, it might go a long way toward calming him down."

"I can do that."

"I don't know that he'll ever get past this, but please offer him whatever he needs. Tell him whatever you feel he needs or wants to know when he's ready. Tell him I'll give him time, I won't bother him. I just want him to feel safe."

"He's not afraid of you, not really. Your boy loves you, he'll come around."

"You didn't see his face, Zavier."

"He's upset now, Gideon, but we'll get him through it. Let me handle this for you."

Gideon nodded then remembered his brother couldn't see him and replied, "All right. Thank you."

"You got it. I'll give you an update later."

They hung up and he leaned forward, head in his hands, scrubbing his face. Completely distracted with thoughts of his boy, he jumped when his phone rang. He saw it was Khaleo and answered it. "Is everything all right, Gideon? I was doing inventory and heard some yelling. Found and cleaned up a mess in the hall down here, so I wanted to check."

Gideon had explained the situation to Khaleo before he'd left him and Roarke in charge, when he'd left to take care of Lars. He had a long history with Khaleo, so he hadn't spared any details when he'd come back, either.

"Boone showed up this morning. Sebastian walked in and heard Boone's accusations. It scared him to death, and he left."

"Fucking hell, Sir. I'm sorry. Is there anything I can do?"

Gideon couldn't think of a thing and shook his head. "No. I did it to myself. As much as I'm pissed at Boone, I'm more pissed at myself for not telling Sebastian about my past. This is on me."

They said their goodbyes, and Gideon realized all he could do was wait. He went to his home office and immersed himself in Custos cases to get his mind off of the situation. His hands were tied at that point, and all he could do was keep busy so he wouldn't go crazy.

Chapter 38

SEBASTIAN

W hen Saturday rolled around, he'd had a cancellation of the one tattoo client he'd scheduled, so he called a car to take him to Sugar n' Spice to grab some coffee and pastries so he could surprise Gideon at his place and maybe finally tell him he'd quit his job. They'd both thought he wouldn't be able to get away until that afternoon, so he was excited to surprise his Dom. He n't in his loft, however, and Sebastian figured he'd check the club before he gave up and left. He should have texted to ask if he was going to be home.

He opened the door to the club from the inner stairwell, let Lola walk through, and then walked down the long, dim hall. Seeing the light on and the door open to his Dom's office made him smile. But when he heard angry voices drift down the hall, he slowed his pace, not knowing what to do. Lola stayed by his side when he drew to a stop, unable to believe what he was hearing.

"…I know you! You fucking murdered the guy in cold blood. You didn't give a shit that he was part of a huge operation, that he was being used to get the bigger fish."

"What the fuck do I care about the bigger fish? And why the fuck are you so worried about the kill? I did it on your payroll for years!"

That was the last thing he heard before the buzzing in his ears took over. He stood stock still for several drawn-out moments, the hum of the voices still muddled in the background. Murder? Oh Jesus. His vision grew hazy, and he lost his grip on the coffees and pastries. He saw Lola dance back and around the mess on the floor, stepping delicately through it to get near him again, but he couldn't move, couldn't think, could barely breathe for the panic sliding through his veins.

His hands were shaking when he raised them to his mouth, and he felt sick to his stomach. When he saw Gideon in the doorway of his office, he slowly backed away, wanting to be anywhere else. Before he could take another step, Gideon had wrapped his hand around his wrist, and he went with instinct when he tried to pull away.

His heartbeat tripled its pace when he couldn't get free. "Let go! Let go of me, Gideon!"

When he heard Lola whine and growl, his efforts became frantic and he didn't know what else to do, losing it completely. "Red! Red, red, red!"

Finally free, he backed away from Gideon, hitting the wall and reaching back to feel for the exit door he knew was close by. When Gideon stepped forward again, he lost his breath and cried out. Lola moved in front of him, obviously reaching her breaking point, barking and growling, leaving no doubt she was trained thoroughly as a guard dog. His heart hurt knowing who she had to protect him against, but he couldn't think about that. He had to get away. As he watched Gideon step back to placate his dog, Sebastian took the opening to turn and shove the door open, fleeing, Lola on his heels.

He called another car to pick him up at the coffee shop down the street from the club. He didn't remember the ride back over there, but he ended up back at the Sugar n' Spice café. When he walked in the door, it was like his mind and body just stopped working. He just stood there, shaking. He heard Maya's voice but couldn't understand what she was saying. Next thing he knew, she was leading Lola over to the pillow with Thor as Braden led him to the kitchen and sat him down on a counter stool.

When he finally got his shit together enough to look around and focus on where he was, he saw he was alone with Braden who was gazing at him in concern. That concern was what ultimately did it. He lost his grip on control and his whole body began shaking, teeth chattering. Braden wrapped his arms around him, holding him tight until he regained control of his body. When he finally calmed down, he didn't move, needing the comfort of Braden's arms to ground him.

When he could speak again, he explained everything he'd heard and what had happened afterwards. Braden just looked at him like he'd grown two heads, held up a finger, and reached in his back pocket as he walked towards the office in the back and made a call. Sebastian just sat there, not knowing what to do or where to go. He didn't want to go home in case Gideon tried to come there. He had a key and the security password to get in, there wasn't much he could do to keep him out.

Braden walked back into the kitchen, taking off his apron. "Come on. I called someone to take my shift. We're going home."

He shook his head, panic lacing his words. "He knows my security code and has a key."

Braden tossed the apron into the break room's laundry basket and walked back to him, a stern look on his face. "First of all, I know you're scared, I would be too if I'd heard it in the context in which you heard it, but Gideon would die before he ever hurt you. You have to know that deep down."

"You're defending him? He killed someone!"

Braden gripped his shoulders. "We don't know what happened, but Gideon's a good man, so my guess is there was a good explanation."

Sebastian gaped at him incredulously. "A good explanation for killing a man?"

Braden gripped his shoulders again. "We don't know what happened, Sebastian. But if anyone knows anything, it'll be Zavier. I only know some of what Z had to do as Army Special Forces, I can only imagine what Gideon had to do as a SEAL."

Braden had been pulling him towards the front when Sebastian stopped, surprised, and yet, somehow not. "Wait. He was a Navy SEAL?" He'd seen the dog tags he usually wore, so he'd known he'd been in the military, but he'd never assumed it was such an elite branch, though he should have, he supposed.

The look of shock on Braden's face morphed into exasperation. "Jesus, that man! Do you know *anything* about him?" He grumbled something that sounded suspiciously like, "He can be such an ass," before he continued, "Come on, we're going home to talk to Z."

They didn't talk much on their way to Braden and Zavier's place. Mostly they chatted about their service dogs, who were, at that very moment, snuggled on the back seat of Braden's car together, already besties.

It made Sebastian wonder if he'd ever have the chance to take Lola over to Gideon's parents' house to play with Thor and Buckley. Soon, they were taking the elevator up to Braden and Zavier's place. He'd been there a couple times since his surgery, but he was still awed by it. It was gorgeous and huge, but it was also comfortable and relaxing. The dogs made themselves at home immediately.

He loved Gideon's place too, but, like the man, it was no frills and mostly free of decoration and homey touches. When you walked into it, though it was close to the same size, it wasn't sterile, it was useful and mostly just set up for need and not want. He'd hoped that in the future he'd be able to make it more of a home for his Dom. But he wasn't sure of anything anymore, and that scared him more than anything else.

Zavier was at the stove, cooking what smelled like eggs of some kind. When he looked up and smiled, Sebastian realized that Gideon had already called him because he didn't seem at all surprised by his presence.

He looked at Braden, his smile warming even more. "Hi, baby." His gaze focused back on him. "Hey, Sebastian."

Braden took his hand and led him to the kitchen. They sat on the comfy counter stools there and watched as Zavier fixed them each a plate with bacon and a vegetable omelette and carried them over to their huge dining table. Braden led him over there and sat beside him, lending his support, Sebastian sitting next to the head of the table where he assumed Zavier would sit.

He started to shake his head when Zavier brought them all orange juice and coffee, and was given a raised brow by Zavier as he sat to join them and thought better of speaking. He knew Zavier and Braden's relationship was partially Dom/sub, but it wasn't strict or contracted like he had with Gideon. But as the man was still Dominant, his automatic reaction was to defer to him.

"Gideon called. I've been expecting you." When he tensed up, Zavier continued, "He's giving you space. He just wants to make sure you're safe and has given me permission to answer any questions you have."

Sebastian whipped his head up at that and asked, "Really?"

Zavier smiled and nodded. "Really. I don't know everything, you know as well as I do that Gideon isn't a talker, and that's no different just because he's my brother."

Sebastian nodded and leaned back in his chair, picking up the coffee mug and drinking a bit.

"You'll eat what I've made you, Sebastian, is that understood?"

Something in him calmed from the order, and he nodded. "Yes, Sir."

"Good. Let me start off by telling you something that I doubt he'll ever tell you. Gideon ended it with you because he thought you'd be better off without him. He never felt he was good enough for you and felt that he'd do you more harm than good even though he loves you."

Incredulous, Sebastian shook his head. "That's not true! That's…"

He broke off there because he didn't know what to say, taking today into account. He sighed and shook his head. Picking up his fork, he took a small bite of the omelet. It was so good, he took another and then another. Next thing he knew, it was gone, and so was the orange juice and coffee. He pushed his plate back, leaving the bacon and smiled a bit sadly when Zavier reached out to grab it and eat it himself, just like Gideon would've done.

"He and I are a lot alike. We were more so when we were younger, but I don't have nearly the amount of demons to battle. I don't know the specifics, but what I can tell you is that he was a SEAL for many years. Under his command, the best men of his team were killed and he saw all of it happen and was unable to do anything to help them."

"Fuck," he whispered. Hearing that crushed Sebastian. He knew how much that would kill his Dom.

"It messed him up for a long time, and he's not been the same since. He left the SEALs then and took a bit of time off. After that, he joined another government organization, one I know made things worse for him in many ways, not better. I think he felt like he had the skill set and it was a new challenge, one that would take his mind off what he felt were his failings. I only know it was for the government because he said he couldn't talk about it, not that he wouldn't talk about it. That, and he was raised with too much of a conscience to go rogue and be a mercenary. Not that that isn't warranted in some cases."

Sebastian's brows drew together at the last comment. He knew Zavier wouldn't have made it without good reason, so he asked, "How is killing ever warranted?"

Zavier tilted his head at that, brow raised. "I've killed a lot of men, Sebastian. It happens in wartime. Hell, it happens when you're not even on the frontlines. Military spec ops aren't only active when there's war."

Sebastian sagged, knowing what he said was true. "All right. I understand that. I guess I never gave it much thought. I'm not completely naïve. But I know that's not what that was today."

Zavier shook his head and answered, "No. It wasn't. And while I have some of the information, I don't have it all. What I will say, is that from my perspective, the lives he took—"

"Lives?!"

Zavier narrowed his eyes and Sebastian calmed, not wanting to push Zavier too far. He sighed. "I'm sorry, Sir. I just…" He shook his head. "I don't know who that was today. I don't know the man who spoke so angrily to whoever was there. I don't know the man that spoke so calmly about killing, so blithely, as if he was shrugging it off as no consequence. It wasn't Gideon, or at least the Gideon I know. And that scares me to death. Makes me wonder who he really is."

"He's the man he lets you, and only you, see. That's who he really is. I've never seen him happier than he has been with you. The old Gideon, the one I grew up with, is finally back and I have you to thank for that."

"I don't know. Today seemed pretty real too. How can he be two different men?"

"It's called compartmentalization. He quit government work about five years ago. He's been better since then."

"What does that even mean?"

"It means that we grew up in a military family and three of the five of us felt compelled to serve our country. It means that we've all had some of the world's best military training and served our military branches with pride and a sense of duty that was instilled in us at an early age. It means that we were trained how to kill and that we did so without hesitation. It also—"

Sebastian sighed. "I understand all that—"

"Don't interrupt me, boy."

He stilled and nodded. "Sorry, Sir."

Zavier continued, "It also means that even though we did so, we weren't unaffected. It doesn't mean we didn't care that we were doing it. And it doesn't mean that we don't have regrets, some worse than others. And sometimes those regrets can eat you alive and come with a sense of feeling tainted, soulless, and not deserving of love and happiness."

"That's bullshit!" Sebastian exclaimed before he realized he was going to say it. He sat back in his chair again and sighed, continuing more calmly. "Everyone is deserving of love and happiness. He's not tainted or soulless. I just… I don't know how to reconcile the two. This obviously was a recent thing, and he's no longer in the military or working for the government."

"I'll leave Gideon to tell you the rest, but what I know is that the man he was talking to used to be his handler at the government agency he worked at after leaving the navy. He came, months ago, to Custos, seeking help from Gideon, and Gideon allowed that only because that help was tied to the murder of his team so long ago. Gideon's always felt the blame for that even though he couldn't have done a thing to prevent it. For him, his sense of duty and loyalty would have been impossible to ignore."

Sebastian sat, contemplating that, and while he did, Braden cleared the table. When he looked up at Zavier, who was waiting there patiently, he nodded his head and said, "Thank you. I couldn't have sat down with him today to hear that. I'm grateful that you shared what you could with me. I don't really know what to do or what to think, yet."

Zavier nodded and stood, placing a hand on his shoulder. "Keep in mind, he's one to double-check everything even if he's handed the information. Whatever assignments he got, he'd have done enough surveillance to be sure what he was handed was in fact the truth. He wasn't just out there killing for the sake of killing."

"Yeah, you said that, and while I understand, I'm having a hard time keeping my emotional reaction in check."

"I understand that. Just know that in the past when we'd speak in generalizations, he spoke of things like going after the heavy hitters in human trafficking, illegal drug development and trafficking, illegal arms brokering, and biological weapons of warfare. I can tell you what I know about my brother, he's a good man but a damaged one. His moral compass is sound even if he doesn't believe that's true. And he'd do anything for you."

Sebastian had a lot to think about. He thanked Zavier and watched as he stood. Zavier gave him a sad smile and said, "I'm going to go next door to The Knockout to get some sparring in. You can stay here for as long as you want. Take your time. We have spare bedrooms if you'd like to stay with us, but know that he won't come to your place until he's invited. He knows you need time."

All Sebastian could do at that point was nod as he watched Zavier grab Braden by the ass and draw him in close for a scorching kiss. He blushed and turned away, knowing how good it felt being manhandled like that by someone so much bigger and so much more dominating. It felt thrilling and wonderful. It felt like you were being possessed, owned. It felt right.

He sighed, unsure how he'd feel if Gideon did that to him right then. He had a feeling he'd forgive him, eventually, but at that moment, he was still confused and hurt that Gideon had kept so much of himself hidden which left him afraid of how much he didn't know about the man he was still irrevocably in love with.

He heard the ding of the elevator and turned to see Braden pouring more coffee for them both and doctoring it up. He walked toward the family room section of their loft, and Sebastian followed. They sat down facing each other, and Braden handed over his coffee silently. He could tell Braden was waiting him out, so he offered, "I need to talk to him."

"You do."

"I'm scared. This is like nothing I've ever dealt with."

Braden reached over and grabbed his hand, holding it. "I know. But, knowing what you know now, think for a minute and ask yourself, are you scared because you think he'll hurt you, or are you scared because it's the unknown?"

Sebastian didn't have to think. He knew, deep down, that Gideon would never hurt him, but that didn't make the rest easier to swallow. He needed to know more, but regardless, he had to admit the truth. "Because it's the unknown."

They sat for another minute, and Sebastian realized he needed to talk to Braden more than he'd known and not just about what happened that morning. "It's going to take time to sort this out in my mind. But, if we can get past this, I think I want to be his submissive twenty-four seven. It's the decision I've been mulling over and had made. But now...I don't know."

"You'll get past it," Braden said with conviction. "Does that mean you'd be his slave?"

Sebastian looked down at his lap and shrugged, not knowing for sure if they'd get past it, but offered an answer anyway. "No. We'd have a contract, I'd have safewords, and I'd work outside of the home. He said he doesn't want a slave, and I believe him."

"All right. You sound nervous about it though."

He sighed. "We had a short conversation about it recently, and he said he wants to take care of me financially. I don't like that."

"You don't like that or you think he feels you're incapable of taking care of yourself?"

He huffed. "Must you always be able to read my mind?"

Braden chuckled. "Z pays for everything unless it's a gift from me to him or I set up something for us like a date, a weekend away, or even a longer vacation. At least, that's what we agreed to. I asked because I had some of the same feelings."

"Does that bother you? I feel like he wants to save me because I'm weak and can't save myself."

Braden shook his head. "No, it doesn't. One, because the McCades have more money than they can ever spend in a lifetime, and they don't care about it. Money isn't a thing to them. Two, because I can do things I wasn't able to do before. I can put more of my money back into my business, I can donate more money to good causes, and I can buy things for the house to make it our home and lavish him with gifts and vacations and do the same for my friends. And there will be more to give our kids. Let me ask you this, do you really believe he thinks you're weak, or do *you* feel weak and like you can't save yourself?"

He glared at Braden who raised his hands in a placating gesture and sat quietly a moment, giving it some thought. When he did, he grumbled. "I never felt weak and like I couldn't take care of myself until recently."

Braden looked at him like he was being an idiot. "So, to clarify, was it weak when you got yourself to all of your doctor's appointments? Was it weak when you made the hard decision to have a craniotomy instead of just suffering because you were scared? Was it weak when you scheduled and paid for half of your own surgery then sold your house to pay for the second half and had to move because of it? And was it weak when you packed almost your entire house yourself, while having seizures I might add, and set everything up to get your stuff moved to a new apartment? And, just to drive the point home, you did all of that alone."

Tears burned his eyes, and he shook his head. "So why do I feel like he swooped in and saved the day?"

"Probably because he's protective and you see him as a hero. But if you sit and think on it a moment, all he really did was help you with what you already did for yourself. Your own surgeon would have done just fine, Gideon just wanted to even the odds. You would have gotten the house packed up yourself even if you lost sleep to get it done. You would have recovered just fine too, all he did was help."

"It still makes me feel like I couldn't do it on my own."

"That's not true at all. You could. You did. But you no longer have to. That doesn't make you weak. You have family now. Friends. You didn't have that before, and it's probably a lot to get used to when you've always done everything alone."

Sebastian nodded, deep in thought, when Braden continued, "What if he gets sick. Wouldn't you do the same for him?"

"He said the same thing."

"Soooo…"

"So, of course, I'd help him. Why doesn't it feel the same? Why do I still feel weak?"

"Because you're used to negative self-talk. And your mind is stuck on his physical size versus yours, probably. But it's all about mental and emotional strength which you have in spades."

"I'm seeing someone for that."

"Let me guess, Dr. Price?"

"You too?"

Braden nodded. "Eric fucked me up. I don't see him as often now, but I still see him. There's no shame in seeking help whether it's from family, friends, your partner, or a psychologist for mental health issues. You know that, right?"

Sebastian shrugged, noncommittally. "I've always hated what I see in the mirror. I think my parents fucked me up from the beginning and made me feel worthless and like a freak, so I've been trying to prove them wrong since then if only to myself and feeling like I'm failing."

"Does Gideon ever make you feel that way?"

He shook his head. "No, never. He's truly attracted to me; I can see it in his eyes, even though I don't understand it. But Gabe explained it like my brain has receptors that are shaped like squares, and when people give me compliments or something really good happens, those things are shaped like circles, so my brain can't receive positive feedback because it doesn't fit the receptors. It only responds to negatives and rejects positives. I'm fucking that up, I'm sure. It made much more sense when he said it and drew it on his notepad."

Braden smiled. "No, it makes sense and sounds like a good way to describe it." He chuckled. "He loves that damn notebook of his."

"He does."

They both laughed and continued to chat. Though their talk was making him feel better, he knew he needed to take some time alone without the clutter jumbling his thoughts. He needed to get through his final days at the station and get things ready for full-time tattooing. He shared those thoughts with Braden who thought he was on the right track. Maybe things would become clearer when he had stepped away from everyone and everything for a bit. He hoped so anyway.

Chapter 39

GIDEON

Gideon had gotten a text from his boy the day after Sebastian had heard his conversation with Boone. He'd asked for some time away from everyone and everything. As much as Gideon wanted to call him or go see him so they could talk, he knew they had time for that and what his boy needed was quiet and solitude to think about what he really wanted. The time for fighting for him, for them, would come later if his boy decided he no longer wanted his Dom. But after that, if he truly didn't want Gideon because of what he'd heard or learned, Gideon would have to live with that.

He had to think positively, or he'd make himself crazy. Thinking the only possible outcome was that of them together in the end was what got him through. He'd spoken to Zavier at length. He'd learned what they'd told Sebastian and gave him a heads-up that he might have to give his boy time. The fact that Sebastian had taken the steps to let him know that himself gave him another reason to think positively. If he was too upset to contact him in any way even if it was just a text, things could go either way.

Regardless of what he'd learned from his brother, he wasn't about to be idle. Zavier asked him to consult on another big case after he'd provided his input on several others. He knew his brother was just trying to help keep him busy, but he knew he'd have plenty of work of his own. The club would always keep him busy, and if he worked out twice as much as usual, no one could blame him. He contacted his Realtor Sunday afternoon and let her know what he was looking for. If the property he was trying to find didn't work out, he'd rent it out indefinitely, or at least for a while and resell later.

He wanted to move fast, and he'd be paying cash, so he knew he could move things along. Cash always made people jump. He knew underwriting would take most of the time, so he'd figure out who he needed to incentivize to expedite the process. It took two days of searching with his real estate agent,

Natalie. She was a gem and dropped everything to take him around the city until he found what he wanted at the last minute when she got a call from her assistant about a location very close to him.

He didn't know if it was a sign or if the gods—that he wasn't sure existed in the first place—were smiling down on him because he'd had such shit luck with Sebastian, but three days after that fateful morning, he was standing in what used to be a hair salon. It had gone on the market just hours before, and they were the first visitors. The place had been fully cleared of the work stations, the outlines of them still visible on the flooring.

It was two streets over from the club, amongst the trendy shops, cafes, and a few tiny art galleries. It would be perfect. He could see Sebastian there. He learned the salon had gotten too popular and moved one street over into a bigger building so they could expand their services. That's what sold it for him, really. He asked his Realtor to put in a cash offer for the asking price, contingent on an inspection and appraisal. He wasn't going to haggle over money. This was the place, and he'd pay more than they were asking for it if it was needed.

Making that clear to his Realtor, he watched her walk off to make the call to the seller's agent. He'd wait on Sebastian to make most of the decisions, but he'd be sure to get it set up exactly as his boy wanted it. The thought of it made him smile, the first one he'd had in three days.

The bones of the building were perfect. He took the stairs to the second floor looking around, he didn't know what Sebastian would do with this space and with a pang, realized that if things didn't work out between them, he may never find out. But he couldn't think like that.

He'd have to see what needed to be done and see how quickly he could do it, as long as the inspection came through clean. He walked down the stairs and out toward the front of the shop. One of the doors from the private rooms opened and closed, and he heard Natalie's heels clicking on the hardwoods. His heart beat faster when she came around the corner and had a huge grin on her face. "They accepted. So, unless there are huge issues with the inspection or appraisal, you're looking at your new tattoo studio. I never did ask. Did you start tattooing since we last did business?"

Gideon chuckled and answered, "No. My partner is a really talented tattoo artist. I hope he'll love it."

Her eyes widened. "Do you want to call him and have him check it out first?"

He shook his head. "No. It's a surprise. He has a little studio that he does business out of, but his dream is to own his own shop. I wanna make that happen for him."

Natalie smiled at that. "That's so great. I just love your family. It's always fun to learn what you all are up to next."

He grinned. "We do keep you in business, don't we?"

Natalie snorted and said, "Uh, yeah. Between finding your parents' house, the building for your club, your sister's house, Finn's house, Aiden's abandoned old church he converted to a home, and Zavier's security warehouses, you keep me busy."

"Yeah, well, no one knows the city better than you do or has the right connections to push past all the barriers we've been met with. Not to mention, you treat your customers like friends. We appreciate that."

Natalie blushed and waved it all away like he knew she would. "Thank you. I love working with you all. I'm just glad I can help. All right, I'm going to make a call to a few inspectors and appraisers to see who can make it out here the fastest. I'm assuming you want to put it in his name only, and that you want this to go through as quickly as possible?"

"Yes, to both. And if I need to pay extra to get them here faster, or the paperwork through to the title company faster, let me know. I'll throw cash at whatever problems we find. Unless there are huge structural challenges with the building, there's not much I won't do. I want to close before two weeks are up, faster if possible. Let me know."

Apparently, what she could do was work miracles. They closed on Sebastian's shop eleven days later, on a Friday. During which time, he hadn't heard a thing from Sebastian. He did his best to ignore that and go about his business. He'd already arranged for workers to arrive to update the things that needed it. He wanted a new A/C unit installed, an upgraded furnace, and a new water heater. The floors were a gorgeous hardwood, but he wanted them refinished and re-stained. He wanted the walls to be bright, so he'd picked out a cream color that Sebastian could change or add to later, if he chose to.

He freshened up the break room and bathroom but didn't want to put in new countertops or make any sweeping changes. He'd make sure Sebastian chose the best but to his own tastes. He had new windows installed, a new door, and had Sawyer and Jackson, Zavier's best guys from Custos, come over and install their security system. Money talked, so he had all of that done by the following Monday, fifteen days since he'd gotten Sebastian's text.

But he wasn't counting. Nope. Not at all.

It wasn't until late Thursday evening, eighteen days from that text, that he received the call he'd been waiting for. When he finally heard his boy's voice, he actually got goosebumps from it. He closed his eyes, so grateful he called that he could scarcely believe his own reaction. He knew he loved Sebastian, but it wasn't truly until that exact moment he realized he wasn't whole without him any longer and he wasn't just in love with him, he needed him in a way he could hardly put into words.

"Hello? Sebastian?"

Did he hear his boy let out a relieved breath? "Hi, Gideon."

"Baby…"

"Yes, Sir."

He knew. Right then, he knew they'd be okay. Not that things would be easy by any means. No, he knew he had a lot to make up for, and a lot of talking to do. But he couldn't remember feeling such hope in his life, and he smiled and let out a calming breath. The plaintive way he said Sir said it all.

He wasn't going to hide for one second how happy he was to hear Sebastian's voice. "Goddamn, boy. I'm so glad you called. So fucking glad."

Another relieved breath escaped across the line, louder this time. "Me too, Sir. Um, I was wondering if I could come see you tomorrow night? If we could talk? I know you're usually working—"

"Yes. Please, come over. Plan to stay the weekend."

"I don't know. I just… I think we need to talk first, Gideon. I'm not sure this is going to work out. I'm scared still, and I need you to talk to me."

Those words put a hitch in his euphoria, but they didn't change his mind about believing things would be all right between them. He'd make sure Sebastian wasn't afraid of him, could fully trust him and still loved him, whatever it took. He'd been sure, not too long ago, that Sebastian would be better without him. He'd been wrong. You're never better off without your soulmate, and that's what he fully believed they were.

"I know, Bastian. Believe me, I do. But we need time together. I know you probably work on Saturday…"

"I don't."

"No? I thought you'd have clients at the studio."

Sebastian cleared his throat. "Um, no. I gave myself a weekend off. We can talk about it tomorrow night."

Suddenly, tomorrow night wasn't soon enough, and he took a chance that Sebastian was feeling the same. "Baby?"

"Yeah?" Gideon heard the emotional quiver in his voice.

"Can I come see you? Right now?"

"It... It's late, Sir."

"I know. But it's been eighteen days since I got your text saying you needed time." He took a deep breath and admitted in a whisper, "Goddamn, it's felt like a lifetime without you."

There was a long silence. Gideon thought he'd gone too far until Sebastian finally replied, quietly, "Eighteen days is very specific."

"I've been keeping track. I just need to see your face. Please. I won't stay longer than five minutes, if you don't want me to. I just..."

"All right," was whispered so softly he barely heard it. Suddenly, he couldn't wait to touch his boy, to hug him, if he allowed it.

"Okay, I'll be there soon."

They hung up, and he was jogging down the building's inner stairwell in less than a minute, an idea forming in his head. When he got in the car and started driving, he turned on the Bluetooth and made a call. When it rang and rang and rang, he was worried he'd missed her, but when Rowan answered the phone, out of breath, he grinned and asked, "What's got you so winded?"

"Oh, shut up, Gideon! I was downstairs getting ice cream if you must know. What do you want? It's late."

"I fucked up."

This perked her right up. "Do tell!"

He sighed and explained, "It's a long story, but I messed things up with Sebastian. It's been eighteen days, and I haven't seen him. He finally called, and I'm headed to his place now. I want flowers but don't want shitty grocery store flowers. You always have beautiful flowers in your kitchen from your garden. Can I have them?"

"They're like four days old, kinda wilty."

"Uh, can you maybe go pick some new ones?"

"Go outside, in the dark, and pick flowers?"

"Come on, Ro! Please? I'll owe you, big!"

She growled, "Ugh, FINE! But only because I love Sebastian."

"I'll take it. Thank you!"

He hung up and then thought of something else. Grinning he called right back.

"Oh my god! What do you want?!"

"Chocolate milk."

"What?!"

"Can you make some chocolate milk and put it in one of your plastic bottles? The chocolatyer, the better."

"You're a big pain in my ass. And chocolatyer isn't even a word!"

Gideon laughed, realizing she was right. "Yeah, yeah. Just make it extra chocolaty, okay? It's for Sebastian!"

"You know I'll do it for him. But, you'll owe me. I mean it!"

"Can you run it out to my car? Please, Ro? There's never parking on your street."

"I'm in my pajamas, you moron!"

"I'll buy you anything you want. No! I'll buy two things you want. Doesn't matter how expensive. You tell me the things you want, I'll buy them. A trip to Paris. A diamond tennis bracelet. Anything!"

"Anything?"

"Anything."

"Deal."

"I'll be there in less than ten minutes."

"Then stop talking to me so I can get this shit together."

"Love you!"

"Yeah, yeah. Be ready to pay up, big."

She hung up, and he laughed. He was just glad she lived on the way to Sebastian's place. Not that he wouldn't have gone out of his way, but he didn't want to delay getting to him any longer than necessary. When he pulled up to the front of her house, nine minutes later, he had to double park and put on his hazards. She must have been watching because she came running out, hands full.

When she got to the passenger side, he leaned over and opened the door. She pulled it open the rest of the way and lay the flowers, wrapped beautifully in tissue paper—*god, she was the best*—on the seat and handed him the huge water bottle full of chocolate milk. He grinned and she grinned right back.

"Anything?" she asked.

"Anything," he replied.

She smirked and wished him luck as she shut the door. One minute later he got a call from her on the Bluetooth.

"I want a Lite Brite!"

He snorted. "You can't be serious! They're thirty years old!"

"You broke mine when you plugged it into the wall in the kitchen."

"I didn't break it! Finnegan did! I got it out for you when I was babysitting. He tripped on the cord, and the thing fell off the table and broke."

"It wouldn't have been there if you'd put it where I usually played with it in the family room! Of course, someone's gonna trip on it when you have the cord hanging from the wall to the table!"

He shook his head, incredulous. *God, he loved her.* He offered her a trip to Paris and diamonds. She wanted a fucking Lite Brite. "Fine, Squirt! What else?"

"Well, now that you mention breaking things. I want a Makit & Bakit Oven!"

"You… What? No! You've got to be kidding me!"

"You said anything! You dumped like twenty packets of Pop Rocks on one of the trays. You wanted to see if they'd heat up and explode. Pop Rocks got on the heating element somehow, and it nearly caught on fire! It never heated my ornaments after that!"

The fact that she was still so angry at him had him laughing his ass off. He was wiping his eyes when he finally got out, "A Lite Brite and a Makit & Bakit Oven? *That's* what you want?"

Satisfaction in her voice, she answered, "That's what I want. And they better be vintage and in mint condition."

"You're crazy, but okay. I'll start my search for them soon. I love you, Ro. Thanks for the help."

"You're welcome. You better grovel really well. If you don't fix things with Sebastian, I'll trade you in for him."

"And I wouldn't blame you a bit. Bye."

"Bye."

He ended the call just as he parked near Sebastian's place. He was nervous. Suddenly wondering what he'd say, how Sebastian would react. Would he let him touch him? God, he needed to touch him. He went up the elevator and knocked on Sebastian's door before he could overthink it.

When his beautiful boy opened the door, he could do nothing but stare. It seemed Sebastian felt the same way because neither of them did anything but look at the other for what seemed like forever. The only thing that broke their gazes was the growling of Lola in the background. And just like that, the magic was broken, both knowing why she was doing it. The last time she'd seen Gideon, in her eyes, he'd been threatening her charge. His shoulders sagged when Sebastian took a deep breath and called her over, hushing her.

He repeated what Killian had said, petting her. "Lola, Gideon is a friend. Friend."

He heard her whine, and she looked up at Sebastian to confirm what she was hearing. Sebastian repeated it, and Gideon held out his hand until she sniffed it, whined again, and moved closer to him. He knelt down and let her smell him some more. Eventually, she licked him then moved closer, and he was petting her. Her acceptance humbled him, and he took a deep breath and gazed up at Sebastian who was watching them, a sad smile on his face.

He stood again, grabbing the chocolate milk and flowers from the floor by the door and smiled tentatively. "Hi."

Handing him the flowers, Sebastian softened a little and sniffed them. Gideon handed him the milk. "And your favorite."

Sebastian held the bottle of chocolate milk in his hand, a laugh escaping. When Sebastian turned to look up to him, to thank him, his heart melted. God, he'd do anything to get his boy back. Sebastian welcomed him inside, went and put the flowers in a vase, and poured some of the chocolate milk in a glass and drank it down.

"Do you want anything to drink?"

"No, baby. I'm fine."

He watched closely and felt some of his tension ebb when he saw Sebastian's small smile at the endearment. Sebastian asked him to sit down, and they sat facing each other on the sofa, not touching. It was killing him, not tugging him close to hold him.

"How has it been, getting settled in?"

Sebastian looked around and shrugged. "Fine, I guess. Just been busy at work." He looked down, fidgeted, glanced back up. "I... Um, I gave my notice. Tomorrow is my last day."

Happiness flooded him, and it was so goddamn hard not to scoop Sebastian up and hug him. He reached over, touched his boy's hand, and gave him a wide smile. "I'm so happy for you, Bastian. When did you do that?"

Sebastian blushed and looked away. "Before I left your place."

That hit him square in the chest and knocked him back a pace. He spoke as gently as he could. "Why didn't you tell me?"

Picking at the seam of his jeans, he shrugged. "I thought you might have used it to try to keep me from moving back here. I wanted to wait until I'd moved back to share it with you. I was... I was coming to tell you...that morning."

Gideon let out the breath he'd been holding in a whoosh and nodded. He could see where Sebastian would want to wait, but he still felt shitty about it, especially since he'd ruined the moment with his monumental fuckup. "I'm sorry, Bastian. You'll never know how much. I had always planned on telling you as much as I could, eventually. I hope you'll believe that. I'll tell you whatever you want to know if I'm able to. You can ask me anything."

Sebastian nodded. "Can we talk about it this weekend? I'm too tired to start this conversation so late."

Ecstatic his boy was contemplating a weekend with him, he couldn't keep the smile from his face when he said, "Yeah. Of course."

"Can I ask you one thing?"

"Anything."

"Are you still doing that type of work? 'Cause, I don't think I can—"

"No. Baby, no. It was... God. It's a lot to explain like you said. But the answer is no. I promise you."

"All right. Can I still come over tomorrow after work?"

"Of course. Please. Anytime you want."

Sebastian nodded then looked down at his lap. Gideon knew it was time to go, but he couldn't leave until he at least asked his boy for what he needed most. Taking a deep breath, he touched a finger to the back of Sebastian's hand, making him look up. "I know you're tired and I've already been here longer than the five minutes I promised. Can I hug you before I go?"

He watched indecision war on Sebastian's face, and it killed him. But then he watched as his boy's shoulders relaxed, he smiled a tiny smile, bit his lower lip, and nodded. Gideon smiled in return, scooting forward until their knees were touching. He leaned forward and wrapped his arms gently around Sebastian's shoulders, tightening them when he heard his contented sigh. Sebastian's grip tightened and a choked, "Sir," escaped.

Gideon tightened his grip, and suddenly, his boy climbed in his lap, hugging him even tighter. He lowered a hand to cup his boy's ass, pulling him in closer, and murmured, "I've missed you so much, boy. So much."

Sebastian didn't respond, but he nodded into the side of his neck, and they held on tight, Gideon rocking them gently, his boy's still too small body tight against him. He didn't know how long he held him; it felt like forever and only a couple seconds all at once. He didn't want to, but he knew he needed to let him go.

Rubbing both hands gently up and down Sebastian's back, he turned his head and kissed Sebastian's temple, whispering, "I love you, boy. Never forget that. I'm so sorry I scared you. So sorry I disappointed you. I'll fix it, Bastian, I promise you."

Sebastian didn't respond but nodded into his neck and gripped him still tighter until his arms shook. Goddamn, his boy was killing him. Knowing he needed to be the strong one, he rubbed his back again then slid his hands up and down Sebastian's arms, gently tugging them until Sebastian pulled away, still on his lap, looking down.

Gideon tipped his chin up and placed a soft kiss on his forehead. He stood, lifting Sebastian with him and placing him gently on the floor, clasping his hand in his and walking them to Sebastian's door. He turned before he opened it and kissed Sebastian's head, breathing in the smell of his shampoo. He spoke, his lips still on his boy's short hair. "Come over anytime tomorrow."

His boy nodded, and he opened the door, stepping out. Sebastian looked up, and when he did, Gideon said, "Lock your door after me and set the alarm. I'll see you tomorrow."

Sebastian smiled and nodded. "Yes, Sir. See you tomorrow."

———

It turned out Sebastian's last day was more perfunctory than anything because he showed up just after one in the afternoon. Gideon had gone upstairs from the club to grab some lunch and was just about to eat when he heard the ding of the elevator. He set his sandwich down and walked toward the doors as they slid open. He had to grin when he saw Slap and Tickle in

Sebastian's arms, a bag over his shoulder, and Lola's tongue lolling out of her mouth.

He gave the dog a rub on the head, pulled the kittens out of Sebastian's arms, kissing them and setting them on the floor, and then pulled the bag from over Sebastian's shoulder, hooking it on his own. He leaned in, tipped Sebastian's chin up and saw a bit of wariness still in his eyes, yet, but also hopefulness which made up his mind for him. He leaned the last scant inches and kissed him softly, chastely on his lips.

They gazed at each other, and Gideon asked, "Are you hungry?"

Sebastian shook his head. "No. They had a little going away party for me that included lunch."

Gideon tilted his head. "You gonna miss it?"

"In some ways. I didn't love the job, but I liked it, and the people there were always kind."

"Sit down with me, while I eat lunch. Let me just put your bag in our room."

"Yes, Sir."

When he came back, he noticed Sebastian had grabbed himself a glass of water. It was a small thing, but it made Gideon happy he'd felt at home enough to take that simple step. He sat down and made quick work of his lunch and pulled Sebastian up to lead him to the couch. Again, they sat facing each other, and Sebastian began to fidget nervously.

"I'm going to just tell you what I can, about my past. If you have questions, you can cut in and let me know, all right?"

Sebastian nodded, and he began by telling him about his career in the military, how he'd loved being a SEAL and thought he'd stay in until he just couldn't physically do it any longer. He talked to him about his contract with his first submissive, Mason Alexander, a Naval Intelligence Specialist. How they'd been having a rough time, and finally, he'd ended it when Mason kept asking for more than Gideon had in him to give at the time.

Mason had started seeing Alan Lewis. Alan worked closely with the military as an IED and Insurgent Network Analyst for a science and technology company. Because they specialized in intelligence, defense, and homeland security, Mason and several SEAL teams—including his own—had worked closely with Alan. Not only worked with him but trusted him.

Alan had been using Mason to gather information, and when Mason had found out, he'd been taken, tortured for more information, and killed. While that was going on, Gideon had been pulled away from his team to provide tactical analysis in an intelligence briefing regarding intel gathered from the Germans.

While he was away, his team had received last-minute orders to be pulled from their counterinsurgency mission in order to guard a munitions bunker that was a possible hideout for insurgent militants selling guns to a known terrorist group. As soon as Gideon had been pulled from his team, Alan had provided information to the base commander to reassign his men and ultimately send them to their deaths in a well-planned ambush.

Upon his return, Gideon learned of his team's new assignment. He didn't trust the intel or the timing. He left immediately to intercept his men, but he was too late. Arriving in time to see Alan use a detonator to set off the explosions that killed his men before disappearing into a building that exploded moments later.

It came to light that Alan's company had been selling military weapons to the highest bidder, the information he'd stolen from Mason proved to be extremely lucrative for Alan and the man giving him orders. Alan's team had successfully stolen the munitions a few days before his team had arrived. The orders were to infiltrate the bunker, document the inventory, and await transport out.

Gideon's men had been brought there to be killed to prevent the military's efforts—and his team's efforts—to keep munitions out of enemy hands. So many explosions were set that day it was made to look like the munitions were destroyed along with his men. His commander said the search was underway for Alan's team and the munitions.

"I'd been assured that Alan was dead by my superiors. My promises to my men's families to not make their deaths be in vain, to find out what had happened, being so much bullshit when the man responsible was dead already. I still wear my military ID tags, just as my dad and brother do. To honor the men that died on my watch."

Sebastian reached out and pulled the tags from inside his shirt, rubbing his thumb over them. "You couldn't have known. It wasn't your fault."

Gideon nodded, knowing the truth of it, but not pardoning himself. He went on to explain that he'd left the military as soon as his time was up. Several months later, he was approached by a three-lettered agency. They'd needed him to verify the intelligence they were given to ensure they were targeting the guilty parties. Once verified, he was sanctioned to take them out. They used his painful past to fuel his desire to lose himself in his anger, causing him to lose more and more of himself in the process.

He went on to explain seeing Boone at Custos, and with his men's deaths on his conscience, he couldn't let it go. He had to seek vengeance on the men responsible for the deaths of his men and likely so many others. He wasn't about to gloss over the reality of what he'd done. If Sebastian was going to be with him, he needed to make an informed decision. He needed to see the reality of who Gideon was, he admitted that he didn't feel worthy of Sebastian, and that working for the agency had siphoned off his humanity until he was a shell of the man he used to be.

"I'm done with that life. I don't have it in me to do it anymore. I put off telling you everything, but I made a promise to myself we wouldn't take any more big steps in our relationship until I shared my past with you. Unfortunately, Boone's visit took that out of my hands, and you found out in the worst possible way. I can't apologize enough for that." When he finally met Sebastian's eyes, the sadness there pulled at his heart. Gideon considered himself lucky that his boy didn't flinch away from him when he reached over to touch his face.

He took a leap of faith and put himself out there, one last time. "Sebastian, I know what I've done in my past isn't forgivable. If I can't forgive myself for the kind of man I am and the things I've done, I can hardly expect others to forgive me. And, I know that I'll never be who or what you'd wish for yourself in a partner."

His gut twisted, but he continued, "I'm holding onto my humanity by the skin of my teeth and asking you to have faith in the fact that I have no reason to ever go back into that world ever again. I have everything I could ever need right here in front of me."

He leaned forward when Sebastian looked down at his lap and shook his head, clasped his chin, and tilted his head back up looking him in the eyes. "I'm asking you for another chance. I know I don't deserve a man like you, and I probably never will, but I have to believe that if I work at it for the rest of my life, it might be enough to earn your love and eventually your respect again."

When Gideon saw Sebastian shake his head and look away, he started to worry that maybe his confidence from yesterday was naïve. Perhaps he should have waited to make that judgement until he'd explained everything because looking at Sebastian now didn't bring him any of that confidence. He rubbed his hands back and forth on his legs, wiping away the nervous sweat on his palms. Christ, he'd done a lot of things in his life that warranted fear and felt none, but sitting here looking at the man who meant most to him in the world and knowing he might lose him made him more scared than he'd ever been.

When Sebastian still didn't say anything, Gideon finally asked, "Do you have any questions for me? Do you need some space, some time alone?"

Sebastian nodded and got to his feet, not meeting his gaze. He dug in his pocket for his keys. "Don't go." Gideon stayed his hand and then snatched it back, worried Sebastian wouldn't want to feel his touch. He scrubbed his hands over his face. "Fuck. I'm not good at this. I just meant, you don't have to go, but of course, you can if you need to. It's just, I have plenty of work to do downstairs to keep me busy. If you decide you need more time than today, obviously, it's all right if you need to leave. I'm not trying to rush you."

Jesus, he was babbling, he realized, when Sebastian sat again and placed his fingers over his mouth. He closed his eyes at the feeling of his boy's soft, warm skin against his lips. Those fingers brushing over his brow had him opening his eyes again and gazing down at Sebastian who said, "I'll stay for now. If I need more time, I'll let you know."

Gideon nodded and added, "Just text me if you're leaving or if you have questions and want to talk, and I can come back up to answer them. You can…" Gideon rubbed a hand over his mouth. "You can call Braden and talk to him. You can tell him anything I told you. Zavier, as well."

When Sebastian nodded, Gideon made his escape, not wanting to say the wrong thing or scare him off even more. He did have a lot of work to do at the club, and some Custos files he could use to occupy himself. He wouldn't return to his place until he heard from his boy. He didn't want to seem like he was rushing him. He shut his mind off to everything but work and got busy.

Chapter 40

SEBASTIAN

Sebastian watched as Gideon made a quick exit. His heart tugged at the obvious distress he'd seen in his Dom. He'd wanted to reassure him. He'd wanted to say he didn't need more time. He'd wanted to say Gideon should forgive himself, and that he was forgiven. He'd wanted to say Gideon was worthy of his love. Goddammit, he'd wanted to say so many things.

The pain on Gideon's face, the shame and self-loathing was so clear Sebastian still felt the remnants of it in the room after he'd gone. It was a sticky, cloying, heavy thing and the fact that Gideon felt it for himself, so strongly it remained in the air after he left, nearly stole his breath. He didn't know why he'd never seen it. How could he not have seen it?

He'd been blind.

Gideon had always been one to lift him up, tell him how wonderful he was, how beautiful. Assured him that he was enough, that he didn't want Sebastian to change, that he was perfect exactly as is. And even after all that reassurance, Sebastian had always assumed Gideon hadn't wanted something permanent with him because he was lacking, as a sub and as a man, he was somehow found wanting. It never occurred to him that Gideon was protecting Sebastian from himself. It never occurred to him that Gideon felt he was the one that was lacking.

His emotions were so close to the surface. He'd needed time. Not to figure out if he could forgive Gideon, not to figure out if he could look past Gideon's violent history. More to figure out his own emotions about it, to sort out how he felt and be able to articulate it. He knew, deep down, that he wanted a future with Gideon, regardless of what his Dom had done in the past. Perhaps because of it. No matter how bad that sounded, he knew that his past had shaped who he'd become, and Sebastian loved Gideon, as is.

As much as he'd wanted to offer that reassurance, he couldn't. Not yet. He didn't want to jump into a conversation about forgiveness and their relation-ship until he figured out exactly what it was he wanted from it. He admitted to himself he'd been a coward. He'd known his feelings all along and had ignored them in fear. Fear of the possibility he'd be rejected again.

He admitted to himself he only thought Gideon would reject him again because somewhere deep down he felt he deserved that rejection, that he was lacking. Weren't they a pair? Maybe they both needed to talk to Dr. Price. They were a mess. But regardless, he'd resolved to give himself time before they talked about forgiveness and a future. Time to sort out his feelings regarding his past. Time to sort out his feelings regarding Gideon's past. And time to admit to himself what he wanted and stop prevaricating.

He needed to think, and he smiled when he realized the best place for him to do that here was Gideon's Jacuzzi-sized bathtub. He filled it up with his favorite bath salts and nearly scalding water. He turned on the jets, got in, and promptly lost himself to his thoughts. And even when he had to let the water out and refill it to keep it hot enough, two times, his thoughts remained on everything he needed to sort out.

It was a couple hours later when he finally realized his fingers were so pruney he had to get out even if he didn't want to. He got dressed in some of his lounge pants and one of Gideon's shirts, feeling better and more peaceful than he had in weeks. He'd thought a lot while he'd been bathing, but he hadn't come to any conclusions, and his thoughts were still jumbled. He thought it might help to talk to Braden, after all. He pulled out his phone and was about to make a call when it rang, jolting him.

"Hey, I was just going to call you."

Braden chuckled. "You were?"

"Yeah. Did Gideon or Zavier put you up to this?"

"Put me up to what?"

"Calling me."

"Uh, no. I hadn't heard from you all week and wanted to check in, see how your last day went."

"It went well. I'm at Gideon's."

"Really?"

"Really."

"Have you guys talked?"

"Yes. He's told me about his past. As much as he feels I need to know at least, or maybe rather what he's able to tell me."

"That's the more realistic of the two. And, to be honest, he probably told you more than he should, but he knows he can trust you. That's how it was with Z."

Sebastian nodded. "Yeah, that's probably true."

"So, what are you doing now?"

"Thinking, thinking, and more thinking. He went downstairs when he realized I needed some time."

"Do you want to talk about it?"

Sebastian sighed in relief, knowing that's exactly what he needed. "Yeah. That would be great."

"Give me twenty minutes, and I'll be there."

"You don't have to come over. We can chat on the phone."

"Not for this kind of conversation. I'll be there soon."

He was there in twenty-five minutes, Thor making a beeline towards Lola as soon as Sebastian opened the stairwell door. They sat on the sofa in the same spot he'd sat with Gideon earlier. They talked for hours. He shared everything Gideon had told him, and he shared a lot of things from his own past. He'd needed someone to talk to, a sounding board, and Braden turned out to be a great one.

When they wound down, Braden finally asked, "So, do you forgive him?"

Sebastian shrugged, looking down at his lap. "I don't know that there's anything to forgive." He fidgeted with a cat toy he'd found on the floor and glanced back up. "I believe Gideon would have told me before we moved in together. What I don't understand is his need for revenge. Why he couldn't just leave things as is when he'd found out."

Braden smiled at him. "Think about it from Gideon's perspective. Think of the lives of men who've fought wars together, saved people's lives together, saved each other's lives. Think of them as a military brotherhood, a brotherhood that means just as much to him as his biological family, and every single one of those brothers' lives was targeted, every single one snuffed out."

Braden clasped his hands, stilling his fidgeting. "Think of what Gideon must've felt, talking to the parents of his dead team, the wives, the children. How much anger would that build when he found out why it was all done. He'd lost family because someone thought making money was more important than the lives of his men, his brothers. He'd been trained to protect at all costs. Trained to kill, yes, but only to protect those that needed protection. That was his reality. I'm not saying what he did was right, but that's not for me to judge. That need to protect was ingrained in him so deeply, it will probably never leave."

Sebastian, thinking of it that way, realized Braden was right, that Gideon still lived that way. From the very beginning, he'd known Gideon was fiercely protective. He'd opened his club and did everything in his power to protect and take care of the submissives there. He'd protected Sebastian from the first day they'd met and continued doing so throughout their contract. He'd moved mountains to help him through his surgery, not just emotionally. He'd used his lawyers, his own family, Finn's expertise, and his own money to protect him from something he had no control over. It must have killed him to not have that control.

It turned out, making his mind up about his feelings regarding Gideon's past was the easy part. What was harder on him was deciding what he wanted from their relationship. Was his decision to move out the right one? Perhaps he'd made it in fear rather than the practicality he'd forced himself to believe he'd made it in. He chatted a little longer with Braden then told his friend he wanted to think on it a bit.

He had to admit he was frustrated with himself. He'd thought that finally quitting the job he wasn't passionate about and deciding to go out on his own full time doing what he loved would give him that sense of rightness he'd been reaching for. But it had merely highlighted what still wasn't right. He'd given himself a taste of freedom and happiness, but only a taste.

He'd kept himself from admitting he'd only be completely happy, completely free from all restraints, when he could finally let go of control completely. When he could finally trust himself with someone. No. Not some-one. With Gideon. When he could finally entrust himself to Gideon.

He walked into their bedroom, pausing his thoughts at that. Their bedroom. It was their bedroom. That felt right, obviously, if that's how he thought of it subconsciously. He needed to stop second-guessing himself every goddamn second of every day. He glanced over at the sound of kitty mewling. He laughed at Slap and Tickle on their kitty condo, playing together.

That prompted him to look around, really check out his surroundings. There were pieces of him everywhere. Cat dishes, dog dishes, toys for both.

His favorite moisturizer was still on the dresser. Walking back into the living area, he saw his yoga video was where he'd left it. He didn't have to look to know his shows would still be recording and sitting on the DVR, waiting for him to watch them.

His throw blanket, because he was always cold, was still folded on the back of the sofa. One of his drawing notebooks and a box of charcoals was still on the end table. The slippers he'd realized he'd forgotten were where he'd left them, tucked under the coffee table. He walked to the kitchen and into the pantry. His favorite foods were there, some that hadn't even been there when he'd left, foods he loved and Gideon didn't were still in the fridge and freezer.

He knew his clothes would still be in the closet, his toothbrush, and other toiletries still in the shower or in the drawers. Hell, he only had to glance in the bedroom to see his favorite colored sheets that he'd purchased for their bed were there. They hadn't been on the bed when he'd left. Approaching it, he ran his hand over the soft cotton and sat there.

Glancing over at the nightstand, he couldn't help but laugh when he saw the wind-up hopping penis toy he'd found one day in the nightstand drawer. One of Khaleo's hidden penis party favors had finally made an appearance, and he remembered laughing so hard he couldn't breathe and then setting it on Gideon's pillow until he found it later that day. They'd both had a laugh when Gideon growled, "Dammit, Khaleo!"

He realized everything was where it was supposed to be. He was where he was supposed to be as well. He was home. His apartment was a pitstop, a place to sleep until he was home again. Why was he doing this to himself? He lay his head down on Gideon's pillow, smelling his Dom. He gripped it in his arms, holding it close, rubbing his cheek on its softness. Why was he punishing them both by keeping them apart when it wasn't even what he truly wanted?

He was letting his fears get the better of him, and he was suddenly ashamed of himself. He knew his moving out had hurt Gideon, deeply. He'd seen it on his face, though as always Gideon had protected him by hiding his own hurt and giving Sebastian the space he needed. Realizing that, he gave up his tight hold on his emotions and just let himself feel.

His heart broke for Gideon and the way he felt about himself and for himself for the same reasons. He felt cheated of their time together since he'd moved out, and he grew angry about those eighteen goddamn days he'd let another kind of fear take over and for the missed opportunities and his stubbornness. When all was said and done and the emotions battering him like a monsoon had finally slowed to a stop, the headache he had and the exhaustion he felt dragged him into a deep sleep.

He was licked awake by Lola's tongue and a bit of whining. He looked at the clock and bolted upright. Shit, shit, shit. Lola pranced to the door and back a couple times before he realized she was telling him she had to pee and was probably starving. Where was Gideon? The club was closed. It was the middle of the night. Did he really have that much work?

Fuck.

No, he didn't have that much work. He wouldn't come home until Sebastian called him and asked him to come back. *Jesus.* He got up, put on his slippers and took Lola out to do her business. He'd normally have let her out hours ago, down at the tiny park a couple streets down, but he was in a hurry and wasn't about to walk that far in the dark with no shoes, even with a guard dog. No, he had to get to Gideon. So, he ignored his feelings of guilt as he let Lola pee and then, oh god, poop on the little square of dirt on the sidewalk, where a tree was planted.

He made a mental note to get a baggie in the morning and pick up the poop as he key coded himself back into the stairwell and out the other side into the hallway of the club. He refused to think about the last time he'd been in that hallway with Lola and walked quickly to Gideon's office, his desk light the only thing lighting the way for him. He felt awful when he saw Gideon sprawled out on the sofa, a sofa that was much too short for his huge frame, his feet dangling off the edge of the sofa's arm. His phone was resting on his stomach, his left arm thrown over his eyes to block out the light, his right one tucked into his unbuttoned pants and boxers.

Sebastian chuckled quietly and sat on the wooden coffee table in front of the couch. He slowly ran his fingers up and down Gideon's arm, jolting his Dom awake. Bleary-eyed, Gideon looked over at him, and Sebastian saw the sleepy smile slowly appear before he said, "Hey. Everything all right?"

"Yes, Sir. I'm so sorry. I fell asleep upstairs and slept for hours. I meant to call you earlier."

"Don't be sorry." He sat up and must have seen the sadness in Sebastian's eyes and misread its meaning when he took a deep breath and asked, "It's late. Do you want me to drive you and the menagerie home?"

Sebastian smiled at that and shook his head. "No. We're already there."

Gideon looked around his office and rubbed his hands over his face a few times to help wake himself up. Obviously confused and not catching his meaning, he glanced up. "You're already... What?"

Sebastian watched Gideon closely when he whispered, "We're already home."

Shock made itself clear on Gideon's face and he slouched into the back of the couch just staring at him, hands folded together behind his head as if he was afraid to reach out, afraid it might not be real. Sebastian's grin broke out when he saw the absolute joy and relief spread across Gideon's face. They stared at each other, smiling stupidly. His Dom let out a relieved breath, still grinning, brows winging up, he whispered, "Really?"

Sebastian, ridiculously charmed by his Dom's incredulity, nodded and whispered back, "Really."

Gideon shot to the edge of the sofa reaching out for him. Sebastian fell into his arms and hugged him tight as Gideon pulled him in to straddle his lap, all the while murmuring, "Oh Jesus. Baby, I love you. I love you so much."

He buried his face in Gideon's neck, telling him he loved him too, and wrapping himself around his Dom. Gideon's arms banded around his back even tighter, nearly cutting off his breath, and he'd never, ever felt happier or more at home than he did at that moment, in his Dom's arms.

They sat there for what felt like hours, only separating when they felt a paw patting at them repeatedly. Lola obviously feeling left out and seeking some attention. They pulled apart and gave their girl lots of love. She wagged her whole body, tongue lolling out, and practically crawled into their laps. They laughed at her and hugged again, her between them.

Gideon pulled away first and helped Sebastian to his feet, then Lola, and then himself. He wrapped his arm around Sebastian, kissing his head, and made a kissy noise to Lola who followed them out of the office and around the corner to the elevator.

Once upstairs, they both undressed and crawled into bed, Gideon told him he wanted to talk in the morning, that all he wanted to do at that moment was hold his boy. Sebastian was okay with that. They kissed and whispered softly to each other until they both fell asleep in each other's arms.

When Sebastian woke the next morning, he smiled shyly when he realized Gideon was watching him. "Good morning, Sir."

He squirmed when he heard the deep rumble of satisfaction in Gideon's chest. "Good morning, boy."

They kissed, and Sebastian realized right away Gideon's breath was minty fresh. He squeaked and jumped out of bed. Gideon tried to catch him, but he had evasive morning maneuvers down pat and was in the bathroom immediately, relieving himself and brushing his own teeth before returning to their bed. When he gazed at Gideon, however, he saw the serious expression and knew he'd need to sideline his libido for a while.

"You're calling me Sir and you said this was home, but I don't really know what that means."

Sebastian ran his thumb over Gideon's brow, smoothing out the confused wrinkles marring it. "It means exactly what you want it to mean. Or, at least what I hope you want it to mean. I want to move in here, permanently, and I want to be your submissive twenty-four seven. It's what I've wanted from the beginning but wasn't brave enough to allow myself."

Gideon's eyes roamed over every inch of his face several times, a gentle smile finally blooming before it slowly melted away. "I still can't fully believe you've forgiven me."

Sebastian moved in closer, their faces only inches apart. "I haven't."

When Gideon tried to pull away, confusion in his eyes, Sebastian pulled him back in and whispered, "Because there's nothing to forgive. You didn't cheat, you didn't lie, and you never hurt me. I was scared because I didn't know anything of your past, but I trust that you would have told me before we'd taken the steps I'm hoping we'll be able to take together now."

Gideon sagged in relief and pulled him closer, grabbing his upper thigh and pulling it over his hip, hooking Sebastian's heel behind his leg and rubbing his large, calloused palm up Sebastian's thigh to his side capturing his arm and wrapping that around his neck. They kissed for several minutes until Sebastian pulled back.

"I can't understand what you went through in your past. I've tried to put myself there and I failed because that's not the life I've lived. But I can't place blame on you for things I don't understand. No matter what you think of yourself, I know you're kind, you're strong, you're brave, and you're loyal. You give of yourself freely, you're protective, and you're generous. You're a good man, Gideon."

When he saw Gideon look down and away from him, he recognized himself in that gesture and clasped Gideon's chin to tilt his head back up. "You don't have to prove yourself worthy of me. You are worthy of me, just as I'm worthy of you. I think you may have some form of PTSD from your past, and it probably wouldn't hurt for you to seek help. But I at least want us to see Dr. Price together, to see how we can become stronger as a couple. Would you be willing to do that with me?"

"Yes. I'd do anything for you," Gideon replied, immediately.

"I think you mentioned you were consulting for Custos—"

"If you want me to stop, I will."

Sebastian kissed him and shook his head. "No. No, I don't want you to stop if it's something you enjoy. But I'm hoping it won't be fieldwork. I don't think I could handle you going off and possibly getting hurt."

"No. I'm done with fieldwork. Zavier understands this and is only seeking my expertise when he knows my expertise might help with a case or I might be able to gather some information he can't get with his sources."

"All right. Thank you."

"You don't have to thank me. I'd do anything for you. If it bothers you at all, I can stop."

Again, Sebastian shook his head. "No. I don't want that. I like that you're close with your brothers. I want you to help if you can."

Gideon drew him closer and they kissed before Gideon finally asked, "What made you change your mind about moving in with me and becoming my submissive twenty-four seven?"

"I haven't been happy on my own. I got the apartment before you came back to me. I never wanted to be alone; I was just scared of being hurt again. But it didn't feel right. It felt like I was still only in a contract with you, and I wasn't giving us a chance. When I would think about coming over here, I felt like I'd be visiting. I don't want to visit my life, I want to live it, full time. So, I'm done with that. I've been in control of everything in my life since my sixth birthday. I'm tired, and I need more than anything to hand that control over to you. It's the only time I feel at peace. So, I'm all in, if you'll have me."

Gideon leaned in and bit the juncture of his neck and shoulder, Sebastian's favorite spot. "You know I will. That's everything I've wanted. But are you sure you want to be under my control twenty-four seven? Meaning I make our decisions and I care for your needs: physical, emotional, and financial?"

Sebastian grinned and answered without hesitation. "Yes, Sir."

Gideon nodded and his deep voice rumbled out when he ordered, "Get out of bed, boy. Let's take a quick shower. There's something I want to show you."

T hey were walking down the street, hand in hand, carrying cups of coffee from a local café. It wasn't Sugar n' Spice coffee, but it was almost as good. They were a couple blocks from the club when Gideon stopped and pulled a key out of his pocket. Sebastian watched as Gideon slid it into the lock on a shop door, opened it, and ushered Sebastian inside.

He looked around the empty space, not understanding what they were doing there, but feeling a prickle at the base of his neck, his hair standing on end. The floors were gorgeous hardwoods, and the walls were freshly painted. The windows were sparkling and the front door had a huge glass cutout, letting more natural light into the space. It was a big, open room with a hallway in the middle of the back wall that had rooms on either side leading to an exit out the back and what Sebastian thought might be a staircase on the left side.

Before he could ask what was going on, Gideon set his coffee down on the low windowsill and walked to the center of the room. "I thought this might be a good place for your new tattoo studio. I've had the walls painted a neutral, light color, the windows and front door are new. You've got a new A/C unit, water heater, and furnace. And the floors have been refinished and re-stained."

Sebastian, setting down his own coffee, waited a beat to make sure Gideon was done and then took a deep breath, barely believing what he was hearing. He turned around in a circle. "You got me a tattoo studio?"

"I did."

He turned again, taking it all in, and faced Gideon. "You got me a tattoo studio."

His Dom's grin melted his heart. "I did."

Sebastian let out a whoop, ran across the room, and jumped into Gideon's arms, wrapping himself around him. He peppered Sir's face with happy kisses in between his words. "You. Got. Me. A. Tattoo. Studio."

Gideon's hands flexed and squeezed his ass cheeks as he took Sebastian's mouth in a heated kiss. When they came up for air, Gideon answered yet again. "I did."

Not bothering to get down, Sebastian pulled back enough to look him in the eyes. "So, you own the whole building?"

Gideon shook his head. "No. You do."

"What? How is that even possible?"

Gideon shrugged. "Money makes everything possible. You'll have to sign the paperwork, obviously, but other than that, it's done."

"When have you even had the time to close on a building?"

"It closed in eleven days. You've owned it for nine."

"How the hell did you do that?"

"Cash."

Incredulous, Sebastian asked, "No mortgage payments?"

"None."

Sebastian carded his hands through Gideon's hair and gazed into his eyes. "I shouldn't accept this."

Gideon raised a brow. "But you will because I'm asking you to."

Sebastian kissed him sweetly. "And because it pleases you, Sir."

"It does, boy."

"Then I accept. Thank you, Gideon."

"You're welcome, baby."

They kissed for a few more minutes then Sebastian slid down Gideon's body and grabbed his hand. "Show me the rest."

They walked down the hallway and into the office and then the break room on the left-hand side, and the two rooms on the right-hand side. Sebastian already started making plans. He'd want to make sure he had a fully outfitted clean room for employees only. And he'd use the other room for a piercing room. He'd want two gender neutral bathrooms, so he'd be adding one, which might make the clean room smaller, but that was just fine.

As they reached the stairs, Gideon took the lead, holding Sebastian's hand behind his back. When they got upstairs, Sebastian fell even more in love with the space. It was a huge open room with windows on one end, letting in a lot of light. He knew immediately that he'd be working up there. He'd hire two, possibly three tattoo artists to work downstairs, ensuring that one or more of them was also trained in piercing, and figure out how to arrange the studio to fit the needs of the clients they'd serve.

The upgrades, additions, and changes he'd be making to the space, both upstairs and down would be costly, but he had quite a bit of money at his disposal now with the house selling, the surgical costs being refunded, and moving out of his apartment. He could afford to do what he wanted, and he could visualize all of it. The possibilities were endless and he couldn't wait to get started.

He might have to work only three days a week for a while so that he could focus his other days on getting up and running. The mental checklist he was making was interrupted when he realized Gideon was speaking to him. "I'm sorry, Sir. I missed that."

Gideon smiled patiently at him and began again. "You've been added to all of my personal accounts and been given your own business account. Anything you purchase for or spend on the studio will be put on that account. You'll not spend a dime of your own, boy. Am I understood?"

Shit. He wanted to argue. He so wanted to argue. But from the looks of it, that's exactly what Gideon expected, and he'd literally *just* agreed to being his submissive and allowing him to make any and all decisions. One thing was for damn sure, Gideon was going to be getting lots of gifts from him and extravagant vacations were going to be a regular occurrence, and that was that.

He smiled wide, and when he saw Gideon's answering grin, he nodded and replied, "Understood, Sir."

"Good. Let's get going, shall we? There's plenty of time for planning later. I think we're in need of an intense session, don't you?"

Sebastian hummed at Sir's choice of words, knowing intense would mean painful but also cathartic. He knew he needed both. His heart picked up its pace, and he sucked in a breath, nodding. "Yes, Sir."

"That's my good boy. Come."

Chapter 41

GIDEON

It was the first day of June, Gideon's forty-first birthday, and about six weeks since Sebastian had permanently moved in with him. Since they'd had Sebastian's recovery time together, there had really been no adjustment period, but he knew it helped tremendously that they'd had multiple therapy appointments together with Dr. Price to help with the transition. As a result, things couldn't have been better. His boy had been seizure free since the surgery, and even though he'd have to keep on the anticonvulsants for the next year or two before they tried to wean him off them, they both felt the surgery had been a success.

Sebastian was becoming more confident by the day. He held his head high, and he no longer wore his colored contact to hide his different colored eyes. He didn't hide behind hoodies and sunglasses, and he made eye contact wherever he went. That confidence was growing in his professional life as well. After Gideon had given it some thought, he realized Sebastian's taking ownership of the tattoo studio had been a turning point. So much confidence had stemmed from that alone.

Gideon could practically see him becoming more and more excited about his personal and professional lives. He was so damn proud of his boy. Sebastian would be opening the studio by the beginning of July. He'd already found two talented tattoo artists that he'd rent space to and was searching for a third. He'd also found a piercer that would work as the front desk clerk, so he'd have one employee to manage.

Gideon had commissioned a permanent, bespoke chastity belt for his boy, and it was the sexiest fucking thing he'd ever seen and could be worn comfortably twenty-four seven. It wrapped around his waist just above his hips and was extremely strong, but so thin it appeared delicate and lay flush against his skin. When he'd opened the beautiful display storage box to show Sebastian, his boy had gasped and then smacked him on the arm and chastised him for getting him a gift when he wasn't the one having a birthday. Gideon had argued that it was just as much a gift for him, and his boy had blushed at that and conceded the point.

He'd been so excited to be in full-time chastity again that Gideon had had to take matters into his own hands, quite literally, to soften Sebastian's excited cock. Afterwards, he'd locked on the most revealing of the three cages he'd purchased with the belt itself, the blush his choice caused his boy's beautiful cheeks made it all the sweeter.

Gideon could still remember the feeling of his sub's hands in his hair when he'd kneeled to attach it. Sebastian hadn't been able to keep his hands to himself, and Gideon couldn't fault him for knowing just how much his Dom loved the feel of his hands in his hair. Sebastian never failed to do what he thought would please his Dom, and Gideon couldn't be more grateful that they'd found each other.

That night was going to be a huge night for them and the chastity device was just the beginning. Besides that, he'd also be wearing the markings from Gideon's ropes. Two days prior, he'd found some of the thinner jute he had for adornment knotting. Creating a spider web effect on both arms and legs and his torso, he'd covered most of his boy's body, leaving the throat bare for Sebastian's collar. His boy had even surprised and pleased him earlier that day by using his clippers and buzzing his hair down to half an inch all over and shaving his face bare. The night of the scene, he'd have a bit of scruff, which suited Gideon just fine.

Gideon had continued the intricate knotwork over the beautiful landscape of alabaster skin, interspersed with intricate inked artwork. He'd been so proud of him as he'd tied off the last of the ropes and thought back to when things had started for them. He'd had no clue they'd end up where they had, but he'd known the second he laid eyes on his boy that he was special and that parting from him would be next to impossible. They'd come a long way since last fall. The confidence he could sense in his boy was a beautiful thing to see. He was happier than he could ever remember being, and Sebastian had said nearly the same to him.

He knew he'd love seeing the lines in his skin from the knotwork when he was up on that stage, but as he removed the two-day old adornment knotting from Sebastian's lithe body the night of the public scene, the dents and grooves left behind turned him on, knowing how visible they'd be in the spotlights of the stage. Next, he took the time to lube his boy's ass and inserted a lubed butt plug. Squeezing those beautiful cheeks.

Afterward, he watched as Sebastian pulled a pair of soft, gray, threadbare jeans on. They were ripped in several places, his beautiful skin framed in denim, tantalizing and teasing him. As he hadn't put back on all the weight he'd lost, they hung low on his hips, showing off the chastity waistband. His boy looked delectable, and he wondered if he'd feel the confidence to remove the pants for their scene. He hoped so, but he'd understand if it felt like too much in front of so many people.

As far as Sebastian knew, Gideon had no idea they were doing a public scene on the main stage. His sub had tried to plan something to surprise him on his birthday, having no idea that Gideon had found out, quite by accident. It seemed they both had a few tricks up their sleeves, but he knew Sebastian would be the most surprised at the night's turn of events.

Two weeks into their new living arrangement, Sebastian had taken Lola out in the morning for a quick walk to do her business. It was something they usually did together, but Sebastian needed to get to the studio early to let in the construction crew, so he was up earlier than normal, and after they'd had breakfast, Sebastian had been on his way and Gideon had been working out in their home gym when he heard his phone ring.

It was Taryn, one of his bartenders, checking to see if she'd left her cell phone behind the bar. She'd tried to call Khaleo down in the club, but he wasn't answering. He told her he'd give her a call back and jogged down the stairs to check. He found it behind the bar and was rounding the corner back to the front entryway when he heard Sebastian talking to Khaleo. He was about to make himself known but thought better of it when he heard what Sebastian was saying.

"Would you be willing to give me another shot to take pictures for him during a public scene? I want to do one on the center stage as a gift to him on his birthday and have some of the pictures framed for him."

Khaleo asked, "Are you sure you're up for that? I don't want to stress you out when it's your first public scene with him."

"We've performed a couple public scenes before," Sebastian said, somewhat defensively.

Khaleo's voice softened. "I know you've done a couple in the voyeur rooms, but that's a small audience. I'm not trying to discourage you, Sebastian. I just know doing it for the whole club is different."

"It's scary, yes, but I'm actually excited to do it. I'm so proud to be his. I've come a long way with my anxiety, and he has so much confidence in me, it's hard for that not to rub off on me. I want to show him I'm finally beginning to feel that confidence in myself. People seem to have accepted me fairly quickly."

Khaleo's voice was serious when he replied, "That's mostly because of the type of person you are, but even if you weren't so kind to everyone, they wouldn't really have a choice, Sebastian. Gideon's word is law here even the Doms defer to Master G. You belong to him, so they'll always treat you with the respect you deserve. But, being the Master's boy, you're gonna draw a huge crowd when you perform on the center stage. Are you ready for that *and* pictures?"

"Yeah. I want to give myself to him in that way, and I want you to capture it. Look, I know I don't have any pull there, but subs have already started coming to me for advice and seem to look up to me in a way, regardless of the fact I didn't do a damn thing to earn it. I don't know what to do with that yet. I need to talk to Gideon about it, but by having a public scene, I feel like I'm also making a statement to them that it's okay to be imperfect and still thrive in this community. I think it's important they know that."

Khaleo's voice softened again. "I agree. And I think you'll be a great role model for them. I just wanted to be sure."

"I appreciate that. And thanks for agreeing to help. I want it to be perfect."

"We'll make sure it's perfect for him."

"Thanks again. I'm gonna get going. I need to get to the studio to let the workers in. Have a good day."

Gideon waited a beat after he heard the club's front sliding door close after his boy and Lola left. He was just about to round the corner when Khaleo said, "You can come out now, Sir."

He heaved a put-upon sigh and strode out. He didn't even bother asking how Khaleo knew he'd been there. Some kind of weird voodoo witchcraft, he was sure. They chatted about what Sebastian wanted, and how to go about making sure it went off without a hitch.

Afterward, Gideon quickly called Taryn back, telling her he'd leave her cell at the front desk for her to pick up and Khaleo would let her in when she got there. Khaleo nodded at that and sent another text on his phone. When he was done, Khaleo flipped it over so he could see it, making Gideon roll his eyes at Sebastian's "name" in Khaleo's phone.

Master G's Boy: K, I forgot to tell you, I want it to be a whipping scene.

Khaleo: Not a suspension rigging?

Master G's Boy: No, that's just for Gideon and me. It's too personal to share.

Khaleo: All right, we'll work with that.

Master G's Boy: Thx

Khaleo: YW

Gideon hadn't worried, but he'd wanted to make sure his boy was ready for a scene of that intensity. They'd only done a few sessions with whips in the past, so he'd begun to work more of those sessions into their private and public play to warm his boy up and get him ready. The fact that he got to stripe his boy's beautiful skin was a bonus.

Part of him was glad they weren't doing a public suspension rigging session because it really was such a personal thing to him, but another part wanted pictures of Sebastian rigged and suspended, displayed beautifully in a web he'd woven. He just figured they'd have to do another private session for that and have Khaleo capture it for them.

He didn't want to tip his hand that he knew everything Sebastian had planned, so he'd had a few conversations with his boy, making sure to twist things just enough for Sebastian to ask for more whip play. During that first week after finding out, Sebastian had come home while Gideon was still at the club. Once he'd gotten the notification on his phone that his boy had turned off the security in their loft, he'd gone up.

Sebastian had apparently been planning for that to be the case because he'd left a trail of his clothes from the elevator through to the bathroom, priming Gideon's libido. His boy was in the shower, naked, soaping up that beautiful body. He'd stripped down immediately and gone into the shower enclosure, noticing that Sebastian had brought in several toys for them to use, taking things into his own hands. The thing that caught his eye was a whip.

"Boy, that's a leather snake whip. Leather and water don't mix."

Sebastian looked horrified that he'd made that mistake. Apologizing, he moved to take it out, but Gideon had just kissed him on the head and taken the whip back to the playroom, returning with a short silicone whip. He'd used it on his boy and watched as it had Sebastian flying high. Afterward, his boy had apologized again, but Gideon had been too busy contemplating an idea prompted by his sub's enthusiasm to worry about the leather whip.

He made some calls the next morning and hired the team that had renovated the club to make a few changes for their upcoming scene. He'd taken Sebastian through his paces with the whip he'd be using and other whips as well during the last month leading up to their big scene.

He'd finally felt like he could go into the evening without any reservations, and that was a load off his mind. As they travelled down in the elevator to the club, Sebastian began to fidget. He placed his hand on the back of his neck and spoke low, near his ear. "Settle, boy."

A calm came over Sebastian, and he answered, "Yes, Sir."

They stepped out of the elevator to the sights and sounds of the club, and Gideon breathed it all in, excited for the evening to come. He leaned over the bar, ordering a round of non-alcoholic drinks for them and walked towards the table he'd reserved, surprised to see Zavier with Braden and Finn with Zoe, both subs kneeling for their Doms.

His boy had surprised him after all. He hadn't expected his brothers and their subs to be there. He hadn't wanted to invite them if having family and close friends in the audience would make his boy nervous. The fact that Sebastian had reached out and invited them meant the world to him and made him even more confident that his boy was truly ready for the night ahead.

Finn and Zoe had been inseparable since he'd gone with Gideon to Sebastian's house months ago. If he was honest, he loved seeing his brilliant, bookish younger brother fall head over heels in love with a tattooed, voluptuous Betty Boop look-alike. Finn had admitted that he wanted to be trained as a Dom so he could give Zoe what she needed. He'd trained with Roarke and had taken to it like a duck to water, admitting that he was getting just as much out of their D/s relationship as she was. The two couldn't have been more different, and he knew that's exactly why it worked.

Glancing over at Zavier, he couldn't help but smile at the way he was sitting sideways, legs splayed wide so his boy could kneel between his thighs, fully surrounded and protected. He'd joked with him about their version of BDSM lite. They didn't enjoy the giving or receiving of anything too painful but loved sensory play; light impact play and bondage.

Both of his brothers did what worked for them, and he loved that he could share the life with them. They'd bonded more over the last several months, and he was immensely grateful for that, feeling as though he was getting his family back again after a long stretch of being absent even if he'd been right there all along.

He watched as Sebastian hesitated and looked to him for guidance. He tilted his head toward Braden, and his boy sat as close as he could get to his friend without touching Zavier. He settled into his own chair smiling at Zoe, whose eyes were closed as she leaned her head against Finn's crossed legs, his brother threading his fingers repeatedly through her hair.

They chatted for some time, enjoying the company, Gideon wondering when his boy would make his move. It was an hour into their evening when Sebastian asked to be excused to go to the restroom. The other subs asked the same of their Doms, and they walked toward the submissives' bathroom.

Several minutes later, they heard the telltale sound of the microphone turning on and the background music was lowered. He heard murmuring, a few gasps, and then everyone got quiet. He only turned towards the stage when he heard his boy's voice ring out loud and clear over the rapt audience.

"Master, for your birthday, and for so many other reasons, I wanted to give you the gift of my first public scene. If it pleases you, Sir, would you join me on the stage?"

He'd always hated being called Master G by those at the club. He'd never felt as if he'd earned the title, and it hadn't ever been something he'd had a desire to attain. But he'd secretly yearned for Sebastian to call him that. When he'd said it, Gideon's heart tripped, and he immediately stood, moving towards his boy as if pulled by a magnetic force.

Those who had drawn closer to the tables and chairs arranged around the stage parted to allow him through. His boy, looking both nervous and confident, a rather interesting mix, gave him a shy smile, and if Gideon hadn't already been in love with his submissive, the look he was giving his Dom would have done the trick.

When he got up on stage, all he could do was take in every inch of his beautiful boy. He wanted to gather him in, touch him in some way, but he knew he needed to take care of something even more important. He took the proffered mic from his boy's hand, affixed the mic to his ear, and clasping his boy's hand and raising it to his lips, he kissed it and looked into his boy's eyes, admitting, "So, you planned all of this out for me tonight, but what you didn't know is that I've known about it from the beginning."

He had to chuckle when his boy growled a bit and shot a glare at Khaleo whose eyes popped comically wide, hands lifted in an "it wasn't me" gesture. Sebastian huffed and turned his glare towards Gideon who laughed along with the crowd. "It's not Khaleo's fault. I overheard you that morning when you asked him to help you plan this. But I'm glad I did because I was able to make some plans of my own."

Khaleo stepped forward and handed him a box. "I'm lucky enough to have found my perfect match; someone who looks past my many flaws and loves me despite or even because of them. Someone who wants to live this lifestyle with me, who craves not just my love, but my ownership, my control, and my desire to protect and nurture their mind, body, and soul. With that in mind, I want to remove your temporary collar and replace it with a permanent one."

Gideon opened the box to reveal a solid, half-inch wide, matte, gunmetal gray, titanium collar. He'd vacillated about whether to go with one that could be hidden or one that fit more like a choker. In the end, as Sebastian had recently asked him to have a lot of the links in his other collar removed so that it was always visible, he'd gone with the choker style collar. It was simple, solid, masculine, and suited his boy perfectly. It had a recessed, sliding channel opening just wide enough to put it on and then slide it back in place to lock it on using a hex-screw locking closure with a matching hex-key he'd be able to hang from his military tag chain.

He lifted the collar from the box and tilted it toward Sebastian. Gideon knew the moment he saw the engraving. The irony not lost on his boy as a small, shy smile appeared when he read the engraving, "Forever Master's boy" on the inside of the collar. Their eyes met, and the happiness on his boy's face was radiant.

"Will you accept my permanent collar, boy?"

426

"Yes, Master."

Removing his old collar, Gideon used his key to lock Sebastian's new one in place and kissed his lips gently, once, twice, three times, before he pulled away. He stood back to admire it and took in the rest of his boy from head to toe. He'd left the jeans on but unbuttoned the top button. Gideon let that guide him as he trailed his finger from his boy's fly, just above the chastity belt, circling both nipples, pinching each one in turn, eliciting a gasp from Sebastian. Walking behind him, he leaned down, grabbed Sebastian's chin in one hand, snaking his other into his boy's pants, titillating the audience.

He tilted Sebastian's head back at an angle, exposing the long column of his throat to the audience and nipping, none too gently up the side, laving his tongue over each bite as he went, reveling in the gasp and moan that had the audience sitting on the edge of their seats, some of them adjusting their dicks in their pants.

After biting his earlobe, Gideon lowered his mic down, whispering only for his boy, "Check in, Bastian."

Sebastian did the same with his mic and responded, "Green, Master." That answer, murmured so sweetly for his ears only, had his dick pressing against the zipper of his pants.

"I love you, my beautiful boy."

"I love you too, Master."

They both raised their mics back in place, and he took a step back from Sebastian to pull the simple, pleather covered kneeling table in place. He'd wanted everyone in the audience to see his beautiful boy, and he'd wanted him at the perfect height for a flogging and a whipping. "Remove your pants and kneel on the bench, knees spread wide. I want everyone to see every beautiful inch of you."

His boy did as he was told without a hint of hesitation as the audience sat, utterly transfixed by his submissive. He knew the feeling. As Sebastian followed instructions, Gideon approached and moved his boy's ankles, shackling them to the bench to keep him in place.

Sebastian reached to take off his own mic, but Gideon stopped him. "Not a chance, boy. Keep it on. I want the audience to hear every single sigh, whimper, and moan." He turned to the audience and asked, "What do you think, do you want to hear him?"

Everyone in the place hooted, hollered, and a resounding yes clinched it.

Stepping back, he reached up, clasping one of the chains he'd hung from one of the exposed I-beams, he pulled, and with a clang, more of the length fell. His eyes were still on his boy, and while Sebastian jumped at the noise, he didn't turn. Good boy. Letting the chain swing beside Sebastian, he could see him tense up as it swung gently by his side, letting him know exactly what it was.

Gideon moved to the other side and pulled down the second length of chain and let it swing. He reached out to grab the first length that had slowed to a stop beside his boy. "Lift your right arm out to the side."

As Sebastian complied, Gideon wrapped the chain several times around his wrist, knowing the new sensation would pique his boy's interest. After he locked it, he wrapped Sebastian's hand around the chain. He did the same to Sebastian's other arm and the sight of both of his arms spread wide, open and vulnerable, did something to him. He heard the camera's telltale snick and glanced up to see a captivated Khaleo, camera held at the ready for another perfect shot.

Giving Khaleo some time to get some shots of just his boy, he walked to the other end of the stage to the rack containing various and sundry impact toys. He picked up a leather flogger for a nice warm-up. He wanted Sebastian's skin nice and warm before the real fun began.

He approached his sub. "Grip those chains, Bastian, and lean forward a bit. I want that ass exposed to me now."

"Yes, Sir," Sebastian said as he complied.

"Tell me your safewords, boy."

Sebastian paused and then breathed out audibly, thanks to the mic. "Red, yellow, and green, Master."

"Use them if you need them."

"Yes, Sir."

"Let's begin then."

He started off slowly, warming himself up and pinking up his boy's back, ass, and thighs. Soon, the slap of the leather falls on his boy's skin was a musical cadence in his ears. He set up a rhythm and didn't stop until he heard the telltale moan of his boy's arousal. Knowing it was time, he slowed to a stop, stepped over to the rack and hung the flogger on its hook, picking up the two whips he'd be using. He tucked one of them at the small of his back under his belt and kept the other in hand.

He moved toward the back of the stage, several paces back from his boy's beautifully reddened back, ass, and thighs, turned the vibrating plug on mid power and grinned at the gasp he heard. "Check in, boy."

"Green, Master," his boy choked out.

He waited several long, drawn-out moments before he lifted the lid on the small electrical box and flipped the switch.

Chapter 42

SEBASTIAN

Sebastian, lulled into a floating calm after having been flogged until he was nearly in subspace, gasped when the butt plug Master had inserted earlier—which he'd nearly forgotten in his blissed-out state—began to vibrate. He was so surprised he nearly missed it when he was asked to check in, but managed to do so before losing himself again.

The last time he'd worn a similar plug and cage, he'd somehow managed to come without an erection. Wondering what Master had in mind, he was completely distracted from everything going on around him. The tight stretching in his arms and shoulders combined with the warm, dull ache of the entire back side of his body, even the audience members and Khaleo's camera so front and center in his mind only short moments ago, seemed to disappear as his mind fixated on Master's endgame. And he always had an endgame.

With his mind unfocused on his surroundings, he barely registered the hiss coming from overhead, but when warm water showered down on him from above, his body reacted like it had been electrocuted, and he let out a startled gasp followed by a desperate moan as he realized Master was recreating the shower scene he'd never been able to get out of his head.

He didn't even know he'd begun to mumble, "Oh god, oh god, oh god, oh god," before his whole body started to shake and his words cut off as his teeth started to chatter, the reactions of his body out of his control.

He distantly realized Gideon would see his body's response and worry. "Green, green, green, Master. Please, please, more, Sir."

"That's my good boy. You know what I like to hear."

The first dull thud of the thick rubber whip was almost a relief. Master was easing him into it and with his whole body reacting in ways he could hardly fathom, he was grateful. The thuds got harder and faster and centered around his upper thighs and back, making him realize the next whip would be focused purely on his ass and the thought of that made his body quake.

He knew he was making noise, but he was only half aware of the whimpers, gasps, groans, and moans. And the begging. He was pretty sure he was begging. He was being battered and overcome by all the different sensations; the chains around his wrists, gripped in his hands, the shackles keeping him in place, his shoulder muscles being stretched by the weight of his body leaning forward, the heat remaining from his flogging, the thud from the rubber whip now feeling more like a sting as it moved faster on his over sensitized skin, and the water, oh god, the water was making his nerve endings sing. And finally, there was a brief pause, followed by a resounding sting of the paracord whip he knew Master was now wielding over the swell of his ass cheek.

That whip fell again and again and again, making him cry out over and over and over. He was so close to losing his control. So close, but he knew he couldn't disappoint himself by coming without permission. He was floating and control felt like it was slipping further and further from his grasp. He was lost in a maelstrom of emotions and sensations, and he realized he was close to not being able to take anymore.

And then, everything stopped.

The water had been turned off, the whipping had ended. Water sluiced down his naked body, off the chains, and from the showerheads as well, and fell with a drip, drip, drip on the floor below. Eyes closed, he was only aware of sensations and sounds. He heard the thunk, thunk, thunk of Gideon's heavy boots on the wet surface of the stage and waited.

His heart was beating a mile a minute and breaths panted out of him as if he'd run a mile. The tether holding him to Earth nearing its breaking point. The anticipation was driving him wild. And though he knew the scene was nearly finished and the water was a huge component of their session, he still wasn't convinced that was Master's endgame. He couldn't imagine he'd want his boy to come in public, hell, he'd been shocked when he'd asked him to strip. But stranger things had happened.

His chastity device left nothing to the imagination. It sat flush against his hips, and the cage was the most revealing of the three. The audience was seeing every bit of his Master's boy and though it wasn't something he'd normally do, something about everything they'd done that night felt right. He no longer felt ashamed about his appearance and knew Master was so proud to call him his.

He felt a hand at his wrist and then one chain was gone, the ache in his shoulder fierce, but not too painful, when his arm was finally down by his side. The second chain was gone, moments later, and that same fierce ache made itself known on the other side. He felt his ankle shackles being released, and he was eased back on his heels, finally relaxing all his muscles at once, unable to move any further, feeling boneless, and weightless.

And then Master was there, pulling Sebastian's back flush against his solid, warm, chest, murmuring, "Lean all your weight on me. That's it. You're such a good boy."

He continued to murmur, though the mic projected everything to the crowd he knew was still watching in complete and utter silence. His eyes remained closed as the feeling of floating consumed him, finally in Master's arms. He thought for a moment it was over, and then the vibrator in his ass was set to stun and he cried out, throwing his head back against Gideon's shoulder, bringing an aching arm up to grip the back of Master's neck and sliding his fingers up into his hair, needing to find purchase.

Master reached up and gripped his throat tightly prompting Sebastian to suck in a breath and hold it, his control nearly gone. His hips started undulating, trying to find friction, his cock doing its best and failing to get hard. And then it didn't matter, because Master ordered, "Come for me, boy." And he did. He squeezed his eyes tightly shut and his hips moved in tandem with the volleys of cum shooting from his limp, caged, cock. It felt like it would never end, and as the ribbons of his spunk continued to erupt out of his slit, the audience gasped and murmured as he cried out and Master continued to encourage him through to the end.

When it was all over, his arm fell loosely to his side and Master's grip on his throat eased, allowing him to exhale. His breathing began to slow, and he heard a murmured thank you, which prompted him to open his eyes to see Khaleo handing off a blanket to his Master. Still unable to move, he stayed where he was, sitting back on his heels, knees spread wide, in full view of everyone still watching every move they made. He was too blissed out to care and closed his eyes again as he felt the blanket being wrapped tightly around him.

The ear mic he'd forgotten he was wearing was removed from his ear and so was Gideon's, the soft words of praise coming from Master's lips were only for his ears. He lost track of anything and everything that wasn't that voice and the feeling of his Master's arms around him. When Gideon lifted him up, he opened his eyes again and realized everyone was standing, watching them still.

Gideon held him tight against his chest and walked down the steps off the stage, carrying him through the throng of the crowd which parted for them in respect and some of what Sebastian realized was reverence. He'd known of the rule about not clapping or making noise at the end of public scenes in order to help keep the sub in subspace, but he had to close his eyes at the intensity of the moment. Walking through the crowd, being so close to those that had watched every last intimate moment of their scene play out was too much. He tucked his head under Master's chin and got a kiss in return.

Gideon walked him directly to the elevator, the doors closing, affording them the privacy they needed. Master continued to murmur to him, but he was gone, no longer able to focus, everything around him seemed hazy, and he was floating along in bliss.

Next thing he knew, he was being placed gently on their bed and Master made to walk away, but he quickly clasped his hand and whispered, "Please, don't leave."

"Baby, I was just going to get us a towel."

"Mm mmm. Please, Master. Make love to me. I need you."

A deep rumble came from Master's chest. "I could never turn down a request like that, boy."

Sebastian watched as he made quick work of toeing his boots off and dragging his soaked tactical pants down his legs and off, onto the floor. And then he was quickly removing Sebastian's chastity device and they were skin to skin, each moaning their pleasure at the contact. Sebastian's recovery time was ridiculously fast, as his cock became hard the second he felt Master's hips and hard cock rubbing against him.

He heard the snick of the lube bottle and then before he knew what was happening, the butt plug was out, and Gideon was deep within his body, and they were moving as one, all lips and teeth and hands. Desperation drove them both. Their coupling frantic, their releases coming fast, and all-consuming.

He'd thought they'd drift to sleep afterwards, but Master had other ideas. He was up and starting a bath in moments. As they waited for the enormous tub to fill, Gideon came back and had him turn over. He rubbed his shoulders down while they waited and then carried him to the tub, put him in the steaming water, and turned on the jets, leaving a bottle of water beside him and ordering him to drink up.

Sebastian soaked for twenty minutes and just as he was about to call for Gideon, he came into the bathroom, helped him out of the tub, and dried him off. He picked him up, carried him to the bed, and had him lie down again then proceeded to rub him down from head to toe, rubbing arnica cream where it was needed. He felt completely relaxed, blissed out, and strangely ravenous. He figured he could just drift off and sleep and he'd eat in the morning, but in walked Gideon, a cheese board to rival all cheese boards in his hands.

There was a variety of cheeses, nuts, cured meats, fruit, and crackers. They ate every last morsel. When Gideon had cleared it all away, they both lay down in each other's arms, talking late into the night. Hours later, when they both got tired and words no longer sufficed, they made love once more, and finally, fully sated, they fell asleep in each other's arms, more content than either of them could ever remember.

Epilogue

SEBASTIAN

Sebastian walked with Lola to Meta Ink, frustrated that he had to work on the day of his twenty-eighth birthday when Gideon had planned their entire day. Phuong (Phoenix) Nguyen, his piercer, scheduler, and all around front desk clerk, had scheduled him for one tattoo at 9 a.m. Instead of trying to reschedule at the last minute, he'd promised Gideon he'd be done in an hour, scheduling a second session if it looked like it was going to take longer.

Phoenix had felt awful when she'd realized what she'd done, nearly crying when she offered to reschedule for him. He'd felt so bad that she'd gotten so upset, he'd just agreed to the hour-long appointment. She'd never made a mistake like that before, and he figured it wasn't that big of a deal. She was so great, he wasn't going to quibble about a tiny scheduling mistake.

Phoenix's girlfriend, Posey Hughes, was one of his three tattoo artists. Luca Delaney and Gunner Torres rounded out his team. They'd become a close knit little family unit, and Sebastian couldn't be happier with his crew at the studio. It had been an amazing four months since the day he'd opened his place. He'd vacillated on the name, but because his own specialty was transforming people's scars into beautiful works of art, he'd finally settled on Metamorphosis Ink.

The studio was thriving, his previous as well as his backlog of customers followed him, and the same could be said about his other artists, so they'd had a solid starting point. On the morning of his birthday, his whole team was there. Strange, that. He didn't think Luca had been scheduled. They were busy setting up their stations though, so he figured there had been some last-minute changes. Phoenix turned on the sound system and opened the laptop, he assumed, to make her morning social media posts for the studio.

He'd shown up with only fifteen minutes to spare so he told everyone good morning, received a resounding happy birthday greeting, and then watched, bemused, as they all went about their business. Curious. He didn't have enough time to think on it though, so he went upstairs to what was now the loft, overlooking the studio below, and got himself ready for his new client. Lola, needing to say hello to everyone and nab a couple puppy treats from the suckers down below, meandered on up the stairs a couple minutes later, collapsed in a heap on her bed, and began gnawing on her rawhide bone. Spoiled rotten, that one, but worth her weight in gold.

He distracted himself with setting up his own station then washed his hands at his sink, as ready as he could be without knowing what he'd be doing for his new client. He was about to go downstairs to greet his client but apparently, they were early, and he'd missed the bell ringing when the front door opened because he could hear footsteps on the stairs. Strangely enough, instead of playing the role of the laziest dog on the planet, as per usual, Lola was up, her ears perked and tail wagging, approaching the stairs. Weird behavior for his girl.

What the hell was going on today?

He made a kissy noise and admonished her, "Lola, move back and give them some room, girl."

Completely ignoring him, she started hopping around, her whole backside moving in her excitement. Confused, he approached and was shocked when Gideon walked up the stairs, a grin on his face, his favorite coffee in a drink carrier and pastries in the fancy box Braden used at Sugar n' Spice. No wonder he'd left twenty minutes earlier than he and Lola had left. Things just got stranger and stranger.

Handing over his cup of coffee, Gideon smiled. "Hey, baby. I wanted you to have your favorite on your birthday."

He kissed and hugged him, and replied, "Thank you, Sir. You've probably got another five minutes before my client shows up, though."

"Nah, I'm your next client."

"What? But…"

Gideon smirked. "Your appointment is with M. G."

Sebastian snorted then folded his arms as a herd of buffalo made their way up the stairs. Phoenix, the last of them, holding a bag that she set down on the counter by the sink, pulled out festive paper plates and napkins. They crowded around him singing happy birthday and hugging him. Gideon set down the box and Sebastian watched as his team nearly tore the thing open to get to Braden's pastries.

They were devoured within minutes and his crew went back down the steps, presumably to get to work. Gideon approached him with a sheaf of papers, pulling the last one down, to reveal signature and date lines. "Can you sign this doc so I can get it to my dad? He's going to see our financial advisors today and I need your signature to add you to an account."

Sebastian scrawled his name and the date across the lines on the page then looked at his Master giving him a bewildered smile. "You know, you didn't have to make a fake appointment to come in and visit me at work."

"It's not fake. You're giving me my first tattoo today. I know what I want and everything."

"What? You don't have to do that, Sir. It doesn't bother me that you don't have tattoos." And it didn't. His Master didn't have any ink, and he'd assumed tattoos just weren't for him. Strangely enough, they'd never talked about it. Tattoos weren't for everyone, and he had to admit, he loved Master's un-inked, beautiful, tanned skin. Obviously, he'd thought about what he'd do if he'd ever be given the chance—he was a tattoo artist after all—but, it wasn't something he'd bring up. If Master wanted it, he'd ask, and it had been months since it had even crossed his mind.

Gideon smiled indulgently at him. "Do I make it a habit of doing things I don't want to do?"

"Um, no."

"I've wanted your ink on my body pretty much since the day I found you in your old studio, beat to shit from your tumble down the stairs. This is just going to be my first and a small one at that. I'll want more in the future that you can draw for me."

A grin spread slowly across his face as he looked at Gideon. "Yeah?"

"Yeah. My skin is your canvas. It's one thing I'll allow you to take control of after my first one. Here." He pulled something out of his pocket and Sebastian gaped at him when he saw what he was holding.

"But…"

"That's what I want."

"Sir, that's a doodle."

"It's a good doodle."

"But…"

"I want it on my chest, over my heart."

Sebastian's jaw dropped then he started laughing, tossed the scrap of paper aside, and shoved at Gideon's chest, letting out an indelicate snort. "Yeah right. Come on. What do you really want?"

Gideon grew serious, picked up the paper and handed it back to him. His voice was a little growly and brooked no argument when he said, "I want this. Over my heart."

"Sir, I could do something so much better than this. I was just fooling around. I thought I threw it away."

"You did. I took it out of the trash. You were drawing it for me."

"No, I…" Sebastian looked back down at the paper then realized he was right and his eyes flicked back up to Gideon. "Maybe I did it with you in mind. But, will you give me some time to make it better? I can make it fancier. Bigger. Something."

"Fancy? What would I want with fancy? I wear long-sleeved t-shirts and tactical pants ninety-five percent of the time, regardless of where I'm going."

"Yeah, but…"

"Do what you want to it while you're inking it on my skin, but don't embellish it much. I want a simple visual reminder of us inked onto my skin by your hand. My darkness, your light. I can't think of anything better than my ropes tying us irrevocably together. Can you?"

Goddamn he loved his man. "No, Master, I can't."

"Good boy. Let's get started. I've got a full day planned for us."

"Yes, Sir."

Sebastian glanced down at the simple, double infinity design he'd drawn of light and dark ropes entwined on the back of a receipt, of all things. Just like his Master, he'd liked the symbolism of forever being tied to Gideon with his ropes.

He'd obviously been thinking about Master at the time, but he'd just been fooling around with an idea he thought he might want to add to his own skin. The thought of putting it on Master's skin had never crossed his mind. And thinking about it then had his palms sweating with nervous anticipation. He'd drawn it in pencil, but if he was going to do it, and it looked like he was, he was going to do it in color.

They always used jute rope for bondage, and Gideon had both light and dark colors he used interchangeably. The pictures they'd had Khaleo take when they'd finally done a private rigging session again, came to mind. They'd mostly had prints made in black and white, but some of them were in color, and he recalled how the light had shown on the rope itself—the beautiful golden brown and mahogany brown colors highlighted in contrast to his skin—some of the fibers showing in what Master had explained was a lay of medium twist, naturally colored jute rope, appearing almost silky in texture.

He watched as Gideon removed his shirt and sat down on the tattoo bed, moving his military tags to hang against his back. He pulled out his drawing pad and began to draw a bit more of a stylized double infinity symbol. He made a frustrated noise at not having rope to look at. Pulling out his phone he went to look for the images he knew were saved on his phone, when two small coils of light and dark ropes were dropped onto his pad. A grin split his face. Damn, his Master knew him so well.

He got up from his stool and straddled Gideon's lap on the tattoo bed and kissed his gorgeous face, delving in to sip from his lips. Gideon groaned and grabbed his ass, squeezing and massaging the round globes. Sebastian moaned and Gideon growled low, "Boy, you better not offer these services to your other clients."

"Only you, Master."

Another growl. "I want you on this chair. Why haven't we made that happen yet?"

Sebastian sat back, a bit dazed, and blinked at Gideon. "On the tattoo bed?"

Gideon smirked and nodded. "Oh yeah. We're gonna make that happen, boy. One of these days."

Flushed and desperate for "one of these days" to be right then, Sebastian leaned in to devour Master's lips once more, receiving another groan, a muttered curse as he sucked on Master's neck, and a reprimanding slap to his ass that pulled him somewhat out of his hyper aroused daze. And he was completely pulled from it when Gunner chuckled and yelled up, "Keep it PG up there, guys!"

He slapped a hand over his mouth, and Master chuckled, squeezing his ass again while Sebastian covered his face with his hands and leaned his forehead on Gideon's chest, embarrassed heat flooding his cheeks, he whispered, "Oh my god, oh my god, oh my god."

Gideon clasped his shoulders, still chuckling and moved him back. "Maybe we should get started and put this on the backburner."

"Fuck. Yeah, probably a good idea, Jesus." He snorted at the absurdity of it and used Gideon's shoulders to steady himself as he climbed off his lap, snickering when they both had to adjust themselves in their pants.

He set the ropes down on his tray in the light from the windows and proceeded to finish the drawing and the transfer after they'd conferred on its location. The tattoo took an hour and a half, and though it was small, Sebastian put everything he had into it, wanting to do his best work. He thought it was coming along nicely and knew that he'd eventually find a spot to put the same tattoo on himself.

He'd always been confident in his work, even so, he worried the whole time whether Gideon would like it. But, when his Master looked in the mirror, the happy grin he gave him was answer enough. They kissed for several minutes then Sebastian finished him up, and they were on their way, Sebastian's cheeks burning when he got knowing smirks from his team.

They left, Sebastian not knowing what they were doing. Gideon had asked what he'd like to do when he'd been planning the day, and all Sebastian had given him was that he didn't care as long as they were together. Sebastian didn't know what he'd expected, but when they pulled into The Castro Theater's parking lot, surprisingly empty even though it *was* just shy of 11 a.m. on a Tuesday, he was strangely excited.

They'd never been to the movie theater together before. Sebastian was a huge movie fan, and he'd basically forced Gideon into being one as well, but it was always movies at home on their giant plush sectional sofa, Sebastian with his head in Gideon's lap and Lola keeping his feet warm.

They got out of the car, Lola right there with them, and rounded the building to the entrance where Sebastian turned giddy to see a classic horror double feature starting in ten minutes. He bounced on the balls of his feet, and Gideon grinned, wrapped his arm around Sebastian's shoulders, and kissed his forehead, pulling his wallet out of his pocket to pay for their tickets. They walked to the concession stand and dropped a shit ton of money on a huge tub of popcorn, three types of candy, and a gigantic Coke Slurpee. He was ready for a carb coma and scary-as-shit movies.

They spent the next four hours watching *Psycho* and *Silence of the Lambs,* and he couldn't remember ever having had a better time at a movie theater.

When they walked out of the building, the sun was shining and it had warmed up a bit, warmer than he'd expect for the beginning of November. They hopped back in the car, and Gideon told him to change into his walking shoes.

Ever since they'd started walking together when he'd been recovering from his surgery, they'd kept up the habit to spend some time together and give Lola some exercise. From there, they'd started taking hikes as well. They were coming up on Mom and Dad's house, and he turned in his seat in confusion. "Aren't we going to see them at dinner?"

"Yeah, but my dad needs the paperwork you signed, and I figured we could pick up Buckley and take him with us."

He got out of the car when they pulled in the driveway and whistled, opening up the passenger door. Buckley came racing around the back of the house and hopped in like he'd been expecting them. Gideon walked up to the side door of the house just as Duncan came out to wave at them. He handed over the paperwork and walked back to the car. Sebastian laughed as the two dogs wrestled around in the back like they hadn't seen each other in years rather than the previous weekend.

They spent several hours hiking around Lands End, the dogs having a blast together, Sebastian having a wonderful day and feeling better now that they'd hiked off some of the carb coma he'd been in after the double feature.

It was nearly time for dinner, and from the direction they were heading, it looked like they were going directly to Braden and Zavier's place. He turned in his seat and saw what he was looking for. "Glad you brought us a change of clothes, I'm kinda sweaty."

"I figured we would be. We can take a quick shower, and then you'll have more time with Bray."

He smiled at Gideon and clasped his hand, bringing it up to kiss it. "Thank you for such a wonderful birthday. I love you, Sir."

Gideon pulled his hand towards him and kissed his in return. "Love you too, baby."

They were buzzed up to Braden and Zavier's loft and chatted for a few minutes before they excused themselves to make use of the guest bathroom to get ready. They took a shower together, and as much as he'd have liked to climb Gideon like a tree and be fucked silly against the shower wall before dinner, he knew they'd have to wait.

When they got back downstairs, Maya, Braden's best friend, business partner, *and* his surrogate, was there looking enormously pregnant and happy, surrounded by all three big dogs. She grinned up at them from her spot on the couch, Lola's head in what was left of her lap, and waved. "Hi, guys. I'd get up, but I have Lola and a baby making me lazy. Happy Birthday, Sebastian!"

He leaned down and gave her a hug while thanking her. They sat with her for a few and chatted. Braden brought them both a beer, and the others started to trickle in: Nana with Ira; Finn with Zoe, a shiny new permanent collar around her neck; Rowan and Marcus, the man she'd been dating for the last six months; Aiden, Gideon's youngest brother that he'd only met one other time but had hit it off with; and Gideon's parents, Siobhan and Duncan, who'd both insisted he call them Mom and Dad since that's what Braden called them. He didn't understand the logic, but he didn't argue. Calling them Mom and Dad meant so much more to him than doing the same for his own parents ever had.

Sebastian, Braden, and Zoe all gathered in the kitchen mixing drinks and serving everyone. He'd thought at first that being submissive in front of Gideon's family would be awkward, he'd even thought about repressing that part of himself around them, but when he'd talked about it with his Master, Gideon had said he wanted Sebastian to feel comfortable around his family to be himself and he wasn't going to be strict about his behavior in that setting.

Sebastian had listened, but instead of easing back from submitting to Gideon around his family, he'd decided if Master wanted him to feel comfortable and be himself, that was exactly what he was going to do. Besides, they knew all about the club and who Gideon really was, so he'd just thrown caution to the wind and done what felt right. After the initial shock from everyone when he'd kneeled at Gideon's feet in the family room of his parents' house during one of their visits, it hadn't been a thing.

He always served Master in some capacity around his family. Sometimes he kneeled or served him food and drinks, but other times, like when they were eating meals, he'd sit at the table with the others. They always ate together, and Master would order him to sit at the table with him just as often as he'd have him kneel at his feet to wait for Master to feed him.

While Gideon wanted them to be true partners, it was in their contract that Sebastian would defer to him in all things. As that was exactly what Sebastian wanted as well, things seemed to come together on their own. It had taken some adjustment, but they'd made their own rules up as they went, and if and when he needed permission for something, he'd cut his eyes to Master and wait for his subtle nod or shake of his head.

The family got used to their dynamic fairly quickly, their easy acceptance of their unique relationship made him love them more. He realized as they made their way up the steps to Braden and Zavier's rooftop oasis that his whole life had led him here, to this spot, and because of that, he wouldn't change a thing. A grin spread across his cheeks as he watched all three dogs running off towards the grassy area that always had dog toys waiting for them. The table setup was festive and the Happy Birthday streamers and banners made him smile.

He was given the place of honor at the head of the table, and though he preferred not to be the center of attention, it was no longer something that would trigger panic. Gideon held out his chair and he sat, watching while Gideon sat beside him. It was a beautiful night, and Braden had all the twinkle lights lit and the heaters on, music softly playing in the background. It was one of his favorite places to visit.

The more time Sebastian spent there, the more he wanted something similar for their own home though far less elaborate. Braden and Zavier entertained much more often than they did. Zavier's team at Custos Securities was very close knit, and it seemed there was always something going on there, be it a small gathering of close friends or a large one with everyone and their dogs too. Literally. They were always invited but begged off more often than not. Neither of them was particularly social, and they stuck to their inner circles for the most part, preferring to spend time alone together more than anything.

People had apparently brought gifts early because there was a whole table set up with them, even though he'd asked Braden to tell everyone not to. The one catching his eye at that moment was a ridiculously enormous one sitting by his side between him and Braden. Big enough to hold a Great Dane, the thing was wrapped in beautiful paper with an enormous bow on top. Gideon had seen him looking at it several times, and his mischievous grin made him realize this birthday was going to be unlike any he'd ever had. Hell, it already was, and it had barely begun.

Everyone sat and chatted, enjoying their drinks and the company. It wasn't long before the caterers began to serve hors d'oeuvres. People laughed and teased each other as they ate. They talked over each other, broke off into separate conversations, and then rejoined others, enjoying the meal together. The first time he'd had dinner with the family, it had been a shock to him. He'd never had that experience, and he remembered telling Gideon and being kissed and cuddled in bed later that night, and he promised they'd do it more often if it made him that happy.

And they had.

GIDEON

He'd done his best to give Sebastian a birthday to remember. He hoped he'd been successful. From the look on his face, he had been. His cheeks had to be hurting from the perma-smile he'd had all day. As the whole family ate dinner, he sat back and observed everyone, but especially his boy who was involved in many of the conversations. He did that a lot; watch his boy interacting with his new family. It was a sight to see.

His sister would pull him aside to chat with him, his brothers would rib him and help him gang up on Gideon, his parents would hug him and chat him up about his business, his mom, already having gotten a tattoo from his boy over her own mastectomy scars, always showered him with attention. Nana would love on him like she'd been his grandmother all along, and Zoe was constantly trying to feed him and take care of him, probably still a reaction from taking care of him when he was at his most vulnerable. It never seemed to bother Sebastian as he'd grown close to her as a result of his earlier trauma and having her be the first person he reached out to.

Braden and Sebastian had a special bond that others outside of the family might think was strange, but it worked for them. They were very demonstrative with each other, Zavier and Gideon joked about them being side boyfriends when they'd huddle together on the couch and talk animatedly about something, occasionally holding hands and even cuddling when they'd had movie nights and he'd gone out with Zavier to grab dinner.

They did the same with Zoe when she was with them. Zavier had likened them to a little sub club, and Gideon had just chuckled at that, not refuting it in the least. His boy needed friends, close friends, as they'd been absent from his life up until he'd met them both, and he'd never in a million years interfere with their dynamic. Their friendship was a pure thing, you could see it in the way they laughed with each other, the way they told each other everything, and the way they protected each other.

All he wanted to do as Sebastian's Master was cultivate those sorts of relationships for his boy. There wasn't a single second he'd ever thought his sub had any romantic feelings for his friends. He was the only one for Sebastian, and Sebastian was the only one for him. Those friendships were a huge part of Sebastian's newfound confidence, and he wouldn't stand in the way of that for any reason.

He'd watched in awe as his boy—his confidence still a new and evolving thing—had taken on somewhat of a leadership role for the submissives at Catharsis, or perhaps more accurately, he'd kind of fallen into it by circumstance.

He thought it had started before "The Water Scene" as the members had dubbed it, but afterwards, it had been cemented in people's minds that not only should he be respected by the members of the club for being his submissive, but also because he'd earned that respect with his striking performance, proving his utter devotion to his Master.

Since the scene, submissives would approach Sebastian for advice. If he could help, he would, but if he couldn't, he'd often speak with his Master about it, keeping each sub's confidence but asking him for guidance. Gideon had realized then that the discussions he'd had a while back with Dr. Price, Sebastian's psychologist, about the doctor being a resource for subs who needed more help than a Dom or a fellow sub could give them was something he needed to put in place sooner rather than later.

They'd only recently decided on how to go about it, and only because Gideon remembered the doctor's Halloween costume of the previous year, when he'd dressed as a priest. That had been the beginning of The Confessional, a room they'd designated as support for the submissives. Anonymous sessions could be set up, or there was a scheduled one-hour block set aside for drop-ins once a week. The room had been set up so that it truly was a closed off confessional where submissives could discuss issues they were having anonymously. So far it had been successful with some of the stress of being the go-to submissive being taken off of Sebastian's shoulders.

Not having to provide so much guidance to his peers, Sebastian had been happy to have more time at the club with Gideon, playing, or simply spending time with their friends. Gideon wasn't one for performing on stage and frankly, neither was Sebastian. If he was needed for a demo in a training session, he'd always happily oblige, using Sebastian as his submissive. And when Sebastian wanted to scene in the voyeur rooms, it was never a hardship. But for the most part, he let others take the stage.

A boisterous laugh from Aiden jolted him out of his reverie, and he glanced around at everyone finishing up their meals. As he caught his boy surreptitiously looking at the big box beside him again, he chuckled, leaned forward, clasped his small hand in his, and kissed it. The fact that a blush bloomed on his cheeks whenever Gideon did something unexpected like that, always made him want to find other ways to bring that sweet rosy color to his cheeks and other parts of his body.

There was always that twinkle in Sebastian's eyes when he did something like that, simple joy at being loved so thoroughly that his Master had a hard time keeping his hands off him. It was hard to resist that twinkle, so he didn't try, preferring to shower his submissive with enough love and affection to make up for his earlier years without. He tugged on Sebastian's hand, drawing him near.

He couldn't help but breathe in his boy's sweet scent, Gideon's one true aphrodisiac. He whispered in his ear, "Are you having a good time, boy?"

"Yes, Master." His boy's answering whisper was breathy and sent a thrill of desire straight to his dick.

He nuzzled his neck, kissed just under Sebastian's ear, and asked, "Are you curious to know what's in that box?"

Another shaky whisper, "Yes, Sir."

A little louder so others could hear him, he asked, "How about we open some gifts before dessert?"

Braden liked that idea and clapped his hands for everyone to hear. "Gift time, everyone! Head on over to the dessert and coffee bar we set up. Grab whatever you want and bring it back to the table then grab your gifts for Sebastian and we can take turns. Per the birthday boy's request, I baked several desserts that he loves in lieu of a cake. We'll eat while he opens everything."

Everyone seemed to love that idea, scooting back from the table which had been fully cleared by the wait staff, along with any remnants of the catered dinner. When everyone was back in their seats, Gideon clinked his spoon against the side of his coffee mug to get everyone's attention. "Thank you, everyone, for coming to help make Sebastian's birthday a special day." He turned towards his boy and smiled. "Happy Birthday. I love you, baby."

Sebastian grinned and replied, "I love you too, Sir."

They began going around the table giving Sebastian his gifts, and each and every one of the gift givers shared with him what he meant to them. There were more than a few tears, and the love he had for his family in that moment was overwhelming. His boy ended up with a veritable treasure trove of toys and treats for Lola, which Gideon knew made him so happy because, obviously, everyone knew he loved to spoil her rotten.

He got a magazine subscription for a couple tattoo magazines and unbeknownst to Gideon, Braden had worked with MetalSmiths, Inc., the company that had created the sign for Catharsis, the sign for Meta Ink, and his boy's permanent collar and chastity device, to commission a metal sign in old sailor style tattoo font.

Gideon smiled at Braden in surprise, and his brother's husband blushed at him before glancing at his friend and explaining, "I thought you might like it. Kinda has a double meaning." He cleared his throat, embarrassed obviously, and continued, "Gideon is your Master, and you've mastered your craft of tattooing, so..."

Gideon loved that Sebastian had a friend who knew him so well, and he could tell it was Sebastian's favorite gift of the night when he grinned and touched the sign in awe, half stood, and reached to hug Braden. "It's perfect. I love it. Thank you."

When his boy addressed everyone, he fell even deeper in love with him which he hadn't thought was possible. "Everyone, truly, thank you for this night. I can hardly express what it means to me, but I'll try." He smiled and looked at Gideon for support. Gideon clasped his hand and held it as Sebastian continued. "This is the first birthday party I've ever had, and the first birthday gifts I've received since I was five. I want you to know that this day, this night, means everything to me. The gifts, they're absolutely lovely, but the fact that you all came tonight to celebrate with me and took the time to tell me how much I mean to you is more than I could dream of in a lifetime. I love you all so much."

His boy got up and hugged each and every one of his guests, several of which were crying. Braden, wanting to avoid any awkward silences, quipped, "Well, now we're gonna have to top this every year."

Everyone laughed and continued to enjoy their desserts. His boy sat, happiness radiating from him as he smiled at him. And then, like he just couldn't help it, he glanced beside himself, and Gideon could see Sebastian's excitement at finally getting to the end of all the other gifts. When his boy looked at him again and bit his lip, obvious yearning in his eyes, Gideon couldn't make him wait another minute.

"Go ahead and open it."

He bounced in his chair and asked, "Yeah?"

Gideon chuckled, "Go on."

"Yes, Sir."

He practically dove for the box, scooting his chair back he went to try to rip open the packaging but couldn't find a paper seam and then realized the huge top of the box was removable. He stood to pull it up, tossed the lid to the side, looked into the box, and then looked back at him. There was lots of blue tissue paper in the box and another big box nestled inside, but an envelope was on top. He opened the envelope and saw two tickets for London.

Sebastian turned to him confused and excited both. "We're going to London?"

"Do the dates look familiar? Think about it."

Sebastian stared at the tickets in obvious confusion. Gideon watched as a grin slowly spread across his face. "Oh my god! The London Tattoo Convention!"

Gideon nodded and laughed as his boy launched himself into his arms. Kissing his face and repeating an "Oh my god" mantra. He popped him on the ass and said, "There's more, keep opening."

Gideon looked around the table, everyone was smiling and laughing at his boy's excitement. The next box was opened and another box and envelope was revealed, and then three more. Gideon had gotten them tickets to every major tattoo convention in the world, and his boy was beside himself.

"I'm not sure what the rules are for being a featured artist at one of these things. I figured we'd figure it out together. But I think you should apply to each one and see what you hear back."

Surprise at the suggestion made its way across his boy's face. He could see the argument and put a stop to it immediately. "Don't argue with me. You've got a huge following, and you're booked out for months in advance. You're in demand and should be able to showcase at these events."

Sebastian looked at the five sets of tickets and took a deep breath, nodding. "Yes, Sir."

"Now, open up your last gift."

Sebastian looked back at the other box, nestled on the blue tissue paper and moved to pull off the lid. Gideon moved his chair back and took a knee, and when Sebastian gasped at the small, ornate wooden jewelry box inside, nestled in red tissue paper, he grabbed it and turned with it towards Gideon, eyes going wide when he saw him on his knee, a hand flying to his mouth after letting out one more shocked, "Oh my god!"

Before Gideon could do anything, his boy was on his knees in front of him, his discomfort at being above his Master an automatic reflex. As his beautiful boy looked up into his eyes, his tears slipped down his cheeks. Gideon reached to wipe them away.

"Sebastian, thinking back on it, I can pinpoint the exact second that I fell in love with you. It was the moment you woke up in my arms for the first time and smacked me in the face when you thought I was Zavier."

Sebastian gasped and started laughing, covering his mouth with his hand, more tears escaping his eyes as everyone else laughed as well. Gideon smiled and continued, "I thought to myself a boy that could stand up to a Dom like that because he was so distraught over possibly hurting his new friend was someone I couldn't ignore and shouldn't let go. I knew in that moment I had to get you in a contract, but I also knew that would never be enough."

He took a deep breath, Sebastian rubbed his hand along Gideon's knee, offering him strength when he sensed he needed it to keep going. "I was stupid, and I started our contract with the stipulation that it could never be more than a simple Dom/sub contract, knowing that ending it would gut me. I didn't think I was worthy of a man like you, a sweet, beautiful submissive who had more goodness in him than I even knew."

He leaned forward and kissed his boy, reassuring him that he was okay. "From the beginning, we fit together like two pieces of a unique puzzle, one that wouldn't ever be whole until the other of us filled the gap. But I was scared, and I ended it because I thought a man like you deserved better than a man like me."

He made eye contact with Zavier and nodded his way, Sebastian looked over his shoulder, following his gaze. "The night I ended our contract, Zavier said that I was right, I'd never be good enough for you, but that I'd need to bust my ass every day for the rest of my life to ensure that I deserved you. He was right."

He wiped away Sebastian's fresh tears and continued, "So this is me, vowing to you that I'm going to bust my ass, every single day for the rest of my life to ensure that I deserve you, to ensure that I cherish you, and to ensure that I'm worthy of the titles Master and Husband. Will you marry me, Sebastian Phillips, and allow me to prove it to you?"

Sebastian was nodding and crying and throwing himself in his arms before Gideon could even pull the box out of his boy's hands to slide the ring on his finger. A litany of yesses falling from Sebastian's lips. His boy was shaking in his arms, overcome. Gideon just held him, whispering that he loved him and wanted the chance to love him forever.

"You're so beautiful. So perfect for me. You're flawless in your service, and I will work so hard to honor your submission and love forever, to earn the collar you wear, and the ring I put on your finger, but, boy? You need to let me go so I can do that."

His last comment had a watery laugh escaping from his boy, and he finally pulled back and handed over the box. Gideon pulled out the ring from Metal-Smiths that matched his collar and slid it on the ring finger of his shaking hand. Once he did, Sebastian attacked him with kisses, and the table erupted with cheers, whistles, and congratulations, all the while, Sebastian kissed and hugged him, refusing to let go, which was just fine for Gideon.

When his boy finally pulled back, he looked him in the eyes and asked his Master point blank, "When are we getting married?"

Hopeful, so goddamn hopeful he'd gotten it right, he replied, "Whenever you want. It's just a matter of how you want to do it, where you want to do it, and when."

"Tomorrow, at the courthouse."

Everyone laughed, but Gideon was serious when he asked, "Why tomorrow?"

"Because I don't want to wait another day to be your husband."

"You don't care about finding the perfect suits to wear, having a long engagement, or inviting all of our family and friends to a big fancy event and reception?"

"You wear a Henley and some tactical pants, I'll wear some jeans and a concert tee." He'd glanced down, describing exactly what they were wearing, and Gideon's heart sped into overdrive as Sebastian continued, "I've waited long enough for you." Sebastian turned and asked the group, "Can you come to the courthouse tomorrow to see us get married?"

As everyone agreed, clapping, and some of them rubbed tears from their cheeks, Gideon stood and pulled his boy up with him. "You're sure?"

Sebastian's laugh rang out, and he nodded. "I've never been more sure of anything in my life."

Gideon grabbed him in a bear hug, lifting him off his feet, and looked into his eyes when he said, "We don't have to wait until tomorrow. We don't have to wait another second. We can do it tonight if that's what you want."

Everyone gasped except for his dad, who stood and asked everyone to move over to one of the larger grassy areas of the rooftop. Excited chatter took over as everyone moved. Sebastian could see the seriousness in his eyes, and he gave his answer, "Yes, please, Master."

Setting him down, he clasped his boy's hand, walked toward the group, and heard his mom ask his dad, "Duncan, you got ordained? When did you do that?"

His dad puffed up with pride, making Gideon chuckle, and replied, "I didn't. I got deputized for a day. All I had to do was pay a fee, show my ID, and bring the wedding license."

He was so pleased with himself everyone laughed. And Sebastian turned to Gideon, eyes narrowed. "That's what you had me sign and date today at the studio?"

Gideon kissed him and murmured against his lips, "Am I forgiven?"

Sebastian laughed and shook his head. "You're crazy, is what you are."

Gideon pulled his own ring out of his pocket and slid Sebastian's off his finger, handing them both over to Braden. They approached Duncan, hands clasped, and faced each other, Lola, tongue lolling out of her mouth, walked and sat beside Sebastian, everyone else looking on. As his dad took them through the ceremony, Gideon couldn't help but be overcome by the moment.

Looking in his boy's eyes, he knew he was the luckiest man alive. "I can see our lives stretching out before us, traveling, maybe even children." There were gasps and happy murmurs from their family. "The possibilities for us are endless. I'm so grateful I set aside my fear and my stubbornness long enough to realize what I had in you. To realize I was better off with you than I could ever be without you. It was the best decision I've ever made."

Gideon felt Sebastian's words deep inside his heart when his boy said, "I think that I've gone through my life alone just so I was deserving of the amount of love you've brought into my life. Your love and the love from your amazing family have helped me realize what real family is. I can barely remember a time when we weren't together. I believe the darkness of our past lives has been eclipsed by the light of our love and happiness. I can't wait to love you, faithfully, as your husband for the rest of my life."

Soon after, they were exchanging rings and sharing their first kiss as husbands. Zavier and Braden brought a case of champagne up from their wine cellar they'd had left over from their own wedding, saying it had been meant to be. Everyone shared a toast, and afterward, as they were all chatting and they were being congratulated, he heard Maya joke, "I gotta stay away from this rooftop going forward, everybody keeps proposing and getting married here," making everybody laugh.

Gideon watched as Sebastian pulled Braden aside and whispered in his ear. Braden pulled out his phone, typed in a few things, and then the music was switched and turned up. As the beginning notes of Sleeping at Last's "Turning Page" began—one of his boy's favorites—he held out his hand, and Sebastian clasped it, moving in to rest his head against Gideon's chest. They danced their first dance together as husbands, their family and friends watching. The day had been amazing, the night had been wonderful, and their wedding, perfect.

When the night wound down, they headed home. He picked a tipsy Sebastian up to walk him through the elevator door to their loft, making him giggle uncontrollably. As the laughter died down and he walked into their bedroom, Sebastian placed his hand on his cheek and kissed him so gently it nearly did him in. He put Sebastian down and watched, rapt, as he stripped. But just as he was about to move in and devour his boy's mouth, Sebastian kneeled and presented, but instead of casting his eyes to the floor, he raised them to Gideon's.

"Master, you vowed to share the rest of your life with me today and I did the same, but I also wanted to pledge my service to you for the rest of our lives. I never thought I'd be lucky enough to find a Dominant like you even for the short term. I still can't believe you want to be my Master forever, but I will always be grateful you saw something in me that I could never see in myself. Something that shined bright in your eyes and yet was shadowed in mine. I'm grateful for your love, but I'm just as grateful for your guidance and your ownership. It will forever be my pleasure to give you the gift of my submission. I love you, Master."

Gideon sank to his knees, capturing his boy's lips with his, their kiss, slow and painstakingly tender. "As your Master, I vow to always put your needs and safety before my own. I pledge to honor your gift of submission to me and cherish it always. I lived in darkness before you, and I have such darkness within me, and while that will never change, you brought with you the light I needed to see the path to guide us. I will forever endeavor to keep your light shining bright for us both so I may one day deserve ownership of you. I love you, boy."

They made love that night, slowly, sweetly, knowing they'd just begun their lives together and joyful for the gift of each day that was to come. It turned out they didn't need fancy suits, they didn't need a wedding planner, they didn't need invitations or save the dates, they didn't need an expensive venue and a gigantic wedding cake.

All they needed was each other, friends, family...and forever.

THE END

Author's Note

Thank you for reading *Saving Sebastian*. This is my third novel and it's been a long time coming. I hope you enjoyed it. Please take a moment to leave a review, if you're so inclined.

I welcome contact from readers. You can find me on Facebook, Twitter, Instagram, Pinterest, and Luna David.

⌘ **Luna David** ⌘

Acknowledgements

To Morningstar Ashley, I'm pretty sure it's not an exaggeration to say that this book wouldn't have been finished this year without you! Sprinting with you is what breathed new life into this book. It's been a pretty rough year and I wasn't convinced I could pull it off, but you were. Your faith in my abilities gave me the kick in the ass I needed to finish. Thank you!

I've met some really great people in this genre. It's felt like coming home. As time has passed, I've become really close friends with several great people and each of them has supported me and given me such wonderful friendships that I know will stand the test of time. Ladies, you know who you are. You've offered up your friendship, your laughter, your love, and your loyalty. I couldn't ask for more. I've truly found my tribe. Thank you for being you.

To my wonderful beta readers, you polished my voice and provided much needed advice. Thank you so much! Morningstar Ashley, Sheena J. Himes, Elizabeth Coffey, Denise Dechene, Jen Barten, Michael Edward McFee and my last minute beta, Miranda Turner Vescio. Every single one of you had unique views on what would aid in making this book great and it's all the better for your help. I can't thank you enough.

And last, but definitely not least, thank you to my cover artist, Kellie Dennis, at Book Cover by Design. Wow, does my book look gorgeous from the outside! This is my favorite cover so far. It's truly stunning and you brought my guys to life in a way I couldn't have even dreamed. Thank you!

About the Author

Luna David is a true romantic at heart who was fortunate enough to find and marry her soul mate. Most of the time she considers herself lucky to have been blessed with having g/b twins, but they're giving her a run for her money. She's a stay at home mom and an author, so when she's not begging her little monsters to behave, you'll most likely find her writing.

She loves anything book, coffee or dark chocolate related and can't think of a better way to pass the time than to combine all three. She reads romance novels voraciously and while she prefers contemporary romance with strong Alpha males finding their soul mates, she's a sucker for any well written, romantic story regardless of genre.

She created the Custos Securities Series because she loves to write what she loves to read. Her books feature strong dominant males and the men they would die protecting. Toss in some BDSM and kink and you've got her Catharsis Novel Series and The Boys Club Series. She loves nothing more than making her readers feel a wide range of emotions with her words. And she hopes you enjoy her stories. Happy Reading!

Manufactured by Amazon.ca
Bolton, ON

13200265R10256